KT- 470- 000

At the Ruin of the World

JOHN HENRY CLAY

At the Ruin of
the World

HODDER &
STOUGHTON

First published in Great Britain in 2015 by Hodder & Stoughton
An Hachette UK company

I

Copyright © John Henry Clay

A CIP catalogue record for this title is available from the British Library.

Hardback ISBN 978 1 444 76136 8
Trade Paperback ISBN 978 1 444 76137 5
Ebook 978 1 444 76139 9

Typeset in Plantin Light by Palimpsest Book Production Ltd, Falkirk, Stirlingshire

Printed and bound in the UK by Clays Ltd, St Ives plc

Hodder & Stoughton policy is to use papers that are natural, renewable and
recyclable products and made from wood grown in sustainable forests. The logging
and manufacturing processes are expected to conform to the environmental
regulations of the country of origin.

Hodder & Stoughton
Carmelite House
50 Victoria Embankment
London EC4Y ODZ

www.hodder.co.uk

For Edmund

Haec uerba
Accipe fraterno multum manantia fletu,
Atque in perpetuum, frater, aue et uale.

It was death, for us, to have lived
Amidst such disasters
And the ruin of the world.

Sidonius Apollinaris

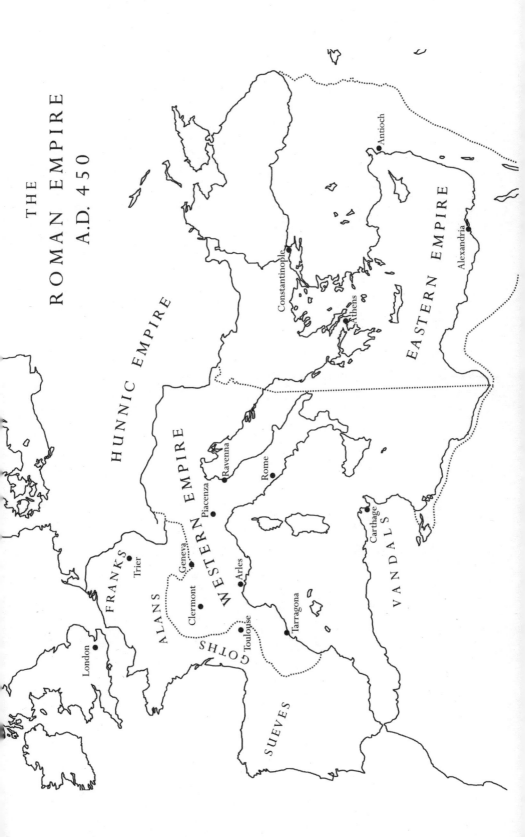

THE
ROMAN EMPIRE
A.D. 450

HUNNIC EMPIRE

WESTERN EMPIRE

EASTERN EMPIRE

FRANKS

ALANS

GOTHS

SUEVES

VANDALS

London

Trier

Geneva

Clermont

Toulouse

Tarragona

Arles

Piacenza

Ravenna

Rome

Carthage

Constantinople

Athens

Antioch

Alexandria

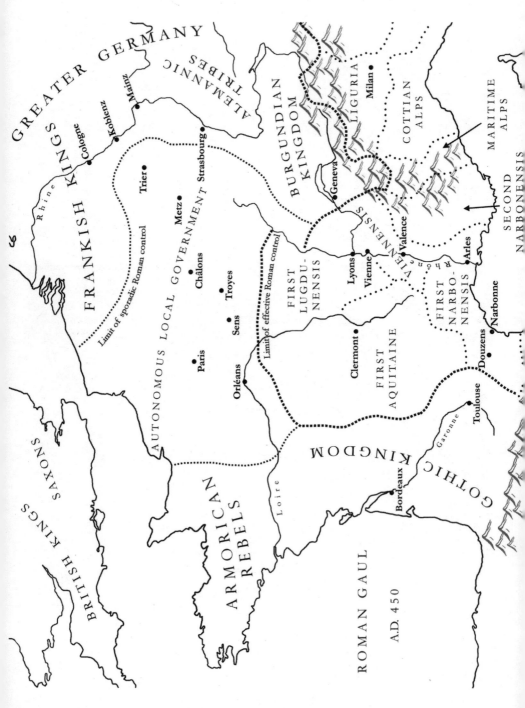

ROMAN GAUL

A.D. 450

GREATER GERMANY

FRANKISH KINGS

ALEMANNIC TRIBES

BURGUNDIAN KINGDOM

LIGURIA

Milan

COTTIAN ALPS

MARITIME ALPS

SECOND NARBONENSIS

Rhine

Cologne
Koblenz
Mainz

Trier

Metz
Châlons
Strasbourg

Troyes
Sens

Paris

Orléans

AUTONOMOUS LOCAL GOVERNMENT

Limit of sporadic Roman control

Limit of effective Roman control

VIENNENSIS

FIRST LUGDU-NENSIS

Geneva

Lyons
Vienne

Valence

Rhône

Arles

FIRST NARBO-NENSIS

Narbonne

FIRST AQUITAINE

Clermont

Douzens

Toulouse

Garonne

Bordeaux

GOTHIC KINGDOM

Loire

ARMORICAN REBELS

SAXONS

BRITISH KINGS

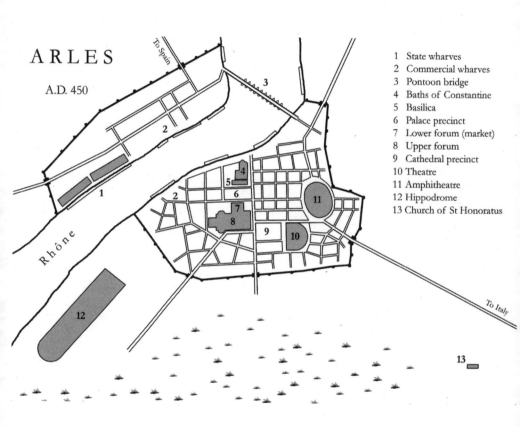

ARLES

A.D. 450

To Spain

Rhône

To Italy

1   State wharves
2   Commercial wharves
3   Pontoon bridge
4   Baths of Constantine
5   Basilica
6   Palace precinct
7   Lower forum (market)
8   Upper forum
9   Cathedral precinct
10 Theatre
11 Amphitheatre
12 Hippodrome
13 Church of St Honoratus

ROME

A. D. 450

1 Tomb of Hadrian
2 Tomb of Augustus
3 Baths of Diocletian
4 Stadium of Domitian
5 Pantheon
6 Church of St Lawrence
7 Odeon
8 Temple of Trajan
9 Trajan's Column
10 Forum of Trajan

11 Temple of Jupiter
12 Senate House
13 Basilica of Maxentius
14 Baths of Trajan
15 Colosseum
16 Imperial palace
17 Circus Maximus
18 Emporium
19 Baths of Caracalla

Quirinal Hill

Viminal Hill

Esquiline Hill

Caelian Hill

Capitoline

FORUM

Palatine

Aventine

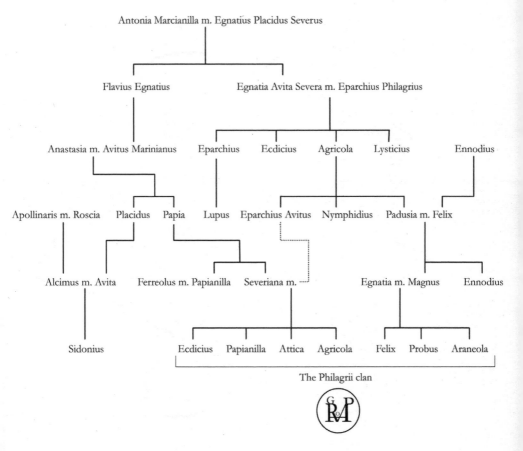

Antonia Marcianilla m. Egnatius Placidus Severus

Flavius Egnatius

Egnatia Avita Severa m. Eparchius Philagrius

Anastasia m. Avitus Marinianus   Eparchius   Ecdicius   Agricola   Lysticius   Ennodius

Apollinaris m. Roscia   Placidus   Papia   Lupus   Eparchius Avitus   Nymphidius   Padusia m. Felix

Alcimus m. Avita   Ferreolus m. Papianilla   Severiana m.   Egnatia m. Magnus   Ennodius

Sidonius   Ecdicius   Papianilla   Attica   Agricola   Felix   Probus   Araneola

The Philagrii clan

Prologue

*M*en say, as much as the sayings of men are worth, that it began with a cowherd. He had lived his whole life in the country beyond the great river Danube. As a boy he had herded his lazy father's cattle between the sweeping grasslands and snowy peaks of that barbaric land, and when his father died the cattle became his.

Because he was a strong and ambitious man his herd soon doubled in size, and he decided to take a wife, who gave him a son. When his herd doubled again, he took a second wife, who gave him two sons; and when it doubled a third time he took a third wife, who gave him three sons.

By this time, judging that he had enough cattle and wives and more than enough sons, the cowherd fancied himself an important man, worthy of the attention of his king. But when he went to see the king he was mocked even before he entered the palace. 'You have nothing to offer him,' the king's guard said. 'You think yourself wealthy, but your entire herd would barely be enough for a single feast in this hall.'

The cowherd returned home dejected. His first wife asked him what was wrong. 'I have seen the splendour of the king's palace,' he replied.

'Now I look at you all and think myself a simple farmer, little more than a beggar.'

The second wife said, 'Make a sacrifice to the gods and ask for their help.'

'How will the gods help me?' he asked.

'Ask them to give you something to offer the king,' said the third wife. 'Something that no other man has.'

And so the cowherd, heeding this wise counsel, went to his herd and chose the finest looking beast he could see. Some say this was a full-grown ox, others a heifer; but whichever it was, when he found it he was dismayed, for it was limping and its front leg was covered in blood. 'This is a bad omen,' the man grumbled to himself as he inspected the wound. 'The gods are punishing me for the laziness of my father.' He saw at once that the wound had been caused by something sharp, and that a trail of blood led across the meadow towards a mound in the distance. Worried that another of his animals might also injure itself in the same way, he began following the blood trail.

Soon he came to a small hollow at the top of the mound, where the trail ended. Peering inside the hollow, he glimpsed something shiny. Straight away he returned to his house to fetch a mattock, before hurrying back to dig out the mysterious object. It was not long before he realised it was a sword. When he had exposed the grip, he pulled it from the earth and held it up to the sun. Never before had he seen such a perfect blade.

So bright did it flash that his wives came running from the house. 'It is a sword of the gods,' they told him. 'They have answered your prayer!'

'I made no prayer to them,' he answered, 'but I know why they have revealed this to me.'

He wasted not a single breath returning to the king's palace. This time the guard took one look at the blade and his face turned pale. He immediately led the cowherd into the great hall. The cowherd fell to his knees when he glimpsed the king sitting on his throne.

'Come closer,' Attila said.

The cowherd approached him, offering the sword in outstretched hands. 'My king,' he said, 'I found this buried on my land.'

Attila's eyes fixed on the blade. He rose from his throne and took hold of the weapon. The steel shone like fire as he turned it this way and that, marvelling at its workmanship, which surpassed anything made by man in any corner of the world.

'Last night I had a dream,' Attila said in a sonorous voice. 'I dreamed that a stranger would come to me with this sword. Today I commanded my guard, if such a man should appear, to bring him to me. Now I see that it was no mere dream, but a prophecy.'

'What is the prophecy, great king?' asked the cowherd.

Attila replied, 'This is the ancient sword of Mars, god of war, lost for countless generations. Now it has been revealed to me for these reasons: that I might be invincible in war; that I might grind the empire of Rome into the dust; that I might sit above the whole world as its conqueror and master.'

This, then, is the tale as told by men. Some call it fanciful, and dismiss it as a tale best told by children.

But they are not the ones who saw Attila amass his hordes and ride on the west. They never saw the fields of the Rhineland turn black with the tide of horsemen, nor did they see the towers of its once-proud cities tumble to ruin before the Hunnic weapons of war, and nor could they have seen the weeping of the women and children as they were led into slavery or death.

Fanciful the tale may be, but Gaul would come to know the truth of it.

I

Vicus Helena, near Tournai, A.D. 448

It was so fine a day for a wedding: one of those days in August
when the sky stretches high and blue towards the sun and not
a cloud can be seen. It was a day of blossom and freshness and
all the scents of summer, a good day for galloping across meadows,
feeling the sure earth beneath the horse's hooves, sucking the air
deep into one's lungs. Such days, Ecdicius felt, were made for
men to enjoy.

For a moment, only a moment, his thoughts wandered. Three
hundred miles, across fields and forests, rivers and towns, his
mind took him to a lake in the hills, where a friendly breeze
played on the water like the voice of an old friend. He saw a
dancing reflection of hills, and above the shore, through the reeds
and bulrushes where the bitterns nested, the white walls of home,
the playing shapes of his sisters and brother . . .

The moment passed. Now was not the time for such thoughts.
Ecdicius made himself sensible to the strap biting into the flesh
beneath his chin, the helmet clamped on his skull, the weight
of the mail on his shoulders. The ranks of cavalry in front of
him, the most experienced of the regiment, made no sound or
movement beneath the cover of the trees. Without turning his
head, for he did not want to appear nervous, Ecdicius felt the
reassurance of the other ranks beside and behind him. One
hundred men of the First Gallic Horse waited in perfect silence,
hidden just within the treeline.

Now he could hear the sounds from beyond the ridge. The
Frankish enemy must have crossed the river. The drums carried
best, each with its own throbbing echo. Less distinctly he heard
a muddle of pipes and flutes, and beneath them the first voices.

The barbarians were laughing and singing, ignorant of what would soon befall them.

Zephyros, sensing that the moment of release was near, shook his mane with a snort and scuffed the ground impatiently, but knew better than to whinny. Ecdicius brushed a calming hand on the steed's neck. He discreetly slipped three fingers beneath the throatlash. There was no cause for anxiety; the bridle was not too tight. This morning at camp he had dismissed his groom and saddled and bridled Zephyros himself, testing every strap, piece and ring over and over again, making sure that nothing might slip or snap in the frenzy of battle. Even so, he could not stop himself reaching back to the javelin case behind his saddle. For the third time he checked that he had left it fastened open, and that each javelin was secure, but loose enough to pull with ease when the time came.

Calm yourself, Ecdicius thought. *You must look like a frightened maiden on her wedding night.* He returned both hands to the reins and breathed deeply, trying to steady his thumping heart. He looked to the commander in the front rank. Dappled light glinted on the tribune's helmet of steel and gilded bronze, and on the immaculate rings of his mail shirt. For half an hour Majorian had been sitting like that, not moving an inch, watching the ridge with the patience of a statue. *That's how a soldier awaits battle.*

Watching Majorian did not help. Ecdicius could think only of how dry his mouth had become. He would have taken a drink from his flask, but he was afraid of fumbling with the cap. Not for the first time, doubts entered his mind. Perhaps he should not have pressed his father so hard to get him this commission. True, the First Gallic Horse were the elite of the field army, and Majorian was second in fame only to Count Aëtius himself, but Ecdicius had never before ridden into battle. He should have joined a lesser regiment, gained some experience. What if he disgraced himself? The slightest mistake, the briefest hesitation, and Majorian would hear of it. Such a commander would not tolerate a second-rate cavalryman in his regiment. Ecdicius would be dismissed and sent back in shame to his father – his famous father, the great hero and general, whose name was renowned the length and breadth of Gaul.

Such a fate would be too much to bear. It would be better to fall in battle.

Ecdicius was distracted by movement at the top of the ridge as the first of the barbarians appeared. Through the foliage he glimpsed them arriving on foot, on horse or mule, in ox-drawn carts, gathering on the high ground to prepare for their celebration. Some hoisted planks of wood from carts and set up tables, which others loaded with fruits and bread. They rolled kegs of beer and raised awnings, stacked faggots ready for the cooking fires. Three boys fixed a post in the earth and tethered a pair of bleating goats. Still the drums and pipes were playing, and now the revellers, dancing, laughing, drunk, were coming into view. There must be two hundred at least, Ecdicius judged, with more coming up the ridge: warriors, garlanded women and girls, boys following their fathers, servants. A large crowd, as one would expect for a princess.

It was indeed a fine day for a wedding, Ecdicius thought. But firm ground, clear air, and an open meadow were fine for many things.

Majorian raised his right hand, fist clenched. A ripple ran through the ranks as men stirred their mounts and prepared to move. That morning the tribune had said there was to be no trumpet when they charged, no battle cry, nothing to alert the enemy. Their only task was to fight through the Frankish warriors guarding the wedding party and capture the barbarian princess, the granddaughter of King Chlodio. If they took her hostage, Chlodio would have no choice but to make a treaty and pay compensation for the war he had started. Justice would be done.

Majorian lowered his fist, and the regiment moved out from the trees. He led the advance, pressing ahead while the far flanks held back. One hundred troopers cantered onto the open ground and flowed into a wedge, nine ranks deep with Majorian and two other riders at the point. Ecdicius, with firm, well-practised movements, kept Zephyros in formation, knowing his place three ranks from the rear in the middle of the wedge, trying not to jostle with the over-eager riders around him.

By the time the Franks noticed the approaching thunder of the cavalry it was too late. They had no time to organise themselves. A few of the men whipped out their axes and swords and prepared to stand their ground, but the rest ran, or stumbled in a drunken stupor. Singing stopped, and laughter turned to cries of alarm.

Straight away the charge lost momentum as the front riders crashed into the chaotic throng of barbarians and carts. Ecdicius found himself hemmed in among the rear ranks, slowed almost to a standstill. Ahead he saw blades rise and fall and awnings topple, heard the horrified screams of the barbarians, of women and children trampled underfoot. His comrades cursed and shouted at the men in front to move on, impatient to reach the fighting. The trooper on his left, whose name Ecdicius could not remember, was pressing against him, trying to push him aside so he could cut across to the right edge of the wedge. Ecdicius pushed the man back with his shield and struggled to keep Zephyros straight. 'Hold your position!' Ecdicius snapped. In response the trooper yanked aggressively on his reins, twisting his horse's head so sharply to the right that it squealed; Ecdicius was forced to lean back to avoid a mouth of furious square teeth, froth bubbling over the bit, and a frenzied dark eye; Zephyros shied, twisting to the right, almost throwing Ecdicius, who stayed in the saddle only with a tremendous effort. By the time he had righted himself the trooper had pushed past. Ecdicius cursed, making sure to remember the face of the reckless idiot. There would be time after the battle to settle scores.

The rest of the rear ranks were loosening as the formation broke apart and individual riders sped towards the fleeing barbarians. Ecdicius, left almost alone, stared after them in disbelief. These were meant to be the flower of the Roman cavalry, yet discipline had broken down at first contact with the enemy. What had been the point of those weeks of drills?

Drawing his sword, he urged Zephyros after his comrades. As soon as he reached the crest of the ridge he looked for where the fighting was thickest, but could not find it. What he saw was not fighting.

Carts and piles of debris were scattered across the grass. The two goats, still tethered to their pole, bleated in distress. The cooking fires intended for them remained unlit. Ecdicius saw barbarians fleeing in terror down to the riverbank or the bridge, but many were too old or too young to get far before being ridden down. Some troopers had abandoned the chase to dismount and fill their satchels with loot, taking finger-rings and necklaces from the dead, or were clambering into carts to seek more precious goods. Others had found different kinds of plunder. Nearby, three soldiers, two on horseback and one on foot, were taunting a brown-haired Frankish girl who wore a garland of summer leaves around her neck. They prodded her with javelins this way and that. She wept, pleading in her barbarian tongue, unable to escape. Eventually the dismounted soldier ripped the garland from her neck, knocked her to the ground, and advanced on her where she lay.

Ecdicius turned away then, suppressing the rising sickness in his stomach. These Franks had invaded Roman territory, he told himself; they had robbed and murdered Roman citizens, enslaved whole families. This was just punishment for their crimes.

He sheathed his sword, not seeing any use for it. The few enemy fighters nearby were already dead, lying in the blood-soaked grass with their weapons beside them. One youngster was curled up on his side, a javelin through his chest. He had the distinctive haircut of the Frankish menfolk, a long fringe at the front and shorn at the back, except where his skull had been caved in by a hoof. His eyes were still open, a startling, living blue.

A hundred yards away was a large group of cheering cavalrymen, above whom rose the regimental standard: a blue, yellow-rimmed star on a black field. If the standard was there, Majorian must be too. Ecdicius headed towards it, riding over the mangled and gutted corpses of the slain. After a few yards the only bodies he saw were of old men and women and children, dressed in what must have been their finest tunics and cloaks. All had been cut down without discrimination. The smell reminded him of the butcher's pen back home, but it was worse; there was the stench of piss and shit as well, mingled with the sourness of half-digested beer.

When he reached the gathering, Ecdicius saw at the centre a dozen women huddled together. One of them, close to elderly, was screaming at the cavalrymen. Ecdicius understood not one word of Frankish, but it was clear that she was cursing them. Majorian stared at her, impassive, and nodded to Primicerius Flaccus, his second-in-command. Flaccus dismounted and marched into the group of women. He grabbed one of the girls by the arm and dragged her away from the others, with his spare hand fighting off the attempt of the old woman to stop him. The girl was stout, big-breasted and rose-cheeked, wearing a long white dress fastened at the shoulders with a pair of gold and garnet brooches, between which hung a necklace of glass beads. As she struggled, Ecdicius caught a glimpse of her golden earrings. She looked high status for a barbarian; the princess, no doubt. She was refusing to weep or show fear.

'Bind her and keep her here,' Majorian said. 'Make sure she is not harmed.' He began to turn away.

'The other women, tribune?' asked Flaccus.

Majorian paused. He looked over the captives. Now even the old woman fell silent. 'Woe to the vanquished,' he said.

The soldiers cheered. As Majorian rode away, Flaccus barked instructions. Two men bound the princess and took her to one side. Others tied the remaining women to a nearby cart by their hands, slapping those who struggled too fiercely. The biarchi pushed their squads into order. Ecdicius watched as the first squad of the regiment dismounted and handed their reins to the second squad. Due to their seniority they were to enjoy the women first.

He felt the bile rise again from his stomach. This time it was too much; he was going to be sick. He slipped clumsily from his saddle. As soon as his feet hit the ground his legs seemed to lose all their strength. He clutched the saddle horn to steady himself. A cloud filled his head with a sudden throbbing. He unfastened his chin strap and pulled off his helmet, gulping the cool air. *Steady, you fool! They are only barbarians. Did they weep for us when their menfolk invaded our lands and raped our women?*

Then the screams started. Ecdicius did not look. He needed to get away. He began to walk, but his legs took him only a few yards before he fell to his knees. With a long, heavy retch he emptied that morning's breakfast onto the ground.

He vomited until his stomach was a lurching, empty bag. Lumps of bread, lentil porridge, and wine were splattered on the grass before him. He spat the last bitter remnants from his mouth and raised his head, wiping a sleeve across his lips.

There was a wet snort by his ear, and the wiry muzzle of Zephyros brushed against his cheek. Ecdicius reached up and stroked it gently, closing his eyes. 'I'm all right, boy,' he muttered.

He became aware of a presence behind him. Raising himself quickly, he turned to see several mounted men watching from a few yards away. One of them was Tribune Majorian. Next to him was a man with a solid, square-jawed face, his dark skin etched with lines. It was Count Aëtius, master of soldiers, supreme commander of the western field army.

'Illustrious patrician,' Ecdicius said, and by instinct fell to one knee. He lowered his gaze.

'He looks familiar,' Aëtius said.

'The resemblance to his father is strong,' said a voice Ecdicius recognised. It belonged to Aegidius, tribune of the Senior Honorians. 'This is the eldest son of Eparchius Avitus.'

'A physical resemblance, perhaps,' scoffed Majorian. 'I don't recall ever seeing Eparchius Avitus shame himself on the battlefield.'

For a moment Aëtius said nothing. The cries from the cart

were quieter now, except for the younger girls. Ecdicius kept his face lowered. One kelt before a patrician, and did not rise until commanded to do so.

Finally Aëtius spoke. There was a note of pleasure in his voice, even amusement. 'Send him home. His father can deal with him.'

II

Bordeaux, the Gothic Kingdom

The facts were these. Three days before the kalends of August, one hour after dawn, Lupus the merchant had been driving his ox-cart towards the city market. The cargo was sixteen amphorae of North African wine, and his ten-year-old son was sitting by his side. They started to cross the bridge over the river. They had almost reached the far side when the last arch of the bridge collapsed. Lupus was able to jump to safety, snatching his son just in time. The cart, however, fell into the river, taking with it both cargo and beast. The amphorae were smashed, the wine washed away in the water. Both front legs of the ox were broken, and the beast had to be killed before its corpse was unfastened from the cart and dragged to the riverbank by a team of men. Thus by God's mercy Lupus kept his own life and the life of his boy, but he lost his cart, ox, and the goods in which he had invested the last of his cash.

The orator Sedatus laid out these facts before the judges in the forum, and paused to give a sympathetic shake of his head. He dabbed the sweat from his brow, using the hem of his cloak. Then, with exquisite timing, he raised a single finger. 'Of course this is a tragedy,' he said. 'But who, I ask you, is to blame?'

The panel of judges – Bishop Frontinus, the chief civic administrator, the two city magistrates, and Count Wulfilas, who represented the king – watched him from the podium, awaiting his answer. Sedatus faced the crowd that filled the forum, pointed his finger into their midst, and slowly turned. His finger swept over the silent faces of the people, and came to rest on the two figures sitting on a separate bench next to the judges. They were the aediles, the councillors responsible for civic maintenance, who normally would have been sitting with the judges themselves. Today, however, they were the ones under judgement, accused by the merchant of negligence for failing to keep the bridge in good repair.

But Sedatus lowered his finger. 'My fellow citizens,' he said, '*why* must we place blame? These two aediles before you are well known by their reputations for good public service. Their very names are spoken with reverence throughout Bordeaux – nay, throughout the whole of Aquitaine. Have they not already begun to repair the bridge? So why, I ask you, must we place blame? Misfortune breeds anger, I admit. When we are hurt it is natural to lash out like an injured animal, heedless of where our blow might land. But if, because of this, one misfortune leads to another, who has been helped? These innocent men should not suffer because of another man's bad luck. Yes, *bad luck* I say, and mean it; and yet was God not watching over the unfortunate Lupus, so that he and his son survived the disaster unscathed? We should be thanking God for His mercy, not seeking to ruin good names. Why, if we condemn these two innocent men, where will it end? Shall we accuse the ox, for being too slow to cross the bridge? Shall we prosecute Neptune for theft, because the ocean drank the spilled wine?'

The absurdities attracted laughter from the crowd and from the panel of judges, even the bishop. But not everyone looked amused. The two aediles remembered to keep their expressions sombre, the better to win the sympathy of the crowd. The prosecuting lawyer, fidgeting on his stool at the edge of the podium as he awaited his turn to speak, seemed too nervous to react at all. Next to him was his client, the unfortunate Lupus, his face red from the summer heat and his own impotent anger. And at the edge of the forum, standing in the shade of the portico among a small group of students, a certain young man spat into the gutter.

'It's as good as over,' he muttered. 'Lupus has lost.'

His tutor, a balding, rat-faced man called Concordius, gave him a sharp look. 'Quiet, Arvandus,' he snapped. 'Watch and listen. Dare I suggest that at the grand old age of sixteen you still have something to learn from your elders?'

The other students glanced at him. A couple of the younger boys tittered. The boy standing closest to the tutor gave Arvandus a well-practised stare of contempt, breathing out loudly and slowly through a wrinkled nose. That was Pontius Leontius, the second oldest boy in the class after Arvandus, tall for his age and with the shoulders of a wrestler. He came from the wealthiest family in Bordeaux, and he never let his classmates forget it.

Arvandus decided to ignore Leontius and their old fool of a tutor, and turned his attention back to Sedatus, who had not yet finished winning over his audience. He was a well-known orator who rarely took on legal cases, and so when he did, he always drew a large crowd, and professors throughout the city would cancel their regular classes and bring their students to watch him. Arvandus could not deny that Sedatus was worth watching. He was a master of his craft, as well as a natural entertainer, and he never failed to put on a good show. It was simply a shame that he was now using his talents to defend two men who were obviously guilty.

'Now comes the prosecutor's final statement,' said Concordius. 'Watch carefully, my boys.'

It was exactly as Arvandus had expected. The prosecuting lawyer forgot to bow to the judges, remembering to do so only halfway through his opening sentence, which made him forget his place and stand for a moment in dumb silence. When he started to speak again, he mumbled his words, gulped with every breath, and was afraid to look anyone in the eye. His material was also uninspiring, full of the most hackneyed tropes about a poor honest man struggling to feed his starving family; a man whose hopes, like his wine, had now been washed away into the ocean. Concordius snorted at that pathetic image, his snort quickly echoed by Pontius Leontius. A few of the crowd began to hiss. Lupus the merchant seemed ready to explode from humiliation.

The more he listened, the angrier Arvandus became. The

whole trial was a sham. Any half-decent advocate would have won the case for the merchant with ease. Both aediles were well known by their reputations, as Sedatus had said – except they were known to be negligent, lazy, and cruel-minded. But it happened that one of them was related by marriage to the family of Pontius Leontius, and the Pontii were like every aristocratic clan. When threatened in the courts they closed ranks, mustered forces, and hired the most expensive advocate they could find. The prosecuting lawyer, meanwhile, needed whatever meagre fee the poor merchant was paying him, but was clearly unwilling or unable to put up a real fight. He did not want to cross the Pontii.

It wasn't even that these two aediles were especially bad. The dire state of the bridge had been obvious to the whole city for years, yet one aedile after another had done nothing. The Pontii and the other noble families, those who claimed senatorial status, cared nothing for the public good. They cared only about their countryside villas and their sprawling estates. When they came to the city it was to strut about the forum amidst their fawning admirers, or to petition government officials for undeserved tax relief, or, as today, to crush in public any poor citizen who dared challenge them.

As they had once crushed Arvandus's family. It had happened thirty-five years ago, long before he had been born, but Arvandus felt the lingering injustice of the crime as though he had witnessed it himself – as though he, not his grandfather, had been forced into exile during the Great Invasions, when Goths and Vandals and Alans had swept across Aquitaine and laid the country waste. Along with thousands of others, his grandparents had sought refuge here in Bordeaux. Eventually the wars had ended and this small corner of the empire was handed over to the Goths. Barbarian rule had brought peace; but when Arvandus's grandfather had tried to take the family home after five long years away, they had found their modest ancestral estate occupied by a Roman steward who claimed to be in the service of the Gothic king. The property had been empty for too long, they were told.

It was forfeit to the imperial fisc, and had been surrendered to the Goths as part of the settlement treaty.

Such was the official story. In truth the vacant land had simply been stolen by a local senatorial family. They had forged documents of ownership, and then, eager to ingratiate themselves with their new rulers, had handed it over to the Goths. Arvandus's grandfather had appealed in the courts, only to be accused himself of forging documents. The legal fees had almost ruined him. They had never been a wealthy family, but they had been comfortable and respectable, with a history of dutiful service in the imperial bureaucracy since the time of Diocletian. That now changed. Because they no longer held any property, they had been demoted from the equestrian class to the ranks of the *humiliores* – in the eyes of the law, mere peasants.

The family had lived in this city ever since. Only by sacrificing everything they had left, by surrendering their pride for a three-room hovel above the docks, had they been able to pay for Arvandus's education. Five years ago he had watched his grandfather die a broken-hearted old man. He had watched his grandmother follow soon after. His parents had buried his little brother and little sister when they got the bloody flux and no money could be found for the doctor. Now it was just he and his mother and father, and whatever future Arvandus could hope to build for them.

The rising jeers of the crowd brought Arvandus back to himself. The prosecuting lawyer had finished his ineffectual address and was shuffling back to his stool. Although the judges made a show of conferring with one another, the outcome was certain. The aediles would be acquitted, and Lupus the merchant would get nothing. Of course, Arvandus thought bitterly, the Pontii were rich enough to compensate him with ease, but by accusing the aediles of incompetence he had angered them, and thus condemned himself to this public humiliation. The injustice of it made Arvandus sick. He felt the same anger in the murmuring crowd: they had jeered the prosecuting lawyer not because they were against his case, but because he had argued it so poorly. The common people of Bordeaux were no lovers of the Pontii. They merely lacked a voice and the courage to speak out.

Concordius told his students to gather around. The nine boys did as they were told, except for Arvandus, who remained leaning against his portico column. 'Now,' Concordius said, looking at each boy in turn, 'do you see how Sedatus has won the day? His opponent could not hope to match him. Eloquence, my boys, is the force that rules the world.'

Arvandus laughed. Were they truly meant to believe that?

'Do I amuse you, Arvandus?'

'I don't know about the world, Master, but it seems to me that Bordeaux is ruled by the Pontii.'

'But the Pontii hired Sedatus for his eloquence,' said Concordius. 'And thus my point stands.' He gave a conceited smile. 'Now, boys, as you'll see when Bishop Frontinus returns the verdict—'

'And what of justice, Master?' interrupted Arvandus. 'Shouldn't justice rule the world?'

Concordius scowled at him. 'Eloquence is a tool to be used in the cause of justice. Now be quiet, Arvandus. Why must every lesson with you descend into moral philosophy?'

Arvandus was stunned into silence by his teacher's words. *Descend* into moral philosophy? Did he truly say that, as though morality were a shameful topic? He looked to his fellow students, but they were oblivious. That was no surprise; they were young, half of them not yet twelve years old, and were awed by the facile old grammarian. The only boy who met Arvandus's eye was Pontius Leontius, and that was to give him a scornful, triumphant look. *This is what happens when someone like you crosses my family,* he seemed to say. *Mark this well, peasant.*

Arvandus could no longer contain his anger. Something had to be done. He stepped out of the portico and began to push his way into the chattering crowd. He would give Leontius a lesson worth heeding.

He positioned himself close to the front of the crowd, where the leading citizens tended to gather at such events. Nobody paid him any attention. He was small, not much over five feet, and well used to being ignored until he desired otherwise.

Up on the podium the judges were still in feigned conference, but it would not be long before they declared their verdict. At one end of the bench, next to the bishop, sat the Gothic count. He represented the king in public legal cases, and was the only one of the judges who would not be under the thumb of the Pontii. 'A word to the count!' Arvandus cried. 'A word to Count Wulfilas!'

Small he may have been, but Arvandus knew the strength of his voice. Wulfilas was engaged in discussion with the bishop, but looked up at the sound of his name. It was a moment before the men standing around Arvandus realised it was he who had spoken, and when they did, their surprise at hearing so commanding a voice come from a youth so small in stature bought him the precious moment of silence he needed. They stepped back to give him space.

'Noble count,' Arvandus said, 'we beg the protection of your master, the munificent King Theoderic, glory of the Gothic people!'

One of the Roman magistrates spoke up. 'Hold your tongue, boy. This is a public legal case, not the count's private audience.'

Arvandus ignored him. 'Noble count, I appeal to your kindness.'

'Are you deaf?' snapped the magistrate. 'You are disrupting procedure.'

Count Wulfilas raised a hand. 'Let him speak,' he said, his Latin thick with the tones of his Gothic mother tongue. 'Who are you?'

The crowd had quietened. The bishop and the other judges stared down at him with a mixture of annoyance and bemusement. 'I am a humble citizen of Bordeaux, noble count. A person of no consequence and no great family, begging the king, on behalf of this city, for protection.'

'Protection from whom?'

'From the ravages of time. Noble count, it was time that

destroyed the bridge. It is time that blocks our harbour, tears up our roads, breaks down our walls.' He indicated the aediles, still sitting on their bench. 'These honourable men have battled this enemy in vain. But what can two men do against so relentless a foe? Every citizen of Bordeaux knows how keen is their sense of duty, how honourable and pious their conduct.' That attracted sniggers from those in the crowd who recognised the sarcasm. *Careful, now*, Arvandus warned himself. *Do not fly too close to that sun.* 'Our city is crumbling, noble count. By God's mercy Lupus and his son were spared. But how long before lives are lost? If only Bordeaux had a benefactor who could truly protect her people! We strive hard to please our king, to pay our taxes. But what does it profit the most glorious King Theoderic when merchants are ruined through no fault of their own?'

'The aediles are having the bridge repaired,' Wulfilas said. 'What more can be done?'

'The honourable Sedatus was right. This is not a matter of placing blame. I do not say that the worthy Lupus deserves compensation – how can there be compensation, when no one is at fault? He is a proud, honest man. He would never beg. And so let us beg on his behalf. Pray let the king grant him not compensation, but a gift of largesse. Let the king show how his heart is pained by the misfortunes of the people entrusted to him. There is a story of how Julius Caesar, upon hearing that a certain merchant bringing wine to his army had been wrecked off the coast of Gaul, at once granted the man the cost of his ship and cargo. Such a noble act, worthy of a man like Caesar! And what is one cart of wine compared to a whole shipload? By this gift may Lupus be saved from ruination, and may he and his son pay their taxes for many years to come, giving thanks to God for the goodness of the great King Theoderic.' He extended both hands to Wulfilas, palms upwards in a gesture of supplication. 'We beg the king!'

Almost at once a voice in the crowd echoed his appeal. Another voice followed. Then suddenly more, until hundreds of mouths were chanting the same words, resounding between the porticos of the forum: *We beg the king. We beg the king.* The bishop leaned close to the count and whispered in his ear, evidently unhappy with what was happening. The count looked exasperated. People began to bunch towards the podium, crowding around Arvandus, obscuring him. He took a step backwards, slipping between two men who paid him no heed, and kept his face low. It was a simple matter to work his way to the rear without being recognised.

The chanting ceased only when the count rose from his bench and raised his arms. 'I have heard your plea,' he said. He was squinting into the front of the crowd, trying and failing to find the young man who had started the commotion. Arvandus could not help but smile to see the confusion in his face. 'King Theoderic is generous,' Wulfilas declared, addressing the whole forum. 'Speaking in his name, I swear by Christ that the honest Lupus will receive his largesse.'

Arvandus did not stay for the cheers. He had made his point to Pontius Leontius, and that was enough. Besides, he was hungry and it was time to return home.

He was almost at the south porch of the forum when he found Concordius blocking his path. 'There is no such story about Caesar,' the tutor said.

Arvandus shrugged. 'Now there is.'

'You think it is permissible to tell lies in the pursuit of justice?'

'It's better than telling lies in the pursuit of injustice.'

Concordius twisted his mouth in anger. 'You need not attend any more of my lessons. Clearly I have nothing more to teach you, since you care for nothing but simple tricks and rabble-rousing. May God help you.'

Arvandus pushed past him.

'You'll never find a patron in this city,' the old man shouted after him. 'I'll see to that!'

His walk home led through the web of busy market streets behind the docks. Fishmongers called out, urging him towards their squirming bowls of eels, baskets filled with cod, tables stacked with lobster and ray; boys pestered him with trays of freshly shucked oysters whose vinegar dressing made his stomach yawn.

He ignored them all, fuming at the words of Concordius. The chicken-brained dotard, talking as though Arvandus cared more about patrons than about justice.

He tried hard to calm himself. He had just won the greatest triumph of his young life, turning the heart of a city and helping an innocent man by using nothing but words. Why should he let Concordius spoil it? Despite his best efforts, he was still irritable when he reached the side alley that led to his home, and he stopped before heading down it. He did not want to upset his parents with another of his dark moods, or disappoint them by confessing that Concordius had expelled him from the class. Instead he took another lane down to the wharves.

It was late in the afternoon, and the last of the fishing boats was coming in, the sails drooping low as the sailors cast ropes to the dockhands. Arvandus walked along to a quiet stretch of the wharves and sat on a large coil of rope. Nobody paid him any attention. He breathed in the pungent river air, listened to the shouts and laughter of nearby men, to the jabbering of gulls, to the lapping of the waves on the moss-faced stones below. He closed his eyes. Slowly he felt his frustration dissolve.

Did it really matter that Concordius had expelled him? His grammatical education was due to end in a few weeks anyway. In the autumn he would start his rhetorical training under a different professor, and three years after that he would be ready to start his legal career. One day Concordius would be nothing but a bitter old memory.

Opening his eyes, Arvandus looked to his right, tracing the course of the river south. Why did he even have to stay in Bordeaux? A hundred years ago this had been the greatest university city in Gaul, famed throughout the empire for its poets and professors. Now it was no longer even part of the empire. Its buildings were crumbling, its old glories forgotten. There was no future here. If he took a barge upriver, within a week he would reach Toulouse, the capital of the Gothic kingdom. True, King Theoderic was known to be illiterate and uninterested in culture – he was a barbarian, after all – but he still needed educated men to run his government. Surely there would be professors of rhetoric in Toulouse, not to mention more opportunities for young lawyers. Most of all, nobody there would care about the Pontii. It would be a fresh start. Arvandus could ask his father about it. Provided they had enough money to live on, he was sure that his parents would not be sorry to leave Bordeaux.

As Arvandus watched the placid blue-grey waters, another thought occurred to him. Toulouse was not the end of the world, either. Not far beyond it lay those provinces of Gaul that were still part of the empire. There was Arles, the greatest city this side of the Alps, where the praetorian prefect ruled in the name of Emperor Valentinian. Once Arvandus completed his education in Toulouse, what was to stop him from applying for a post in the prefect's offices? A couple of months ago he had heard of a student from Bordeaux who had managed to start a career in the imperial civil service. Admittedly the youth had been from an equestrian family and had relied on family contacts in Arles, but it still showed that one might cross from the Gothic kingdom to the empire. Arvandus would just need a good recommendation from a reputable professor. It would get him through the door, at least – even a humble clerkship would be something. From there it would be a matter of talent and patience before he rose through the ranks. He could save up enough to buy some property and have the family restored to the equestrian class, where they belonged.

Arvandus smiled, his head filling with dreams. He saw himself ten years from now, wearing the cloak and belt of an imperial civil servant, standing in the garden of a pleasant little villa somewhere far away from Bordeaux. There was a small vineyard, a few acres of ploughland, some well-behaved house slaves. His parents were sitting in the shade of the orchard, content in their old age. There was a pretty girl with them, Arvandus's wife; she was sensible and kind, from respectable parents who had not judged him or his family for their temporary misfortune.

This was all he wanted. It was not much to ask.

Arvandus rose from the coil of rope. He felt happier than he had done for a long time, as though Concordius had not so much expelled him as liberated him. He no longer had to endure those tedious grammar classes, with their endless recitations and stilted dialogues. He would never again have to put up with the smug bullying of Pontius Leontius. A few weeks from now he might even be in Toulouse, with this city long behind him.

The last of the fishing boats was mooring as Arvandus steered his way back along the wharf, weaving between dockhands as they unloaded crates of squirming fish. He passed by the rope-makers' warehouse, by traders' offices, by the bars that sold cheap wine and fish stew, until he came to the alleyway that led up to his home. He hopped over a fetid gutter in the middle of the lane, and climbed the external staircase to the upper floor apartment where he and his parents lived.

He was already reaching for the latch when he saw that the door was open. In fact it was not there at all, but had been smashed down by force. He stepped across the threshold, peering into the gloom. 'Mother? Father?'

'Arvandus!'

The voice came from his mother, Flacilla, who was sitting on the bed over his reclining father. She held a wet linen cloth to his father's head. At her feet was a bowl of bloody water.

Arvandus came deeper into the room. Fragments of pottery vessels crunched under his feet. A shelf had been ripped from the wall, leaving smashed jugs and pewter strewn in chaos across the floor. Garments and blankets had been torn from a chest.

'Your father tried to stop them,' Flacilla said, 'but they struck him down.'

Arvandus knelt beside her. 'Who?'

'I don't know. They just came and took everything.'

He took his father's hand. He was conscious, but his eyelids were flitting and he made no sound but for a vague murmur deep in his throat. Arvandus lifted the bloody cloth on his forehead and saw the gash beneath it. 'We need to get him a doctor.'

His mother shook her head. She looked so much older than her years. 'We have no money for a doctor.'

'We still have my great aunt's jewellery. I can sell it, pay for a doctor and have plenty left over. Mother, I have a plan for us to leave. It'll be all right.'

But she was starting to weep. She looked away, seemingly unable even to look him in the eye.

A fearful knot rose in his gut. He got to his feet. 'No.'

He raced into the back room where he slept. His cot was lying on its side. The floorboards were covered in the straw from his mattress, which had been torn apart. He plunged his hands into what remained of the mattress, feeling into every corner. This is where they had kept the leather bag containing the last of their family wealth – a pair of gilded brooches, three gold armlets, an engraved silver bracelet, a necklace set with gemstones.

It was all gone.

He stood up, his head spinning. It was gone. His eyes darted over the rest of the room. He threw the mattress aside, kicked over a chair. It was no use. They had taken it.

'We tried to stop them,' his mother said when he returned to the front room. She rose, clutching the cloth in both hands. It dripped blood onto the floorboards between her feet. 'I'm sorry, Arvandus,' she sobbed. 'I had to tell them, they were going to kill your father. Please, I'm so sorry.'

'Don't,' Arvandus muttered. She had always borne their poverty with such guilt, as though she herself were to blame for it. But no one had suffered more than she. Newly wed when the Great Invasions tore a swathe through Aquitaine, she had chosen to stay with her husband rather than return to her own family. She had endured poverty and shame, and had buried one child after another until grief and sorrow were the bones that held her together. She had denied herself everything to make sure they could pay for Arvandus's education. It had meant living in this miserable hovel with no comforts or servants, wearing out her knees and shoulders at the grinding stone. Now this last hope had been taken away.

'I'm sorry,' she said again, this time barely above a whisper.

Arvandus took her in his arms. 'I'll get it back,' he said. 'I'll get us out of here.'

Whether or not she believed him, he could not say. He breathed deeply, fighting the tears. Without that jewellery they could not even buy their passage to Toulouse, let alone afford a professor's fees. It was over; all his dreams, all those stupid boyish fantasies – they would come to nothing.

He closed his eyes, desperately seeking calm, but all he could see was the mocking face of Pontius Leontius.

III

Clermont

The situation was becoming desperate. The brigands held the stronger position, having encircled both flanks, and were ready to press on to the centre. The Roman forces were sorely outnumbered, with just a small guard left to protect the duke, and a few soldiers scattered across the battlefield. It was only a matter of time before the end.

'You're beaten,' said Papianilla.

Attica ignored her elder sister. She studied the board closely, planning her next move. It had been a mistake to make that impetuous frontal assault without first securing the centre of the field. Such a tactic always worked against her younger brother, but she should have known better than to try it with Papianilla, who had calmly drawn the Roman forces in, surrounded them with her brigands, and cut them up while taking possession of both sides of the board.

'You should concede,' Papianilla said, growing impatient. 'I'd like to get back to my reading.'

Attica would not give her the pleasure. Win or lose, she would hold out until the bitter end. Annoying Papianilla would be a small victory, at least.

She moved a piece one square closer to the duke, drawing in her defences. Papianilla frowned in irritation, her dark eyes focused on the board, and made her counter-move. 'You might have won if you weren't so distracted.'

'I'm not distracted.'

'You are. You know he'll be back any moment.'

Attica moved another piece. 'Who?'

'You know who I mean.'

'Our beloved elder brother, I assume?'

'Don't be facetious.'

Attica said nothing. Naturally she knew whom Papianilla meant. Their brother Ecdicius was due to arrive that afternoon, but it was their house guest who had been most in Attica's thoughts for the last few days. Consentius, currently out at the city forum with their father, would soon be returning. She had promised to show him her herb garden.

'It's pathetic, you know,' said Papianilla. She moved one more piece towards the increasingly encircled duke, cutting off his escape. 'You're too young for him, anyway.'

'I'm fourteen,' protested Attica, adding quickly, 'not that I am interested in him. But if I were, what's pathetic about it? He'd be a good match.'

'A good match for the family. A good match for him, and for Mother and Father. Marriage is never a good match for the wife. Saint Paul told the Corinthians it was better for nobody to marry at all.'

Attica was tiring of her sister's biblical references. They were growing more frequent by the day. 'Well, if we all listened to Saint Paul, the human race wouldn't last long, would it? Marriage only makes a great woman greater.'

'Empress Galla Placidia isn't married.'

'She's widowed. Besides, she was married not just once, but twice – first to King Athaulf, then to General Constantius.'

Papianilla scoffed. She moved one of her brigands back a space, consolidating the centre of the board. She was being cautious, as always, trying to win the game with as few risks as possible. Their brother Ecdicius would have charged in for the kill by now. 'Both times Galla Placidia married,' Papianilla said, 'it was at the point of a sword. If you want to be free, Sister, then you should forget about men.'

'Free to do what? A woman can't hold political office. Nor can she lead an army, write laws, or sit as judge, or even deliver a speech from the public podium.' She moved her duke forwards one square – a defiant, reckless move, but she enjoyed seeing the consternation disturb her sister's normally sedate features. Attica leaned forwards and whispered, 'Men are the podium we must climb if we are to rule the world.'

Before Papianilla made her counter-move, they heard the front door open, and male voices entered the house. Attica recognised the laugh of Consentius – deep and rich, alive with joy.

'It sounds like your podium has returned,' said Papianilla, rising from the table and smoothing her dress. These days her clothes were ostentatiously modest: a dark linen tunic, plain leather shoes and belt, a yellow mantle fastened with a single brooch, and a simple pair of bronze earrings.

It was her perverse way of trying to get attention, Attica thought as she went with her sister from the day room into the atrium, their handmaidens following. When an eligible girl from a noble family chose to dress in such a common way, of course it would be remarked upon. Attica was the younger and prettier of the two, and so Papianilla had decided to impress people with how pious she was. The bishop might fall for it, but Attica knew her sister better than that.

Their father entered the far end of the atrium, followed by Consentius, whose athletic, confident strides seemed to give him command of the room. Attica almost hated the way her heart leaped at the sight of him.

'Welcome home, Father,' Papianilla said. 'How was your morning?'

'Busy,' he said, removing his cloak and handing it to a servant. He bent down to kiss each daughter in turn. 'By now everyone and their bath attendant knows Count Aëtius will be passing through the city next month, so the petitioners are out in force, all wanting me to get them an audience, as though Aëtius cared a jot for my recommendations. Well, then, how have you been occupying yourselves?'

'Playing brigands, Father,' said Papianilla. 'I think Attica could use your help. Her duke is on the brink of surrender.'

'That's rubbish,' said Attica.

'I have him surrounded!'

'That may be so, but he is *not* going to surrender.'

'You'll get no help from me, I'm afraid,' said their father. 'I'm officially retired as a general, isn't that so, Consentius?'

'I could petition the imperial court to have you reinstated,' said Consentius.

Her father laughed. Attica missed seeing him in such good spirits. He seemed to have aged so much in the last couple of years; his shoulders and arms still looked thick and strong, the light was still in his eyes, but the paunch around his belly had grown, and his blond hair had turned grey and retreated from the top of his head. With his trimmed silvery beard he looked an old man.

'I need to discuss some business with Soranus,' he said, slapping Consentius on the back. 'Go on, Attica can show you her garden. I know she's been pestering you about it for days.'

'And I've been looking forward to it,' Consentius said. 'Attica will be one blooming flower amongst many. Papianilla, will you join us?'

'I don't think so. I'm sure Attica wants you all to herself.'

Attica blushed as her father and sister left the atrium, irritated by their teasing. Were her feelings for Consentius so obvious? Did the whole household know? She must learn to be more subtle.

When Consentius bowed and invited her to lead the way, she made sure not to smile, and tried not to betray the mixture of excitement and fear that was turning over her stomach. She led him through the house towards the small walled garden at the rear, where they would be alone – except for her handmaiden Cyra, but Cyra already knew how she felt about Consentius. One did not keep such secrets from a handmaiden. Cyra knew that Attica thought Consentius the handsomest man she had ever seen. He was not too old, either, still only twenty-five; Attica had known girls her own age to be married to men of fifty or more. Why, her father had been more than twice her mother's age when they married. Yet more important were Consentius's wealth and prospects. Whoever became his wife would find herself moving in the highest circles of the empire. Attica intended to be that woman.

The garden had a wide central path, framed by flowers and hedges closest to the house, with vegetables, herbs, and orchard trees towards the back. The kitchen servants managed the vegetables and trees, but Attica had taken on the herb garden for herself. She had directed the servants where to plant everything, and sometimes she even did the trimming and harvesting. 'Papianilla doesn't approve of my herbs,' Attica told Consentius as they started walking slowly down the path. 'She says I'd be better off looking after just the flowers.'

'So why don't you?'

'Flowers are so useless. We hardly do a thing with them. But look at this mint here – it can cure a sick stomach or a sore throat, soothe an insect bite, calm the nerves, and a hundred other things.' She picked up a small basket and pruning knife that had been left on a bench. 'But one must be careful with mint. It's a greedy little barbarian, always wanting to invade its neighbours. That's why we grow it in a box.' She knelt by the plant, cut a bunch of leaves, and placed them in the basket. She offered Consentius the knife. 'Would you like to cut some?'

'Gladly.' He took the knife and crouched beside her. She did not move, thus obliging his knee to brush against hers as he leaned over to harvest the plant. That slight touch provoked a warm rush through her whole body. She felt the heat rise to her cheeks as she gave him a sidelong glance. His clear skin, glowing from the sun, that strong jaw with its dusting of stubble, those deep brown eyes that narrowed with such earnest intent on the task at hand . . . she was sure that there never had been, nor ever would be again, a creature as perfect as him.

'Enough?' he asked, wielding a handful of mint leaves.

'Quite enough,' she said. Before he could drop them into her basket, she took them from his hand. *That was our first touch*, she thought as they both rose. It would be a moment to remember for the rest of their lives.

She took him around the remainder of the herb garden, aware of her handmaiden in the colonnade watching their every move. Consentius seemed charmed by the rich beds of parsley and dill, the basil and the bay leaf, the hyssop with its sweet purple blooms. She kept a larger summer garden at their country estate of Avitacum, she told him, but this small one was enough to keep her busy whenever they stayed in the Clermont town house. He was interested, judging from the way he asked questions, and he smiled when she told him that the ancient Egyptians had worshipped garlic as a god.

'You shouldn't make fun of my ignorance,' he said. 'Cats are one thing, garlic quite another. It's an odious plant. Who could possibly think it was a god?'

'I didn't say they thought it was a *good* god.'

He laughed, throwing his head back. Even his teeth were perfect.

'What are you doing?' came a voice from the colonnade.

Attica, with a pang of irritation, saw that it was her younger brother Agricola. He had become insufferable since Consentius had arrived, trailing him everywhere and pestering him with questions. It was all because he missed his big brother Ecdicius. That was one more reason Attica was glad that Ecdicius was returning today, after six months' campaigning with the army in the north; with him back, she might have Consentius to herself.

'Your sister is showing me her garden,' Consentius said, smiling. 'And what are you doing, young master? Don't you have lessons?'

'My lessons are finished,' said Agricola, sauntering towards them. He whacked the leaves of each plant as he walked by. 'I want to hear about the chariot race again.'

'Again?' said Consentius, with mock amazement. 'I've told you that story so many times, you surely know it better than me by now.'

'You mustn't keep bothering our guest,' said Attica.

'It's quite all right.' Consentius beckoned to the boy. 'I'll tell you one more time, but this time with a difference. This time, *you're* going to win it for me. Come on.'

Agricola rushed forwards and leaped onto Consentius's back. Once he was secure, Consentius carried him to the far end of the broad garden path, next to Attica's handmaiden. 'Here's the track,' he said, nodding down the length of the path. 'A bit shorter than the Circus Maximus, but it'll do. You see your sister? She's one turning post. Her handmaiden here is the other. We're the white team – we're partnered up with the blues, remember, so we have to work together against the greens and the reds. Now, are you ready? Hold those reins tight!'

Attica could not help but smile as Consentius took on the persona of four eager racing steeds, scuffing the ground, snorting, shaking his head, jostling the excited boy on his back.

'Go, go!' cried Agricola.

'Not until the trumpet – Attica, you must be our trumpeter! Quickly, before I smash through the starting pen!'

She obliged, using her hands to form a makeshift instrument in front of her mouth and making the nearest sound she could to a trumpet blast. The chariot team burst from its pen and came hurtling up the path towards her, Consentius urging Agricola to keep the reins firm, for they needed to make the turn as tightly as possible. She kept her place as they brushed around her, only for Consentius to lament that they had been overtaken by their opponents, and so had to shift to the outer track and hope that their partner could hold the lead until the seventh lap. Down the path he raced, turning around the hand-maiden at the far end and charging back up towards Attica, rushing around her for a second time, hurtling away again, to the screaming delight of Agricola.

She watched him as he made his circuits. It was not just that Consentius was a masterful poet, loved and respected by all who knew him; it was not that he had served at the imperial court and earned the personal esteem of Emperor Valentinian, who had sent him as his special envoy to the eastern court in Constantinople; it was not even that last year in Rome he had triumphed at the magistrates' races, driving his chariot to a bold and death-defying victory that had earned him a golden torc from the emperor himself. Any of these would have been enough, but that he was beautiful and kind as well – what else could she do but want him?

With the fifth lap things became more desperate, as Consentius's invisible partner bowed out from exhaustion, leaving him to beat both opponents by himself. The race came to its critical stage. Consentius nudged close behind the blue team, causing its horses to veer away across the track and crash into the basil patch. The red driver, thinking that his partner still held the lead, had shifted to the outside track to receive the adulation of the audience. Only when he noticed Consentius passing him on the inside did he realise his mistake, and he swung his horses in, seeking by foul play to put his rival out of the race; but by a fatal misjudgement he made his own beasts stumble, and with a terrible explosion of squealing horses and splintering wood he was hurled from his chariot.

The way forward was clear. Consentius gratefully slowed for the final two laps while Attica, standing in for one hundred thousand people of Rome, clapped and cheered Agricola's triumph. At last the race was over.

Consentius deposited Agricola on the path. 'Shame we don't have a prize to give you. Perhaps your sister will make you a victory wreath from those mint leaves, what do you think?'

A new figure appeared in the shadows of the colonnade. It was Ecdicius, still in his travelling cloak. He looked sunburned and dusty from the road, his blond hair bleached by the sun, an unruly beard covering his lower face. Agricola, seeing his older brother, ran to embrace him around his middle. Ecdicius put a tender hand on his head, but did not lift him for his usual hug, and did not smile.

'Such a pleasure to see you back safe, Ecdicius,' said Consentius. 'How are you? How was the journey?'

'Tiring.'

'I see you've grown a beard, it looks quite fearsome on you. Don't you think, Attica?'

'Yes,' she said, making her way down the path towards her brother. He had yet to look her in the eye, and it upset her that he had not bothered to greet her properly. 'I almost mistook you for a Frank.'

'The Franks prefer moustaches, I believe,' said Consentius. 'Isn't that right, Ecdicius? You should know, I dare say you've seen enough at close quarters by now. So, did you win the war for us already?'

Ecdicius did not reply. He stared into the garden. 'Are Father and Mother home?'

'Yes,' Attica said. 'Father's with Soranus, going over some business.'

He nodded. 'I'm going to take a bath.'

Consentius clapped his hands. 'Excellent idea. I'll join you. I could do with a wash after that chariot race.'

'I'd rather take it alone,' said Ecdicius, a hard edge in his voice. He turned and walked back into the house.

'He's tired, no doubt,' Consentius said to Attica. 'He's been riding a long time to get home. This time of year, that would be enough to wear out anyone.'

But Attica watched him go with concern. Her brother did not seem himself. There should have been hugs and laughter between all of them, joy at his safe return home. He had always brought such light and life with him, but not today. Something was wrong.

IV

Edicius had not known how it would feel to arrive home. Over the last two weeks, during the long ride south after his dismissal, when he had been mostly alone with his thoughts, he had tried to imagine himself crossing the threshold of the Clermont town house. He had imagined relief or joy; he had pictured himself falling to his knees and weeping. But even during the ride those images had appeared to his mind as though through dark-tinted glass, and he had never truly seen himself in them.

When he had stepped through the front door for real he had felt nothing. Following the sound of laughter, he had walked through the atrium to the garden, where he had seen first Agricola running to him, and then Consentius standing on the path. Then he had seen his sister, and it was as though an iron gate closed within his breast. He had been unable even to look at her.

The warmth of the bath suite was the first pleasure he had felt for a long time. He did not mind that the servants had not had time to fire up the hypocausts properly. He sat on a wooden stool in the caldarium, wrapped in the pleasant heat, feeling the sweat ooze from his open pores while the attendant scraped him clean. He let the dirt of weeks and months leave his body. He closed his eyes and imagined everything else from the last half-year leaving with it: the miserable campaign food, the drudgery of the endless paperwork, the envious prejudice of his comrades, who had hated him for having a famous father, the final disdain of Tribune Majorian and Count Aëtius . . . all of it.

Except the one thing he dared not touch. He did not need to think of it now. It would be in his dreams again tonight.

After the bath he had the attendant shave him. In his old

bedroom he found another servant waiting with a fresh tunic. Ecdicius dismissed the boy, whom he did not recognise, saying he could dress himself. He did so slowly, making sure to brush out every crease, to pluck every loose thread from the embroidered hem, to tighten his belt and the straps of his shoes.

He prepared himself for what was to come. He did not expect to be shouted at or beaten; that was not his father's way. But there would be anger, disappointment, shame. His father had always wanted him to finish his rhetorical education in Arles before entering the military, and it was only through stubborn persistence that Ecdicius had won him over. He remembered stepping onto the barge that had carried him away from Arles, away from his pedantic tutor, away from the lessons that had always left him feeling like a dullard. He had felt like a liberated prisoner. Back then he had seen nothing but glory ahead, the promise of joining a heroic campaign against the barbarian Franks, of proving himself as a warrior and defender of Rome. And now he was back home, disgraced and despised.

Ecdicius drew himself up to his full height, holding his chin high. It was time.

He found his father in his private office with his secretary Soranus, who was dictating to a scribe. His father was listening carefully to Soranus's words. Ecdicius waited just inside the open doorway, hands clasped at his front. When Soranus had finished speaking, his father nodded. 'Good. Have a copy drawn up and sent to the bureau of petitions.'

Soranus bowed. 'Yes, Lord Avitus.' He gestured to the scribe, who hurriedly rolled up the parchment, and the two of them walked out past Ecdicius. Neither acknowledged him.

'Close the door,' his father said.

Ecdicius obeyed. It would have been too much to expect a warm welcome. It was not his father who now stood before him, but Eparchius Avitus, the illustrious general, former praetorian prefect, hero of Clermont and saviour of Gaul, oldest living descendant of Flavius Eparchius Philagrius. It was the man who ten years ago had brought an end to the Gothic Wars by negotiating a treaty with King Theoderic, establishing a peace that had endured ever since. This man did not abide weakness in the servants of Rome.

'I received a letter from Majorian regarding your discharge,' Avitus said. 'Do you have anything to say?'

'Father,' Ecdicius began, and hesitated. He cleared his throat. 'Father, I was not treated fairly by Count Aëtius.'

'Indeed?'

You sound pathetic, Ecdicius thought. *No matter what you say, he will despise you.* 'It was the weakness of a moment,' he continued. 'I believe it was something I ate, maybe some bad wine. But when the count saw me, he . . .'

'He sent you home. With your tribune's consent. In his letter Majorian says you disgraced yourself on the field of battle. He also expresses his disappointment in your performance as staff officer. He speaks of orders left unissued, letters left uncopied, and those which were copied were half illegible. He describes accounting errors that not even a halfwit would commit.'

'I didn't join the regiment to be a scribe. I was there to fight.'

'That hardly matters, since you failed in both.'

'Father, if you had been there—'

'That's enough. Don't compound your fault with childish pleading. When a soldier fails in his duty, he takes the punishment like a man. You ought to thank God that Aëtius sent you home. He could have had you lashed and branded as a coward.' He held up the letter. 'Instead he and Majorian have decided to punish *me* with this. "The boy lacks a soldier's disposition," they tell me. "He may be better suited to the civilian life."' He tossed the letter on the desk. 'I can see them smiling as they wrote it. Do you have any idea what this will cost me? The honour and respect I stand to lose from this humiliation?'

The door opened. Ecdicius turned to see his mother enter. She closed the door behind her and went to stand by her husband.

'Mother,' Ecdicius said, bowing his head.

'I'm glad to see you home safe,' she replied. He could hear the restrained affection in her voice. It was clear that both parents had already agreed on how to deal with him.

Ecdicius addressed his father. 'I need another chance. If I've harmed your reputation, let me repair it.'

'That's beyond my power now. So long as Count Aëtius is the master of soldiers in Gaul, he'll never approve another commission for you.'

'Then I can go to Italy, join a regiment there.'

'No,' said his mother, Severiana. 'If you cross the Alps you won't see your family again for years. Who knows where they would send you – Africa, Pannonia? It would be as good as exiling yourself.'

Ecdicius felt a rising worry. He had expected to be reprimanded, but not to be banished from the army for ever. It was all he had ever wanted to do, all he was good for. He had never had the brains or temperament for a civilian career. 'Then what would you have me do?'

His father paused, and glanced at Severiana. 'There are other ways of serving the empire,' he said.

V

As the homecoming meal for the eldest son, and in honour of their guest, dinner that evening was to be more lavish than usual. For hours the scent of eastern spices had been drifting from the kitchen: ginger and costum, spikenard from the snowy peaks of India, pepper of Malabar for Ecdicius's favourite dish of prunes and lamb. The large semi-circular couch in the dining room had been polished and newly furnished with feather cushions. Attica had the central position on the couch, at fourteen still young enough to enjoy the novelty of reclining with the adults instead of sitting on a chair. To her right was her mother, and then her father in the host's position at one end of the couch. Her sister Papianilla was to her left, with Ecdicius beyond her, and finally Consentius in the guest's place of honour, facing the host across the table. Young Agricola sat quietly on a chair next to their father.

None of them spoke as the courses were brought into the room on plates of engraved silver and set with almost religious solemnity on a table covered with a cloth of the finest Tarsian linen. Attica stole glances at Consentius, dreading to see any hint of disappointment. Her father, despite being the senior member of the Philagrii clan, was not the wealthiest man in Gaul, nor even the wealthiest in Clermont. At the imperial courts Consentius must have seen opulence that she could only imagine. He seemed delighted, however, smiling with anticipation as each dish was placed on the table. Once the feast was ready he tugged out his personal napkin, flourishing the embroidered Chinese silk for all to see, and placed it on the cushion before him.

Her father nodded to the two musicians standing at the door, one bearing a lyre and the other a flute, who began playing a soft

melody. 'That's an impressive napkin, Consentius,' he remarked
as a servant approached to pour the wine.

'Thank you, Lord Avitus. It was a gift from the prefect of the
east. While at court I helped his daughter with her Latin compo-
sition, and this was his thank-you.'

Attica felt a stab of jealousy at the thought of Consentius
tutoring this girl. She might have asked a discreet question to
learn more, but protocol required her to remain quiet for now.
It was the duty of the host to invite each diner to speak in
turn, beginning with the guest of honour, which meant that
Attica would be the last on the couch to say anything. Perhaps
if she was lucky, her father would ask about the prefect's
daughter.

He did not. 'I'm glad to hear you've kept up with your poetry.'
He reached for an olive. 'Too often these days young men don't
appreciate the importance of literacy. I would have liked to be a
poet myself, had I the brains for it.'

'That would have been a sad loss for Gaul, if I may say so.
She needs soldiers more than she needs poets. Isn't that right,
comrade?' He nudged Ecdicius, who stared at the table in sullen
disinterest. He had not yet taken anything to eat.

'Ecdicius might surprise you yet,' her father said. 'In two weeks
he's returning to Arles to complete his education.'

'Good heavens,' said Consentius. 'Back to school? I had you
down as a career soldier through and through. Surely there
are still some barbarian tribes in the north in need of a good
pummelling?'

If Ecdicius intended to reply, his father did not give him the
chance. 'Count Aëtius has negotiated an honourable peace with
the Franks; they've given hostages and sworn not to raid our lands
again. I don't foresee any more trouble in the Rhine provinces.'

'Assuming one can trust the pledge of a barbarian,' said
Consentius.

'King Chlodio is old and tired of war. I'd say the same of King
Theoderic – he's kept the peace for ten years now. There's no
sign of trouble from the Alemanni, not since Aëtius settled the

Burgundians next to them to keep them in check. Even the Armoricans are quiet for once.'

Their mother nodded. 'With everything looking so calm, we've decided it's time for Ecdicius to finish his schooling. Soldiering is a young man's game, but he must think of his later career.'

'He doesn't look very happy about it,' said Attica, attracting a disapproving look from their mother.

Papianilla gave her a slight slap on the arm, and hissed, 'You shouldn't speak until you're invited to.'

'Well, for that matter, neither should *you*,' replied Attica, slapping her back.

'Stop it,' snapped Severiana. 'Both of you. Or Agricola here can take the couch, and you can go back to your chairs.'

'Mother,' Attica said with indignation, 'I merely observed that Ecdicius doesn't look very happy about going back to school, which is a plain fact.'

For the first time Ecdicius spoke. 'I'm going to Arles. Whether I'm happy or not has nothing to do with it. I'm going.' He snatched a piece of bread, dunked it in olive oil, and stuffed it in his mouth. 'Consentius,' he said as he chewed, 'for God's sake tell us more about your precious napkin.'

A heavy silence hung over the table. Such an outburst was not like Ecdicius at all; Attica did not know whether she ought to be anxious for his sake, or angry that he was embarrassing her before Consentius. She knew how fiercely her brother had always wanted to follow their father into the army, but that did not excuse him acting like a brat in front of such an important guest.

'Ecdicius won't be the only one going to Arles,' said Severiana, clearing the air with her pleasant tone. 'Attica – your father and I will be sending you after him next month.'

That was unexpected. She stared at her parents in surprise. 'I'm going to Arles? For how long?'

'Until spring at least. You and your brother will live with Uncle Ferreolus and Aunt Papianilla. You'll be fifteen soon; it's time you became accustomed to the world. Your cousin Felix is also very eager to meet you.' She smiled as she brought her wine cup to her lips.

So that was why they were sending her to Arles. This was not the first time her mother had mentioned Felix. Attica had never met her first cousin once removed, and did not particularly want to do so, given that Ecdicius had already described him to her as dull and plain-looking, a humourless pedant with the charm of a wet rag. She did not want to marry someone like that. She wanted Consentius.

She looked up to see him smiling directly at her. 'She seems thoroughly awed by the prospect,' he said. 'Don't worry, Attica. I'm sure your brother will take good care of you.'

Her father grunted. 'Or perhaps we should ask *her* to take care of *him.*'

At that Ecdicius reached out and grabbed a lump of bread, depositing it on his napkin, followed by handfuls of olives and cheese, and a pair of boiled eggs. He bundled up the napkin and rose from the couch. 'Now that we've won our *honourable* victory against the Franks,' he said, 'I have no purpose other than to chaperone my sister like a slave. I'm obviously not worthy to dine in this company.'

He stalked towards the door. Avitus barked his name and made to rise, but Severiana held him in place. 'Let him go, husband.' She looked to Consentius. 'Forgive our son.'

Their guest seemed undisturbed. 'Of course, my lady. Ecdicius is as passionate in disappointment as he is in joy.' He cleared his throat, and turned to Attica. 'Now, tell me, Attica – what excites you most about going to the little Gallic Rome?'

VI

Bordeaux

The doctor arrived three hours later than promised, excusing himself by saying that those patients he could help would not die in so short a time, while those who did die were beyond his help. He laughed at his own joke, wheezing as Arvandus led him up the staircase to the apartment.

'Here's your patient,' Arvandus said. 'My father. His name is Patroclus.' His father was lying on the bed, a moistened towel across his brow. He had been like this for two days. The bleeding from his head had stopped, but he had been suffering from crushing headaches ever since, and was unable even to stand without crying in pain like a man under torture. His wife Flacilla was sitting beside him on a stool. She had hardly left his side since the attack.

The doctor, a bald, sweating man who went by the name Galenos but sounded about as Greek as Arvandus, went over to the bed. His large Gothic companion remained at the top of the staircase outside the still-broken door. It concerned Arvandus that a doctor might feel the need for a bodyguard, but he had not had time to investigate the man before agreeing to hire him. He had come recommended by the owner of the nearest tavern, who knew Arvandus's father well and had said Galenos was an expert at dealing with the results of dockside brawls.

Galenos took the damp towel and tossed it aside. 'That can go for a start. Chills are what cause migraines.'

'It's obvious what's causing it,' said Arvandus. 'Just look at his head.'

'Please refrain from giving me your medical opinion,' said Galenos, leaning down to press his fingers against Patroclus's temples. Patroclus winced at his touch. 'Has he been suffering nausea? Darkened vision? Ringing in the ears?'

'Yes,' said Flacilla. 'Lots of pain, and he's hardly eaten a thing in two days. Can you give him some relief?'

'That depends. Has he been sleeping?'

'Very little.'

'Regular bowel movements?'

'Passing water, nothing more.'

Galenos straightened up, looking down at his patient. 'I may need to induce an evacuation just to be sure. A case this severe normally ends up with leeching, but I prefer to try other things first.' He opened the wooden box hanging from his shoulder, rummaged inside it, and brought out a small pouch. 'This is a mixture of knotgrass and endive,' he said, handing it to Flacilla. 'Mix it with olive oil and pig fat to make a plaster, and apply it to his brow. He's to have two cups of watered wine every day, and a third of his regular amount of food, if he can keep it down. And make sure to keep him on his back, with his head up. It'll help to rub his limbs, too. I'll be back in three days, and we'll see how he's doing.'

'I understand, doctor.' She took hold of his hand. 'Thank you.'

He smiled, pulling his hand free, and turned to Arvandus. 'Now, about the fee.'

This was the part Arvandus had been dreading. 'We can give it to you next time you come.'

'Oh! Can you, indeed?' Galenos snatched the pouch from Flacilla's hand. 'I'm afraid not. Payment on service, or no service.'

'I swear to you, we'll have the money in three days.'

'Then I'll start treating him in three days. Until then, I have paying patients to see to.'

'I give you my word,' said Arvandus. He reached out and gripped the doctor's sleeve. 'You can't leave my father like this. What kind of healer are you?'

At once the Goth stepped into the room, a great looming block of a man. He took hold of Arvandus by both shoulders, lifted him as though he were a sack of grain, and threw him backwards. The floorboards shook as Arvandus crashed onto them, knocking the back of his head with a sudden, shuddering pain.

Flacilla cried out and rushed to him. He felt her cradle his head and rest her hand on his cheek. The room seemed to tilt as if the whole city were sliding into the river.

'Be careful there, boy,' said Galenos. 'Your mother already has one injured patient to look after. I doubt she wants another. Send for me again when you have money. Not before.'

The doctor and his Goth were making their way down the staircase when Flacilla began to weep, still cradling her son. Arvandus felt the wetness of her tears on his forehead, her warm breath in his ear.

So this was all he amounted to: a pitiable scrap of a man to be tossed aside at will. No, not even a man. He was a boy. He had been an idiot to think he could save the family, an idiot to think he could stand up to the Pontii in the forum. It had to be Leontius who had sent thieves to ransack his home and torment his parents in retaliation. And there was nothing Arvandus could do.

Except one thing.

Anger drove Arvandus to his feet, taking hold of him with a force beyond conscious thought. He did not hear the words his mother spoke as he went to the shelf where they kept the cooking utensils.

It was an old blade, blunted and dull, but it would be enough. It was no longer than his index finger – short enough to conceal in the hand, long enough to reach the heart. Arvandus took it and walked out of his home, fighting off his mother's hands. He shouted for her to stay with his father, and such was the fury in his eyes that she did not argue.

His anger settled into a deep, steady force, like the swelling of the river in the springtime floods, irresistible and relentless. It drove him towards the forum. He knew that Pontius Leontius would be there at this time. It was a quiet hour of the afternoon, when most public business had either been concluded or was being conducted in the bath houses, and the forum was abandoned to idlers and prostitutes and gangs of youths.

Arvandus entered the forum by the south gate. As expected, his former classmates were in their usual north-east corner, where the steps of the basilica offered the best place to soak up the late afternoon sun. Pontius Leontius was lounging at the top of the steps, his gaggle of friends arranged around him.

Arvandus clutched the smooth wooden handle of the knife in his right hand, with the blade pointed upwards and out of sight, and began to stride across the forum, ignoring the youths and whores and the boys playing their ball games. Fury and excitement pulsed through his limbs. He would have to get close to Leontius, right up to his face, without anyone glimpsing the weapon. Whatever happened to him, the world would see that not even the Pontii could escape final justice. That was worth any price.

Before he was halfway across the forum, a strong hand took his shoulder and veered him away. Arvandus found himself being guided towards the side of the forum. He struggled, but the stranger held him fast until they reached an empty stretch of the portico, where he released him.

'Be calm,' said the stranger.

Arvandus, breathing heavily, gathered himself and looked at the man. He was of medium height and dark complexion, bearded, with his greying hair combed flat down his forehead almost to his eyebrows. It was his eyes that struck Arvandus: quiet, warm, but with a strange intensity that was almost threatening. There was a cloaked slave standing behind him, silent and attentive.

'Who are you?' Arvandus asked. 'What do you want?'

'My name is Simeon,' said the stranger, with a curious half-smile. His accent was foreign; Greek or Levantine, Arvandus guessed. 'I want to talk to you, ideally before you get yourself killed.'

'Talk to me about what?'

'About your future. I saw you speak here the other day. What you did was cunning. You could not openly offend the Pontii, so you ignored them. Nor could you offend the count, so you appealed to the mercy of the king to get what you wanted. But this is not why you won. Do you know what you did?'

Arvandus knew exactly. 'Of course I know. I used the crowd.'

'Yes. You understand the mob.' He glanced at Pontius Leontius and the other students on the basilica steps. They appeared not to have noticed Arvandus. 'What does it matter if you are small and weak, if you can convince a hundred people to rise up in your name?'

'It matters when your home is invaded by thugs.'

'Yes, I have heard about your recent misfortune,' the stranger said. 'I believe my master will be pleased to assist you.'

'Really? And who's your master?'

'He is not local. I am his agent, and one of my tasks is to find new talent – especially talent that is not appreciated by others. You understand the mob, and you understand the meaning of justice. Finding both qualities together is rare in these times.'

'You flatter me.'

'I hope so. On behalf of my master I'd like to make you an offer. He would be willing to pay for your further education.'

'Then I hope he has more influence than the Pontii. No respectable professor is going to take me on in this city.'

'Not in this city,' Simeon said. 'You will go to Arles.'

Arles . . . the imperial capital of Gaul. Arvandus did not know what to say. He studied the man closely. Who was he?

Simeon smiled. 'I see from your silence that the idea intrigues you.'

'It confuses me. Who is your master, to be so generous to a simple peasant from Bordeaux?'

'Someone who for the time being wishes to remain anonymous. That will change if your performance is satisfactory.'

Arvandus laughed. An anonymous benefactor, building up a stable of educated, penniless young Romans? It could only mean one thing. 'Your master is the Gothic king.'

Simeon looked amused. 'Believe me, my master is *not* the Gothic king. Let us consider your options, Arvandus. Your family is destitute and of no name. Here in Bordeaux you have – rather imprudently, if I may say so – earned the hatred of the Pontii. You will never find a patron in this city. Regardless, I can see that you will never be satisfied here. Your ambitions will never be realised, and your talents, to be frank, will be wasted. But I am only stating what we both already know, so let us cut to the heart of the matter.' He snapped his fingers, and the slave handed him a small pouch. 'This is enough silver to see you safely to Arles, and a three-month living allowance. All rent and tuition fees will be paid for.'

Arvandus did not take the pouch. 'I want to know the name of my patron.'

'Not yet. That will change when he desires it. Rest assured he is as Roman as you are. For now, you need only ask yourself: "How badly do I want what I want?"'

Arvandus looked across the forum to his former classmates. Two of the younger boys in his group had started to scrap at the bottom of the basilica steps, cheered on by Leontius and his friends. Arvandus's anger had faded now, to be replaced by a distant feeling of contempt. He saw the two young boys rolling in the dust, and pitied them. This was all they knew, all that life in this city had taught them: petty cruelty and vain bluster, the little people dancing to the tune of the powerful. They would play and fight like fools till their dying day.

Perhaps that was enough for them. Perhaps it was enough for most people. It was not enough for Arvandus.

He turned to Simeon. 'My father is unwell. I want you to pay for a doctor. A proper doctor, the best in Bordeaux. And I won't come to Arles until he's strong enough to come with me.'

'The doctor will be arranged. However, you must leave for Arles at once if you're to make the start of classes.'

'I can't leave my parents alone.'

'They'll be quite safe. Your father will have the best care, I assure you. I'll have them moved to a new residence, somewhere more suited to a family of equestrian background. If it will reassure you, by all means stay here for a few more days to make sure they're comfortable, and follow me on to Arles. But it's a two-week journey, and you must be there on the ides of September.'

Arvandus could not shake off his instinctive distrust. His family had endured nothing but misfortune for years, and it was hard to imagine that Fate did not have one more cruel trick in store. Yet nothing the stranger had said gave Arvandus cause to doubt his word. By refusing to reveal the patron's name he was not telling the whole truth, but at least he was doing so honestly. Besides, what would anyone hope to gain from exploiting a penniless, futureless nobody? He was offering Arvandus a way to achieve everything he had dreamed of.

He reached out and took the pouch of silver. 'I accept your offer.'

VII

Arles

Ecdicius crept slowly out of the bed, wiping the sleep from his eyes. His head throbbed. Aotlind was sleeping on her side, her red hair spilled over her shoulder. Still in his tunic, Ecdicius needed only to pick up and fasten his cloak, tug on his boots, and leave a silver coin on the bed beside the girl. He was careful to leave the room quietly.

The morning light was sharp, unkind. Ecdicius crept blinking out into the street. He moved slowly so as not to upset his stomach. Resting his back against the wall of the brothel, he closed his eyes and took in a few deep breaths. He tried not to gag on the pungent odours of urine and rotting vegetables, and the stale beer from the smashed mug at his feet.

He opened his eyes. A small child and a dog were sitting in the open doorway of the opposite house. They stared at him blankly.

A figure shuffled out of the brothel. 'Ecdicius, where are you?' It was Frontius. He shielded his eyes from the sun, squinting painfully, and looked up and down the street. 'There you are,' he muttered when he saw Ecdicius.

Marcus came out of the door after him. 'In the name of Christ, I feel awful.'

Frontius grunted in agreement. He asked Ecdicius, 'Where's your ward?'

'He's not my ward.'

'Ward or not, you'd better make sure he's all right.'

Irritated, Ecdicius went back into the brothel. The front room served as a small tavern. It was now empty except for the slaves, who were busy cleaning the tables and sweeping and mopping up the detritus from the night's revelry. He went down a corridor towards the back rooms. 'Sidonius?' he called, pausing to listen briefly at each door. He had no recollection of which room his second cousin had been led into last night. 'Sidonius, where are you?'

At the end of the corridor was a door leading to a back yard. One of the prostitutes came through this door towards him, a bundle of blankets in her arms. 'The lad's out back,' she said as she passed by.

He found Sidonius in the yard. He was on his knees, doubled up, with his face over a bucket that he was clutching in both hands. Chickens strutted and clucked around him. 'Sidonius, come on. We need to go.'

In response Sidonius retched into the bucket. It was some time before he was finished. Ecdicius stood at the door, waiting. When Sidonius was done, he spat into the bucket and wiped his sleeve across his mouth. The girl came back into the yard with a cup of water. She gave Sidonius the cup. She stroked his hair tenderly as he drank from it.

'He spoiled a set of bedclothes,' she said.

Ecdicius gave her two silver coins, and guided Sidonius out onto the street, to where Frontius and Marcus were still waiting. The four of them began to walk back to the main street.

Frontius slapped Sidonius on the back and laughed, 'Good fun, eh, lad?'

Sidonius stopped, clutching one hand to his stomach and leaning on Ecdicius with the other. His face was drained of colour, his eyes glassy.

'Better not be rough with him,' Ecdicius said.

When Sidonius was ready, they continued. They reached the main street, where Frontius and Marcus went in one direction, Ecdicius and Sidonius in the other. They were passing the arches of the amphitheatre when Sidonius stopped again. His stomach heaved a couple of times, his eyelids fluttering. Ecdicius guided him beneath the arches and kept his hand on his cousin's back as he bent over and vomited.

They continued down the busy street that ran from the east

gate of the city to the forum, Ecdicius holding Sidonius by the elbow so he did not get lost in the crowd. It was not far to the house of his uncle Ferreolus; just a few blocks to the forum, then north as far as the city basilica before turning west towards the neighbourhood of the imperial palace. He was already starting to regret the previous night. It had been a mistake to bring Sidonius with them. He was too innocent to be visiting brothels, especially common ones like that. Even worse, he had embarrassed Ecdicius in front of his friends, as though he did not already humiliate him enough in class. It was bad enough that they shared a slave attendant and a professor, and that Sidonius was much the better student even though he was two years younger. But the most insufferable thing was having to live with Sidonius in his uncle's house. Every dinner was like another lesson, as Sidonius and uncle Ferreolus competed to see who could make the most obscure allusion to some ancient republican hero or Greek myth. With each course Ecdicius felt more stupid, especially when they invited him to join in.

Still, he thought, as they came to the house – a high-walled villa compound that took up half a block – at least his uncle was not the most controlling of guardians. After spending the afternoon in the public baths Ecdicius might skip the family dinner, head back to the eastern quarter, and find another tavern in the alley-ways around the amphitheatre. He was getting to know the local crowd there: actors and vagabonds for the most part, young men on the make, down-at-heel imperial clerks like Frontius and Marcus; cheerful people with little to be cheerful about, which made them good company.

Sidonius was still unsteady on his feet as they passed through the entrance hall into the atrium. Uncle Ferreolus was standing beside the central pool discussing something with his secretary. He had obviously just returned home, and was still wearing what he called his 'peacock clothes' – green tunic beneath a heavy blue cloak, the latter embroidered with bright corner roundels, an elegant border of silver thread around the hem. This was the costume for his morning promenade in the upper forum, when he ruffled his feathers and the clients flocked to his side. He was tall, too, which gave him presence, and just stout enough to be imposing without seeming corpulent. When he spotted his wards, he waved them over. 'Tell me, my boys,' he said, 'of what shall we speak over dinner this evening? Of fleet-footed Atalanta, cunning Hippomenes, and the three golden apples of Aphrodite? Or of Eteocles and the seven bold captains of the Argives? Or perhaps we'll have a reading from the *Pharsalia. Of wars worse than civil on Emathian Plains we sing, and of justice surrendered to crime.* Marvellous. That would be much more your thing, I expect, Ecdicius? Some good old-fashioned Roman history, none of this flowery nonsense about Greek heroes and frolicking in the woods. Well, the baths are heating up; you'll both be joining me, I trust?'

'No, Uncle,' said Ecdicius. 'I'm meeting some friends at the public baths. I won't be here for dinner, either.'

'As you like, as you like. What about you, Sidonius? Shall we spend an afternoon singing of the doom of the old republic?'

Sidonius tried his best to stand up straight. 'I think I'd prefer to lie down for a while, my lord.'

'My lord? *My lord?* Really, Sidonius, we're cousins, and only once removed at that. Call me Ferreolus or disown me entirely. All right, off you go, then; I need to speak to Ecdicius.'

Sidonius started to bow, stopped himself, seeming unsure of how formally to take his leave, and settled on a nod before scuttling through the atrium with his slave attendant in pursuit.

Ferreolus dismissed his secretary. He beckoned for Ecdicius to come close, put his arm around his shoulder, and began to guide him in a slow walk around the central pool. 'So where are the choice taverns these days? When I was a student there was a place behind the old theatre owned by an African called Agbal, who'd been forced to leave Carthage because of the Vandals. He'd been caught seducing the daughter of a Vandal prince, or so he said. Short man, big scar on his cheek.'

'I don't know him.'

'Oh, that's a shame. Not too surprising, though, considering the crowd he used to bring in. The number of times his place was torn apart! Needless to say, my friends and I learned to sense the precise moment when to move on, before the tables started flying. It could get messy, all right. Speaking of which, I heard the most atrocious tale in the prefect's palace this morning. It seems that a dozen bodies have turned up in the reeds downstream, on the right bank.'

This was the first interesting thing his uncle had said. The right bank of the Rhône was dominated by the military factories and warehouses, and the commercial wharves that stretched for half a mile down the river. It was the realm of shipbuilders and rope-makers, tanners and butchers, infamous for its violence. Hardly a week went by there without a murder in some drunken quarrel or gang feud. But twelve bodies was unusual. 'Who were they?'

'That's the most gruesome part: they were naked and decapitated. Who knows where the heads are? The shippers hate the dockers, the dockers hate the bargemen, and everybody hates the saltworkers. It could have been any of them. Bishop Hilary was saying it's high time the prefect sent troops across the river to clean out the gangs, but of course he won't do that. Do you know what the prefect said? "According to law, soldiers are exempt from paying the head-tax." It's as though we've already given up that half of the city to the barbarians. So I hope you weren't planning any forays over the bridge?'

'No, Uncle.'

'Excellent. Your father would be most displeased if I sent you back to him without a head.'

'Not as displeased as you might think.' He released himself from his uncle's arm. 'I must go and change. My friends are expecting me.'

'Of course. I just wanted to make sure you hadn't forgotten about your sister.'

'What about her?'

'Well, she's arriving tomorrow.'

'I haven't forgotten.'

'Good, good. While she's here, though, remember that you're

responsible for her. Your parents wouldn't want you doing anything foolish, getting yourself hurt, anything like that. For the hundredth time, I wish you'd take a couple of my men with you when you go out drinking. But I suppose as long as you keep to the safer establishments, and don't over indulge, there won't be a problem.'

'No, there won't be a problem,' said Ecdicius. 'Uncle, I'm not a child. I don't need to be told how to look after myself or my sister.'

'Of course not.'

'But that's what you're doing. Has my father written to you?'

Ferreolus looked taken aback. 'No. But even if he had, as your guardian, I—'

'I didn't ask for a guardian, Uncle. I don't need to be coddled or looked after. And I don't need you or my father watching my every move.'

As Ecdicius turned to leave, his uncle placed a firm hand on his shoulder, holding him in place. His grip was surprisingly strong. The pleasantness had vanished from his face. 'Do not test me, Ecdicius,' he said. 'I did not ask to be your guardian any more than you asked to be my ward. I agreed because your mother happens to be my sister.'

'She should never have sent me back to this city.'

'Do you want to serve the empire, Ecdicius?'

'Of course I do. But I'm not a politician.'

'No. You're a boy, and you live under my roof.' He leaned close. 'I do not approve of your behaviour, Ecdicius. I do not approve of you wasting time with idle friends and prostitutes, but, provided you do not run up debts or get any free-born girl pregnant, I will tolerate it because I see that to forbid it would be pointless. Yet while I will tolerate this, I will not tolerate your disrespect. Now apologise.'

Ecdicius gritted his teeth. He took the frustration and wound it up tight inside himself. 'I'm sorry, Uncle. I spoke rashly.'

Ferreolus released his grip. He brushed the creases from where he had disturbed Ecdicius's cloak. 'Good. I am not unsympathetic to your situation, Ecdicius. But you must learn to be patient. If you disgrace yourself now, it will only be harder for you to restore your reputation when the time comes.'

'When the time comes? Aëtius himself banished me from the army. Do you think he's just going to change his mind?'

'Other things might change first. Today word arrived from the Rhine that some tribes in Germany have pledged themselves to Attila. Even some Franks have sworn oaths to him, according to the rumours. Of course, rumours would also have us believe that beyond the Rhine live unicorns and dog-headed men. But if Attila is building a new confederation and turning his eyes to the west, Rome will soon have need of men. She will have little need of boys. Do you understand?'

'Yes, Uncle.'

'This is confidential information I'm entrusting to you. Swear you will tell no one.'

'I swear it.'

'Good. Now you can leave.'

Ecdicius was distracted as his wardrobe slave helped him change into a plain linen tunic and hooded cloak. *Be patient,* his uncle had said. It was easy for someone like Ferreolus; years of service had won him free access to the prefect's palace. He had been playing his part for so long he could surely not remember what it was like to be young, ignored, impotent – to know that the empire was under threat, and to be forbidden from defending it. There was nothing worse than that.

The midday heat was already rising as he left the house and started out for the baths. At this time of day he would normally be looking forward to meeting his friends, lounging and laughing for an hour or two before heading over to the amphitheatre quarter. But he could not forget what his uncle had said about Attila. Everyone knew that for years the Huns had been ravaging the lands of the eastern empire, pillaging countless cities, advancing even to the gates of Constantinople, while Emperor Theodosius trembled behind its walls. They were not like Franks or Goths. They were said to be ugly, twisted creatures who lived on horseback, with no knowledge of farming or towns, driven by a bestial lust for blood and gold. They ate half-raw meat, and cut the faces of their infants so they grew up scarred and beardless. The eastern empire had limitless wealth and soldiers, and still the Huns had brought it to its knees. The west, meanwhile, was fractious and infested with barbarians. So far it had been protected from the Huns by Count Aëtius and his personal friendship with Attila. But if that friendship failed . . .

Ecdicius came to a stop in the busy courtyard of the bath complex. His heart was racing, his breath short. He went to the nearest column and rested against it on one hand, waiting for the moment to pass, banishing the unbidden images of devastation from his mind.

The thumping in his chest calmed. This had been happening ever since the battle, and it was getting worse. Almost every night he was revisited by the screams of those Frankish women. He had not even been able to fuck since arriving in Arles – he had tried, to his humiliation. It was as though a curse had robbed him of his manhood. He was thankful that Aotlind let him lie with her, gave him comfort, and had promised not to say anything. She seemed to understand.

Ecdicius took a deep breath. He glanced about himself, relieved that none of his friends had been around to see his moment of weakness. So far the only respite he had found was in drink and companionship, but that would not help for ever. He did not want to become a drunken wastrel, wrapped up in his own self-pity and scorned by his father. He wanted to serve the empire with honour and courage. But that meant getting another commission, with or without his father's approval.

The biggest problem was money. Ecdicius had only a small allowance, enough for baths and drinking, nothing more. He still had Zephyros in the stables at Avitacum, but his armour had been supplied by his father, and he had no means to support either himself or the groom he would require, let alone pay the cost of a commission. He would need to find a patron. In any case he had no hope of joining a regiment in Gaul, not so long as Count Aëtius had approval over all new appointments. In Italy, though, there was hope. The Italian master of soldiers was Ricimer, a former protégé of Aëtius who was said to have fallen out with his old master. Another possibility was the household guard of Emperor Valentinian, whose mistrust and dislike of Aëtius was well known; that hatred went back more than twenty years, when Aëtius had tried to oppose Valentinian's succession during the last civil war. Either Ricimer or the emperor would surely welcome another ally against Aëtius, provided he came with a good recommendation. But whom could Ecdicius find to vouch for him?

He entered the reception hall of the public baths. It was busy with comings and goings and with groups of chatting friends, their conversations echoing in the barrel vaults of the roof. As Ecdicius walked through the hall, the answer came to him. Consentius – he would soon be arriving in Arles. He wasn't military, but he was a friend, and he had connections at the imperial court. Surely he would know someone who could help. Ecdicius simply needed to enlist his aid without his parents finding out.

He clicked his fingers, and one of the waiting slave attendants followed him into the changing rooms. He felt better already, knowing what he had to do. If serving the empire meant abandoning his family and going to Italy, so be it.

VIII

P erhaps it was the heat and the exhaustion of travel, but
Arvandus felt as though in a dream when he caught his first
glimpse of Arles. For two weeks he had journeyed from Bordeaux
across the countryside of Aquitaine, passing peasants as they
brought in the last of the wheat harvest. Armies of labourers
had been toiling among the vineyards of Marmande. He had sat
by the road for lunches of bread and honey, watching the wind-
pushed waves in the meadows beside the Garonne. He had stood
aside for the troops of bearded Gothic soldiers as they rode to
or from the royal court at Toulouse, horsehair crests flowing
from their tall helmets. Closer to Arles the road had passed
through forests where slaves burned charcoal and felled trees
for the shipbuilders of the Rhône and Durance. He had not
wasted a single day resting. A few times he had paid to jump
on the back of a wagon, but for the most part he had walked,
and his shoes were worn through almost to the soles of his feet.
His tunic and cloak were heavy with dust and sweat. Every
muscle in his body ached.

None of that mattered now. Arles was before him, its walls and
towers becoming more real with every step. As soon as he had
settled into his lodgings, he could buy new shoes and clothes,
and throw away these old rags.

There was salt in the air, carried by the southern wind from
the great marshy plain that lay between Arles and the coast. In the
distance Arvandus spotted the rising clouds of steam from salt
pans. As he neared the city gate, farms and woodland began to
give way to olive groves and suburban houses bunched along the
main road. The houses closest to the walls looked newer, he

guessed built since the end of the last Gothic war ten years earlier. The Goths had long coveted Arles for its port, its famous walls and palace, its fertile lands and valuable saltworks. Four times they had marched on the city, and four times they had been beaten back by Count Aëtius. Arles was the jewel of Gaul, a prize too precious for the empire to lose. Now, as Arvandus came to the western gate, with its vast double gateway, with the thick projecting towers looming one hundred feet above him, he could understand why.

He joined the crowd of people waiting to enter the city. For the most part they were merchants bringing wagonloads of grain and other goods from the provinces, but there were many pedestrians, among them peddlers, labourers, monks, a troupe of acrobats, and more youths than Arvandus could count, all brought to the city by dreams of their own. Soldiers walked up and down the road, guiding wagons and mule-drivers to one side and pedestrians to the other, making sure that nobles and priests had swift passage without being molested by beggars. They looked much like Gothic soldiers, Arvandus thought, except that their helmets lacked plumes and their shields were uniformly painted with double red rings on a green background. Otherwise they wore the same sort of breeches and tunics, the same thick leather belts studded with brass fittings, the same steel helmets with broad cheek guards. They even had the same swaggering arrogance that Arvandus had learned to dislike in all armed men, Romans and barbarians alike.

Arvandus had been waiting in the line for half an hour when he saw Simeon approaching from the city gate. He was alone, wearing a plain cloak and sturdy boots. He might have passed for a legal clerk or a small-scale merchant, or any other such nondescript person, and attracted little attention. He smiled when he spotted Arvandus.

'It's good to see you arrived safely,' Simeon said, at once taking Arvandus by the arm and leading him down the road towards the gate at a brisk pace. 'I hope the journey wasn't too hard?'

'It was fine,' said Arvandus. The soldiers were letting them pass down the line as though the two of them were invisible. 'I was expecting to meet you inside the gates.'

'How are your parents? Were they comfortable when you left them?'

'Very comfortable.' As far as Arvandus's parents were concerned, Simeon had been as good as his word. He had moved them into a house on the outskirts of Bordeaux. It was small, but it had a courtyard garden, and the household chores were managed by an affable domestic freedwoman and her daughter. The new doctor, who had called every day while Arvandus had been there, was serious and optimistic about his father's recovery. It was the first time in years Arvandus had seen his mother smile, though she had wept when he left.

'Good,' said Simeon. 'I'll take you to your lodgings first, and we can talk there.'

When they came to the city gates, where low-ranking newcomers to the city were being questioned by soldiers and registered on the official rolls, Simeon merely nodded to the commanding officer. The officer nodded back and waved the two of them straight through the right-hand arch into the city. Arvandus thought better of asking why they had received special treatment, and was soon too distracted by the commotion of the place to care. Simeon led him up a broad, busy street lined with shops and filled with wagons, pack animals, and pedestrians. Outside a bakery Arvandus spotted a pair of imperial civil servants, not much older than him, identifiable by their military-style brown cloaks and leather belts. A few years from now, he thought with excitement, perhaps he would be able to don that uniform.

The street led directly to a bridge over the river Rhône. 'You're about to walk upon one of the wonders of Gaul,' Simeon said as they passed through a gatehouse that stood at the near end of the bridge. 'Do you see?' After the gatehouse was a drawbridge that shook with the traffic passing over it, and then a long, flat wooden structure that Arvandus saw had been hammered into place across a series of mastless triremes, their prows pointing upriver. Each ship was joined to its neighbours by huge iron chains, with the outer two ships fastened to stone towers further upstream. Arvandus had heard of such constructions, but never seen one. 'The current here is too strong for a normal bridge,' Simeon explained, 'hence this pontoon bridge. In case of siege, the draw-bridges at each end can be raised. If all else fails, the boats can be released so the whole bridge floats away.'

Arvandus was still marvelling at the bridge as they passed through the opposite gatehouse and came to the city proper. They turned right and walked along the east bank of the river, past the fishermen's wharves. Arvandus was strangely comforted by the smell of freshly caught fish, mingled here with the scent of salt in the air. Behind the brick and timber buildings of the wharves towered a massive edifice of barrel roofs and high latticed windows that Simeon told him was the main city bath house. After this they took an alley to the left, into a web of narrow lanes where the two- or three-storey buildings crowded close together, leaving scarcely enough space for a cart to pass between them. They passed several taverns, none of which looked especially disreputable.

Eventually Simeon brought him to a door set in a cleanly plastered wall. He hammered on the door, and it was opened to reveal a tall, thin woman, at least half skeleton, with sharp cheek-bones and deep-set eyes. She acknowledged Simeon with a nod, and appraised Arvandus. She did not look impressed. 'He's small,' she said. 'Well, that's all for the best. Small ones are less trouble, in my experience.'

Simeon gave her a broad smile that was not returned. 'Arvandus, this is Maria, your landlady.'

She led them through the entrance hall, which was plainly furnished but clean, with bundles of fresh herbs hanging from the ceiling, through the inner courtyard, and up to the first floor, explaining the house rules as she went. Open flames were forbidden except in winter; Arvandus was to empty his bedpan every day, lest the smell annoy the other lodgers; he was not to use impious language while under her roof; he was not to entertain actors, charioteers, barbarians or prostitutes, or to molest the cleaning girl. Rent was six silver coins, to be paid on the ides of every month without fail.

'This is your room,' she said, opening a door to let him and Simeon enter. It contained a bed, mattress and chest, all in good condition. In one corner was a small table upon which sat a bowl and water pitcher. The floorboards were well-fitted, the walls smoothly plastered. A decent-sized window overlooked a court-yard at the back of the building.

'I like it,' Arvandus said.

'Most of my lodgers are students. I don't care who you are, if you break the rules you'll be out on the street. I can always find another to replace you.'

'You don't need to worry about this one,' said Simeon. 'He comes from a respectable equestrian family of Bordeaux.'

She pursed her lips. 'He doesn't look very respectable.'

'Neither would you, dear lady, after two weeks on the road.'

Maria said nothing, but her displeasure at Simeon's remark was clear enough in the narrowing of her eyes. Giving Arvandus a final glance, she left them alone, closing the door behind her.

'Maria doesn't trust anyone from the Gothic kingdom,' said Simeon. He went to the chest, opened it, and lifted out a fresh white tunic, which he tossed over.

Arvandus caught the tunic. He was more concerned, however, with Simeon's lie about his status. 'Why did you tell her my family was equestrian?'

'Because she has no idea that it isn't true,' Simeon replied. From the chest he fished out a cloak of dark grey wool, throwing it on the bed. There followed a pair of breeches, a belt, and shoes. 'New clothes for the new man,' he said. 'Get changed.'

Arvandus did not move. 'First tell me why you lied.'

'It's a necessary deceit, I'm afraid. All of your fellow students will be *honestiores* – either equestrian or senatorial. Surely you don't think anyone here will take you seriously as a plebian? In Arles, the only thing people worry about more than their own rank is the rank of everyone around them. And *honestiores*, my friend, do not mix with *humiliores*.'

'But it's fraud.'

Simeon shrugged. 'By the letter of the law, perhaps, but who writes those laws? Remember that your family used to be equestrian anyway, and one day will be again. Don't think of it as lying. Think of it as pre-empting a future truth.' He smiled. 'If you're unable to do this, Arvandus, I will admire your honesty. But we will also have to cancel our arrangement.'

Arvandus ran a finger over the tunic. It was a high quality weave, better than anything he had ever owned. The clothes on the bed looked no less fine. Yet he could not pretend that he was happy with this revelation. 'You should have told me this in Bordeaux.'

'Would it have made any difference? If I'd told you, would you honestly have stayed in that miserable hole? Would you have marched off across the forum and murdered that boy, and buried your parents under yet more shame?'

They both knew the answer to that. There would have been no choice. It was no great dishonesty, Arvandus supposed. It was certainly nothing measured against the injustices committed by the real noble classes.

Simeon seemed satisfied by his silence. 'Remember, your father is an equestrian of middling rank, a *centenarius*. Above you are the two higher equestrian ranks, and then the three senatorial grades: *viri clarissimi, viri spectabiles* and *viri illustres*. Do not forget that.'

'I understand how the senatorial grades work.'

'Good, then I can leave you to devise the rest of your story. I suggest you invent some close relatives who have held minor posts in the civil service – nothing too impressive, just enough to sound believable. Now get changed.'

Arvandus pulled off his travelling clothes, splashed water on his face and neck from the bowl, and dressed in his new wardrobe while Simeon watched. The tunic and breeches were a little too large and would need adjustment, but even the softness of the cloth against his skin made Arvandus feel like a different person. He had known enough boys from equestrian and senatorial families that he would have no trouble affecting a noble bearing, and in his education, at least, he was already their equal. As he fastened the short cloak at his shoulder, he could not deny himself a certain satisfaction. He could easily pass for one of the *honestiores*.

'You would fool Empress Galla Placidia herself,' Simeon said, nodding in approval. 'Now to the forum. There is someone speaking there today whom I want you to see.'

They left the apartment building and headed up the lane, away from the river. At length they came to a wide thoroughfare that Simeon explained ran between the palace precinct and the forum. 'There are in fact two forums in Arles,' he said as they passed from the street into an entrance hall packed with stalls. Through the hall was a large open space surrounded by raised porticos on every side. 'This is the lower forum, the common market,' Simeon continued, waving at the collection of stalls and bustling buyers, from the corner where butchers displayed their cuts of meat and boys used palms to keep the flies away from hanging sheep carcasses, to tables piled high with tubs of olives and beans, to the sellers of fish sauce and ceramic wares, to the wine merchants and basket weavers; Arvandus spotted a pair of acrobats, one balancing on the head of the other before an applauding audience, while nearby a dark-skinned man wearing nothing but a leather thong provoked gasps with his grotesque contortions. There was music, too, a frenetic melody of pipes that carried over the heads of the crowd.

Simeon placed his hand on Arvandus's shoulder and pointed to the opposite side of the forum, where a flight of marble steps led up to another monumental entrance. 'Through there is the upper forum,' he said. 'That's where you'll find the higher-class wares – jewellery, silks and so on. Only *honestiores* and their servants are allowed up there.'

'Can we go up?'

'Another time. Look, this is why I brought you here.' He indicated the far left corner of the forum, where a dark-clad man was standing on a wooden podium and addressing the crowd. Simeon pulled Arvandus closer, easing their way through the throng. A sizeable number of citizens from all classes, men and women, had gathered before the podium. 'This is the monk Salvian,' Simeon said. 'They call him Brother Doom. Listen to him.'

Arvandus was curious. He had heard that the southern cities had preachers like this. The monk looked old, emaciated, his rough tunic hanging loose on bony shoulders. In his right hand he carried a staff, which he waved and thrust as he spoke. Arvandus could tell at once that he had had rhetorical training; the clarity of his diction and the strength of his voice belied his simple appearance.

'See how the rich, great Romans behave!' the monk was shouting. 'See how they open their arms to the common folk; they welcome them, they offer protection. "Come, come," they say, "work on my land, I shall protect you from the taxman." But they are wolves, my brothers. They offer protection to the weak only so they might despoil them further. They steal the lands of the poor and drive them to destitution and the shackles of servitude. Why do you wonder that our citizens long to live under the barbarians? They would rather live free under a barbarian king than be a slave under Roman tyrants. And so for these sins of the well-born, God scourges us all.' He pointed his staff at the crowd. 'Oh, pity the republic! Pity yourselves, for God looks upon us and says, "You are not my people! You are *not* my people!"'

'Is he allowed to say this?' asked Arvandus. 'It almost sounds like treason.'

'You're not the first to think so. But Salvian is a friend of Bishop Hilary, and Bishop Hilary is a friend of Count Aëtius. Now watch the crowd, and tell me what you think.'

Arvandus glanced around the audience. Most faces watching the monk were serious; only a few youths at the edge of the crowd were chuckling to one another. An ancient woman standing nearby was weeping into the hem of her scarf. Others were grumbling. 'He has the sympathy of the people,' Arvandus said. At that moment he noticed a group of three young men descending the steps from the upper forum. They were wealthier members of the nobility, as was clear from their crisp tunics and finely embroidered cloaks, and the assurance with which they carried themselves – bolstered, no doubt, by the half-dozen armed retainers behind them. Pausing on the steps, two of the youths laughed as the monk went on to describe the terrible fate of Trier, that once great imperial capital of Gaul that had been sacked four times by the Franks and now lay in ruins.

The third youth, pasty and dour-faced, with the eyes of an old man, was not smiling. He waited until Salvian had made one more attack on the arrogant nobility of the empire, and then called out across the heads of the crowd, in the clipped, nasal tones of the high senatorial class: 'And what would you have us do, monk? Shall we save the republic by dressing in rags and living on rocks in the sea, like you and your friends?'

Salvian spotted who had spoken. He raised his staff and aimed it at the young man. 'I would have you repent!' he cried, and was met with jeers and applause in equal measure.

His challenger was unmoved. '*We* have nothing to repent. If you love the barbarians so much, perhaps you should go to Toulouse and leave us alone!'

'I know you,' replied Salvian, shouting over the laughter of the crowd. 'I know you, Felix, son of Magnus. It was your great-grandfather, Flavius Agricola, who settled the Goths in Aquitaine. It was he who despoiled honourable Romans of their property.'

Anger rose in the young man's voice. 'You dare slander a consul and prefect?'

Salvian turned to the crowd. 'And what is the prefectship, I ask you all, but a license to pillage?'

Felix roared in outrage, his pale face flushing red. His friends took hold of him, as though he were about to launch himself through the crowd and drag the monk from his podium.

Simeon laughed. 'Oh, Salvian is surpassing himself today, picking a fight with Felix of the Philagrii!'

'They're a big family in Arles?'

'The Philagrii are *the* big family in Arles – and Narbonne, and everywhere else. Felix can count more prefects and consuls among his ancestors than anyone else in Gaul. He's likely to be prefect himself one day.'

Arvandus watched Felix being hurried across the forum by his companions. He was staring directly ahead, his face set with fury, oblivious to the commoners as they were scattered before him by his bodyguards. Salvian's voice came after him in triumph, demanding repentance before the sins of his class led to the utter destruction of the empire. Only when Felix had left the forum did the monk end his sermon and descend from the podium. He left his audience alive with chatter and argument.

Arvandus had been captivated by him. It was not his prophecies of doom, which sounded like the rantings of a zealot. It was the way he had openly challenged one of the noblest citizens of Arles and driven him out of the forum. Such boldness was extraordinary. What was more, he seemed to have the support of the common people. Not one of them had leaped to Felix's defence.

Simeon spotted the excitement in his face. 'Mad or not,' he said, 'you should pay heed to what Salvian says. The old families are frightened of him – not because of what he can do, but because he speaks the truth and reveals it to all.'

'So you agree with him?'

'To a certain extent.' Simeon put his arm around Arvandus's shoulders and pointed at a large marble statue on the left-hand side of the forum, raised on a plinth above the surrounding stalls. It was of an armour-clad emperor wielding an orb in one hand and a sceptre in the other, his eyes raised to heaven. 'Do you see this man? He is Emperor Valentinian, the last truly great ruler of the west. In his day the Gallic prefecture reached from the deserts of Africa to the frozen north. Roman soldiers guarded the frontiers. Roman law ruled in a thousand cities. Now look at you. Romans kneel before Vandals in Africa, before Alans and Sueves in Spain, before Saxons in Britain, before Goths, Burgundians and Franks in Gaul. Many great old cities are in ruins, just like Salvian says. Law has vanished, just as he says. He claims it is the judgement of God. There your patron and I disagree with him. The same families have been running the Gallic prefecture for a hundred years – they, not God, have brought us to this state of affairs. We believe it is time for new men to rise up.'

'So my patron isn't a nobleman?'

'Not by birth, no. Let us just say that he sympathises with your family history, and believes that you have common goals. You are not the only one who has suffered at the hands of the mighty.'

'Have you?'

'I am a Jew,' said Simeon. 'I know what it means not to belong.'

'So to challenge the powerful families, I must pretend to be one of them?'

'Such is the way of the world they have created. It is not pleasant to deceive, I know. But families like the Philagrii have become too powerful; they have confused the good of the empire with their own good, and they destroy any who oppose them. Only by deception can they be removed, and honest men be put in their place.'

Arvandus did understand. Amidst the energy of the crowd, still seething with debate, he saw for the first time that his story did not belong only to his family – it was the story of Gaul. The powerful families had corrupted the country, sinking the rot deep into its roots. They had built up mountains of gold and turned honest men into paupers, driving them from their land or crushing them beneath unfair taxes while the state coffers drained empty and the imperial armies grew weaker. Over the past forty years one barbarian group after another had settled itself on Roman land, and the empire had been powerless to resist them. The Goths claimed to rule Aquitaine on behalf of the emperor, but nobody truly believed that. King Theoderic bowed to no one. Simeon was right. The empire was crumbling.

One thought was kindled in Arvandus's mind like a fire: just as the empire had been brought down by men, not God, so it would need men to restore it. And he would be one of them.

IX

'Have you ever seen a Moorish dwarf, my dear?'

'I saw dwarves performing once in Lyons,' Attica said.

'But a *Moorish* dwarf?' said her aunt Papianilla. 'He's called Zerkon. The prefect had him entertain us at a feast last month. Oh, I wish you'd been here then! Wasn't he wonderful, Ecdicius?'

'Yes, Aunt,' said her brother. He did not take his eyes from the arena, although it was still empty.

Shielding her eyes, Attica gazed into the upper tiers of the amphitheatre. Her heart leaped to see the great stone arcade climbing halfway to heaven, the flags of purple and gold fluttering in a brilliantly blue autumn sky. The higher seats had already been filled with the commoners, a teeming mob who watched as the last of the noble families entered and took their seats. She had never seen so many people in one place. Her native city of Clermont did not have an amphitheatre, and even its theatre had not been used for years. There must have been twenty thousand voices humming all around her.

In the last two weeks Arles had proved to be everything Attica had imagined it would be. She loved the towering walls of the imperial palace near their house, the never-sleeping sounds of the streets, the markets with the sweet smells of perfume and incense, and piled-up rolls of eastern fabrics, and the upper forum where men and women from the noblest families in Gaul could be found: the Philagrii, Syagrii, Aviti, Ennodii, and a dozen others. Nor was she disappointed by this amphitheatre. She was proud to be sitting between her uncle and aunt. Behind them were the equestrian families of civic officials and lesser imperial clerks, but she was in the most prestigious place of all, right next to the prefect's box, on the cushioned seats reserved for those of senatorial rank. As she looked over the crowd she felt the satisfying weight of her new earrings, and imagined how fine they must look with the sunlight flashing on the gold pendants, and on the inlaid emeralds, garnets and pearls. Aunt Papianilla had given them to her, along with a pair of fur-lined leather shoes and a mantle of pale blue silk. She was pleased to see that she was already attracting looks from many people, men and women, highborn and low. Uncle Ferreolus and Aunt Papianilla seemed to know every person of note, judging from how often they smiled and waved to the other noble families taking their seats. Attica recognised some faces, having been introduced to more people than she could remember since arriving in the city.

There was only one face that interested her, though. She gave another discreet glance to the right, where, in the next section of seating, Consentius was with a group of other young men. He was still too busy joking with them to notice her. They had not seen one another since her arrival in Arles. It was agony to be sitting so near to him, after all this time, and not be able to get his attention. In two days she was to meet for the first time with her cousin Felix, which would be the first step towards the betrothal desired by both their families. If only she could get Consentius to declare his interest, her parents might allow her to choose him instead. With luck she could somehow bump into him as they were leaving the amphitheatre.

Her aunt was still talking about Zerkon the Moorish dwarf in her usual excited manner. 'He used to belong to Attila's brother, if I remember rightly. Then after Attila killed his brother, poor Zerkon had to flee, and ended up in the east. Now he wants to go back to Attila, apparently to reclaim the Hunnic wife he left behind. He's like a little Odysseus. It's dull to hear me tell it, but I wish you'd seen him, Attica. He had a whole clown performance in Latin, Greek and Hunnic. He even had the bishop in hysterics, and I do believe Count Aëtius almost cracked a smile.'

'I wouldn't go that far, my darling,' said Ferreolus. 'Anyway,

Zerkon may be a clown, but he's no fool. He knows he's useful to us. Aëtius is planning to send an embassy to Attila next year, and it'll be helpful to have Zerkon go along.'

He was interrupted by a blast of trumpets from the prefect's box. There was a roar of applause as the praetorian prefect entered, accompanied by his family and the members of his privy council. He led the crowd in acclamations for the health of Emperor Valentinian, before signalling for the games to begin.

The air filled with cheers. Despite her disappointment at remaining invisible to Consentius, Attica could not help feeling the excitement of the crowd. Ecdicius, though, seemed immune to it. He was still hunched over, staring into the arena with a severe intensity in his eyes.

Attica looked at her brother with concern. He had not bothered to shave again today, and was still wearing that tunic with the dark stain down the left sleeve. Ever since her arrival in the city he had treated her with the same cold distance he had shown back at home. Half of the time he did not even eat with the family, instead venturing into the city and often not reappearing until the next day. When he was at dinner he spoke little. At first she had feared he resented having to be responsible for her, but she sensed something much deeper than that. Whatever darkness he had brought to Clermont he had brought here, too.

'I saw the list of wild animals ordered by the prefect,' Ferreolus said. 'Thirty stags for the mounted archers, bulls, half a dozen bears from the Alps, a giant aurochs from beyond the Danube. It'll be quite the show.'

Her cousin Sidonius, who was sitting beyond Ecdicius, leaned over. 'Will there be any lions and leopards?'

'Don't be stupid,' scoffed Ecdicius. 'Arles hasn't seen lions or leopards for ten years.'

'Why not?'

'Because the Vandals captured Africa, why do you think?'

Sidonius nodded. He said nothing, but Attica could tell his feelings had been hurt, and felt sorry for him. So far she had had little luck engaging her second cousin in conversation, but he seemed harmless. There was certainly no cause for her brother to have been so brusque.

'The aurochs will be outstanding,' Ferreolus said. 'I saw one last year. Tore a man to shreds. They're not like the bulls they breed around here – they're wild, all right, those German beasts. Big as houses, you'll see.'

The first entertainment was the stag hunt. It was good to bloody the sand, although Attica found the horse-archers were more interesting than the animals, which loped predictably around the arena, terrified. The bears were large and fierce, frightening even seen from safety. Most of all she enjoyed the bull-leaping and bull-baiting, and cheered to see the young acrobats defy death by hurling themselves between the sweeping horns.

But when the arena was cleared and sprinkled with fresh sand ready for the aurochs, the crowd hushed. The gate was drawn up. The monster emerged with a bellow and thunderous hooves. Her uncle had been right. She had never seen such a creature. A cry of fear caught in her throat as she watched it charge around the arena, churning up clouds of sand, as though it might at any moment crash into the wall and bring the whole amphitheatre tumbling down.

Three riders with lances entered from a different gate, and two riders with javelins. Each rider wore the same costume of red and green, with strips of fabric flowing from their shoulders like wings. They circled the aurochs, drew it on, taunted it, teased it with the points of their lances, tiring it out. This was a famous team, Uncle Ferreolus told her, and they knew what they were doing. After a while they began to thrust their weapons into its flanks. One lancer was thrown from his rearing horse, but another rider distracted the beast with a javelin, and the first was able to climb the webbing to safety.

The contest lasted for half an hour and ended the only way it could. 'That was a good fight,' said Ferreolus when it was over.

'The aurochs didn't have much of a chance, did it?' said Sidonius.

'Of course it didn't,' said Ecdicius. 'That's the point.'

'What do you mean?'

Ecdicius did not reply. He was watching Consentius, who had left his friends and was making his way towards the entrance that led into the gallery below the seating. At once Ecdicius jumped up and headed after him, pushing past Sidonius. With scarcely a thought, Attica also rose.

'Where are you going, my dear?' asked her aunt.

'I'm going to get some refreshments with my brother. I won't be long.'

She joined the throng heading down the steps into the cool air of the tunnel, which was reserved for the use of nobles seeking respite from the sun. Slave attendants stood at tables, serving wine and water to those who desired it. Attica, having lost sight of her brother, felt momentary alarm at the press of unfamiliar bodies around her; but then she spotted the back of his head further down the curving gallery, and went after him.

By the time she caught up, Ecdicius had found Consentius and was talking to him in a quiet, gloomy stretch of the tunnel. They were standing close together as though in secret confidence. Ecdicius was speaking with such urgency that Attica hesitated before approaching. Consentius, with his back to the tunnel wall, looked evasive and uncomfortable.

She was about to turn back when Consentius noticed her. He smiled and waved. Ecdicius stopped talking, saw his sister, and gave her a look of deep irritation.

'How lovely to see you again,' said Consentius, walking over and taking her hand. 'How are you, Chromatia?'

'Attica,' she said.

'Attica, of course! Can you forgive me? It's the heat of the sun, it always slows my brain. Are you enjoying the games?'

'Very much.'

'Splendid. Well, I need to get back to my friends. It was a pleasure to see you again, Attica. I'm sure we'll meet again soon.'

With that he nodded and left them. She watched him go, her heart sinking. He had not even remembered her name. Who was this Chromatia?

'Thank you for the interruption, Sister,' said Ecdicius, giving her a sarcastic bow. 'Thank you.'

'He forgot my name,' she said, trying to fight the lump in her throat. She felt like a fool.

'Of course he did. What did you expect?' He noticed her distress, and laughed. 'By God, Sister, don't say you've infatuated yourself with *Consentius*? You have, haven't you? Well, let me save you a broken heart. The charming Consentius is most unlikely to return your affections. You'll be an old maid by the time he marries, believe me. His predilections lie elsewhere. Oh, poor, innocent Attica!'

'Don't you mock me,' she said. She used her anger to steady the tremble in her voice. 'I'm not the one moping about like a spoiled brat.'

'*Moping about*? Don't be ridiculous.'

'You've been a miserable wretch ever since you got home. The way you talk to Sidonius is horrible. You're disrespectful to Uncle Ferreolus and Aunt Papianilla. All because you're not allowed to play soldiers any more.'

He took a sudden step towards her. His voice became sharp. 'I don't have to explain myself to my little sister.'

'Don't you dare bully me. It's not my fault you got sent home for being a coward.'

At first she did not feel the pain of his knuckles against her cheek. There was only the naked force of the slap, and the shock as her neck twisted to the side. The pain came a moment later, flooding across the side of her face. She gasped. Steadying herself, she looked at her brother, blinking as her eyes filled with tears.

He was frowning, with his mouth half-open as though in shock himself. He held out a hesitant hand.

'Don't touch me,' she snapped, stepping away from him. 'You're a coward. A *coward*.' She might have said more, but instead she turned around and headed back down the gallery, pushing her way through the jovial crowd, and headed up the steps into the blinding afternoon light.

X

Maximinus was old and white-bearded, a hunched-over Greek who seemed small even to Arvandus. He scratched his cane on the floor as he walked up and down the length of the classroom. In his crackly, weirdly-accented little voice he was explaining in careful detail the principles of panegyrics, the formal poems of praise delivered on ceremonial occasions, while his students took notes on their wax tablets for later memorisation. The panegyric was merely one of the rhetorical forms they were expected to master. Over the next three years Maximinus would also instruct them in epic, comic and lyric poetry, in philosophy and history, satire, geometry and arithmetic, astrology and law. This was the intellectual armoury of the cultured Roman.

Over the last month Arvandus had grown used to the daily routine of rising before dawn to congregate with the others at their tutor's house, where they had lessons until midday. He enjoyed the classes, finding Maximinus to be a demanding but fair-minded teacher, and he took some satisfaction from being the cleverest of the nine students. Three of his fellows were from senatorial families, the remainder equestrian, and they came from every corner of the Gallic provinces. Besides Arvandus only one of them, Lampridius, came from the Gothic territory, but his family lived in Toulouse, with no connection to Bordeaux, and so Arvandus had no fear of being found out. Not only had Lampridius accepted his story without question, he had even adopted him almost as a long-lost brother. 'After all,' Lampridius had said at their first meeting, 'we barbarians must stick together, mustn't we?'

It was a joke, of course. Except for the accident of their

birthplace, the two of them were as Roman as the others. Yet
Arvandus liked having someone who had also grown up under
barbarian rule, with whom he could complain about the rough-
ness of Gothic soldiers, 'those seven-foot piles of hair and
grease,' as Lampridius called them.

When the day's lessons ended and the class spilled out onto
the street, Lampridius, as usual, took Arvandus by the arm. 'Will
I see you at the baths later, comrade?' he asked.

'Certainly you will,' said Arvandus. 'Just let me go home and
change.'

'As you wish. Be there within the hour, though, or suffer the
consequences!'

They parted, laughing, as Arvandus took the road that led to
his lodgings. Lampridius was good company, but he could be
overbearing. He did not walk so much as strut, rarely spoke
except to shout, and if oxen could laugh, Arvandus thought, they
would laugh like him. Since Lampridius had also undertaken his
grammatical education in Arles, he already knew the city and
had taught Arvandus some basic rules – where students drank,
when and where they bathed, which chariot faction they supported
(the blues), and above all never to go to the west bank of the
river. And he had told him where to find girls. 'Head over to the
amphitheatre quarter if you want actresses, dancers, gymnasts,
that sort of thing,' he had said. 'The high-class courtesans don't
look twice at our sort, so don't even try. Go to the new cathedral
on one of the feast days if you want a respectable girl. Give her
a fistful of flowers and you're as good as married. But if you
want *real* excitement, head for the artisans' district down by the
river. There, my friend, you'll find whores from every corner of
the world. Flaxen-haired, white-limbed Fenni from the distant
north, ebony Nubians from the deserts of the south, Parthians
and Thracians, Scythian she-wolves whose mastery of pain and
pleasure is beyond even my ability to describe.'

In Bordeaux, Arvandus had been with only one girl, the daughter
of a fishmonger, in a few brief ruttings under the staircase outside
his parents' apartment. Apart from that, because of his shortness,

girls had never shown much interest in him, and he had never had the money for prostitutes. Now that he wore the clothes of an aristocrat, things were different. The last month had brought many new experiences.

Arvandus entered his lodgings quietly, hoping to avoid Maria. He had passed through the empty entrance hall and was climbing the steps to the upper floor when he saw her waiting at the top.

'Arvandus,' she said, peering down at him with a contemptuous narrowing of her eyes. 'I explained the rules to you, did I not? Rent on the ides of every month. The ides was two days ago.'

'And I promised to pay. I just need a couple more days.'

She took in a long, slow sniff. 'This is your final warning. One more day. If you haven't paid by noon tomorrow, you will leave. Is that clear?'

Arvandus climbed the steps, pushed past her, went into his room and kicked the door shut. He cursed under his breath. The tight-fisted hag. He had been here a single month, and she was ready to throw him out. Was he the first person ever to suffer bad luck at the races? That had been a stupid bet, to be fair, but necessary to gain face with the others. The favourite topic of conversation among his classmates, aside from sex, was chariot racing. By placing such a large bet Arvandus had impressed them, at least to begin with. How was he to know that the blues' third horse had sprained an ankle last month, and that the team wouldn't even complete the third lap?

He shouldn't have made the bet while drunk. That was true. Maybe he shouldn't have bought this new tunic, either, with its red and gold embroidered collar of Dionysiac revellers, or the brass-studded belt and fine shoes.

He sat on the end of the bed, realising the depth of the problem. Maria seemed to mean what she said. Even if he sold his clothes, he would never be able to scrape together enough coin by noon tomorrow. What was he going to do?

There was a knock at the door. It did not sound like Maria. 'Enter,' he called. The door opened to reveal a familiar figure. At once Arvandus jumped to his feet. 'Simeon.'

Simeon nodded. His slow, critical gaze passed over the room, then settled on Arvandus. 'I see you've renewed your wardrobe.'

Arvandus felt suddenly uncomfortable in his tunic.

'And I understand that you have failed to pay this month's rent. Maria has complained to me, and so I have been obliged to pass her complaint on to your patron. He is most displeased.'

'I'm late by just a few days. If he wants me to explain myself . . .'

'Oh, he does. I'm to take you to him.'

Arvandus's words caught in his throat. He coughed. 'Now?'

'Yes. This is not his usual custom, I must tell you. He's only agreed to see you at my personal urging.' He placed a hand over his heart. 'So if you disappoint him, I will also pay the price. He is not a man who forgives easily.'

'I won't disappoint him.'

'Good. Then get your cloak, and follow me.'

Simeon, not saying another word, led Arvandus from the apartment building and through a part of the city he did not yet know, passing by the new cathedral and leaving the city by the south gate. They came to a suburban neighbourhood of orchard gardens and meadows, where the busy sounds of the city were softened by the wind rustling through branches, and by the cries of herons from the marshes to the south. Passing down a gravel path lined with pear trees, they approached a secluded compound of ivy-clad walls. Standing at the gatehouse were two armed men with a leashed guard dog. They opened the doors and nodded to Simeon as he led Arvandus inside.

They came into a courtyard surrounded on all sides by a portico. Well-kept paths ran between tidy rectangular beds of colourful flowers and shrubs, most of which Arvandus did not recognise. Even more striking than the garden were the statues lining the portico: nymphs, dryads, an array of emperors, heroes, gods and goddesses. He saw a pair of strange birds walking slowly along one of the paths, dragging immense feathery tails of shimmering green and purple, their purple necks raised with regal dignity. They were peacocks, he realised. He had seen images of them before, but never imagined that they were so glorious in reality.

'Wait here,' said Simeon. 'Your patron is called Paeonius, *vir clarissimus* and former governor. You will refer to him as "Master".'

Simeon walked down the central path towards a canvas awning that had been erected on a lawn on the far side of the courtyard. Beneath the awning a large man lay on a generously cushioned couch. Another man sat at a small table; he seemed to be an accountant of some sort, and was counting gold coins from a pile, placing them into small sacks, and scratching on a wax ledger as he did so. Simeon went to the reclining man, bowed, and began talking with him.

Arvandus tried not to look as intimidated as he felt. He attempted to plan what he would say. It would do no good to make excuses. He would have to admit his fault and plead naïvety, while not appearing too pathetic. Or would Paeonius expect abject humility? It was impossible to know, never having met him before. He was not among the noblest families of the city; *vir clarissimus* was the lowest senatorial rank, looked down on by the likes of the Philagrii, whose menfolk frequently attained the rank of *vir illustris* through serving in high office. But he was clearly a man of taste and substance.

Simeon turned and with a brief gesture beckoned for Arvandus to approach. He straightened his posture and walked along the path towards the awning. Paeonius, on the couch, was a long-limbed, rotund man. He was dressed in a loose linen tunic that was finely cut but not extravagant. His elbow-length sleeves and broad neckline revealed sagging fat that wobbled as he wiped his hands on a napkin before throwing it on the low table before him. A sheen of sweat gleamed on his balding head. 'So,' he said. 'You are Arvandus?'

'Yes, Master,' said Arvandus, bowing.

'I have received complaints about your conduct.'

'I beg your forgiveness, Master. I'm new to the city, and in my innocence—'

'Don't try your sophistry on me, boy,' snapped Paeonius. 'I'm told you've failed to pay your rent for this month.'

Arvandus spoke his next words almost without thinking. 'I haven't failed,' he said. 'I just haven't succeeded yet.'

His patron's eyes widened, shocked at the insolent reply. Simeon coughed. Arvandus glanced at him, and thought he saw a subtle smile.

Paeonius, if he was offended by the remark, chose to ignore it. 'Be that as it may,' he said, 'you've exhausted a three-month stipend in four weeks. I have a good pair of eyes in my head. I can see you're wearing half of it, and I understand you've gambled the rest away. Well, I won't have my money wasted. Simeon here claims he saw you work wonders in Bordeaux, which may or may not be true, and your tutor is satisfied with your progress so far. But for their testimonies, you'd be on your way back home already. As it is, I'll keep you on – for now. But I'll reserve my forgiveness until I think you deserve it. Is that clear?'

'Yes, Master.'

Paeonius fixed him with an unblinking stare. There was a frightening hardness in those eyes. He made a brief wave of his hand that seemed to indicate a dismissal.

Arvandus did not move. 'Master,' he said. 'About my rent . . .'

'That's not my concern. You receive your next installment two months from now, as agreed – assuming you don't starve to death before then. Now get out of my sight.'

Simeon took Arvandus by the arm and guided him away from Paeonius, back down the path. 'You were fortunate to get him in a good mood today,' he said.

'But how am I to pay my rent by tomorrow?'

Simeon shrugged. 'However you can. Surely you didn't expect Paeonius to give you more money?'

'Could he at least ask Maria to give me a few more days?' As he spoke there was a rush of wind through the trees. Arvandus felt a spot of rain on his neck.

'He is not that kind of patron. After he raises his clients up, he expects them to stand on their own feet. If they fall, they fall. There are always more ready to replace them. Think of it as a test of your ingenuity.' He glanced into the sky. 'There's a storm coming. You should return to the city.'

Simeon bowed and returned to his master, leaving Arvandus

to walk back to his lodgings alone. The rain began to fall before he reached the south gate, but he scarcely noticed. As he passed through the gate he was met by a faint rumble of thunder from the north.

Once back in his room, he closed the door and sat again on his bed. He had no money. Could he ask to borrow some from his fellow students? That was a possibility. Lampridius would be his first choice, except that he too was penniless at the moment, waiting for his father to send more money. Of the other students, the equestrians Arcadius and Salonius always seemed to have money to spare, but they were devious and mean-hearted, not the sort he wanted to be indebted to. The moneylenders in the markets and taverns would be even worse. Behind their every smile was a knife.

He leaned forward and grasped his head in his hands, closing his eyes. *Think.*

Another peal of thunder rolled over the city.

Then the answer came to him. It was so simple it made him laugh out loud. Why did he have to pay his rent at all?

XI

As soon as the last echo of thunder had faded, the rain began to patter on the tile roof above, reverberating through the quietness of the day room. Even louder was the din from the atrium, where the rain fell straight into the central pool.

Attica turned her attention back to the small copper mirror held by Cyra in front of her. The bruise was not as bad as she had feared; Ecdicius had tried to stop himself at the last moment. He had left a yellow blush on her left jaw, but it was not too large, and the colour was barely noticeable. It would soon fade. Her uncle and aunt had not yet noticed it, anyway, and she had not told them about the incident. 'Thank you, Cyra,' she said.

Her handmaiden replaced the mirror on the table and picked up the make-up cloth. 'I could still try to hide the mark, mistress.'

Attica pushed the cloth away. 'No, don't bother. I want Ecdicius to see what he did, assuming he ever shows his face again.'

Cyra nodded, placing the cloth back in the ivory cosmetics box. As she closed the lid she gave a wet sniff.

'Don't cry, Cyra,' Attica said. '*You're* not the one he hit.'

'I should have been there to protect you, mistress.'

'Protect me against Ecdicius? No, don't be silly. I was the one who told you to stay at home, remember? My brother's the one to blame. He's a coward. He hasn't even had the courage to apologise.'

'Your brother isn't himself, mistress. He hasn't been since he came back to Clermont. It was the same with my father. He was always so gentle, and then after the wars sometimes he would hit us for no reason.'

'I remember.' Attica knew that sad tale. Cyra's father had been a centenarius in her father's regiment during the last Gothic war. He had been decorated for valour at the siege of Narbonne, holding the walls until the Roman relief force arrived, but afterwards had never been the same. In the end he had walked into a public privy and sat down as though to relieve himself, before taking out a dagger and thrusting it into his heart. He had expired to the sound and smell of his own bowels emptying, with a dozen strangers looking on in horror. To help repair the shame of such a death, Attica's father had taken the old soldier's widow and daughter under his wing, and Cyra had been trained as Attica's handmaiden.

Although Ecdicius had not told her what had happened to him in the north, the awful thought occurred to Attica that he was heading down the same road as Cyra's father. She felt some of her anger dissipate, to be replaced by anxiety. The signs were there: the darkness in his looks, the strange distance, and now the violence . . .

She heard the front door of the house open and close. Felix had arrived. She straightened her back, squared her shoulders, tried to clear her thoughts. Cyra withdrew quietly to the side of the room. Meeting with Felix was the last thing Attica wanted to do today. A few days ago she had been planning to feign illness, but what was the point now that Consentius had shown her the way things really were? She could not forget her brother's mocking laugh at her infatuation, as though she were the last fool in the city to realise the truth about him. All of his charm had been a mere joke, a pantomime. So she had decided to meet with Felix after all, to see what kind of man he was.

Her uncle appeared at the open door, accompanied by a pale, thin-faced young man. 'Dearest niece,' Ferreolus said, 'I have the pleasure of introducing you to Felix, son of your cousin Magnus.'

Attica rose from the chair and gave a brief, meticulous bow, tilting her head demurely to one side as she had seen other noble girls do in the upper forum. 'Cousin Felix,' she said, meeting his gaze. He was wearing a white tunic with swirling green borders, perfectly embroidered. Every hair of his receding hairline was in place.

'Cousin Attica,' he said. His voice was unattractive, nasal and sharp. He did not smile.

'Well,' said her uncle, 'I'll leave you alone for a little while.' He walked out, leaving the door open. Only Cyra remained with them.

Felix was inspecting her face with narrowed eyes. 'Someone has struck you.'

'I wasn't struck,' she said, alarmed at his bluntness.

'I know where a bruise like that comes from. Who was it?'

'It doesn't matter.' She gestured at the chair beside hers. 'Would you like to sit?'

He did not move. 'It matters to me. Who was it?'

'If you sit, I'll tell you.'

There was anger in his expression, but Attica could not tell whether it was due to her stubbornness or because he was upset for her sake. Eventually he sat, placing himself in the chair in a single smooth movement. He continued staring at her, his back straight. His grey eyes were fixed on her like a pair of grappling hooks. 'Well?' he said. 'Who was it?'

It was clear that there was no point resisting him further, and no point lying; she could not blame her uncle, and any slave she blamed would pay for it with his life. 'It was my brother.'

He sniffed. 'Of course it was. He's been disgracing the whole family ever since he arrived in the city. Associating with layabouts and catamites like that clown Consentius. Half the time he's still drunk when he arrives for morning class.'

Attica did not know what to say, torn between an instinct to defend her brother and her abiding anger with him. It was hard to imagine Felix and Ecdicius sharing the same tutor. Nineteen years old, Felix was speaking like a man of forty.

They sat together in silence while the rain hammered overhead. Felix appeared to become aware of the awkwardness he had created. He cleared his throat. 'I apologise. I shouldn't speak harshly of your brother. I am simply concerned for your well-being.'

'It was nothing,' she said. 'Just a silly squabble between brother and sister.'

'I see.' He looked at the cosmetics box on the table before them. It was carved with scenes from Virgil and Ovid. 'Dido,' he said, tracing a finger on a carving of the queen climbing onto her funeral pyre. '*May the Trojan drink in this fire with cruel eyes from afar,*' he recited, '*and may he carry with him the omens of our death.*' His eyes returned to Attica. 'I won't have any man harm you, not even your brother.'

'That is kind of you, but I'm sure he won't strike me again. Cyra here has sworn to slay him if he does.'

The joke was misjudged; Cyra looked startled, Felix merely confused. 'A handmaiden can't always protect you,' he said. 'That is the job of a husband – someone like me. Our parents anticipate our betrothal, Attica, and I can assure you that I desire it just as much as they do.'

He did not lack confidence, that much was clear. 'I hope to have some say in it myself,' she said.

'Of course, but I have no doubt that a union would be in your interests as much as mine. We're of similar age, which people say can be a great advantage. I won't complete my education until next summer, true, but I expect to be made tribune and notarius at the imperial court within two years. Certainly we can be wed before you reach seventeen, which will leave you plenty of time to bear children.'

He had everything planned out, it seemed. Her role was to breed his heirs. 'Tell me then,' she said, 'how many male and female children would you like? I could try to give you a boy, then a girl, then another boy, and keep on like that. Or perhaps just boys to start with?'

For a moment he seemed to think she was serious, as though she were revealing to him the feminine secret that women could choose the sex of their unborn children. Then, slowly, he detected the sarcasm. 'You're making fun of me, I see.'

'A little, yes.'

'If we wed, Attica, I can promise to treat you with the respect you deserve. Once I return from the imperial court, a post here on the prefect's staff seems assured. By that time my father may even hold the Gallic prefectship. Then one day, should the emperor deem me worthy, I may be given the honour myself. I have no interest in a wife who sits at home weaving all day. I want a wife who can stand beside me at every step of my career. I hope that you are that woman.'

Her interest was rising, though there was still something amusing about his precocious ambition. 'You only want to be prefect? I'm disappointed in you, Felix. I thought you'd settle for nothing less than a consulship.'

For the first time, something like a smile creased his lips. 'Indeed,' he said. 'My great-grandfather was consul, and my grandfather. I'm sure my father will be, too.' His voice lowered. 'But why even stop at the consulship? I mean to achieve what no one in our family has since Philagrius himself.'

He could only mean one thing. Only two consuls were appointed each year, one by the eastern emperor and one by the western; an honorary title, but it assured eternal fame for the man's family. Such fame would be enough for almost all men. But Felix's great-great-grandfather Philagrius had won a further honour. 'You want to be named patrician,' she said.

'I'd be a fool not to reach that high.' He leaned closer. 'The prefecture, the consulate, Gaul itself – it's as good as my inheritance. *Our* inheritance. You're as much a descendant of Philagrius as I am, and you have consuls on your side of the family, too. Your father has already held the prefecture. Gaul belongs to you, Attica, as much as it does to me.' His voice dropped almost to a whisper. 'We could share it together.'

She was no longer ready to mock him. There was nothing boyish about him, nothing silly. Suddenly she saw her infatuation with Consentius for the foolishness it had been. Consentius might be wealthy and charming, but inside he would always be a boy, pleasure-seeking and wilful, and boys did not run empires. Attica wanted more than that. Although Felix was not pleasant to look on, he seemed to be offering it. And she could tell that he desired her in a way that Consentius did not.

'Perhaps we could share it,' she said.

He straightened in his chair. 'Forgive my presumption. I didn't mean to startle you with my passion. I'll have my father write to yours at the first opportunity, if I have your favour. It should be done properly.'

'Let me speak to him when I return home,' she said.

'But that won't be until after winter, surely?'

She frowned. 'Will you not wait?'

'Of course. You know I will.' He made an awkward shift in his chair, as though deciding to move and not to move in the same instant. He hesitated a moment longer, then lurched forwards, placed his hands on her shoulders, and kissed her. It was a brief, chaste kiss, his closed lips pressing against hers, not the kiss of a lover. 'I would like to see more of you,' he said, rising awkwardly. 'I'll talk to your uncle now. If he approves, perhaps you can come and stay at Lupiacum for a few days, before the cold weather sets in.'

'Will Ecdicius be invited too?'

'I can hardly not invite him.'

'Perhaps getting out of the city will do him some good.'

'Perhaps,' he said, though he looked doubtful. 'I will see you very soon, Attica.'

She enjoyed watching him try to recover his composure as he walked out of the room. Was it really so easy? She had felt no excitement at the kiss, but it was exciting to think of Felix's quiet audacity – reaching for not just the consulship, but the *patriciate* – and no less exciting to think that she, with no great effort, could strip him of his self-confidence. Becoming his wife would give her real influence. She could be like her great aunt, Padusia – not *quite* like her, she corrected herself; Padusia had been arrested and executed for treason by Count Aëtius. She would be more careful. She would be like Sidonius's grandmother Roscia, who ruled the Apollinares clan, or like her own mother Severiana, whose opinions were respected by governors and bishops across Gaul. She would certainly not be like her sister Papianilla, who seemed determined to shut herself away in religious isolation for the rest of her life.

As for whether she truly wanted to marry Felix, she had won herself a few months to decide. If he proved to be unbearable, she could simply refuse him. There were other ambitious men in the world.

She smiled to herself. This was a game better than brigands, one it seemed she could play by instinct. It was a game Papianilla would never know how to play.

In fact, there would be no harm in reminding her of that. 'Cyra,' she said. 'Fetch a tablet and pen. I wish to compose a letter to my sister.'

XII

Maria was not a happy person. She especially despised the morally misgoverned, who, as far as she was concerned, comprised the majority of the human race. Her only uncertainty was which kind of iniquity was worse. Drunkenness, gambling, or licentious perversion? Arvandus, at any rate, was guilty of all three; and he had only made himself more suspect by coming from Bordeaux, which lay in the domain of King Theoderic. Maria was just about old enough to remember the time when Aquitaine had not been ruled over by savages. The Goths, she knew, were the rod with which God had decided to punish the empire for the sins of the wicked. For thirty years Aquitaine had festered under them. And now this small, degenerate creature had come crawling out of that swamp to her doorstep. Was it any wonder that he had proven to be a reprobate?

This was how Arvandus imagined himself through Maria's eyes, at least. It did not make him want to mend his ways, but it did make him feel less guilty about stealing her furniture.

He arranged for the men to come in the early hours, when Maria was at church and the rest of the tenants were either asleep or had not yet returned home from the previous night's dissolution. They took the bed, mattress, table and chest from his room, and even the wooden stool. They did not want the jug. Arvandus was tempted to sell them the floorboards and window frame, but that would have made too much noise and taken too much time. They carried everything downstairs, loaded it onto the back of a mule cart, and headed off down the lane, trundling through the puddles left from the previous day's rainstorm.

Arvandus did not wait, but started walking in the opposite

direction, a sack containing his few belongings over his shoulder. He smiled as he felt the satisfying weight of his newly filled purse against his chest, where he had it tucked beneath his tunic and cloak. He had not nearly made good his losses, but the quality furniture had fetched a good price, enough to last him for the next couple of months. Paeonius would hopefully appreciate his boldness and ingenuity. There was the pleasure of imagining his former landlady's face when she saw the room, too. Now he simply had to find a new place to live, a safe distance across the city.

That proved to be harder than he had expected. Anywhere near the east bank dockyards was too close; he wandered further into the city, first around the well-paved streets near the palace, where he sensed at once that he would not be welcome, then towards the new cathedral, and after that to the south-eastern district, between the ruins of the theatre and the old cathedral. The few apartments with spare rooms were too expensive. Finally he went to the north-eastern quarter, but had no more luck.

By this time it was mid-morning, and the city was bustling. He walked without aim down towards the river, hunger and rising anxiety twisting his gut. He bought a plate of mussels from a seller near the bridge and sat on the edge of the wharf, in the shadow of the vast public baths. From its high windows he could hear the sounds of laughter and splashing water. Impatient gulls strutted nearby, watching him as he ate the mussels and flicked the empty shells into the river. He wondered what to do. Had it been a mistake? It had seemed an ingenious solution. Perhaps he should have demanded more coin for the furniture. No, that wouldn't have helped. The buyers had known perfectly well what he was up to, and he would have been even more foolish to push them further.

A merchant ship was coming in to dock to his left. The captain was leaning over the starboard side, yelling commands at the steersman and at the dockhands as they pulled on tow ropes. The yard was crooked, evidently damaged in the storm and now held together by lashes of rope. Arvandus wondered where this vessel had come from. Spain, perhaps, or Corsica, or Italy. Perhaps it had come from Portus itself, at the mouth of the Tiber. Wherever it had come from, the captain would need a fast turnaround if he intended to head back; the sea would soon be closed to traffic for the winter months. He would unload, spend a few days restocking, repair the yard, load up, push off, and sail back down the river to the sea, leaving Arles behind him.

Arvandus almost envied him. Even with the dangers of the sea it would be good to have such purpose, to know exactly where to go and what to do, to have a place in the world. Instead he was sitting here on the docks, homeless and half destitute. His gaze fell on the discarded mussel shells, bobbing aimlessly on the lazy water below. He pondered how long they would take to be carried out to sea. Would they one day wash up on the shores of Africa?

There was a flurry of feathers and whiteness in his face that knocked him over backwards. By instinct he brought up his hands to protect his eyes, dropping the plate of mussels. At once a flock of seagulls descended on the feast, and the air around him was filled with screeching and the rushing of wings. He cursed, scrambled to his feet and retreated, his face reddening with indignation at the laughter of the dockhands. Fucking gulls. In Bordeaux they had never been so bold. His breakfast was lost.

He picked up his sack, ignored the dockers, and walked away, heading towards the bridge. *Fuck it*, he thought. There was only one part of the city he could afford to live in.

Arvandus had not been back on the west bank since arriving in the city a month ago. He would have been happy never to cross it again: the road at the far end of the bridge led directly to the west gate of the city, which in turn led to the Gothic kingdom. He planned to bring his parents to Arles when he had enough money, but since arriving here his memories of Bordeaux had become like the remnants of a bad dream, and he would be content never to set foot on that road again. Yet now, just for a short while, he would have to cross the river to find lodgings.

Once over the pontoon bridge Arvandus turned south down the riverside wharves, pulling his cloak tight. He wished he had not been shaved so recently, and was starting to regret his fine clothes, which would surely mark him out as a likely victim for a mugging. He would not venture too far away from the docks, he decided, but would take the first passable lodgings he found. He picked his way carefully between coils of rope and passed-out drunks, down an alley that was thick with the stench of an open sewer, and across a rickety plank into a tavern.

It was early enough that the only patrons looked to be sailors, or layabouts who had not bothered to go to bed the night before. They sat alone or in small groups around the dark room. Nobody spoke as they watched Arvandus enter. From the kitchen came sounds of food being prepared: sizzling meat, clattering plates, gushes of steam. A strong-shouldered, square-jawed woman emerged from the kitchen with a trencher of steaming sausages. She stopped when she saw him. 'And what are you looking for?'

'A room,' he said, adopting a common accent that would have scandalised his professor. 'Do you keep lodgers here, or is there someone nearby who does?'

'You have money?'

'I can pay four silver per month.'

The woman went to a table, deposited the trencher in front of two red-haired barbarians who were among the largest men Arvandus had ever seen, and came back over to him. She held out a hand. 'Let's see.'

He reached down the front of his tunic and extracted a silver coin from his purse. The woman took it, licked it, tested it in her teeth. She nodded. 'Four silver up front. There's a spare room upstairs, at the back.'

Arvandus gave her three more coins and she returned to the kitchen, yelling at someone to watch the stew. She seemed uninterested in finding out anything more about him, which suited Arvandus perfectly. No doubt the sort of lodgers who ended up in this part of the city didn't welcome too many questions. He glanced at the two barbarians, who were busy stuffing sausages into their mouths through beards thick with grease. They were enormous, even bigger than the Gothic soldiers of Bordeaux, with thick necks and arms like trunks from the Hercynian Forest. They didn't look like Goths, either – their beards were thick and unruly, reaching down to their bellies, whereas Goths tended to keep theirs shorter and carefully groomed. More likely this pair was straight out of Germany, perhaps criminals banished by their tribe, looking for work in the empire as bodyguards or hired killers. Arvandus made a mental note to avoid their company.

One of them looked up and saw him watching them. The barbarian's eyes were a cold silvery blue, animal-like. Arvandus turned away, his heart suddenly beating with primal urgency, and headed up the staircase to the upper storey.

At the end of a short corridor he found two doors, one on the left and the other on the right. Which was his room? The left-hand door was slightly ajar, so he knocked lightly on the door-frame. There was no answer. He pushed the door open. It was dark inside, with curtains covering the single small window. The noises of the west bank seeped into the room: barking dogs, the voices of children playing in the street, clucking chickens in their cages, a persistent clinking of steel on steel from the nearby armour factory. He went to the window and pulled the curtains apart, illuminating a room that was empty except for a small bed, a pile of blankets that looked like a makeshift second bed, and a table.

It was the table that caught his attention. Upon it was a pair of leather satchels, beside which lay half a dozen knives and cleavers of various sizes, all arranged with exquisite care. Next to them was a well-used whetstone. The steel blades were so sharp they seemed to cut the sunlight itself.

Arvandus felt his fear rise like an ocean wave. This clearly was not his room.

He heard two pairs of heavy footsteps coming up the stair-case, and a deep, German-sounding belch. He made a step for the door, but stopped. There was no time to get out; they would see him leaving their room and catch him in the corridor, and assume he was a thief. He spun about and looked to the window, but it was blocked by an iron trellis.

The footsteps continued up the corridor, so heavy that Arvandus could feel the floorboards shuddering beneath his feet. A desperate instinct urged him to grab a blade, but he knew it would be pointless against two men of that size.

The first barbarian appeared in the doorway, almost entirely blocking it with his bulk. He froze when he saw Arvandus. His companion bumped into the back of him, uttering what sounded like a curse. Then he, too, noticed the diminutive intruder. Both men stared at him, saying nothing.

'I can explain,' said Arvandus. 'It's an honest mistake.'

The first barbarian took a step into the room. He had to bend his neck to avoid the lintel. His eyes narrowed as he looked Arvandus up and down. Finally, with clenched fists, he muttered a single word. '*Thief.*'

XIII

O f course he should not have hit his sister. But then she should not have called him a coward. He might be many things, but he was not that. Nor should the stupid girl have followed him down into the tunnel. Consentius had all but agreed to help him find a commission in the Italian field army. Then Attica had blundered along, and Consentius had used the distraction to slip away. He would no doubt try to avoid Ecdicius in the future. A real cultivator, that one, collecting friends and treating them like flowers – pleasant only while fresh.

In the days following the games Ecdicius spent as little time as possible at home. He did not want to see his sister, not after what he had done. He attended lessons, took his meals in taverns, and returned home to sleep for a few hours and to change his clothes. If only his father were to give him a decent allowance, he could rent his own lodgings, keep his own slave, perhaps take on Aotlind as a companion, and have as little as possible to do with his relatives.

But there was small chance of that happening. He was trapped in Arles, enduring the daily tedium of Eusebius's classes, feeling more useless than ever. He kept himself apart from his fellow students, especially those related to him. Aside from Sidonius there were his first cousins once removed, the Philagrii brothers, Probus and Felix. He had not yet decided which of them was duller. Another distant cousin, Avitus, had come with Sidonius from Lyons. The other students were of even less interest: Philomathius, Gaudentius and the rest, all of them from the noblest families in Gaul, and civilian to the bone. They were forever composing poetic ditties to one another, and gossiping about former students who

had entered the imperial civil service – such-and-such had been
appointed tribune and notary at the imperial court, or so-and-so
had been taken onto the staff of the prefect's chief legal advisor.
Every class began with them chattering about what strings had
been pulled by whom, what favours called in, what debts
compounded. It was all a game to them. They had no idea of the
real danger lurking beyond the borders of the empire, of Attila
and his growing confederation.

One morning, four days after the amphitheatre games, Eusebius
entered the classroom at the back of his house as usual and called
the students to order. He was the most famous professor in Arles;
a tall man, stiff and thin as a cane shaft, with a bald head that
sloped evenly down to his flattish nose, and small eyes beneath a
deep brow. His intelligence was like a simmering cauldron, never
still, quick to rise to a brilliant rolling boil. He liked students with
a head for arcane mythology, who could declaim with the elegance
of Cicero, who could conjure up verses in the leaping feet of
whatever poetic measure was demanded of them.

He did not like Ecdicius.

'There are two species of barbarism,' Eusebius began as he
paced up and down the classroom, ignoring the chair in which
he almost never sat. 'First, there is the barbarism of the world
beyond the empire. Against this barbarism we are defended by
soldiers with swords of steel. Second, there is the barbarism of
the soul and spirit, the barbarism that lies within each of us.
Against this barbarism we must defend ourselves with the virtues
of civilised men. Ecdicius!'

He looked up. 'Yes, Master?'

Eusebius stopped pacing and stared at him. '*Yes, Master?*' He
raised his cane to touch his shoulder. 'I say again: we must defend
ourselves with the virtues of civilised men.'

Ecdicius stared back. He had endured a year of Eusebius's
tutoring before he had left to join the army, and had never learned
how to read his obscure prompts. What did he want? He looked
around at his half-dozen fellow students, but they were avoiding
his eyes, as usual.

Eusebius glowered. 'Have you been struck dumb, boy?'

'No, Master. But I don't understand—'

'And have you suddenly become lame?'

He did not know what to say. Eusebius swished the cane down, striking the stool a hair's breadth from his leg. He instinctively jumped to his feet.

'So you're not lame, I see. In my class, when you are addressed, you stand, and then you speak. Once more: we must defend ourselves with the virtues of civilised men.' He pointed the cane at Ecdicius's chest. When Ecdicius still did not answer, Eusebius said: 'Hold out your hands.'

Ecdicius did so, his palms facing upwards. Eusebius raised the cane, held it for a moment to make sure that the other students were watching, and brought it down with a sharp *snap*.

Ecdicius did not mind the pain. After so many years of education his palms were thickly callused. At least pain was easy to handle. Being made to look a fool was far worse.

After the third stroke, Sidonius sprang up from his seat. 'Prudence, justice, temperance and fortitude,' he said.

'Good, Sidonius,' said Eusebius. He turned away. 'You may both sit.'

Ecdicius took his seat, feeling no less humiliated. His hands were burning. Of course it had to be his cousin who showed him up in front of the rest of the class. He never missed an opportunity like that. When they were boys Ecdicius had always soundly beaten him at athletics, and now Sidonius enjoyed beating him in the classroom.

'Like it or not, Ecdicius,' said their tutor, pacing again, 'I intend to train you to think on your feet, not just kill from the back of a horse. This is true for all of you. I will train you to speak clearly and confidently. You will not equivocate, mumble, or waste a syllable. In debate you will pay attention to what is said and to what is not said, so that you might anticipate the thoughts and intentions of your opponent, and always be two steps ahead of him.' He stopped, clutching his cane in both hands, and looked each student in the eye. 'But why must you learn this? Because the essence of civilisation is public life; and the essence of public life is wisdom and eloquence. The empire needs lawyers, judges, governors and ambassadors. It needs men whose words can preserve peace and justice. And as the world lapses into barbarism, my boys, this need becomes all the greater.'

The empire needs armies, you old fool, Ecdicius wanted to say. *It needs gold, and generals, and men with swords to kill its enemies.* He wanted to tell Eusebius and all the others that the Huns were building their strength in the east. But he held his tongue, as he had promised his uncle.

Once the day's lessons ended at noon, Ecdicius was the first to leave. Eusebius's house was on the edge of the fashionable quarter near the forum and imperial palace, a little too close to the docks for the noses of the wealthiest citizens of Arles, but impressive for a mere professor. Normally Ecdicius would set off immediately for the baths, where Frontius and some of the others would be awaiting him. Today, though, he was not in the mood for their frivolous company. His sister's accusation would not leave his thoughts. *Coward,* she had called him. *Coward. Coward . . .*

A sickening thought came to him. What if she was right? What if cowardice *had* made him disgrace himself at the battle? Was that what cowardice felt like?

His stomach yawned, reminding him of his hunger. He would find a tavern to buy lunch and think about this. Somewhere near the baths would be most convenient, but there was the risk of running into his friends. The amphitheatre was a long walk. The fish market on the east bank would be best.

He had already started to walk when a new thought occurred to him. Why not go to the west bank instead? He had not been over there yet. Not because Uncle Ferreolus had warned him against it – if anything, that had only made him more curious. When he had tried to entice Marcus and Frontius across, they had refused. But civil servants were a timorous breed, and Marcus and Frontius were not with him now. Why should he not go over by himself? It was stories, that was all; in a city like this, where gossip spun in the air like a whirlwind, a single

mugging could become a massacre, and a handful of delin-
quents could become a criminal army that was threatening to
topple the entire city into anarchy. It was all nonsense. Ecdicius
would prove to himself that he was no coward. He would go
to the west bank by himself to buy lunch.

This new sense of purpose made him feel good. He continued
down the sloping street to the docks, where he could walk
upstream to the bridge. Almost at once, however, he heard scurrying footsteps behind him, and his cousin appeared at his side.
'I hope you didn't mind what I did earlier,' said Sidonius. 'I was
trying to think of some way to signal to you, but then I thought
I could just as well tell him, spare you the agony. It was the four
cardinal virtues he wanted. Of course, it would've been easier if
he'd just *asked* you for them.' He gave a nervous laugh.

Ecdicius did not reply, displeased at the distraction. His cousin
had always been like this, a fawning, frightened creature. Ecdicius
had not taken him out drinking again since the first disastrous
outing to the brothel, when he had left that trail of vomit halfway
across the city. Sidonius was exactly the kind of student Eusebius
liked: one who could proclaim the glories of empire, but who
had never even seen the frontier. He had humiliated Ecdicius in
class, and was now pathetically trying to apologise for it.

Ecdicius stopped those thoughts. Attica had been right about
that; it was wrong of him to treat Sidonius like this. He had only
been trying to help. Ecdicius looked over and forced a smile. 'I
admit I'm hopeless in the classroom.'

'Don't feel bad about it. I'd be just as hopeless on the battlefield. Are you heading down to the docks for lunch?'

'Yes – actually, to the west bank.'

Sidonius grinned. 'The west bank! May I join you?'

Ecdicius had not expected such a reaction. 'It would be better
if you didn't, cousin. You know what people say about that side
of the river.'

'I know, but it can't be all that bad, can it? It'll be an
adventure.'

Ecdicius laughed, surprised at his cousin's enthusiastic spirit.

Perhaps he was not such a frightened creature after all. 'All right,'
he said. 'But we'll make it a quick lunch.'

Ecdicius felt a swell of excitement, not fear, as they crossed
the pontoon bridge and headed down to the docks of the west
bank. It wasn't the same as galloping into battle, but it was what
he needed. The north end of the wharves was lined with river
barges, the sort used to ferry the imperial grain tax down the
Rhône from the inland provinces. They were empty and idle now
that the harvest was long finished, their cargoes transferred to
the military warehouses further downstream, or onto bulky cargo
ships for transport to Rome. Gangs of shipwrights were working
on a number of new vessels, filling the air with the noise of saws
and hammers. Only a few ocean-going ships, the last of the year,
were tethered further along the wharves.

The open-fronted bars along the waterfront seemed to be
doing good trade, though. Ecdicius chose one of the first and
led Sidonius inside. They entered to find the air rich with the
smell of sweat and leather, and crowded with sailors who glared
at them with squinting eyes set in gnarly, sunburned faces. The
place babbled with provincial Latin, Greek, Punic, Coptic, and
other languages Ecdicius could not name. There were plenty of
women, too, who looked almost as tough as the men, a wholly
different breed from the delicate-limbed prostitutes on the east
side of the city.

They went to the bar at the back of the room and ordered
some wine. Sidonius took the first sip. 'This is Falernian,' he said
in surprise.

'That's what I've heard,' Ecdicius said. 'When the ships from
Latium come in, a few amphorae always go mysteriously missing.
It's a kind of unofficial tax levied by the guild of dockers.' He
raised his cup. 'To your health, cousin.'

Ecdicius had clearly been charged triple for the two cups, but
that was only fair, since the wine was excellent and he could
easily afford it. He leaned against the bar, enjoying the roguish
atmosphere and delighting in his boldness. There was really
nothing to it; aside from a few disdainful looks, the regulars were

showing very little interest in them. Even Sidonius began to relax, though he stayed quiet, sipping his wine.

Ecdicius had turned to ask the barman for some bread and cheese when a hand appeared on his shoulder. It was fat-fingered, scabby-knuckled, the nails cracked and bitten close. The grip was firm, aggressive. On one digit was an expensive silver ring. 'You.'

Ecdicius turned. The owner of hand and voice was a bald man of medium height. His tunic was fastened with the wide, brass-studded belt of a soldier. It was a moment before Ecdicius recognised him as a trooper from the First Gallic Horse. He could not remember the man's name.

'You're Ecdicius,' the soldier said. 'You were in the north with us.'

'Take your hand off him,' snapped Sidonius. Ecdicius looked at his cousin in surprise. The wine had clearly given him boldness. 'How dare you touch one of your betters? This man is of senatorial family.'

The soldier removed his hand from Ecdicius's shoulder. 'Forgive me, my lords,' he said, bowing. He looked around at his two civilian drinking companions, who were sitting at a nearby table. The three of them laughed. 'I just want to drink to the health of your father,' the soldier said to Ecdicius. He raised his cup, and turned to face the room. 'Listen, all of you! Shut up, there! We have here the child of a great man. This is none other than Ecdicius, first-born son of Eparchius Avitus.'

There was a chorus of cheers. Sidonius was grinning, but Ecdicius could not help but feel uncomfortable. Out of the corner of his eye he noticed that the barman had left a knife on the counter. It was within easy reach, should he need it.

'His father is indeed a great man,' the soldier said once the cheers died down. 'Eparchius Avitus would have been proud to see his son ride into battle under Count Aëtius and the tribune of the First Gallic Horse, Majorian.' The cheers for those two names were even louder. A few passers-by on the wharves had gathered outside to watch. 'He would have been proud, I tell you, to see his son ride against the army of King Chlodio – a fiercer horde of savages you never did see, naked as sin, with teeth and blades and cocks all bared ready for us, as we charged from the wood and smashed into them like a wave of death! Here a head was lopped off, here an arm, here a leg! We trampled them, my friends, we crushed them, we slaughtered them like pigs! That day the Franks learned the meaning of Roman justice.' He looked briefly at Ecdicius. 'How proud your father would have been.' Turning back to the room, he continued: 'How proud he would have been to see his son fall off his horse, and piss and shit himself like the cowardly cunt he is.'

Ecdicius, his head filled with anger and wine, did not even think to reach for the knife. He lunged for the soldier, grabbing his tunic with both hands and forcing him backwards to crash into the table where his companions were sitting. The table collapsed under his weight, and he and Ecdicius fell to the ground amidst splinters and broken planks of wood. Ecdicius sat on top of the man and managed to land one punch on his face, cracking something, before he was dragged off and hurled against the bar. His head connected with the brick, stunning him. Through his swirling vision he saw the soldier being helped to his feet by his two friends, blood streaming from his nose.

Ecdicius also tried to rise, helped by Sidonius, and steadied himself with a hand on the bar as the three men stepped closer. The soldier was in the middle, his eyes filled with hate. He wiped his bleeding nose with his forearm, leaving a red smear across his face. 'You're the wrong side of the city,' he growled. 'Sometimes rich boys like you come over here, and they're not seen again till they get dredged up in the river. 'Course, by then not even their own mothers would recognise them.'

'Don't come any closer,' said Sidonius. 'If you lay a finger on us, by imperial law you'll pay with your life.'

'We have our own laws this side of the river,' the soldier said. 'A man starts a fight, doesn't matter if he's the son of the fucking emperor, he stays to finish it. Isn't that right?'

The other patrons shouted their agreement. Sidonius reached out to snatch the knife from the bar, but he fumbled with the handle and it clattered to the floor, out of reach. The men and women around them laughed. None of them looked ready to intervene on either side; they were simply an amused audience. It would be fine entertainment to see two wealthy students beaten up and robbed.

Ecdicius stood in front of Sidonius, shielding him. 'Don't touch him. I'm the one who started the fight.'

'He went for the knife,' the soldier said. 'He's in the fight now, just like you.' He cracked his knuckles, clenched his fists, and began to advance.

That was when a new voice called across the room: 'Leave them alone.'

Everyone turned to see who had spoken. It was a young man, short and handsome, fairly well dressed despite the rough edge to his voice. He pushed through the crowd towards them with a confidence that belied his stature. The soldier stared at him, his expression somewhere between amusement and confusion. 'What do you want, little man?'

'As I just said, I want you to leave them alone.'

'Maybe we'll deal with you first.'

The young man grinned, and called over his shoulder. 'Gunthar! Guntram!' From the table where he had been sitting there now approached two enormous barbarians, bearded and blue-eyed. 'These are good friends of mine,' the young man said. 'Gunthar and Guntram, brothers from Germany. They're butchers by trade, very efficient ones too. I'm afraid their Latin isn't very good, but they know a few words for types of blades, cuts of meat, that sort of thing. "Cleaver", "dagger", "slice", and so on. I'm sure they'd enjoy giving you a quick butchery lesson, if you like.'

The soldier studied the two Germans. He turned back to Ecdicius, and spat at his feet. Then he walked out, followed by his two companions.

Once he had gone, the young man thanked his German friends and handed them each a coin, before approaching Ecdicius and Sidonius. He looked them over, and laughed. 'Now, you two look *very* lost.'

Ecdicius could still feel his heart pumping with excitement. He had not felt any fear, merely the sharp exhilaration of the fight. 'We're in your debt, friend,' he said.

'Don't mention it. What else are barbarians good for, if not protecting honest Romans like ourselves?'

'Now you sound like my father,' Ecdicius laughed. 'This is my second cousin Gaius Sidonius Apollinaris, son of Alcimus of Lyons.'

'I'm Arvandus. Pleased to meet the two of you.'

'Not as pleased as we are,' said Sidonius. 'Will you let us buy you a drink?'

Their saviour grinned. 'I certainly will. A new friendship is best anointed with wine, wouldn't you say?'

XIV

T he last big cargo ship of the season had docked the previous
evening, and it seemed as though the entire city was flocking
to the markets. In the lower forum were wholesalers, domestic
slaves, hawkers and thieves, all hoping to find a bargain or a
profit; students and workmen ambled through the crowds,
seeking their friends or trying to catch the eyes of girls, while
colourfully-clad acrobats and musicians entertained the people.
The sea would now be closed for the winter, and the city was
determined to enjoy this last party of the year.

Attica stepped from the litter. At once she was enfolded by
the tumult of the lower forum, with its noisy sellers and gaggles
of drunken young men, and smells of fresh bread and meat
drifting through the air. It was exciting, but also dirty and
dangerous, and she preferred to observe it from a safe distance.
Sidonius, who had exited the litter after her along with Cyra,
ordered their four armed attendants to clear a path to the upper
forum. He took Attica's arm to lead her up the staircase and
through a portico, passing the soldiers who stood guard at the
top. This was where the better citizens came; here they could
promenade in peace, meet with clients or patrons, view the stalls
laden with fine eastern silks, luxury wine, gloves and shoes, ivory
trinkets, precious jewellery and spices, all above the hectic
hubbub of the common folk.

Attica wished that Ecdicius had come with them. He had
finally apologised to her a week ago, begging forgiveness for
his shameful loss of control in the amphitheatre tunnel. She
had forgiven him quite readily, hardly torturing him for his
guilt at all, and over the last few days he had revealed some

of his old self again. He had joined conversations at dinner and had even started joking with Sidonius, which he had never done before. The two young men seemed to have discovered a long-lost brotherhood. Attica did not know what had happened between them, but she was glad of it. Recently she had warmed to Sidonius; once she had charmed her way past his shy exterior, she had found him to be more playful and witty than she had expected, and less skilled at board games than her sister.

Attica and Sidonius wandered into the forum, looking for familiar faces. They smiled greetings to some friends of their guardians. There was the portly Cethegus, who, judging from his pair of walking sticks, was suffering yet another attack of gout; he was speaking with his brother-in-law Felocalus, and Ennodius, a former proconsul of Africa who somehow always managed to steer any topic of conversation back to the depredations of the Vandals on his old estates outside Hippo. Ennodius's wife Thelasia was nearby with Projecta and Suzane, elderly widowed sisters who lived together in a suburban villa and ran their household with the strictness of a nunnery. Attica gently pulled on her cousin's arm so that they veered in another direction. 'We need to avoid those two,' she said.

'Don't you like them?'

'Not remotely. They make me feel judged. Let's find someone wicked to talk to, so we feel better about ourselves.'

'I see just the fellows.' He pointed towards a curious-looking pair of young men working their way along the market stalls. One was very large, with a big, puffed-out chest and curly beard, and the other was short, no taller than Attica, but with a strong jaw and attractive face. Despite the difference in size, they were both dressed in the latest fashion of well-to-do youths: embroidered footwear cut low to the ankles, and tunic hems well above the knees to show off their legs, with brass-fitted belts worn loosely on the hip, slanted rakishly to one side, and deep v-shaped necklines. They were discussing the goods laid out before them with ostentatious cheeriness. The small one picked up a ream of expensive fabric and held it up to his shoulder as though thinking of having it cut for a tunic. At the next stall he raised up a gold ring to glitter in the sunlight, laughing as he haggled with the merchant.

By this time Attica and Sidonius were close enough to hear him. 'I could buy your entire stall if I had a mind to,' he was saying. 'You're a thief, asking for so much! You may keep your ring, and I'll be back in two hours to pay half the asking price.'

'I pity you in your loneliness,' said the merchant, shaking his head as he laid the ring back on its cushion. 'For only a man with no sweetheart can afford to be so miserly when it comes to precious things.'

The young man slapped his large friend on the chest. 'No sweetheart, he says! Never mind, Lampridius. The glass cameo didn't match your eyes anyway.' The one called Lampridius let out a booming laugh as the merchant shooed the two of them away in pretended annoyance.

As the small one turned, he spotted Sidonius and called a greeting. Something about his face was familiar, she thought – his dark, earnest eyes, maybe, or the pleasant openness of his smile. Had they met before?

'Arvandus,' said Sidonius, kissing his friend and taking him in an embrace. He did the same for Lampridius. 'Comrades, let me introduce you to Attica, my second cousin on my mother's side, youngest daughter of Eparchius Avitus. Attica, meet my two newest comrades: Arvandus and Lampridius, a pair of barbarians from Bordeaux and Toulouse.'

'I'm very pleased to meet you both,' she said, intrigued that her cousin had found friends from the Gothic territory. 'Are you also students of Eusebius?'

'Ha!' bellowed Lampridius. 'Eusebius, the finest rhetor in all of Gaul – or at least the most expensive. No, we two suffer under the birch rod of Maximinus.'

'Not that we hold that against them,' said Sidonius. 'Lampridius here can actually string a sentence together when he puts his mind to it.'

'That sounds like a challenge! I accept. Let us have a poetry contest.'

'Very well. On what theme?'

Arvandus stepped between them. 'I'll set the themes as independent judge,' he said. 'Here are the rules. You walk one complete circuit of the forum together, composing in your heads. At the end of the circuit you each reveal your masterpiece. Lampridius, you must tell the story of Andromeda in hendecasyllables. Sollius – let me think. Yes, I have it! Your task is to describe the first time you met me, using dactylic hexameter.'

'Unfair, unfair,' cried Lampridius. 'Sollius has by far the more epic theme.'

'Then your verse will simply have to rise to the occasion,' Arvandus said. 'Go, now. And don't dawdle.'

Attica watched as Sidonius and Lampridius began to stroll towards the portico surrounding the forum, already deep in thought. She noted that Arvandus and Lampridius had called her cousin Sollius, the name used only by his closest friends and family, not even by her.

'There's no stopping them when they smell a challenge,' said Arvandus. 'If they were boxers instead of poets, they'd both be toothless by now.'

She still had the odd feeling that she knew him somehow, although it was impossible; she had never been to Bordeaux, and did not mix with people of his class. 'Is it true what your friend Lampridius said?'

'About what?'

'About how you and Sidonius met. Was it more epic than the tale of Andromeda?'

He smiled, looking down modestly and shaking his head. 'It wasn't half as epic as it might have been, thank God. Has Sollius not told you about it?'

'No.'

'It's a tale of roguery and mischief.' He looked at her closely, as though judging her trustworthiness. 'First I must swear you to secrecy. This clearly isn't a tale Sollius would want to be widely known, but I feel I can trust you.'

That sounded intriguing. She was not used to such bold familiarity from a stranger. 'I swear to keep the secret.'

'Very well. We met about a week ago. He came with your brother to a dockside bar I happen to frequent. I won't tell you which side of the river it was on, but let's just say there's a fair bit of water between here and there. In walk the two of them, middle of the day, dressed in their finest rags, strutting up to the bar like they own the place.'

She listened, fascinated, as he told her about a belligerent soldier, and how Ecdicius attacked him for a slight on his honour, and Sidonius's valiant, inept attempt to defend his cousin with a knife. It sounded incredible, but explained why the pair had become so comradely over the last few days. When he reached the part where the three assailants scurried from the shadows of his two hulking German friends, she laughed with him. 'Where did you find such beasts?'

'Well,' he said, and started to explain, but interrupted himself with a laugh. 'Oh, let's just say I arrived here back in September, fell in with a bad crowd, made an unlucky bet at the races. You know how it goes. Anyway, I ended up having to move lodgings, just for a short time until my father sends more money. So I've found a place to share with some other ill-starred wretches – a lame old blacksmith, a very pretty actor who calls himself Demetrias, and these two German brothers. First time I met them, they caught me in their room by accident. The older brother, Gunthar, he leans over me and calls me a thief. Stares at me with eyes as cold as ice.'

'It sounds terrifying.'

'Not at all. Well, it was at first. I'm there, ready to be pulled limb from limb, and Gunthar starts laughing, and I don't know if that makes it better or worse. Then his brother joins in. Turns out they thought it was hilarious. They're soft as lambs, really.'

'But what are they doing in Arles?'

'It was the Huns, they tell me. They left Thuringia when the Huns attacked their village, crossed the Rhine, and they've been wandering from city to city ever since, selling their trade where they can. They've lost their wives, families, everything. I think they did, anyway. Their Latin isn't the best. I've agreed to help them. I teach them Latin, they keep me alive. It's a splendid arrangement.'

'And have they taught you some German?'

'A little, yes. But nothing I'd be prepared to repeat to a lady.'

She laughed, delighted at his easy company. At that moment she noticed Felix walking towards them across the forum. His bodyguards, as usual, were hovering a short distance behind him.

'Attica,' he said as he reached them. He kissed her on the cheek. 'Are you enjoying the market?'

Arvandus remained where he was, smiling even though Felix seemed intent on ignoring him. 'Cousin Felix,' said Attica, 'this is Arvandus of Bordeaux, a friend of Sidonius. He was just telling me about two barbarian friends of his.'

Felix inspected Arvandus. 'Barbarian friends,' he said, his flat voice turning the two words into an insult. He looked back at Attica. 'I'd like to buy you a new pair of gloves for when you come to Lupiacum.' He took hold of her hands. 'The weather is turning cold. You must make sure to keep warm.'

She did not like his possessive tone, nor his rudeness towards Arvandus, who seemed perfectly inoffensive. Why did he have to be like that? She pulled her hands free. 'I already have a pair of gloves,' she said. 'Several, in fact.'

Felix's lips tightened. His nostrils flared. There was a hint then of something deeper in him that Attica had not seen before, but he soon disguised it. 'I'm glad to hear that,' he said, trying to appear gracious. He turned to Arvandus. 'You're a student?'

'I am. My father sent me here to complete my education. He said I'd have no future in Bordeaux so long as the Goths ruled.' His voice had lost its playful edge. He was now serious, measured, reflecting Felix's sombre demeanour. 'It pains me to admit it, but Bordeaux's becoming less Roman with every year.'

'The Goths are a problem,' said Felix. 'King Theoderic will seize the rest of Aquitaine given half the chance, and Narbonne for good measure. If things keep going as they are, we'll be speaking Gothic before we know it.'

'I hope you don't mind me saying, but I'm glad you understand. In Bordeaux most Romans have forgotten they were ever part of the empire. Here in Arles, I've found most people hardly think about the Goths at all. It's as though there isn't a barbarian court less than a week's ride from them. Or do you think I'm being unjust?'

Felix gave a grim nod. 'It's true. At least during the war our people understood the danger of the Goths. Ten years of peace, and they act as though every Gothic sword has been melted down and hammered into a ploughshare.'

'Oh, their swords are very much unmelted, believe me. And I pray to God I never see them unsheathed this side of Toulouse.'

Attica decided it was time to contribute. 'My father negotiated the treaty, and he says Theoderic is a man of peace.'

'With respect to your father,' said Felix, 'Theoderic is simply too old to start any wars. When he dies the kingdom will likely pass to his eldest son Thorismund, and he's no man of peace. The Goths might sit in Roman palaces and eat and drink Roman food, they might even learn to speak our tongue, but their hearts still lie beyond the Danube. And if you ask me, *that's* where they belong.'

'I'm glad we agree,' said Arvandus.

Felix seemed to look at Arvandus properly for the first time. Attica could see the curiosity in his eyes. 'You're from Bordeaux, then. Your father – would I know his name? Are you related to the Pontii?'

'I'm afraid not,' said Arvandus. 'My father owns a modest estate outside Bordeaux, and in former days we served Rome with honour. My grandfather was tribune and notary at the imperial court. My great-uncle served in the treasury. That was before the Goths came and took half our land. Since then opportunities to serve in the empire have been few, despite my father's best efforts. But we uphold the dignity of our family.'

'Rome was built by families such as yours. Treaty or not, the Gothic settlement in Aquitaine was a mistake.'

'I agree entirely,' said Arvandus. 'And there are many back home who feel the same.'

'He should join us at Lupiacum next week,' Attica said to Felix, touching his arm. 'I'm sure your father would be interested to hear all this. And Arvandus is a friend of Sidonius. The two of them could share a room.'

Felix looked momentarily taken aback. Attica could tell that he wanted to refuse, but was caught between instinct and propriety. It would be rude to refuse the invitation to Arvandus's face. 'Why not?' he said. 'My family's villa is a day's sail down the coast, towards Narbonne. You should certainly join us.'

'That's a most gracious invitation,' Arvandus said. 'I would be honoured.'

'Good,' said Attica. 'Make sure you talk to Sidonius about the arrangements.' She saw that Sidonius and Lampridius were returning from their circuit of the forum, weaving their way through the crowd. They appeared to be engaged in spirited discussion, but when Sidonius noticed Felix his smile faded. He brought Lampridius before Felix and introduced him. Felix nodded his usual curt greeting. Even Lampridius was suddenly subdued. Felix, whether he knew it or not, had a talent for killing joy.

'Well?' she asked Sidonius. 'Have you composed your masterpieces?'

'Not yet,' he said, with a wary glance at Felix. 'I fear the muses have forsaken me today.'

A few more pleasantries were exchanged – about the weather, about the various delights of the market – but Attica could see that Felix's patience for such idle talk was wearing thin. Arvandus seemed to recognise it, too, and she was grateful when he engineered a polite excuse for himself, Sidonius and Lampridius to take their leave.

'Sidonius's new friends are a curious pair,' said Attica, watching them walk away.

'You shouldn't have invited him like that,' Felix snapped. 'It put me in an impossible position. We hardly know the man. Who is his father? What is his rank?'

'Oh, he's clearly respectable enough. Sidonius would hardly be associating with him otherwise. Besides, one should be hospitable to strangers. I thought it was generous of you to invite him. Won't it be useful to know someone from the Gothic kingdom?'

'Well, I suppose he'll make up the numbers at dinner,' Felix grumbled. 'I hate having eight people on a couch made for nine. He'll spare anyone else going in the lowest position.'

Of course Felix, who would refuse to wear a tunic if he spotted a single loose thread, would need the perfect number of guests at dinner. Yet she could tell that Arvandus had intrigued him, even if he did not want to admit it.

And she was intrigued, too. She had enjoyed talking with him more than anyone else she had met since coming to Arles; the depth of his voice and the warmth of his brown eyes were such that she had hardly even noticed how short he was. She was sorry for what had happened to his family, but admired his good humour. He did not seem to be ruled by bitterness, like so many who had suffered at the hands of barbarians.

She even smiled as Felix took her arm and guided her towards Cethegus and the others. The visit to Lupiacum promised to be much more interesting with Arvandus there.

XV

Lupiacum

Though he tried not to, Arvandus could not help thinking of his father. The old man Patroclus, unlike his son, had known a different life, before the Great Invasions that had seen Gaul and Spain overrun by barbarians. Sometimes he would tell Arvandus of their ancestral farm outside Bordeaux, recounting how as a child he had played hide-and-seek in the vineyard, and had learned to ride in the meadows along the river. Or he would talk of the villa, with its cobbled courtyard and modest peristyle of whitewashed columns, and its brightly painted walls where the sunlight played on satyrs and nymphs as they danced amidst twisting foliage. There had been no barbarian kings in Aquitaine then, he would say, and none in Spain or Africa or even Britain. It had been a life of peaceful pleasures.

Patroclus would talk of these things when drunk, with a mixture of wistfulness and anger. It had always come back to the noble classes. They had not only stolen his patrimony, but his past and the life he should have led.

Arvandus had never seen that patrimony. For him it existed only in the memories of his father. His world had been the three-room apartment above the docks of Bordeaux: musty floorboards, scrabbling rats and a crooked staircase. There was always noise, whether from the neighbours or merchants or bickering sailors. On hot summer days the stench from the sewer in the lane had been unbearable. School had been an escape for him, where through Plutarch and Sallust he had come to know the great men of the old republic, and through the words of Virgil had witnessed the deeds of heroes and gods. But this had been no more real than his father's memories, and after lessons there was always the walk back down those gloomy alleys to his home.

It was only now, when he came to the villa of Lupiacum, that he truly understood what his family had lost. From Arles they travelled by ship down the Rhône, sailing before a swift easterly wind along the coast, past the sandbanks and marshy islets of the Camargue, following the flat shoreline where fishing boats sat beneath screeching clouds of gulls. Late in the day they disembarked at a small harbour and were taken a short distance by carriage to the banks of a lagoon, whose calm blue waters they crossed on a raft kept afloat by inflated goat-skins. There was a hamlet on the northern side, a busy-looking clutter of wooden huts above a row of beached vessels and piled-up fishing nets. A group of men and boys was dragging the last boat up the shore. On the west side of the hamlet, as they left the barge and climbed into another pair of enclosed carriages, Arvandus saw pottery kilns and a smithy. They were driven up a track between shrivelled vineyards and scrubby fields for half a mile, the servants following with the baggage. The sun was sinking in the west by the time they dismounted in front of the villa.

Lupiacum sat nestled in the flat country like a contented bird, its white façade looking out over the countless acres of surrounding farmland. It presented no windows to the visitor, merely a plain frontage that stretched a hundred yards across, in the centre of which was an entrance framed by a plinth set upon enormous marble columns. Arvandus had seen such country palaces from a distance before, but he had never been so close, much less entered one. *Those who ruined my family lived like this,* he thought. *With so much, why do they always need more?*

The thought arose again and again in his mind as Felix led his guests into the villa. The entrance hall was paved with types of marble Arvandus could not name. Even the walls were marble-clad. Blue birds, painted between roundels of crimson and gold, looked down on them from the high coffered ceiling. Through the hall, at the heart of the villa, was a vast garden courtyard of plane trees and sandy paths, encircled by a peristyle floored with an intricate mosaic of black and white. A servant was sweeping up leaves that had blown in from the garden. The entire residence was arranged around the courtyard, some of it two storeys high. *It must have a hundred rooms,* Arvandus thought. It was a palace. This was the kind of wealth that even Paeonius could only dream of.

Arvandus remained quiet while his fellow guests complimented the refined symmetry of the garden and the airy lightness of the peristyle. They walked through the courtyard as though God had fashioned it all for them. Arvandus was afraid to speak, lest he give away his true feelings: that this splendour had been built on the ruination of poorer families. He did not find it hard to resent them for their ease amidst such opulence.

Ecdicius was quiet, too, he noticed. During the boat trip Arvandus had noted how he and Felix had kept a distance from one another. There seemed to be a deep dislike between the cousins that they had agreed to keep subdued, for now at least. Sidonius, distantly related to the Philagrii only by marriage, seemed intimidated by Felix and eager to please him. As for Attica – she was a sweet girl, and obviously clever for her age, but one of the Philagrii just the same. It still pleased Arvandus to think of how he had managed to send Sidonius and Lampridius walking around the forum, giving himself the chance to talk alone with the girl. He was aware, too, of how easily he had charmed her. He had never imagined that just one week later he would be a guest in the home of the most powerful family in Gaul. He could not afford to waste this turn of fortune. Such friends as these might open many doors.

Once they had crossed the courtyard, Felix led them down a short passageway and through a pair of heavy oak doors into a large hall. This had to be the grandest room of all. Before their feet stretched a marvellous mosaic floor, this time not just black and white, but red, yellow, blue and green, depicting columns and archways, peach trees filled with fruit, vines swirling from ornate vases, cornucopias spilling their bounty, all of it shimmering in the light of brazier fires and the last glowing sunlight that fell from the windows high above. At the far end of the hall was a great apse, with two smaller apses in the side walls. Heavy embroidered drapes of red and gold hung all around.

Before Arvandus could take the full measure of the room a side door opened and a middle-aged man and woman entered, followed by a younger man. The older couple, he knew at once, were Felix's parents Magnus and Egnatia. The resemblance between Felix and his father was obvious: the same narrow nose and sharp chin, the same tired-looking eyes. Arvandus bowed when Felix introduced him, making sure to address his hosts correctly according to their rank, and giving every impression of a provincial sycophant. The younger man was their second son, Probus. They received Arvandus with politeness, showing no great interest in him, and showed barely more affection to their other three guests. It was not a household of ebullient love, that much was clear. There was a cold formality about it all that Arvandus was quickly finding oppressive.

Only in the bedroom that he was to share with Sidonius did Arvandus feel able to relax, but even then he was almost too nervous to sit on the bed lest he disturb its carefully arranged blankets. He was not used to so many servants – truth be told, he was not used to *any* servants. Here they seemed to inhabit every corner of the house, standing by doors or slipping silently down corridors like ghosts. Dinner would also be a trial. Arvandus was aware of the basic etiquette, but he had never reclined to eat, and was nervous of making some mistake that would expose how humble his roots really were. He would just have to observe the others quietly and follow suit. If he was to feign playing by their rules, first he needed to learn them.

'Did you bring your napkin?' Sidonius asked. He was rummaging in the small chest that contained both their clothes. 'I can't seem to find it in here.'

Arvandus had not brought a dining napkin because he did not own one, and could not afford to buy one of decent quality. He got to his feet and went over, pretending puzzlement as he looked in the chest. 'That's odd. I'm sure I packed it.'

'Never mind,' Sidonius said with a wink. From beneath a folded tunic he pulled out a finely embroidered green cloth. 'I brought a spare. What about your slippers?'

'My slippers?'

'Yes! Unless you were planning to attend dinner in those travelling shoes?'

Arvandus flushed with embarrassment. He had not even known that special footwear existed for dinners. 'Aren't they in the chest? I don't believe it. I packed in such a hurry . . .'

'Well, no need to worry. I'm sure the others won't mind. When we're at table nobody will see your feet anyway. Oh, and try not to be frightened by old Magnus. He isn't renowned for his joviality, but he respects straight talkers. And if talk turns to politics, don't mention Count Aëtius.'

'Why not?'

'Family history. Twenty or so years ago, I forget when exactly, Magnus's parents were both executed by Aëtius. Treason, officially. Anyway, don't bring him up.'

Darkness had fallen by the time they assembled for dinner, and so the winter dining suite, smaller than the great hall, was illuminated by flickering braziers that cast long shadows across the floor. Arvandus was glad of that; it made his shoes less obvious. He followed Sidonius into the room, treading as softly as possible to hide the noise of his hobnailed soles on the mosaics. Fortunately everyone else was already reclining on the semi-circular couch, which made it easy to pick out his proper place once Sidonius had lain down. Magnus and his wife, as hosts, were at one end of the couch, facing the chief guest, Ecdicius, across the table. The others were positioned in descending order of precedence: next to Ecdicius was the family priest Anastasius, followed by Felix, his younger brother Probus, Sidonius, and Attica. Coming from a supposedly equestrian family, Arvandus had been assigned the lowliest place. He walked around the couch and climbed onto the cushions between Attica and Egnatia, laying out the napkin before him and reclining on his left elbow.

A train of servants brought in the food, spreading an array of cold meats, cheeses and bread on the central table. Anastasius, an aging cleric with sunken cheeks and a droning, high-pitched voice, led them in prayers over the food. There was no music, no entertainment, and no wine. It was to be a plain, sober meal.

Magnus began by picking up a chicken wing. 'How is your father, Ecdicius?' he asked. 'Well, I hope?'

'Yes, my lord,' replied Ecdicius with a smile. 'Not as young as he once was, but still determined to be a farmer.'

'At his age? He must be, what, over sixty by now? Marrying so late, that's kept him young. Well, he's earned his retirement. The peace he negotiated with the Goths has lasted longer than any before it. A true Roman hero, your father. Courageous and selfless, always looked his enemy in the eye.' He took a bite from the chicken wing.

'It's very kind of you to say so, my lord.'

'I can't say I was surprised at your discharge, Ecdicius. Not that you deserved it, not at all. On the contrary. If you ask me, you're *too much* of a soldier. That crowd running the army these days don't like that, not from our family. All they want is boot-lickers and lapdogs. You're a threat. Better for them if you're kept out of the way.'

'I hope to attain another commission in the future.'

'As you should. Generals retire, generals die. That crowd won't be around much longer. To be frank, I'm amazed they've lasted as long as they have.'

That crowd, Arvandus realised, was a euphemism for Aëtius, as though even uttering his name at a private dinner might be dangerous. Magnus had clearly learned to be careful after the fate of his parents. It was well known that Aëtius had made many enemies over his long career, most of all in the imperial family, but the common folk of Gaul adored him nonetheless. Arvandus had never heard anything but praise for him in the taverns of Arles. The Philagrii, along with the other noble families, always made a public show of concord with him. Clearly things were very different in private.

As the dinner progressed Magnus invited the priest to speak, and then his sons. He asked Sidonius about his family, and Attica about her schooling. Arvandus prepared himself to say something charming and witty when addressed. Perhaps, being the only person present from a barbarian kingdom, he could make a joke about the Goths. Something about their dining customs would go down well – not that Arvandus had ever attended a Gothic feast, but he could make it up.

The chance never came. It was as though he had become invisible. To his right lay Egnatia, propped up on her left elbow with her back resolutely facing him. Neither she nor her husband even looked at him. Magnus spent some time congratulating Sidonius on the imminent appointment of his father as praetorian prefect of Gaul, an office that would raise him to the very highest senatorial rank of *vir illustris*. The conversation moved from politics to literature and finally religion. Time after time Arvandus felt the urge to speak out, but he forced himself to hold his tongue. If the Philagrii wanted to snub him, so be it. He would endure it. They would not provoke him.

Once the first course was ended, servants came to clear the table of dishes. Magnus snapped his fingers at a blond slave boy who was standing near the door holding a silver goblet, his hands draped in a silk cloth. The boy came forward and offered Magnus the goblet. He drank from it and handed it to his wife, who did the same. With her right hand she then passed it across the table to their chief guest, Ecdicius. Arvandus had heard of this ritual, too. The goblet was to be passed down from the highest ranking to the lowest, always with the right hand. When it came to his turn he took the goblet from Attica and sipped from it. By that point Magnus had already renewed the conversation.

Arvandus held the heavy goblet in his hand. What was he to do with it? He could not pass it on to Egnatia; that might be seen as an insult, and she was in any case ignoring him. Not knowing what else to do, he reached forward to place it on the table, but accidentally knocked the foot of the goblet against the cushion; it tipped from his fingers, clattered on the table, tumbling on its side and spilling the remaining wine. The slave boy shrieked and scrambled forward to pick it up, dabbing at the wine with his cloth. For his efforts he received a sharp whack on the ear from Magnus.

'Clean it up,' Egnatia said, addressing no one in particular. An older servant came and took the sniffling boy away, while a girl set about wiping the table clean.

Arvandus burned with humiliation. He cursed himself. They would think him a clumsy fool, a rustic clown. Now they must surely see through his façade. He should never have accepted the invitation to the villa, understanding so little about the aristocratic way of life. If only he had prepared himself better.

As harshly as he berated himself, he felt worse when he glanced up and caught Felix staring at him. His dour grey eyes were filled with contempt. It was the same look he might have given a stray dog that had somehow wandered into his house. Arvandus realised then that Felix had never truly wanted to invite him. He had done it only to please Attica.

Arvandus looked down at the table. Shame gave way to anger. Who were any of them to treat him with disdain – they whose fortune was built on corruption and theft? That silver goblet alone would have been enough to pay for his education. What right did they have to any of it?

Dinner continued for another course. Arvandus ate little. The conversation went on, but he did not listen to it. Tomorrow morning he would come up with some excuse and return to Arles. He would walk back if he had to. He could not stay here.

Finally the meal came to an end and the others rose from the couch. They were yawning, ready to retire. Arvandus was the last to rise. As he did so he noticed that Felix had left his golden seal ring on the cushion; he had taken it off when eating from a plate of slippery mussels, and had obviously forgotten it.

There was only a brief moment, not even enough to think it through, when none of the others was watching, and none of the servants was close enough to see. Arvandus reached down and snatched up the ring. Melted down, the gold would get him at least twenty silver coins. He clutched it in his fist as he followed Sidonius out of the dining room.

XVI

Attica rose early the next morning, as soon as the first faint light of dawn illuminated her room. She had Cyra dress her and arrange her hair in an elegant yet simple style, and then went to sit alone on a couch in the great hall. A lit brazier offered some warmth, but she was still glad of her thick winter cloak and fur-lined shoes.

The villa was half asleep. Slaves had begun their work for the day quietly, wary of disturbing their masters. Aside from the soft spitting of the coals in the iron brazier, the only sounds Attica could hear were from the birds nesting in the eaves of the windows above. The air of the great hall was solemn.

She was glad for the peace. It allowed her to calm her restless mind, still troubled by the bad dreams of the previous night. She had been a little girl again, running through a labyrinth of endless rooms and corridors, pursued by some invisible horror that she knew nestled at the heart of the building. This was her first visit to Lupiacum since she was a child. In her memory it had always been a place of frightening coldness, of vast arches and columns rising into shadowy heights. The courtyard had been a forest, and this hall the cave of the Cyclops. Magnus and Egnatia had presided over it like the cruel gods of legend. It was no wonder that these old fears had seeped into her dreams.

She was no longer a child. It was stupid to be frightened by a building. Now she saw it for what it was: dumb stone and tile and glass, marble and painted plaster. The building was less than what it represented, which was the power of those who owned it. Her father owned houses in Clermont and Arles, her mother a house in Lyons, but none of them approached Lupiacum. It was all because her father had chosen a military career in Gaul, when everyone knew that real influence came from high office close to the emperor. Honour, duty, sacrifice – he had always praised them above everything else. They were all he cared about. But what of ambition?

She was sure that Felix had ambition; he had made this clear when he said he wanted the patriciate. She had considered his words over the last two weeks, and had been watching him closely. The more she observed him, the more like a statue he seemed: dry and dusty, lacking in life. All he thought about was collecting one title after another for the honour of himself and his descendants. But to what end? It was as though he had already bought his own sarcophagus, and could not wait to start chiselling his accomplishments into the cold stone.

Then she thought of Arvandus. That day in the forum their souls had touched briefly, she was sure of it. It was unlike anything she had felt for Consentius, but so fleeting. During the journey from Arles he had spent most of his time with Sidonius and Ecdicius, leaving her little chance to talk to him. It angered her to remember the previous evening, when Magnus and Egnatia had been so rude as to ignore him for the entire dinner, which meant that she had been unable to find out anything more. He remained a mystery. His obvious awkwardness had only made her more curious. It was as though he had never reclined at a dinner before.

She blamed herself, too. She had invited him to Lupiacum, after all, only for him to be snubbed and humiliated by her relatives. This was why she had come to the great hall. Arvandus and Sidonius were sharing a bedroom that opened off one of the small apses, and so would have to pass through here as soon as they rose. She wanted to speak to Arvandus again – to apologise, to reassure him, simply to find out who he really was.

There was a soft creak from across the hall, and movement in the darkness of the opposite apse, followed by the sound of a latch being lifted gently back into place. A moment later Arvandus emerged from the apse, walking with swift paces across the hall. He did not notice her until she rose.

'Attica,' he said in surprise, coming to a stop. He was dressed in a tunic and hooded cloak, and had a cloth bag slung over one shoulder.

'Where are you going?' she asked.

'I'm going home. Back to Arles.'

'But we're not returning for three days. And why so early? Without saying goodbye?'

'I have a friend in Arles who's very unwell. I left a note for Sidonius explaining everything.'

That did not strike her as a likely excuse. 'Is this because of last night?'

'It was very kind of you to invite me, Attica.' He continued his walk towards the door.

'You should have given it back to the boy,' she said.

He halted at the threshold. Still facing away from her, he said, 'Given what back?'

'The goblet. The last to drink from it always gives it back to the servant.'

He remained in the doorway as though frozen. 'I didn't know that.'

She stepped closer. 'I thought everyone knew that.'

'Not everyone grows up in a palace.'

'I didn't grow up in a palace. Where did you grow up? Tell me the truth.'

He turned to face her. 'Do you remember our talk in the forum?'

'Of course.'

'I haven't stopped thinking about it. I can't, Attica. It was like waking from a dream. I'd never imagined that such a woman as you could truly exist.'

It was those eyes of his – deep, inviting. Pained. They promised answers, and yet more questions. She was drawn into them.

'I asked you to keep a secret before,' he said, his voice almost a whisper.

'About how you met my brother and Sidonius.'

'Yes. Do you know why? Because from the very first moment

I knew I could trust you. I *wanted* to put my trust in you. I want to tell you everything.'

'You can,' she said, her heart thumping.

Before he could reply, the air was pierced by a high-pitched shriek, the cry of a child.

It had come from the courtyard. A look of alarm flashed across Arvandus's face. There was another cry, and this time Attica heard the sound of wood whipping on flesh. She walked past Arvandus, out of the hall and down a short corridor to the peristyle. Between the columns she glimpsed figures in the courtyard. She headed across the grass directly towards them. A slave boy, the blond one who had held the goblet at dinner, had his front pressed against a tree, his arms raised above his head and tied by rope to a branch. He was stripped to his underwear. Felix stood behind him bearing the birch cane, with his personal attendant standing close by.

By the time Attica reached them, Felix had hit the boy three more times. He could not have been older than ten. He jolted violently with each strike, weeping with anguish.

'What are you doing?' demanded Attica. It was brazen of Felix to be punishing a slave so early in the morning, right in the middle of the villa.

Felix lowered the cane. 'I'm sorry if he woke you.'

'What in heaven did he do? Your father already hit him for the goblet last night.'

'This isn't for the goblet. This is for my ring.'

'What ring?'

'One of my gold rings has gone missing. I took it off at dinner last night and accidentally left it on the couch. This one was tidying up afterwards. He swears he didn't take it, but . . .' He raised the cane and brought it down in a swift arc. The boy screamed. He was sagging against the tree now, his legs limp. His back was criss-crossed by half a dozen red stripes.

'Do you have any proof it was him?'

'Not yet.'

Felix lifted his arm once again, but Attica reached out and grabbed his wrist. She stared into his surprised eyes. 'No more.'

Felix's eyes narrowed. 'I'll stop when I choose to.'

'I have it,' said Arvandus. He was walking across the grass towards them, a gold ring in his outstretched hand. He gave it to Felix. 'I found it under the couch last night. I was going to give it to you this morning.'

Felix slipped the ring on his finger. 'Thank you,' he said flatly. He nodded at the bag Arvandus held at his side. 'Are you leaving us?'

'I need to return to Arles. A friend of mine is unwell. I left him alone in bed to come here, but I couldn't sleep last night worrying about him, so I thought I should head back.'

'Your compassion does you credit.'

'Will you please give your parents my thanks for their hospitality?'

'Of course.' He beckoned to his attendant, who stepped forward. 'Give Arvandus here some money to pay for a ship back to Arles.'

'Thank you, but that isn't necessary.'

'Of course it is. If you head across the lagoon to the coastal harbour you can buy passage on a boat. There's a decent westerly wind this morning. Have a safe journey.'

'Thank you,' Arvandus said, taking the coins. He bowed to Felix and Attica in turn, then continued across the courtyard to the villa entrance.

As soon as he had disappeared from view, Felix snorted. 'The filthy liar. He stole that ring.'

'Don't be absurd,' said Attica. 'If he stole it, why did he just hand it back to you?'

'Because he's weak.' Felix looked at his attendant and waved his hand towards the boy. The attendant went to loosen his bonds. As soon as he did, the boy crumpled to the floor. He was still sobbing. The attendant raised him to his feet and guided him away.

Attica felt pity for the slave, punished for something he had not done. Her parents believed in a firm hand when it came to slaves, but they also believed in restraint and justice. They would never have beaten a young boy on a whim like this.

Then it struck her. Felix had not even seemed surprised when Arvandus revealed the ring, as though he had been expecting it. 'You knew the boy was innocent.'

'Of course I knew. I didn't forget my ring, I left it there deliberately to see if Arvandus would take it. If you want to trap a rat, you set a juicy bait. I had a feeling he wouldn't be able to resist. I wondered how many slaves I would have to torture before he gave in. I admit, I was expecting to stand here all morning. So he's not only a poor thief, he's soft-hearted, too.'

Attica felt a sickness in her gut. 'It was cruel to beat the boy.'

'A good beating is never wasted, deserved or not. Now he knows what happens to thieves, he won't ever become one.'

'It was un-Christian.'

Anger edged into his voice. 'That boy's blood is on Arvandus's hands, not mine. Really, Attica, you seem to care more about a slave than you do about the imposter you invited into my family's home.'

'He's not an imposter.'

'You don't honestly believe a word he says, do you? You saw him last night. He's somehow got himself an education and a wardrobe, but he's as cultured as a pig farmer. My parents were right – they knew he was up to no good, trying to worm his way into our house. He may have fooled your brother and Sidonius, but he won't fool the rest of us. Oh, don't worry, I'll find out who he really is. And I'll make him pay for trying to steal from me. I promise that.'

With a final cold smile he walked away, leaving her alone in the courtyard. All was quiet again; even the nesting birds had vanished, frightened off by the sounds of torture. Attica noticed that her left hand was shaking. It was fear. The first time she had ever seen real joy in Felix's eyes had been when he was whipping that boy.

XVII

Arles, A.D. 449

It was the kalends of January, and the new year's consul, Astyrius, was to be ceremonially appointed in the basilica. No one could doubt the importance of the event, for consuls were traditionally inaugurated in Rome; by special benefaction of Emperor Valentinian, to show his affection for his loyal Gallic subjects, Astyrius had been permitted to hold his celebration in his home city of Arles.

First, soon after daybreak, came the procession, as the highest dignitaries of Gaul met Astyrius and his train outside Arles and escorted his four-horse chariot into the heart of the city. The people had turned out in their excited thousands despite the cold and wet, for the ceremony was to be followed by public races at the hippodrome. They cheered Astyrius as he was driven through the streets of their city, past the amphitheatre and cathedral, past the forum and palace precinct, to the basilica, where the noblest men and women of Gaul awaited him.

The richly painted pillars and lofty roof of the basilica had been strung with evergreen garlands. Silver morning light struck airy shafts through the clouds of incense, casting a heavenly sheen on the blue and gold mosaics of the apse ceiling. Astyrius walked in procession down the length of the nave to a resounding chorus of horns.

Ecdicius, standing near the front of the crowd with his uncle Ferreolus, watched as the new consul took his place on the curule throne, its ivory feet carved in the form of lion paws. Astyrius was heavily draped in his robes of office: not the full triumphal vestments, since he was not being inaugurated in Rome, but nonetheless fold upon fold of Tyrian purple, the borders sparkling with golden embroidery; in his left hand he clutched a sceptre surmounted by miniature busts of the emperors of east and west, Theodosius and Valentinian. Behind him stood a pair of green-cloaked attendants bearing the fasces and the insignium of his office. On either side sat the highest officials of the prefecture and representatives from the imperial court, likewise decked in all the splendour of their rank. Sidonius's father was sitting to Astyrius's immediate left, proudly wearing the heavy cloak and brooch of the praetorian prefect. Behind him was Sidonius himself, clad in a plain toga. He stood stiffly amidst the frozen magnificence, seemingly too petrified to blink.

Astyrius directed the distribution of largesse, the pouches of gold that scurrying servants held out to the serving court officers and to members of the Gallic Council. Then it was time for the panegyric. The chosen speaker, a renowned orator of Lyons called Nicetius, emerged from the crowd. With solemn steps he approached Astyrius on his throne, knelt before him, clasped his legs and kissed his knees. The gesture of humility was carried out with meticulous composure. Nicetius rose and withdrew a few paces. He waited for a complete hush to fall over the audience.

'When the pelt-clad deity,' he began, 'wielding her spear point-downward, gazed upon the Palatine rock, and was joined by she whom the Sulmonan bard called the goddess of a thousand works, a frown crossed her immaculate brow . . .'

Ecdicius quickly lost interest in the panegyric, which would go on for a full winter hour. He let his eyes wander over the crowd filling the basilica. He spotted relatives and friends nearby: his uncle Nymphidius, his cousin Ennodius with his sons, Camillus and Firminus, Sidonius's uncles Simplicius, Thaumastus and Apollinaris, and several of his fellow students in the company of their fathers or patrons. Felix was with his father and brother, three stone faces staring at the dais.

Then, to his surprise, he spotted Arvandus about ten yards away. As a young man of equestrian rank he should have been at the back of the hall, certainly not mixing with the senatorial families. He looked nervous, trying not to attract attention while glancing discreetly from side to side. Ecdicius wondered how on earth he had got so close to the front. He seemed to have surrounded himself with strangers to avoid detection.

His anonymity did not last long. Felix had also noticed him. He whispered something to his father, who gave Arvandus a brief, furious glance before whispering in turn to his secretary. The secretary moved discreetly towards Arvandus, coming right up against him and muttering a few words close to his face. Arvandus shrugged awkwardly and shook his head, and began to ease himself away. This only served to confirm his guilt. The secretary attracted the attention of someone in his path, a man of senatorial status who looked like a former consul-governor or a middling court official. This older man blocked Arvandus's way and issued a few brief, curt words to his face.

Arvandus, as far as Ecdicius could see, said nothing in reply. He turned and pushed his way back through the crowd towards the rear of the basilica. Though his face was hidden, his humili-ation and anger were clear enough in the set of his shoulders. He did not stop when he reached the rear of the crowd, but burst through the doors and disappeared into the wintry streets of the city.

The echo of the crashing doors reverberated the length of the basilica, distracting Nicetius and almost causing him to forget his place. A murmur ran through the crowd as men turned to see the cause of the commotion. Ecdicius cursed Arvandus for his stupidity. It was one thing to be bold and ambitious; indeed, Ecdicius respected him for those very qualities. But it was foolish beyond belief to disrupt a consular inauguration.

Two days of celebrations at the amphitheatre and circus followed, as the city enjoyed the munificence of the distant emperor. Ecdicius endured the stiff ceremonies, audiences and banquets in the company of his uncle. The house became lonely; Sidonius, now that he was the son of the prefect, had moved to live in the palace. He was not enthusiastic about it, having so recently escaped the clutches of his father and grandmother, and he confessed to Ecdicius that he was dreading the deluge of new friends who would soon start clamouring for his attention, all of them merely wanting to meet his father. Ecdicius could offer his friend sympathy, if not advice. He had been only nine years old when his own father had served as prefect, too young to be of use to anyone.

Ecdicius was almost glad when the celebrations ended and school lessons started up again. He rose at dawn, as usual, and walked with his attendant from his uncle's house to the praetorian palace to meet Sidonius. It was an imposing, high-walled complex that took up an entire city block between the basilica and forum; its audience chambers, courtyards and dining rooms were furnished to a degree appropriate to the highest imperial officer in Gaul and the direct representative of the emperor.

He found Sidonius in the atrium with his grandmother Roscia. She was wrapped in blankets on a couch that had obviously been placed there for her benefit; an ancient woman now, over seventy years old, with sharp features and fiery eyes. House servants were carrying pieces of furniture through the atrium to the residential quarters of the palace, and she was supervising them in-between delivering advice to her grandson.

'Beware of flatterers,' she was saying. 'Decline all invitations – politely – unless your father approves them. Do you hear me, Sollius?'

'Yes, Grandmother,' Sidonius said.

'Ah, Ecdicius, there you are. My grandson told me you were coming by this morning.' She noticed a pair of servants carrying a bed frame through the front doors. 'That one to my woman's sleeping chamber,' she said, 'and make sure you don't chip the wood taking it in. The doorway is far too narrow.' She turned back to Sidonius. 'Now, about this Arvandus. Of what family is he?'

Sidonius looked startled. 'Who told you about Arvandus?'

'Don't you mind about that. Answer my question.'

'He's just a friend, a student of Maximinus.'

'I don't know who Maximinus is, nor do I care. Your father is now prefect. You cannot be seen mixing with a young man of such character.'

'There's nothing wrong with Arvandus's character, Grandmother.'

She gave him a stare worthy of Medusa. A pair of slaves shuffled past carrying another bed frame, keeping their faces low. 'I heard what he did at the consular ceremony,' she said. 'Atrocious behaviour. I advise you to associate yourself with friends of true aristocratic dignity – the sons of Magnus, for example. You are to stay away from this upstart Arvandus. Do you hear me?'

Sidonius received her words in miserable silence. Ecdicius could see that he was still daunted by his grandmother – with good reason. She was known to be the true head of the Apollinaris clan. Not even her son becoming praetorian prefect would change that.

Ecdicius, though, was not one of the Apollinares. 'This upstart saved our lives, my lady,' he said. 'Sollius, won't you even try to defend him?'

Roscia stiffened in her seat. 'Saved your lives? What do you mean? Sidonius, explain.'

'We were out one afternoon,' Sidonius said, reluctantly. 'A drunken soldier was being difficult, and Arvandus had his friends help us. That's all.'

'And you feel you owe some sort of debt because of this?'

Sidonius shrugged.

'Yes,' Ecdicius said, stepping forward. 'Yes, we *do* owe him a debt. Were it not for him, we'd both have ended up in the river with our throats cut.'

Roscia did not seem impressed. 'Do you know who is paying for his education?'

'His father,' said Sidonius.

'Hah! A dear friend of yours, you say? His father is a penniless wastrel, a peasant. What's more, I have it on good authority that his patron is that common gossip-monger, Paeonius. He's been lying to you, Sidonius. Taking advantage. This is precisely what I've been warning you about. I thank Heaven that your real friends have keener eyes than you.'

Ecdicius could not believe it. Arvandus had told them all about his equestrian family, about their land outside Bordeaux. Had he been lying the whole time?

'Which real friends, Grandmother?' Sidonius asked. 'Who told you this?'

'It was Felix, as a matter of fact. He and his father wrote to the Pontii in Bordeaux, who revealed that Arvandus was at school with Leontius, but belongs among the *humiliores*. Really, Sidonius, you must be more careful. Your father and I forbid you from having any more communication with Arvandus. Very soon he will be exposed for who he is.'

Ecdicius felt a cold chill down his neck. They all knew what that would mean. For impersonating one of the noble class, Arvandus would be arrested, stripped in the forum, and beaten with rods. He would then be expelled from the city in disgrace.

It could not be allowed to happen. 'I'm going to talk to Arvandus myself,' he said.

'You are not,' snapped Roscia.

'With respect, my lady, you cannot stop me.'

'I don't have to. Your father is summoning you back to Clermont. You are to return home to pack immediately, and will leave tomorrow morning. He expects you home within two weeks.'

'Why, just because I'm friends with Arvandus?'

'Your father didn't say why he wants you back, he merely said that your education is to be suspended.'

A clumsy slave dropped a brazier on the atrium floor with a loud clatter. As Roscia began berating the culprit, Ecdicius used the distraction to pull his cousin to one side. 'This can't be true about Arvandus,' he said. 'You need to talk to him. I won't have time before I leave.'

'But my grandmother—'

'Forget about her. Remember what Arvandus did for us. We can't just ditch him on the word of Felix.'

Sidonius glanced warily at his grandmother, who was still scolding the slave. He looked like a man preparing to face an island of harpies. Then his eyes widened. 'I have an idea how we might save him,' he said. 'I need to talk to my father.'

XVIII

A rvandus left the classroom as soon as lessons were over, avoiding Lampridius and the others, and went to buy a plate of stewed fish at a tavern. He had been coming here the last three days, ever since the inauguration. It was close enough to the public baths that he could hear the bell announcing the opening of the doors to male bathers. More important, none of the regulars knew him.

He wanted to be alone. The embarrassment of being ejected from the front of the inauguration still hung too heavily over his head. He did not know why he had pushed so far forward in the crowd. At first it had been because he could not see anything from the back, so he had tried to slip closer for a better view. Finding that no one seemed to notice, he had gone a little further. Step by step, it had seemed so easy. Before he knew it he had found himself surrounded by the long decorated cloaks of the senatorial classes, and it had been too late to go back. It had felt good, being so close to the consul. Nobody else had seemed to mind. It was only Felix who had caused the trouble.

Felix could hang himself. He and his parents had made their contempt for him clear at Lupiacum. Arvandus was only sorry that he had not kept the gold ring, but Felix had given him little choice. What kind of man would whip a young boy like that, even a slave?

The bell from the public baths sounded. Arvandus wiped his fingers around the plate, licked them clean, and left the tavern, pulling his cloak tightly against the winter chill. His friends normally attended the baths later in the afternoon, once the athletes and leering old men had left, and so he was deliberately heading there early in the hope of avoiding them. They would only tease him about the ceremony, especially Lampridius.

For once luck seemed to be on his side; for the third day in a row, none of his friends or associates was among the early bathers. He was able to find a quiet corner of the tepidarium where he was oiled by a slave, before heading into the thick, steamy air of the caldarium. He sat on a vacant bench, leaned his back against the wall, and closed his eyes, trying to shut out the murmur of conversation around him.

Sidonius and Ecdicius had not abandoned him after Lupiacum. That was something. They had believed his lie about the sick friend in Arles, or at least did not enquire further about it, and through November and December the three of them had spent many more hours bathing and drinking together. He especially liked Sidonius, who took delight in words and understood their power. Ecdicius, on the other hand, was not exactly dull-witted, but he always seemed a little lost whenever they played word games or jokingly pretended to be famous figures from literature. At these baths he was also prone to join the athletes in the palaestra, the very sight of which horrified both Arvandus and Sidonius. Arvandus smiled to think of the time Ecdicius had almost managed to tease his cousin into a wrestling bout.

Careful, he warned himself. *You cannot afford to think of them as true friends.* He forced himself to remember why he had intervened in the tavern at all. It had not been to save them; part of him would have enjoyed seeing two well-groomed youths beaten up and dragged out to their fate. He had done it for his own reason: to ingratiate himself with the senatorial classes. Both Ecdicius and Sidonius were members of families who had ruined Gaul, and part of a world to which Arvandus did not belong. Lupiacum and the inauguration had proved that. But if he was ever to rise, he would need to cultivate their friendship more carefully, and not overreach himself again.

'Arvandus?'

He opened his eyes. Sidonius was standing in front of him,

naked and oiled. 'You're here early,' said Arvandus, straightening up in surprise.

'I've been trying to find you the last couple of days,' Sidonius said cheerfully, sitting on the bench beside him. 'I have a question for you.'

'About what?' he said, trying not to sound as nervous as he felt.

'My father's visiting Bordeaux next month on official business, and he wants me to go with him. So I thought, since your family is from Bordeaux, why don't you come, too? It wouldn't be bad, would it, turning up in your home city in the train of the praetorian prefect? I'd enjoy meeting your father. I could even ask my father to give him an audience.'

Arvandus hoped his alarm at this news did not show. 'He's visiting next month? Winter's a hard time for travelling.'

'It's something about the ten-year anniversary of the peace treaty, I don't know the details. During the summer he'll be too busy in imperial territory to make the trip. He has old friends in Bordeaux as well. Anyway, what do you think? You'll need to write to your father to let him know.'

'I'm not sure,' Arvandus said, trying desperately to think of an answer. He felt trapped. He had not prepared for this; as far as he knew, no praetorian prefect had ever crossed the Gothic territory to visit Bordeaux before. 'My father isn't very politically minded,' was the best he could do. 'I honestly think having an audience with a prefect would terrify him.'

'Well, perhaps so. But you and I should still visit him.'

'I don't know,' he stammered. 'Let's talk about it another time.'

'Why not now?'

'I have to go.'

He began to rise, but Sidonius fixed a hand on his thigh, holding him in place. 'Arvandus,' he said, 'is Paeonius your patron?'

Arvandus pushed Sidonius aside and got to his feet, wanting only to get away. How in the Devil's name did Sidonius know about his patron? He would have to forgo the cold bath and get dressed while still hot and covered in sweat, but he didn't care. He was not safe. He had to go at once to Paeonius.

Arvandus walked out of the caldarium, through the tepidarium, and into the covered walkway that surrounded the palaestra, where he noticed that it had started to rain. His friend was still behind him. 'Arvandus, listen to me.' Sidonius grabbed hold of his elbow, forcing him to stop. 'Please, I want to talk.'

Arvandus shook his elbow free, but stayed where he was. There was no point maintaining the deceit with Sidonius any longer. The palaestra was empty. This was as good a time and place as any. 'Yes,' he said, 'I'm a client of Paeonius. No, my father is not equestrian. We used to live in a shack. We ate pork once a month, when we could afford it. There was never any need for napkins or slippers.'

Sidonius stared at him with innocent eyes. 'Why did you lie to us?'

Unable to help himself, Arvandus let out a bitter laugh. 'Why did I lie! Do you know what happened to my family?'

'Tell me.'

'We used to be in the equestrian class, in my grandfather's time. He had land – I mean, it'd be nothing to a family like yours, but it was enough to bring him status and respect. Then the wars came, and he had to flee. When he came back, he found he'd been dispossessed.'

'By the Goths?'

'By a nobleman – one of you. He stole my grandfather's land. My grandfather tried to challenge him in the courts, but of course he failed. And thus my family was ruined, until Paeonius saved us. I owe him everything.'

'I wish you'd told us this before.'

Everything was so simple for the noble classes. Arvandus felt his anger rise – not just anger at the arrogance of Felix and his father, but at the stupid complacence of those like Sidonius, born into privilege and raised with no real understanding of the world. 'Ask yourself this, Sidonius: how do big men become big? By taking from other men. Well, if that's the game, then I'm willing to play it. I might even thank God that I was born into a humble family. Better that than to be born into a family of criminals and thieves.' He leaned forward, bringing their faces close. 'Your class has ruined the empire. It's time for new blood.'

He stood back. The palaestra was quiet except for the pattering of rain on the flagstones, and the occasional splash from one of the adjoining baths. They had both begun to shiver in the cold air.

Sidonius looked shocked, his voice wavering. 'We're not enemies.'

'When one party has everything, and another nothing, what else can they be?'

'I'm not talking about parties of men. I mean you and me. We're friends.'

'Are we? You are born, and you have everything – a name, wealth, influence. And what do I have? Even my clothes are bought with another man's money. Everything, *everything* I must fight for. There's so much between us, and you can't even see it.'

'I believe our friendship is true,' Sidonius insisted. 'Let me help you.'

'I already have a patron.'

'Paeonius won't be able to protect you, not from this. He'll give you up, and claim you lied to him about your status. At best he'll smuggle you out of Arles, never to return.'

Arvandus did not dispute the truth of that. Paeonius already had enough enemies among the noble classes; he would be a fool to risk his reputation defending a nobody like Arvandus. 'Then what do you suggest I do?'

'My father is prepared to take you on as his client.'

At first Arvandus was lost for a response. Sidonius's words made no sense. After being exposed as a fraud, to be taken on by the most powerful official in Gaul . . . 'Why would he do that?'

'He knows you're talented, the best student Maximinus has. He appreciates intelligence.'

'But I'm a peasant.'

'Only by law. As praetorian prefect, he can raise your father to equestrian rank by special dispensation. Such things are not unheard of.'

'So I won't be punished?'

'No. You'll become exactly what everyone else already thinks you are.'

'So you want me to betray my patron?' Arvandus said. 'After all Paeonius has done for me and my family, lifting us out of the dirt, you want me to jump beds like a prostitute?'

'Changing patrons isn't that unusual. Your parents will be looked after, and you wouldn't be expected to say or do anything *against* Paeonius . . .'

'Come on, Sollius, don't treat me like a fool. These are no ordinary patrons. What's really going on?'

Sidonius sighed. 'All right, I'll be frank. My father wants you to swear allegiance to him publicly. It will embarrass Paeonius, which will be good for us. You'll be presented as an innocent who was manipulated by Paeonius for his own ends. Rather than punishing you, my father is choosing to pardon you and take you on as his own. He'll look merciful, generous. It'll send out a good message at the start of his prefectship.'

Arvandus could appreciate the cunning of the plan, and the advantages for Sidonius's father. The risks would be all his own, however. And there was the matter of loyalty. 'Paeonius will accuse me of treachery,' he said.

'Did he make you swear an oath?'

'No, but if I cross him—'

'Then you're not legally bound to him. I know Paeonius has helped you, but think about what he is. A governorship is the highest post he's ever held, and the highest one he's ever likely to. My father is the praetorian prefect of Gaul. How can Paeonius compete with that? He'll rant and complain like he always does, but you'll be the one standing next to the prefect. You deserve it.'

Arvandus turned away. Everything had fallen apart, but once again Fate was offering him a hand. He knew what accepting the offer would mean. No more lying to his friends. Nobody could ask for a more influential patron than the praetorian prefect himself; it would surely open up the path to power and to everything he dreamed of achieving. And the alternative was clear: disgrace, expulsion from Arles, losing everything he had so far gained. He would have to watch his parents sink back into poverty. That would be more than he could bear.

'I'll do it,' he said. 'Tell your father I'll abandon Paeonius.'

Sidonius grinned and embraced him. 'I'm *freezing*,' he laughed. 'Come on, let's get back into the heat.'

XIX

'**A** re you going to tell Father?'

Not this again. Ecdicius prepared himself for the same argument he and his sister had been having every day for the past week. 'No, I'm not.'

'You should. You know Father would never do such a thing.'

'How Felix handles his own slaves is none of Father's business, and none of yours.'

'But the boy didn't do anything.'

'Why are you so bothered about this boy? It was more than two months ago, Attica. Even the slave has probably forgotten about it by now.'

Attica, bundled up in layers of blankets and peering out between the barely open shutters of her window, did not reply. Ecdicius listened instead to the creaking of the wagon, the steady trundle of the wheels, the snorting of the horses as they pulled the heavy load along the track. Not many roads were easily negotiable in the depths of winter, but the one between Arles and Lyons was kept in good repair as a matter of imperial policy, and luckily the last week had been dry. Ecdicius was grateful for this. The sooner they reached Lyons, the better. There they could rest for a day before the final stretch west to Clermont, and to their awaiting parents.

Ecdicius tried not to think too much about what would follow; he had already spent days torturing himself doing that. Word must have reached home about his behaviour in Arles – the drinking, the gambling, the lowly acquaintances he had made. The public behaviour of Arvandus had not helped. He had not even made any academic progress that might have compensated for it. He had proved himself unfit for a military career, and now unfit for a civilian one. There were not many options left.

'It isn't the boy,' Attica said. 'At least, it isn't just the boy. It's about Felix, and me.'

He turned to look at his sister. 'What do you mean?'

'He's cruel. I could see it in his eyes when he had the rod. He frightened me.'

'So? You've decided to come home, you won't be seeing him again for a long time.'

'I pray not.'

Ecdicius waited for her to say more. 'Attica,' he said, nudging her. 'Why does Felix bother you? Did he try to hit you, too?'

'No. It's just . . . I'm afraid I was silly with him. I didn't promise him anything, exactly, but he might think I did. I'm afraid he'll talk to Father.'

'Attica, look at me. Felix will never hurt you. I promise you that.'

'He made a promise to me, too. He swore he'd punish Arvandus for trying to steal from him.'

'I already told you, Sidonius's father is taking on Arvandus as his client. What can Felix do to him now?'

She did not reply, but merely stared through her window at the passing scrub.

They spent the rest of the journey in silence. It was evening by the time the wagon arrived in Lyons and rolled into the stable yard of the town house where they were staying, the residence of Syagrius. He was a cousin of their uncle, Ferreolus, but Ecdicius did not know him well.

Syagrius was waiting in the yard as Ecdicius climbed down from the wagon door. A servant stood behind him bearing a torch. 'Welcome to both of you,' Syagrius said, his voice half-muffled by the thick woollen coat and the scarf pulled up close to his face. 'Horrible time of year to be travelling.'

'Our father would have it so,' said Ecdicius, giving a hand to Attica as she descended. 'There's a second wagon following with our luggage.'

'My people will see to it.' He pulled the scarf down to reveal a wide, friendly smile. 'Are you hungry? My wife has had the kitchen prepare a little something, nothing too heavy. I don't know about you, but I can never get to sleep if I eat too much at this hour.'

'We'd be grateful, thank you,' said Attica.

'Excellent. The food will be brought to your room – one of the servants will take you. Ecdicius, before you eat, my other guest will want a word with you, I suspect.'

The figure holding the torch stepped forwards. He was not a servant, as Ecdicius had at first assumed because of his anonymous winter coat. It was Aegidius, commander of the Senior Honorian Horse. Ecdicius remembered that he also happened to be Syagrius's nephew. The last time Ecdicius had seen him had been at the wedding massacre; he had been with Aëtius and Majorian. It was not easy to look him in the eye. 'Tribune Aegidius,' he said. 'This is a surprise.'

'Not for me. I hope you're not tired, Ecdicius. We've a lot of talking to do, and even more drinking. Come on.'

Leaving the others, Aegidius took Ecdicius into the house, passing through the atrium into a side room. It was dark, lit by lamps that hung from metal hooks on the wall. There was a couch, a desk covered in scrolls and tablets, and a brazier that had been burning for some time, only the dullest glow coming from its heaped coals. Aegidius, still in his coat, went to sit behind the desk. This was the first time Ecdicius had ever had the chance to study the officer properly. He was young, still not thirty, short in stature, and with his russet beard and pointed nose he resembled a fox. That was appropriate enough; he was known to be a crafty soldier, and so Aëtius tended to give him scouting duties. Ambushing the Frankish wedding was said to have been his idea.

Aegidius picked up a large jug from the desk and used it to fill two pewter tankards. He handed one to Ecdicius, keeping the other for himself. 'Take this. I dare say you need a drink, and if you don't now, you will in a moment.'

Ecdicius sipped from the tankard. It was foul; some kind of

weak beer. He was not surprised, as Aegidius was also known to prefer beer to wine, a barbarity that his troops never tired of discussing behind his back. In the ranks there had even been whispers that he was the bastard son of a Frankish chief. Ecdicius thought it was foolish to base such a rumour on a man's drinking habits. Aegidius was one of the noble Syagrii of Lyons and his parentage was not in doubt.

'No, no,' said Aegidius, waving his hand. 'Drink it down, drink it down. You can't drink beer like you drink wine.'

Ecdicius obediently forced down a mouthful of the stuff. Perhaps if he drank as much of it as Aegidius, it would start to taste good.

'That's better. Don't disappoint me, now, Ecdicius. I've heard bad things about you – the *right* sort of bad things. I've heard you like to drink, and you like to fight. Is that so?'

'When I have the chance, tribune.'

'If it's the chance you want, you're about to get it. I'm going to re-commission you in the First Gallic Horse.'

'I don't . . . what about Majorian?'

'Majorian has retired. I'm now tribune of his old regiment.'

This was news to Ecdicius. Retirement sounded unlikely, given that Majorian was no older than Aegidius. 'Was he injured?'

'He was a casualty of politics, you might say. What do you know about Count Aëtius's wife, Pelagia?'

'I've never met her,' Ecdicius said.

'A tactful answer, and a boring one. I asked what you *know* about her.'

'I know she's a Gothic princess of some kind.'

'She and Aëtius also have a son they want to marry off to the emperor's daughter Placidia. Unfortunately the girl's grandmother has other plans – *she* wants Placidia to wed Majorian. She thinks Majorian is the rising star of the army, more friendly to the imperial family. She's right, too. You see how this caused problems.'

'So Aëtius has removed Majorian from his command?'

'From public life entirely. He's been exiled to his estates in Italy. Ironic, isn't it? First Majorian kicks you out of the army, and then Aëtius kicks Majorian out. In the meantime Aëtius has returned to Ravenna and left me as acting master of soldiers in Gaul.' He waved a hand over the chaos of documents before him. 'As you can see, it's a bloody mess. Most of Majorian's command staff were dismissed with him, so I need deputies. You'll have the rank of protector. Are you interested?'

'Yes,' Ecdicius said at once. 'But my father—'

'Your father knows exactly what's happened, and he knows I'm meeting you here. This is why he summoned you from Arles. I believe he's glad to see the back of Majorian, the two of them never got on. And yes, Majorian is my friend, but I have more urgent things to worry about. We must make sure the northern tribes don't take advantage of the situation – this will mean some aggressive patrols along the Rhine.'

'What of the Huns? My uncle Ferreolus said Attila was building a new confederacy in Germany.'

'It's happening as we speak. Aëtius has refused to believe it, so we've been trying to get word to the prefect through other means, including your uncle, hoping to apply pressure on Aëtius from that direction, for all the good it's done us. Even if Attila waits for another five years, we need to start planning *now* – guarding the frontiers, strengthening our alliance with the Goths to make sure they stand by us. Frankly, I'm glad Aëtius has been distracted by this business in Italy. It's freed our hands to do what we need to do. Your father, for instance – he understands that the real danger is the Huns. If Attila turns his attention from the east to the west, there isn't a chance in hell that the Gallic field army alone will be able to stop him. He'll burn this country from one end to the other.' He slapped both hands on the table, rising from his chair. 'Well then, you still remember how to ride a horse?'

So Ferreolus had been right about everything: about Attila, and about being patient. Ecdicius could almost feel the satisfying weight of the armour on his shoulders. The sense of finally being where he belonged wrapped itself around him like a cloak. He grinned. 'Most certainly, tribune.'

XX

'I'll give you twelve for it.'

The merchant placed both hands over his heart. 'Sixteen, and may God forgive you if my children starve to death this winter.'

'Fourteen. No more.'

'Done.'

The merchant held out the ring in his open hand. Its twisted golden wire gleamed brilliantly in the sunlight, the dark garnet stone seeming to glow with a hidden fire. Arvandus reached out to take it, but the merchant clenched it suddenly in his fist. He coughed, extending his other hand. Smiling, Arvandus counted out fourteen silver coins and stacked them in the merchant's palm.

'May it bring you much happiness,' the man smiled, handing over the ring.

Arvandus admired it closely for a moment. It was beautiful; small, but as much as he could afford right now. He could sell it and buy a bigger one in a few months. In the meantime it would show the world that his fortunes had well and truly turned. Now his family was truly equestrian, and had a decree from the praetorian prefect to prove it.

He slipped the ring on the little finger of his right hand, fitting it snugly above the first knuckle, and continued his promenade of the upper forum. It was March, still too cold for his liking, but his new, warmer cloak was helping keep the chill out. The afternoon market was busier than it had been for weeks. Today he was content to amble by himself between the stalls of luxury fabrics and trinkets, of imported pottery, of bread and roasted meat, wine and spices, enjoying the air of pleasure and prosperity. He smiled and nodded as he spotted friends, exchanging short greetings and noting the admiration in their eyes when they spotted his new ring.

Life had certainly improved since shifting his loyalty to Prefect Alcimus. Once again he summoned the memory of the morning a month ago when he had attended the daily public audience at the prefect's palace. He remembered standing with the crowd of petitioners, sick with nervousness, waiting for his name to be called out. He had approached Alcimus on the throne and performed the correct ritual bow, lowering himself to his knees and bending forwards to touch his head on the cold marble floor. From that position he had begged to be accepted as the prefect's loyal and obedient client. Alcimus had asked him who his current patron was. 'The *vir clarissimus* Paeonius,' he had replied. 'Your petition is granted,' Alcimus had said, graciously inviting him to approach. Arvandus had dutifully obeyed, kneeling before the throne with head bowed and hands held out, palms pressed together. Alcimus had grasped Arvandus's hands between his own. With that gesture he had become his patron.

It had all been carefully arranged, of course. Arvandus had had to wait for days until Paeonius had happened to be attending an audience. It was vital for him to be present. As Arvandus had backed away from the throne he had glimpsed Paeonius standing in the crowd to the left. His face had been red, his arms dropped bolt-straight by his side. He had looked about ready to burst with fury.

Arvandus could not pretend that he felt no guilt about it. There had been no real choice, though. His stipend had doubled in size, and he had moved to a comfortable two-room apartment near the amphitheatre. Alcimus had already sent one of his secretaries to Bordeaux to inform Arvandus's father of his new rank, and to move both parents into a country villa with an estate worthy of an equestrian. Arvandus had sent them a letter along with the secretary, explaining his rise in fortunes. He wished he had been there to witness their joy. The long years of hardship were finally over, the family's honour had been restored.

True, aside from these arrangements, Sidonius's father had shown little interest in Arvandus; apart from the audience they had only spoken once, and Alcimus had struck him as aloof and distracted. But Arvandus wanted him as his patron, not his friend. Once his education was over he would not need to toil away for years as a provincial clerk, slowing rising up the ranks of the civil service. A letter of recommendation from a former prefect would surely get him a post in the imperial administration in Italy. After a few years as a tribune and notary he'd be a strong contender for a senior post on the prefect's staff back in Gaul – in the tax office, perhaps, or the legal office. Those were said to be best for men who wanted to rise high. His dreams had not changed, he had merely found a quicker way to achieve them. He would become famous for his honesty and sense of justice. He would protect the weak, stand up to the proud, be the kind of leader the empire needed.

'A most impressive trinket,' said a man close behind him.

Arvandus recognised the voice. He turned to find Simeon's smiling face. 'My business with your master is done with,' Arvandus said. He glanced around quickly. It would not be good to be seen with the agent of Paeonius.

'You made that very clear at the audience last month.'

'What do you want?'

'Just to talk.' He examined Arvandus's new cloak with approval. 'I see your new circumstances agree with you. I can certainly appreciate the material benefits of what you did.'

'Did Paeonius send you to talk to me?'

'He sent me with a simple proposal. Perhaps there is a way for us all to benefit from the new situation. Publicly, Alcimus is now your patron. That cannot be changed. Privately, Paeonius is prepared to maintain a certain discreet friendship.'

'You mean he wants me to spy for him?'

'I would not put it in so crude a way. It is natural for friends to share information from time to time, is it not?'

'And why should I want to be friends with him?'

'Because Alcimus only took you on to hurt Paeonius. Surely you realise that? You will always be the least of his clients, the one of low birth, of no family and no breeding, the last in line for any promotion. The noble families will never truly accept you.'

'You're forgetting that I have real friends among them.'

Simeon sighed. 'My master is a pragmatic man when it comes to politics,' he said. 'But he has his pride, too. He does not like being embarrassed. If you refuse this offer, there may be consequences later.'

'I'm under the protection of the prefect now.'

'Prefects change almost every year. Paeonius has a long memory.'

'I'm not afraid of him.'

'Let's not talk of fear, as though we were common criminals! I merely wanted to plant his proposal in your thoughts. If you change your mind, you can send me a message through your professor. Good fortune, Arvandus.' He turned and walked away, vanishing into the crowd.

Arvandus stood surrounded by the bustle of the forum. He tried to stay calm, but Simeon had unsettled him. There had been an unmistakable threat in his words. But had it been a mere bluff? Surely someone like Paeonius would not dare harm a client of the prefect. For the time being, at least, he was safe.

He reassured himself by finding Lampridius and a couple of other classmates, and the group of them spent the rest of the afternoon in the baths. After that they went to one of their regular corner taverns in the amphitheatre district. The evening was a pleasantly drunken haze of laughter and games, of coins slapped on tables and dice tumbling from towers, of spilled wine and badly sung poetry. Simeon fell far out of Arvandus's thoughts.

He returned home after sunset, stumbling from the tavern into the dark street, winding merrily between the piers of the amphitheatre until he peeled off down a lane to the house where he now lived. Yes, life was much better than it had been a month ago. No more stomping Germans to keep him awake. No more knife-fights in the corridor outside his room. No more sleeping on the floor because of a flea-infested mattress. Life was good, and getting better. He had seen quite a few girls looking his way in the forum earlier. Nice girls, too. Respectable. Maybe he could find himself a proper sweetheart, like the older students. Someone kind and clever and pretty, from a good equestrian family. And not too tall.

The face of Attica came to mind, hovering before him in the moonlit gloom. Those delicate features, her clear skin and lively eyes . . .

'No, no,' he muttered. 'Don't think of that one. Not that one.' He reached the side entrance to his apartment building and steadied himself against the brick wall. As soon as he felt his head stop spinning, he hammered on the door. It was opened by the building's night watchman, a surly old Spaniard called Castus. Arvandus bade him good evening, receiving as usual no reply, and entered, shuffling down the lamp-lit corridor to his rooms. He fumbled with his iron key in the lock for a while, before realising that it was already open. Strange. He must have forgotten to lock it when he left. He ought to leave a note for his sober self in the morning, telling him to be more careful. No matter. Sleep was more important. He staggered into the room.

As soon as the door closed they grabbed him, raised him from his feet, stuffed some cloth in his mouth, carried him to the bed, and put him on his back. He kicked, tried to scream, all to no effect. A voice next to his ear told him to keep quiet.

He did so, relaxing his limbs, though his heart continued to beat like a hammer in his chest, and his breath came short and loud through his nose. Two men were holding him down. He noticed a small candle burning on the table. A third man used it to ignite the wick of an oil lamp.

Its warm, soft light filled the room. The two men holding him looked exactly as large as they had seemed in the darkness. The third man was even larger. They looked like dockhands, the sort of big-shouldered men who could hoist full sacks of grain with hardly a grunt, and who in the off-season would make a living however they could. He began to struggle again, until one of the men holding him punched him in the side of the head. His vision filled with flashing lights.

He felt his new ring being pulled from his finger. *No,* he wanted to scream. The third man had taken it, and was slipping it onto his own little finger. Next he said, keeping his voice low, 'Hold out that hand.'

The man who had punched him grabbed his right hand and stretched it towards the third man, who was obviously the leader. Arvandus felt bile rise up into the back of his throat, making him want to cough.

'Don't choke, now,' the leader said, grabbing the hand. He drew a dagger from his belt and brought it up to the little finger.

No. Please.

The man pushed the dagger point under the fingernail – gently at first, then slowly with more force.

Agony flooded Arvandus's mind, a wave rushing down his arm, banishing every conscious thought. He bit into the cloth, clamping it between his teeth with a muffled scream.

At last the pain subsided. He opened his eyes, blinking. Tears were pouring down the side of his face.

Who are you? What do you want?

The third man now bent the little finger backwards. Again Arvandus tried to scream. It felt like the finger was about to snap off. He craned his neck up to see that the man was holding the edge of the dagger against the middle of the finger. Before Arvandus had time to comprehend what was about to happen, it did. With a swift, sharp flick the man severed the finger at the first joint.

Everything became black for a moment. Then there was a steady slapping on his left cheek, three faces looking down on him, laughter. The cloth was yanked from his mouth. He gasped for air, and something smaller was shoved into his open mouth. It was soft, salty, wet.

The men left, closing the door behind them, as Arvandus turned over on the bed and spat out the tip of his little finger. What remained of the finger on his hand felt as though it were on fire. Blood streamed down his arm. He had to stop the bleeding. He grabbed a bundle of his woollen cloak and stuffed it firmly over the stump.

This time there was nothing to stop him screaming.

TWO YEARS LATER

Prologue

H onoria had always been impetuous, even for a princess.
Sometimes it seemed that her whole world was ruled by people who hated her. The imperial palace was her cell, Ravenna her prison. Life was a web of pomp woven by her mother the empress, who told her what to wear, what to say, how to behave, what to believe, what to think. And every day she was told how fortunate she was.

There were few friends to be found, but the chamberlain Eugendus was one. He treated her kindly. He understood her. He was wary of her at first, but he came to her room when she sent soldiers to get him. He became scared again when he made her pregnant, and then more soldiers came to get him, this time sent by her mother.

Poor Eugendus was tortured for a long time before he died. When Honoria gave birth they took her child and smothered it. She never saw it, never knew if it was a boy or a girl. Then they sent her away to Constantinople, where her cousin Theodosius was the emperor, and there she lived in a nunnery for fourteen years.

'Your sister must be wed,' the empress said one day to her son, the emperor Valentinian. 'She is still young enough to bear children, and the religious life has surely tamed her rebellious spirit.'

And so Honoria was brought back to Ravenna and was betrothed to an old Roman senator who was boring enough that he would never try to claim the throne, even if married to a princess. He was wrinkly, foul-breathed, and his left eye was filled with an ugly grey mist. Honoria refused to marry him. 'The choice is not yours to make,' her mother said.

She did have a choice, though. She chose to take one of her gold rings and seal it inside a little sack with a message written on a piece of papyrus. She gave the sack to the only eunuch she could trust. She swore him to secrecy, and commanded him to take it to Attila, king of the Huns.

The eunuch was loyal, and did as he was told. After many months he came to Attila's palace, a timber-built marvel on the grassy plains beyond the Danube. When Attila heard the message and saw the ring, he knew that the time had come to fulfil his destiny. For Honoria had promised to take him as her husband, offering as her dowry the western half of the empire, if only he would come and rescue her from a hated marriage. At once Attila sent one of his swiftest messengers to Ravenna, asserting his right to the promised dowry.

By now the old empress had died, and so Valentinian received the messenger without his mother by his side.

'My master, the great King Attila, is coming to claim your sister and half of the empire,' the messenger said. 'He commands that you prepare the imperial palace for his arrival.'

Valentinian and his entire court laughed. They denounced Attila's claim as illegal and insane. There would be no wedding, nor would he ever set foot inside the palace. The eunuch was found and beheaded. For her treacherous behaviour Honoria was condemned to perpetual imprisonment in a distant corner of the palace, where her anguished cries would never be heard.

Attila, when news of this reached him, sent riders to every corner of Germany, calling his vassals to arms. A hundred tribes rose up at his word. They sharpened their blades, donned their helmets, said farewell to their loved ones, and marched to war.

XXI

Trier, A.D. 451

They kept coming. An endless train of them from the east, a weary, bedraggled column of men, women and children, of packmules and oxen, dragging themselves up the grey sludge of the winter road. Overloaded carts trundled by with small children and the elderly perched on top. They looked half dead already. Their sullen eyes stared into space. Some of them watched Ecdicius, sitting on his horse just outside the city gate. He found it difficult to meet their stares. They seemed to be accusing him of something. Or perhaps he was just accusing himself.

As well he might. Where had he been – where had any Roman soldiers been – when Attila and the Huns had crossed the Rhine? The city garrison of Mainz had been unable to resist them. The Alemannic kings, pledged to protect the frontier on behalf of the emperor, had not resisted. The rumour was that they had even sworn allegiance to Attila as their new king, along with every other tribe of Germany.

Rumours. Every hungry belly that entered the gates of Trier brought a new one. The bishop, Severus, had asked his priests and deacons to question as many refugees as they could, and had related to Ecdicius the few certainties gathered. Attila had been moving west across Germany for months, arriving near the Rhine just before the onset of winter. At the start of February, in a bold move, he had built a fleet of barges and begun ferrying his horde of steppe riders and German allies across the river. They had swarmed over Mainz and put its surprised defenders to the sword. Even more than gold and slaves, survivors said, Attila had wanted food. His soldiers needed grain for the rest of the winter, their horses needed fodder. They had emptied the granaries of Mainz and every other granary within a day's ride. The countryside up and down the river was plagued by roving bands of Huns. What they could not eat they raped, and what they could not rape they burned. Terror spread on the winter wind. Attila, King of the Huns, had arrived to claim the western throne.

Ecdicius shivered. There had been no snow for three days, but the most recent fall still blanketed the tombs that stretched on each side of the road leading into Trier. Those tombs were crumbling from neglect, their occupants long forgotten. Bare branches sprouted from cracks like long, skeletal fingers. The whole city looked like that. Rome had given up the old imperial capital of Gaul during the Great Invasions almost fifty years earlier, and had never truly reclaimed it. It had been captured and recaptured by the Franks more times than anyone remembered, until now it was hardly worth the taking. Almost every family of note had fled south long ago, abandoning their ancestral estates and town houses.

This was the home of the monk Salvian, Ecdicius remembered. Now the old monk seemed a little less mad. When he had stood in the bustling forum of Arles and raved about doom and devastation, this must be what he had seen. Trier was a foretaste of God's judgement on the empire. It was a foretaste of what Arles might soon become.

Ecdicius wheeled Zephyros to face the gate. 'We'll return to Troyes,' he said to his men. 'We can't do any good here.'

His second-in-command Flaccus, a big-jawed man of about thirty, grunted. Between the scarf wrapped under his chin and the nose-guard and cheek pieces of his helmet, his face was almost entirely hidden. 'So you don't want to ride on to Mainz after all?'

Ecdicius decided to ignore the hint of insubordination. The men were tired, frustrated. It would do no good to antagonise Flaccus now. 'It's too late for Mainz. Form up.'

The scouting party of ten riders fell into place behind Ecdicius as he led them through the city gate. The gatehouse had been turned into a miniature fortress by what passed for the civic garrison, along with the other three gatehouses. Most of the city walls had been left to crumble, being far too large to maintain. Ecdicius led his troops down a wide colonnaded street that had once seen processions of emperors, but was now dilapidated and strewn with rubbish. At the end of the street was the cathedral precinct, around which huddled such life as the city still retained, a measly collection of wooden houses and shacks. Beyond the cathedral, in what had been the heart of the city, lay the sprawling imperial palace. It seemed to have been taken over by squatters, the fine courtyards now used as stables and storehouses. *At least there will be no shortage of space for the refugees*, Ecdicius thought grimly. But who would feed them? Not even the bishop had enough for so many, not in the middle of winter.

They left the city by the west gate and crossed over the Moselle bridge. It would be a long, hard ride to Troyes, especially at this time of year. Ecdicius had made sure his men had sufficient rations for themselves, but Zephyros was tiring, and the other mounts would be no better off. It was hard to forage at this time of year, harder still to keep warm at night. The only consolation was that the winter conditions would slow the Huns just as much. Tribune Aegidius would need every spare moment to prepare for what was coming.

Using every precious hour of daylight available, it took eight days to ride more than two hundred miles to Troyes, passing through the cities of Metz and Reims, most nights camping in barns or under makeshift shelters. Ecdicius did not mind the cold and discomfort. He was used to it, as were his men. Over the last two years of patrolling the northern borderlands, preserving the peace established by Aëtius, putting down barbarians, bandits and rebels where necessary, he had earned the respect of Tribune Aegidius. He could not say the same of the rest of the First Gallic Horse. To some of them, especially to Flaccus, he was still the pampered senator's son who had shamed himself in battle two and a half years ago.

There would be time to deal with Flaccus later; right now there

were more important things to worry about. Ecdicius had learned
how tenuous the empire's grip had become in the north. In these
parts Rome did not impose peace, it negotiated it. Local cities
ran their own administrations, collected their own taxes, supported
the various barbarian contingents that Aëtius had settled in their
territories to act as hired protectors – Teutons, Sarmatians,
Batavians, Alans, Franks, and others. As far as Ecdicius could
see, the barbarians were more interested in extorting their hosts
than protecting them. They fell into line when a regular Roman
unit passed through, their self-styled 'kings' bowed and scraped
and renewed their pledges to the emperor, but Ecdicius knew
that these oaths were forgotten as soon as the Romans moved
on. In truth, the land beyond the Loire did not feel like part of
the empire. The roads and bridges were no longer properly
maintained. The countryside was littered with roofless and weed-
choked villas. The great public buildings of the towns had become
haunted shells. None but old men remembered a time when the
bath houses or amphitheatres had been places of life, and not
mere quarries.

For two years Ecdicius had ridden with Aegidius through this
strange world. He had come to admire the northerners for their
resilience and resourcefulness, for the fierce loyalty they showed
to their cities and their bishops. They were tough, there was no
doubt about that. And in spite of everything, they still thought
of themselves as Roman.

Aegidius had set up his headquarters in the basilica complex
of Troyes, using the adjoining forum as barracks. Ecdicius rode
through the large forum courtyard, Zephyros's hoofs clattering
on the flagstones, surrounded by the noises of camp. Horses
neighed, men shouted, and from every corner came the sharp
clinking of hammer on anvil. His groom, Stephanus, a youth
from his father's estate who had proved himself to be a skilful
and eager horseman, came running from the courtyard colonnade
to take the reins. 'The tribune is inside, master,' he said as Ecdicius
dismounted.

Ecdicius nodded. 'Get Zephyros fed and watered.' Dismissing

Flaccus and the others, he strode up the steps and through the double doors of the basilica. He heard Aegidius's voice booming down the length of the nave as soon as he entered. The tribune was standing at a table in the apse with the commanders of his other two mounted regiments, the Eighth Dalmatians and the Senior Cornuti. They appeared to have been joined by the bishop of Troyes, Lupus.

Aegidius saw Ecdicius and waved his hand. 'Finally! Ecdicius, report! What news from the frontier?'

'Attila has crossed the Rhine, tribune,' he said, snapping a salute. 'Mainz has fallen. We got as far as Trier.'

'Is he advancing up the Moselle?'

'Hard to say. He seems to be stopping on the Rhine for now, sending raiding parties in every direction. My best guess is that he'll be heading downstream for Koblenz, then Cologne. Not all the Franks have pledged allegiance – he'll need to deal with them first or risk an attack from the rear.'

'I agree. His main advance will come in the spring. He wants to secure his hold on the Rhine first, before we can mobilise against him. What about numbers?'

'No clear reports. I'd guess at least ten thousand Huns, with as many Germans, but there may be more waiting to cross the Rhine.'

'May Christ preserve us,' said Bishop Lupus, crossing himself. 'How many soldiers do you have under your command, tribune?'

Aegidius grunted. 'Not enough. Three mounted regiments to hand, four infantry, but all undermanned. Fewer than three thousand, all told. Aëtius took too many men with him to Italy. From what I hear, they've been hit hard by plague and desertions, too, so even if he brings them back they won't be at full strength.'

The tribune of the Eighth Dalmatians, a tough and unpopular commander named Marcus, spoke up. 'What about our barbarian allies?'

'We can count on the Burgundians,' Aegidius said. 'Same goes for the Alans at Valence. Maybe the Armoricans, with some persuasion. We can hold out hope for the Franks, possibly even the Saxons. The Suebes, Sarmatians and the rest will follow. That's maybe seven, eight thousand, assuming we can muster them all in time.'

'You haven't mentioned the Goths,' said Marcus. 'Theoderic is the strongest barbarian king in Gaul.'

'He claims he can field fifteen thousand warriors,' said Tribune Messianus of the Senior Cornuti. Ecdicius knew him as a loyal friend of his father, a cool-headed veteran of the Gothic war.

'I'm well aware of that,' said Aegidius. 'But Theoderic is also far in the south, and he hates Aëtius. He and his fifteen thousand warriors are just as likely to stay at home, safe and sound, and watch Attila grind us down. Then he'll strike when our backs are turned. Win or lose, we'll be in no state to defend Narbonne when he decides to move against it.'

Outrage flared in Marcus's face. 'The Goths are sworn to us by treaty.'

'The Goths keep to treaties only through fear, not honour,' said Aegidius. 'Theoderic has been after Narbonne for years. He wants to control the sea trade with Africa and the east. When he's got Narbonne, he'll be after Arles, then Marseilles, until every last corner of Gaul is his.' He looked at each man in turn. 'Make no mistake: the Goths could be an even bigger danger than Attila and all his Huns.'

'Then we should strike the Goths first,' said Marcus, slamming a fist on the table. 'March on Toulouse. *Force* them to join us.'

'That would make things worse,' said Messianus.

Bishop Lupus seemed ready to despair. 'And if Theoderic refuses to help . . .'

'Perhaps my father can persuade him,' Ecdicius said. The three tribunes and the bishop turned to face him, looking surprised to find him still there. 'He and Theoderic negotiated the last peace treaty,' Ecdicius continued. 'They respect one another.'

Aegidius folded his arms. 'It's been twelve years since that treaty was made. Are you sure Theoderic will still listen to your father?'

'No. But do we have any choice?'

'I suppose not. How soon can you ride to Clermont?'

'I can set off today.'

'You've been on the road for weeks. Take a day to rest.'

'With respect, tribune, I'd rather leave at once.'

'As you wish.' He snapped his fingers, and a subaltern hurried to his side. 'Summon every courier we have,' Aegidius told him. 'We have three months to raise the biggest army Gaul has seen in fifty years.'

After they were dismissed, Lupus fell into step beside Ecdicius. The bishop was first cousin to his father, but there was little resemblance. He was small-boned, anxious. The news of the invasion had clearly unsettled him. 'Greet your father for me,' he said.

'I will, Bishop.'

He gripped Ecdicius by the arm, forcing him to stop. 'Tell him we *must* have the Goths, whatever it takes.' He looked him firmly in the eye. His voice trembled with fear. 'Theoderic must not leave us to these heathen monsters.'

XXII

Arles

It was a typical morning in March. Maximinus's lesson that day was on *chironomia*, the use of gestures in oratory. Many otherwise gifted speakers, Maximinus told his students, suffered for want of proper training in gestures, tending towards either theatrical extravagance and effeminacy, or simple inconsistency. He stood at the front of the class in his toga, the folds draped elegantly over his left forearm, his right arm free. 'Observe,' he said.

Arvandus watched closely as the professor bent his right arm at the elbow so that the forearm was perfectly horizontal, angled slightly away from his body. His hand was palm upwards, held still as though gently cupping a bird. Then he bent his middle finger so that its tip touched the middle of his thumbnail, keeping the other fingers extended. 'Thus.' He lowered his hand a few inches, and held it in that position. Next he slowly raised it until level with his shoulder. Finally he returned it to the original position. 'This is the acceptable range of vertical motion. Restraint is to be observed, especially at the beginning of an address. Plan your gestures carefully once you have memorised your speech, not before. But they must appear natural and spontaneous in practice. Let your motions be in harmony with your words, measured by tempo and emphasis.' He demonstrated the correct movements as he spoke.

Maximinus had his students stand in a line, and instructed them to imitate him as he demonstrated a series of oratorical gestures. Next they were to perform individually, delivering a passage they all knew from Cicero's speech in defence of Caelius and improvising whatever gestures they thought fitting, under the critical eye of their tutor.

Arvandus, since he had won the previous month's class compe-
tition, had the honour of going first. He had hardly begun before
Maximinus interrupted him.

'Too aggressive, too aggressive! We do not swing, punch or
thrust. We are not pantomime performers or the common rabble
on the street. How do you hope to inspire restraint in your audience, if you show none yourself? Start again. Slowly.' Arvandus
tried a second time, and then a third, but each time Maximinus
found fault. 'You're flapping your hand about like a prostitute,
then clenching it like a boxer. Sit down, you can try again tomorrow.
Lampridius, begin.'

Arvandus returned to his bench. He gritted his teeth in frustration. He knew what the problem was. He hated displaying his
right hand with the ugly half-finger. It would take real force of
will to train himself out of a two-year habit of keeping the mutilation hidden.

When lessons ended at noon he went with Lampridius to the
lower forum, as usual. They found their favourite spot midway
along the east side, where a large statue base offered comfortable
steps a good distance from the fly-infested air of the butchers'
stalls. Arvandus watched the market traders selling their goods.
Perhaps he should be a merchant instead of an orator. They flung
their arms about so violently it was a wonder they didn't come
flying off.

'You could have an artificial finger made,' Lampridius said.
'I've seen hands and feet made from wood. Why not a finger?'

Arvandus inspected his stump. That was an idea. It might look
passable from a distance. 'Maybe,' he said.

'It's a shame they never got the bastards who did it. If I ever
catch them, it won't be just their fingers I cut off, believe me.'

'It was my fault for wandering the streets so late at night. I
was more upset about the ring they stole, I hardly miss the little
finger. Who needs it, anyway?'

'Soldiers,' said Lampridius. 'For balancing swords. Charioteers,
for holding reins. Whores.'

'Whores? What for?'

'I don't know. I'm sure they use it for something, though.'

'Well, that's a shame. There go my three best career options.'

Lampridius punched him on the arm. 'Cheer up, comrade. You're still smarter than the rest of us. A year from now you'll have lined up some cushy post in Italy, probably with three or four girls on the go. They'll love the missing finger. Make up some heroic war story about it. You'll be supping with their senator fathers before you know it.'

Arvandus laughed, more to please his friend than because he felt like it. Even after two years, the mere memory of being held down in the dark, powerless, at the mercy of a sharp blade and sadistic mind, was still enough to make him sweat. He had not been able to sleep in that bed for weeks. Paeonius had sent those three men into his room to punish him for his betrayal. Arvandus had not made any public accusations against him, fearful of what Paeonius might do to his parents in Bordeaux. It was hard to forget such an experience, or to make light of it.

Lampridius remarked that Sidonius was walking towards them. Arvandus looked up. Their friend seemed to be in haste, approaching with awkward, hurried strides. He was holding a wooden tablet. 'A letter from Ecdicius,' he said as he reached them. He glanced to left and right as though in fear of being watched. He continued in an excited whisper. 'You mustn't tell a soul. His father is being called out of retirement and is heading south to Arles as we speak. I'm to be on his staff.'

'Slow down,' said Lampridius. 'Catch your breath. Why is Avitus called out of retirement? What staff?'

Sidonius squeezed himself on the steps between them. 'It's Attila,' he said. 'The Huns have crossed the Rhine. Avitus is coming south to negotiate with King Theoderic, and he's prepared to consider me as his secretary.'

'Congratulations,' Lampridius laughed, slapping him on the back.

'Not too loud. It's confidential. Ecdicius and his father will arrive in a few days, but until then we're not to say anything about this. They don't want to spread panic.'

'Still, it's excellent news. Splendid that he's chosen you.'

'He hasn't chosen me yet, but it means I have a chance. Ecdicius says there may be spaces for one or two additional clerks when the army heads back north. Are you interested?'

Lampridius laughed. 'Not me, comrade, though thank you for the thought.'

'Why not? It'll be a great adventure!'

'You seem to be forgetting the part about the Huns crossing the Rhine. No, I plan to reach a ripe old age, which means keeping well away from their sort.'

'What about you, then, Arvandus?'

He did not hesitate. 'I'm with you. When would we leave?'

'I don't know yet – as soon as the army is assembled. But Avitus needs to win over the Goths first.'

'Well,' said Lampridius, rising to his feet, 'since the pair of you seem determined to give your lives for the empire, the least I can do is buy you a cup of wine. Shall we?'

Laughing, arms entwined, the three friends walked together from the forum. Arvandus felt his earlier frustration vanish. So much for the pedantic precision of *chironomia*! This was what serving the empire was about: comradeship, duty, and excitement.

XXIII

E cdicius waited in the entrance hall of the prefect's palace, still in his thick cloak and riding boots. There had been no time to change since arriving in the city. Even through the closed doors he could hear the commotion from the forum across the street. As soon as word of the Hunnic invasion had reached Arles, the city had gone into a panic, and people were flocking to the forum to seek, exchange, or invent news. A crowd had quickly gathered outside the palace. Ecdicius had ordered the gates of the precinct barred until the situation calmed.

His father was in one of the palace audience chambers with his uncle, Ferreolus, who currently held the prefectship. They were preparing to meet a Gothic prince who happened to be in the city on a diplomatic mission. That was lucky, Ecdicius thought: it would allow them to start negotiations with the Goths at once. Over the last few weeks Aegidius had managed to enlist the support of several barbarian groups in northern Gaul, some more certainly than others. The Burgundians looked steadfast, at least. The Alans of Orléans, under their king, Sangiban, were already wavering. The Armoricans, led by Britons who had fled their island after the Saxon invasions, were never happy about cooperating with the empire, but they understood the greater danger of the Huns and had sworn to send two thousand men. Meanwhile the Franks had fallen into civil war after the death of King Chlodio; one of his sons had gone over to Attila, but the other had gone over to Rome.

The army was growing. Even with the troops Aëtius was said to be bringing from Italy, though, it would not be enough. They needed the Goths. The battle-hardened army of Theoderic was the largest and most formidable barbarian force in Gaul, equal to the regular Roman troops of the Gallic field army. Nothing less would stop Attila.

The front doors opened, revealing a glimpse of the tumult on the street outside, and the guards ushered in the spare, thin figure of Sidonius. Ecdicius had recommended Sidonius to his father as a personal secretary, praising his cool-headed intelligence and loyalty. He was a keen judge of character, too, which would be useful. Ecdicius took his cousin in his arms. 'Sollius,' he cried, nearly crushing him in his embrace. 'It's good to see you, though I wish the circumstances were better.'

'How are you, Ecdicius?'

'Strong as an ox and bold as a lion,' he laughed. 'And still as stupid as both, I'm afraid.'

'And your sisters?'

'Both well, safe in Clermont. My father's about to meet with the prince. Follow me.'

As they went through the palace, Sidonius related the horrors he had snatched from the chattering mouths of the forum, the sort of rumours that quickly grew in the telling. Attila had burned Cologne to the ground and had personally raped a hundred women of Koblenz. He had flayed alive the churchmen of Mainz and turned their skulls into drinking goblets. He and his swarm of Hunnic riders would fall upon Arles within a month. 'None of that is true,' Ecdicius said. 'But it isn't too far from the truth.'

Ecdicius led his friend to a small, gloomy audience chamber. On the walls to the left and right hung ancient tapestries. The only light came from a single latticed window set high in the far wall. Avitus stood next to a pair of chairs placed below the window, talking with his brother-in-law Ferreolus, the prefect.

'My lord Avitus,' Sidonius said. 'Illustrious prefect.' He bowed to each man in turn. 'I am pleased to obey your summons.'

'Excellent,' smiled Avitus. 'You're just in time.' He beckoned for Sidonius to approach as he and Ferreolus settled themselves in their chairs. Prefect and former prefect were dressed in the full uniform of their rank: embroidered tunics and belts, with golden brooches on their right shoulders pinning colourful cloaks. 'We're about to meet an embassy from King Theoderic,' Avitus said. 'I want you to stand with Ecdicius and pay close attention to everything. Afterwards I will ask you three questions. If I'm satisfied with your answers, I'll take you on. Do you understand?'

'Yes, my lord.'

'Good.' He waved his hand, and a clerk ushered Sidonius to stand with Ecdicius off to one side. Another clerk bowed, and left the room to summon the prince.

All was silent for a short while. Avitus sat motionless in his chair, his back straight, chin high, his arms resting on either side with an air of relaxed authority, as though he had not been retired from politics for twelve years. He had held the prefectship of Gaul when Ecdicius had been only nine years old, too young to attend him at court. Through his youth Ecdicius had merely heard others praise his father's courage on the battlefield, his integrity as judge, his wisdom as diplomat. His reputation had shone over the family like a distant, unreachable star. A dullard in the classroom, Ecdicius had known he would never make a diplomat; if he was to surpass his father anywhere, it would be the field of battle. He was pleased that he might finally have the chance to do that. His father, too, seemed to have accepted that he belonged in uniform.

Besides, Ecdicius didn't need to pretend to be a secretary when he had Sidonius. It felt good to help his friend. He glanced to the side and gave his cousin a reassuring smile. The poor fellow looked almost petrified with fear. Ecdicius had no doubt that he would be an outstanding aide – sharp, efficient, and loyal. He merely needed a little confidence.

Presently the clerk returned, bowed again to Avitus, and announced the Gothic ambassadors. Ecdicius watched as two men entered. One was a Goth of substance and striking dignity, easy to identify as the prince. He looked no older than twenty, tall and broad-chested, with a clean-shaven jaw, and intelligent eyes beneath a pair of heavy, arched eyebrows. His dark curly hair was thick, brushed back from his temples and over his ears. He wore boots and woollen leggings in the typical barbarian fashion. His green, short-sleeved tunic was edged with embroidered red bands, and fastened with a Roman-style military belt. A longsword hung from his left hip, the pommel, crosspiece and scabbard gleaming with gold fittings. Most striking of all was the bear pelt that he wore ostentatiously over his shoulders. Its fine black hairs shimmered almost silver in the light.

The second Gothic ambassador was the more surprising of the two, at least as far as Ecdicius was concerned, for he was a Roman. He wore no badges of office, but his clothing and demeanour showed him to be a man of education.

Avitus declared a solemn welcome. 'Theoderic, Prefect Ferreolus and I greet you in the name of his excellency, Emperor Valentinian.'

The Goth's thin lips curled slightly into a smile. It did not seem like an expression that came naturally to him, but nor did it look insincere. 'Master, it has been too long.'

Avitus laughed suddenly, and rose from his chair. He clasped the Goth's hands, and they exchanged kisses on both cheeks. 'How fares my former pupil?' Avitus asked.

'Very well, so long as he recalls the lessons of his former tutor.'

The Goth spoke perfect educated Latin, with scarcely a trace of accent. Ecdicius found it oddly disconcerting to see such fluency emerge from a barbarian mouth, and even stranger to see such familiarity between a barbarian and his father. Only then did he remember that many years earlier, when his father had been Rome's ambassador to the Gothic court, he had acted as tutor to young Prince Theoderic, second son of King Theoderic. This was good. Prince Theoderic was said to be friendlier to Rome than his father and brothers were.

Avitus returned to his chair, and called for a stool and a cup of wine to be brought for Theoderic. The Roman, who was evidently acting as Theoderic's secretary, remained standing.

The discussion that followed dealt with serious matters of which Ecdicius had only passing knowledge. Ferreolus said little, leaving the negotiations to his older and more experienced partner. Avitus expressed Rome's abiding annoyance that three years ago King Theoderic had married off one of his daughters to Rechiar, king of the Suebes in Spain. On his way home from the wedding in

Toulouse, Rechiar had allied himself with Spanish rebels and pillaged the region of Saragossa, which might have been construed as a breach of the Roman–Gothic treaty. The prince replied that the wedding had been intended to secure peace between all parties, and so far had succeeded. He also said that his father had not forgotten the fate of his other daughter, who had once been married to Huneric, the son of King Geiseric of the Vandals. Nine years earlier Geiseric had accused her of treason and sent her back to Gaul with her ears and nose cut off.

'I understand a father's anger at such an outrage,' said Avitus. 'But that matter is between Goths and Vandals. Rome was not involved.'

Theoderic shook his head sternly. 'Why was my sister spurned? Because your emperor offered his own daughter to Huneric, knowing that Huneric was already married. He knew that my sister would have to be removed. So how can you say that Rome is not also to blame? Once she was famous for her beauty, and now men cannot bear to look upon her face.'

Avitus tactfully diverted the discussion away from Theoderic's sister, saying that such ancient diplomatic quarrels, though lamentable, served to distract them from the greater threat. The duplicitous nature of King Geiseric of the Vandals, Avitus said, had been suggested by the mutilation of the princess, but it had been confirmed when he bribed Attila to attack Gaul, hoping to weaken both Romans and Goths for his own ends. To prove this Avitus had one of the clerks reveal an intercepted letter from Geiseric to Attila. Theoderic read the letter with furrowed brow.

'It is Geiseric's intention that Goths and Romans remain divided and suspicious of one another,' Avitus said. 'He has seeded mistrust between us. Believe me, he'll rejoice to see both Arles and Toulouse in flames.'

Prince Theoderic handed the letter back to the clerk. 'Or maybe just Arles. The Huns are still a long way from Gothic land. Why should we fight and die to protect Rome?'

Prefect Ferreolus, losing patience, spoke up. 'Because Aëtius is planning to march north with or without you,' he said. 'Every tribe in Gaul has flocked to his side – except yours. When Aëtius defeats Attila, what will happen? He'll be stronger than ever. Those Huns who survive will swell his ranks. He'll be hailed as the greatest warrior in the world. And he will not forget those who refused to honour their treaties.'

Theoderic absorbed those words calmly. He thought for a moment. Then he looked at Ferreolus and said, 'You threaten us.'

'I don't,' said Ferreolus. 'Aëtius might.'

Avitus interjected. 'As an old man, I for one have seen enough war between our peoples. Theoderic, you and I know that Gothic strength and Roman law are destined to rule the world together.' He leaned forward, resting one hand on his knee, and stared intently at his former student. 'We must not let the hatred between your father and Aëtius keep us apart.'

Theoderic's lips curled once more into something resembling a smile. He rose from his stool. 'You should return with me to Toulouse,' he said. 'My father will want to speak with you.'

The audience ended. Avitus and Theoderic said their friendly farewells, and Theoderic left with his secretary. When they were gone, Avitus dismissed the clerks, telling Ecdicius and Sidonius to remain.

'The Goths are more afraid than he's letting on,' Ferreolus said.

'Maybe so,' said Avitus. 'But fear has never been the way to manipulate a Goth. It only makes him more stubborn. You must speak to their sense of pride.' He waved his hand. 'We'll discuss this in a moment, Ferreolus. Let me have a word with my son and Sidonius.'

Ferreolus rose from his chair. He bowed to Avitus and walked out.

Avitus beckoned Sidonius to approach him. 'So,' he began. 'Ecdicius tells me you're the cleverest student in Eusebius's class.'

'I would not say that, my lord,' he said, 'but I work hard.'

'Your modesty becomes you. Now for my three questions about what you just witnessed. First, is Prince Theoderic a man of honour?'

'Yes,' said Sidonius. 'That is to say, he's reputed to be honour-able. He struck me as sincere.'

Avitus tilted his head. 'Sincere in all things?'

'Almost. He pretended that he doesn't want to make war against Attila. Looking at him, I believe he desires nothing more.'

'The boldness of a young man might work to our advantage,' chuckled Avitus. 'Provided he can help me convince his father. Which leads to my second question: considering the diplomatic situation, will the Goths join us?'

'Yes. King Theoderic will lose face with his own people if he agrees too quickly to a Roman alliance, at least one proposed by Aëtius. But if Attila is defeated, he'll want to share in the glory.'

'Very good. Although I believe you mean *when* Attila is defeated. Not *if*.'

That caught Sidonius off guard. He began to mumble a reply, but Avitus smiled and silenced him with a wave of his hand.

'My final question,' he said. 'How many rings was the secretary wearing on his left hand?'

'None,' Sidonius replied at once. 'But he had two on his right.' He had evidently made good use of the mnemonic training that Ecdicius had never been able to master.

'Excellent!' Avitus laughed, slapping his knees. 'Sidonius, you are now one of my personal notaries. You will attend my meetings, take notes, and draft letters. You will learn the names, faces, inclinations and aberrations of every politician in Arles, so that I don't have to. And from time to time, I'll ask for your judgement and advice. Note, however, that my position is not official, and so neither is yours. That means you'll receive no honours for it. I'll support you in my household, but otherwise your only reward will be the satisfaction of serving the state in her moment of direst need. Do you accept?'

Sidonius glanced aside to Ecdicius, who nodded enthusiastically. Sidonius grinned so broadly he had a hard time getting the words out. 'I do, my lord. Thank you. Thank you—'

Avitus rose from the chair. 'You can save your thanks until we've saved our country.'

XXIV

Clermont

'**M**y deacons will supervise the fetching of water from the river,' Bishop Namatius said. 'My priests can tend to the sick and administer the sacraments. We will do whatever is in our power to help the refugees.' He clutched his hands together, and darted his nervous eyes around the atrium.

Attica, standing with her sister at the side of the room, studied the bishop. He looked uncomfortable surrounded by the mosaic floor, the richly painted walls and the fluted columns of the central skylight. It was strange. Considering the fortune he had lavished on rebuilding his cathedral, she would have expected him to be used to the opulence of their Clermont town house.

Their mother, Severiana, seated in a wicker chair before the bishop, seemed equally unimpressed with him. 'But you require our help,' she said.

'Yes, my lady,' said the bishop. He did not look well. His skin was pale, his dark hair matted messily across his head. Today he had chosen to wear a plain white chasuble with frayed edges, no doubt to emphasise his poverty. 'The city council has agreed that the meadow north of the river can be used for the refugees. But they will need food and shelter, and wood and oil for fuel. Some may need clothing.'

'Does the church have no money?' Severiana asked. 'Are your own granaries empty?'

Attica enjoyed watching the bishop squirm. Her mother was playing with him, of course, but he deserved it.

'With the recent construction project, my lady . . . that is to say, the resources of the church . . .'

'Have been squandered,' Severiana said. 'For years you have

let the poor starve at your gates while you mismanaged the construction of the cathedral and bankrupted your accounts, and now you are surprised to find that refugees cannot eat piles of stone and glass.'

'Forgive me, my lady,' he said, bowing his head. 'You are right, as always.'

Bishop Namatius was of equestrian family, traditional in his outlook, too easily intimidated by the senatorial classes. A bishop ought to rise to the dignity of his office, Attica thought. Her mother would respect him more were he less of a grovelling sycophant.

'We will help supply what you need,' Severiana said. 'But our own accounts manager will oversee the distribution of food and materials, to make sure it is used properly. Nor will you receive a single coin in cash.'

'Thank you, my lady. May God bless your charity.'

'One more thing. The river meadow is far too exposed. The refugees have come to us for protection, and should be brought within the city walls. You will shelter the refugees in the cathedral precinct, in your own house, and if necessary in the church itself.'

Namatius looked about to object. He was clearly picturing his fine new mosaics being trampled on by a hoard of filthy homeless peasants. He held his tongue, though. Instead he bowed again and muttered, 'As you wish, my lady.'

As soon as the bishop had scurried out, Severiana turned to her daughters. 'May God forgive me for saying it, but our bishop is an oaf.'

Attica giggled. Papianilla tutted and said, 'You shouldn't speak of him in such a way, Mother.'

'I agree. I shouldn't call him an oaf. But then he shouldn't *be* an oaf.' She rose from the chair. 'Papianilla, are you certain you wish to help the bishop with the refugees?'

'Of course, Mother. Christ commands us to care for the destitute, doesn't he? I'm merely doing my Christian duty.'

Attica contained her irritation. Ever since declaring her firm desire to become a nun, Papianilla's piety had reached new levels. Now that Attila had invaded – a punishment from God for the sins of the empire, as Papianilla had proclaimed more than once – it was becoming excessive. It was as though she even looked forward to the prospect of the Huns galloping over the hills towards Clermont, burning everything in their path.

'And what about you, Attica?' their mother said. 'Will you also lend your aid to the bishop, like your sister?'

Before she could answer, they heard the front door open and close, and some hurried footsteps. Moments later Felix appeared in the atrium.

As always, Attica felt herself harden at the sight of him. He stole from her every desire to smile or show warmth. She did not like it, but it was necessary. Learning to become like a stone was the only thing that made the prospect of their imminent marriage bearable. She wished that he were back at the imperial court in Italy, where he had been for most of the past two years.

'The Huns have sacked Metz,' Felix said. His eyes were wide with anger or fright, or both. 'It was just announced in the forum.'

Severiana gave a sober nod. 'So Trier must have fallen, too.'

'I don't know. Probably. More Huns are heading for Paris and Orléans. If they manage to cross the Loire . . . and there's still no word from Aëtius in Italy. We need to leave for Arles at once.'

'Abandon Clermont?' Severiana said. 'I think not. Soon the city will be flooded with refugees. If the people see us leave, they'll panic. No, this is our city, and we stay.'

'As you like, my lady. But this isn't my city, and I'm not staying. Attica, have your handmaiden pack your clothes. I'll take you with me.'

Attica gasped at his presumption. 'Will you?'

'You're my betrothed. I won't have people say I abandoned you here at the mercy of the Huns.'

'Of course not,' she said. 'Heaven forbid people think you're a coward.'

For once he seemed to recognise the sarcasm. 'I'm no coward. But there's no point sitting here waiting for Attila to start hammering at the gates.'

'There's every point,' she snapped. 'Thousands of people need our help. Papianilla and I are going to help the bishop with the refugees.'

'Leave them to the church,' Felix exclaimed, flinging his arms wide. His fear was beginning to control him, and Attica despised him for it. He looked to Severiana. 'My lady, please command your daughter to listen to me.'

'Very well.' She turned to Attica. 'Daughter, listen to Felix.'

'I *am* listening to him, Mother. I hear every word he says.'

'There,' Severiana said to Felix. 'She is listening to you.'

'I mean, please command her to *obey* me.'

'I can hardly command her to be obedient, Felix. By their very nature, disobedient people tend not to listen to commands. It seems to me that you have only two options. First, you can force my daughter to go with you. I must say, though, that our guards will not take kindly to their mistress being manhandled. Second, you can *ask* her to go with you. Why don't you try that?'

He exhaled loudly, trying to calm his frustration. 'Attica,' he said, 'will you please come with me to Arles?'

'No.'

Felix snorted. 'I do not like being mocked.'

'You have your answer,' Severiana said. 'Stay or go as you like, Felix, but Attica remains. I cannot see what more you can do.'

He stood there for a moment, fists clenched at his side, bitter resentment in his eyes. 'Then I'll stay,' he said. 'But if the Huns cross the Loire, I'm going to Arles – and I *will* take Attica with me – dragging her by her hair if I have to.'

He spun about and hurried out of the atrium back into the entrance hall. The front door slammed behind him.

Severiana sighed. 'Our second oaf of the day,' she said.

'And still I must marry him?'

'You must. Your father has settled on the match, and neither you nor I can change that. But you've started well, Attica. Never let your husband think he can treat you like one of his slaves.'

XXV

Arles

It was late April when Count Aëtius, master of soldiers, finally crossed the Alps with his army. At first the people of Arles were jubilant as they watched his standards marched into the city, but relief soon turned into dismay when they saw how few troops he had brought with him: just five understrength regiments, fewer than four thousand men. There was a famine in Italy, people said, which had sapped the army's strength; furthermore, Emperor Valentinian feared that the Rhine crossing was only a feint intended to draw Roman forces away from Italy, and so had refused to give Aëtius any legions at all, commanding him to hold the line with a few auxiliaries and whatever allies he could gather in Gaul.

Over the following days, life continued as normal, at least on the surface, but Ecdicius could feel a growing nervousness. It was strange that Aëtius had halted in Arles instead of heading immediately north, and the people of Arles seemed to be of two minds about this. The more optimistic took it as a sign that the military situation was not as urgent as had been thought. The pessimists said that Aëtius was reluctant to march against Attila because the two had always been such strong allies. Lovers of tragic theatre embellished this by casting Aëtius and Attila as blood-brothers, thrown against each other by capricious Fate.

Ecdicius knew the real reason for the delay. Aëtius simply did not have enough men. So far Aegidius had managed to enlist the Burgundians of Sapaudia, the Suebes and Batavians north of the Loire, the Sarmatians near Clermont, and the Alans near Valence. The Frankish prince Childeric, exiled by his brother, had reached Aëtius in Italy and pledged himself to Rome. Word had also reached Arles that some of the local garrisons on the Rhine had managed to escape the Hunnic onslaught and were retreating south to join the regular Roman forces. But with every report of new allies came more reports of Attila's army. He had succeeded in winning over most of the Franks, and with more tribute peoples crossing the Rhine in his wake his numbers were now reckoned at more than thirty thousand.

By now Ecdicius's father had been at the Gothic court in Toulouse for a fortnight. Relay riders sped back and forth constantly, covering the two hundred miles in two days, bringing official updates that Prefect Ferreolus shared with Ecdicius. King Theoderic was prevaricating, deflecting, making demands. He wanted trading rights in Narbonne. He wanted more of Aquitaine to be ceded to his authority. 'Your father still believes he can win the barbarian bastard over,' Ferreolus said. 'I pray to God he's right.'

On the third morning after his arrival, Aëtius held a public audience in the basilica along with Prefect Ferreolus. Ecdicius stood to one side of the hall with the other military and civilian officers. Aëtius and Ferreolus sat in the apse on a pair of curule thrones, Aëtius raised on a small platform to signify his higher status, since he was a patrician and had held the consulship three times. He was unassuming in appearance, being of average height and build. He looked both older and younger than his fifty years: his solid, square-jawed face was dark and etched with deep lines, his hair thin and white, the result of a lifetime of strenuous campaigning, but his eyes had a quick, youthful alertness. Behind him, in a place of honour, stood Prince Childeric, whom Aëtius had adopted as his son in order to solidify their alliance. He was a youth clad in a short tunic and cloak, with a sword and long-handled axe hanging from his belt. His long blond hair hung loose about his shoulders according to the custom of Frankish royalty.

Aëtius had always been popular with the common people, and with the noble families who had attached themselves to him out of fear or ambition. Ecdicius had learned to keep his opinion of

Aëtius to himself. He could not deny that the old general had held the barbarians of Gaul in their place for more than twenty-five years. He respected him for that. Nor did he think less of Aëtius for his ancient rivalry with the imperial family, who had never shown much interest in Gaul, and now seemed happy enough to leave it to its fate. But none of that mattered against what Aëtius had done to his family. Ecdicius had been only an infant when his Aunt Padusia and Uncle Felix had been arrested by Aëtius and beheaded for conspiracy to commit treason. In part the charge was true – except that they had been conspiring only against Aëtius, not against the emperor. They had understood that Aëtius would stop at nothing to make himself the most powerful man in the west. He had proved them right. And for the last twenty years no one in Gaul, not even the Philagrii, had dared move against him.

Ecdicius watched a series of petitioners bring their requests and grievances to the count and prefect. There were, as to be expected, complaints about the behaviour of certain soldiers billeted among the civilian population. Troops had been demanding food from their hosts rather than buying it themselves from the market. Some soldiers had gone to the market, but had terrorised the traders, refusing to pay full price for bread or meat. Aëtius promised that any such abuses would be dealt with in the military courts, and the soldiers punished accordingly. That would never happen, Ecdicius knew. If Aëtius started punishing his troops at this stage he would damage morale and risk rebellion in the ranks.

It was noon when the last petitioner was dismissed. The usher was about to pronounce the audience over when a voice came booming down the length of the basilica: 'I will be heard!'

Every head turned. The speaker was already striding down the nave from the western doors. He was a tall, bald man in his forties, dressed in a dust-stained travelling cloak. In his right hand he wielded a staff, which he hammered loudly on the marble floor with every fourth step. When he reached the apse he bowed his head briefly, but did not kneel as he should have done. 'Illustrious Patrician,' he said. 'Prefect.'

'Bishop Anianus,' said Aëtius, evidently surprised to see him. 'You are far from Orléans. Had we known you were coming—'

'The Huns march on my city as we speak,' said Anianus. There were gasps from the assembled court officers. It was unheard of to interrupt a consul and patrician, least of all Count Aëtius. The bishop did not seem to care. 'Trier, Metz and Paris have fallen. Bishop Lupus says he would rather surrender Troyes than watch his people be butchered.' There was no mistaking the anger in his voice. 'In the name of God, where is the army?'

'The army is here in Arles, as you can see,' replied Aëtius. 'Aegidius has a contingent near Lyons, awaiting reinforcements.'

'And meanwhile thirty thousand barbarians lay waste to the north. You must march *now*.'

'Forgive me, Holy Father, but it is not the place of a bishop to dictate military policy.'

'No, it is the place of a bishop to protect his flock. But you know as well as I do that if Orléans falls, Attila will control the best crossing point on the Loire. There will be nothing to stop him striking in any direction he chooses. The Huns will spread like locusts across the south, spreading such destruction as has not been seen since the time of our grandfathers. Limoges and Clermont will be next, and then Lyons and Vienne. Arles will not escape.' He struck his staff one more time on the floor. The impact echoed in the cavernous hall. 'He must be stopped *now*, at Orléans.'

Ecdicius had never before seen Aëtius lost for words. The count was not used to being spoken to in such a way. 'King Sangiban will defend you until we march north,' he said.

Anianus scoffed. 'Sangiban cannot be trusted,' he said. 'He will either retreat, or surrender to Attila. But he will not stand and fight.'

Ecdicius was inclined to agree with the bishop. Sangiban was the leader of a tribe of Alans who had been settled by Aëtius near Orléans some years ago. Their mandate was the defence of the Loire crossings. But Sangiban was known to lack boldness and mettle, and his loyalty to the empire was uncertain. He was most unlikely to stand firm in the face of thirty thousand invaders.

Aëtius rose from his throne. 'You will have your aid,' he said solemnly. 'I swear in the name of Christ, before all those present, that Orléans will not fall.' He nodded to the usher, who declared the audience formally over.

The crowd began to disperse. Bishop Anianus was immediately approached and surrounded by a number of civilian officials. Ecdicius watched Aëtius as he sat back on his throne and exchanged some words with Ferreolus. Then the count happened to turn his head, and he caught Ecdicius watching him. He beckoned for him to come over.

Ecdicius obeyed, kneeling before the throne. 'Illustrious Patrician,' he said, concealing his dislike behind the stiff formality.

'Rise,' said Aëtius. He looked Ecdicius over. 'Back in uniform, I see?'

'Yes, my lord. I serve on the staff of Tribune Aegidius.'

'With the First Gallic Horse, then. And your father is special ambassador at the court of King Theoderic. So far your family is doing well from this war, wouldn't you say?'

Ecdicius tightened his jaw. 'We live to serve Rome, my lord.'

'But you would like more? Perhaps you'd like to be an adjutant to the master of soldiers one day. Or perhaps the master of soldiers yourself? Or even patrician, like your great-grandfather Philagrius?'

Ecdicius considered his response. He had the sense that Aëtius was trying to lead him down a dangerous path. 'I will serve Rome for as long as she needs me.'

'And when she no longer needs you – when you are old, say, or when the last barbarian lies dead at your feet – what then?'

'I don't know, my lord.' He noticed a messenger approaching with swift steps up the nave, weaving between the clusters of chattering court officers. He was holding a sealed document tube.

Aëtius laughed. 'Well, it's early for you to think that far ahead. But if you take my advice, you'll retire as soon as you can and become a farmer like your father. A man can learn a lot from agriculture, more than you think. My first wife used to tease me about it. She used to say I needed only touch an olive tree to kill it. So one summer I thought I'd prove her wrong. I took over a corner of our house garden and planted a basil shrub. I tended it every day for months, cared for it like a first-born child. It was no good, though. It didn't die, but nor did it flourish. Its leaves were small and limp.'

The messenger had reached the apse and was kneeling in front of Ferreolus, holding out the tube. Ferreolus took it, broke the seal, and pulled out the papyrus scroll within.

Aëtius had not noticed the messenger. 'But you see,' he continued, 'eventually my wife told me what I was doing wrong. I was pruning the leaves at the bottom when I should have been pruning the flowers at the top. "But the flowers look so marvellous!" I said. She said, "That may be so, but they are greedy and useless. The leaves at the bottom feed the plant. Cut the flowers," she said, "starting with the tallest." So I did, and she was right. The plant grew tall and strong.'

'My lord,' said Ferreolus, leaning over. 'Forgive the interruption. A message from Avitus. He's done it. The Goths are with us.'

A slow grin crept across Aëtius's face. He stared at Ecdicius. 'Your father is a good gardener. It's a shame that your aunt and uncle never were. Otherwise they would have known that it's always the tallest and greediest flowers that are the first to be cut.' He stood up sharply, clapping his hands. 'Where's my chief of staff? Hurry up now! Summon the war council!'

Aëtius stalked away, heading for the main doors of the basilica. The civilians stood aside while a dozen officers fell into step behind him, their cloaks billowing, the hall reverberating with the sound of their hobnailed boots and clattering swords. Ecdicius remained standing by the empty throne. He realised that his heart was thumping, as surely as if Aëtius had held a knife to his throat.

XXVI

'How long will it take us to reach Lyons?' Arvandus asked. 'Six days,' said Sidonius. 'We'll meet the Alans at Valence, and the Burgundians at Lyons. Then Aëtius is taking most of the army to Bourges to meet the Goths and some other allies, and Aegidius will ride north to Autun, where he'll meet the Franks, Teutons, Saxons, and the local garrisons from the Rhine. Then he'll head to Bourges, too. As soon as the whole army is ready, we march to Orléans – God willing, before the Huns reach it.'

Sidonius seemed to be enjoying the expedition, looking splendid and happy on his bay gelding as they headed up the road to Lyons. Arvandus did not share his enthusiasm. He was ill at ease on his own borrowed mount, a docile pony that was about as much as he could handle. He had never even ridden until Sidonius had started giving him lessons a few months ago. Nor had he ever expected to be part of an army on the march. There was something discomforting about the whole experience – the sound of hooves and tramping feet, the constant yells of officers to keep up the pace, the marching songs of the rank and file, the smell of sweat-stained leather and oiled brass. Arvandus found all of it strange and intimidating, and was frustrated by their unsteady progress. Half of the time they were stopped dead, held up for some reason or other that was never explained; the other half they were racing to make good the delay. And then there was the food. Count Aëtius insisted that everyone in the diplomatic train share the same rations as the soldiers, which meant biscuit and gruel every day. Apparently he always saved the salted meat for the end of a march, to encourage the men and strengthen them for the fight, and he did not believe in pandering to civilians.

Arvandus had to remind himself to be grateful. After all, Sidonius had managed to get him appointed assistant secretary to Avitus, which was no small thing, even if it wasn't an official post. And it did feel good to be part of something that was meant to be great and noble. Every now and then Ecdicius would come galloping down the column, his plumed helmet flashing brilliantly in the sunlight. 'Keep it up, comrades,' he would yell cheerfully as he rode by, grinning at Arvandus and Sidonius. 'Not far to go!'

And so Arvandus pretended to be cheerful for the sake of his friends, and hoped that he would become used to the privations of the march. It was mild enough to spend the nights outside, sleeping beneath the vault of Heaven amidst their own constellation of crackling campfires, but even then Arvandus found little rest. He lay awake, staring into the multitude of stars and imagining that they were an avalanche of Huns coming towards him. His dreams, when he slept, were filled with barbarians and blood.

He was relieved when they finally reached Lyons and pitched camp east of the city. The Burgundian contingent arrived the following day, three thousand infantry and cavalry with King Gundioc in the van. From the hillock where the command tents had been pitched Arvandus could look out over an ocean of tents and smoking campfires. The army of many nations was slowly coming together.

On the kalends of June, Bishop Patiens of Lyons conducted a dawn service and blessed the generals and their soldiers, and then the march renewed. Arvandus and Sidonius said farewell to Ecdicius, who was to go with the First Gallic Horse on the northern road, splitting from the main column.

'I'm relying on you two to look after my father,' Ecdicius said as he fastened the chin strap of his helmet. He turned to grip the horns of his saddle and launched himself onto the back of his horse. Settling himself on the saddle, he looked impressive in his newly polished mail shirt, with the silver-hilted longsword hanging from his left side. His face was almost concealed by the broad cheek pieces and nose-guard of his steel helmet.

Sidonius handed him his shield. It bore the design of a blue, yellow-rimmed star on a green background. 'Your father can look after himself,' Sidonius said. 'We'll see you at Bourges.'

Ecdicius grinned. To Arvandus he said, 'Then you look after my cousin.' He clicked his tongue and flicked the reins, and began to ride to where Aegidius was waiting with the rest of the regiment.

Arvandus was sorry to see him go. He had not set eyes on Ecdicius for two years, since he had left Arles to rejoin the army. Their reunion had brought back memories of those months after their first meeting, when the three of them had been inseparable as they traipsed around the baths and taverns of the city. Arvandus could almost forget that he had been deceiving them that whole time, as they seemed to have forgotten. Their friendship had proved true after all, and the excitement of this expedition had only rekindled it.

'Come on,' said Sidonius. 'We should get ready.'

After another hour of breaking camp, the main column continued the march to Bourges. The first hints of summer were starting to appear in the swelling wheat fields and in the warmth of the air. There were moments when Arvandus almost felt that he was enjoying himself, at least until he remembered what awaited them at the end of the journey.

Five days from Lyons the column stopped to make camp on the banks of a river called the Allier. That evening, as usual, Arvandus and Sidonius were with Avitus in his tent, making copies of his diplomatic correspondence. They each sat at a small writing table on either side of the tent entrance, making the most of the remaining daylight. The old general was hunched over his desk, reading through some reports. He had seemed distracted all evening, and Arvandus sensed that something was wrong.

'Tomorrow morning,' Avitus said suddenly, 'the two of you will take the road to Clermont, and remain there until the war with Attila is concluded one way or the other.'

Arvandus and Sidonius exchanged glances. Sidonius looked shocked, as though he were being punished for some unknown infraction.

'Don't look so distraught, Sidonius,' Avitus said. 'My mandate is all but complete, and your term of service with it. We've done what we had to do: get the Goths to fight with us. In five days we'll join forces with King Theoderic and Aegidius, and after that the outcome will be in the hands of God.'

Sidonius looked about ready to drop to his knees. 'Can't we stay with you until Bourges, my lord?'

'No. I need to stay with the army to make sure Aëtius and King Theoderic don't try to murder each other, or at least to make sure they don't succeed. As well as you've served me so far, Sollius, that's one piece of business I mean to keep you out of. Much better to have you in Clermont.'

'Please, my lord,' said Sidonius, 'let us stay by your side. Have we displeased you?'

'Far from it,' Avitus said. 'Come over here, both of you.' They went to his desk as he unrolled a cloth map of Gaul. He looked down upon it darkly. 'Earlier this evening word came that Bishop Lupus of Troyes has surrendered his city to Attila. The latest news from Orléans is that King Sangiban almost certainly cannot be trusted. I don't see how we can reach the city in time. It may already be under siege.'

This explained why he had been so serious and withdrawn all evening. The war was becoming more real by the moment. Arvandus knew that he and Sidonius would be of little use from this point. They would merely be two more mouths to feed. He would not be sorry to leave the fighting to the soldiers. 'My lord,' he said, 'is there any way we can serve you in Clermont?'

'You can help my wife and children. They're busy dealing with refugees, and a couple more pairs of hands would be useful. Felix is there already, although according to my wife he'd rather be back in Arles, or Ravenna for that matter.'

That piece of news was not welcome. Arvandus had had no contact with Felix over the last couple of years, since Felix had long ago completed his education and had spent some time serving at the imperial treasury in Italy. But Arvandus doubted that he had forgotten the incident at Lupiacum.

Still, he thought, perhaps this would be a good opportunity to put right that old humiliation. He was no longer just some uncultured peasant fresh from the docks of Bordeaux. His father was now of equestrian rank, his patron was Alcimus of the Apollinares, and he was on the staff of Eparchius Avitus. He had learned the rituals and customs of the nobility. He had even remembered to pack his own dining slippers and napkin, a very fine piece of Antiochene cloth. If Felix tried to embarrass him again, he would be in for a surprise.

Arvandus even smiled as he went to bed that night. Facing Felix would be vastly preferable to facing the Hunnic horde.

They left the army on the following morning as commanded, setting out on the south road along with a convoy of civilians and camp followers. The journey took the whole day, and by the time they reached Clermont the evening star was glowing above the western hills. At the city gate Sidonius showed the guards a letter of patronage that Avitus had given him. The guards allowed him and Arvandus through the gates at once, and two of the soldiers even escorted them to the home of Avitus's family.

Clermont did not strike Arvandus as a large city, but it looked prosperous. The gates and walls were well maintained, the streets and buildings in good repair. There was no theatre, but the cathedral basilica was large and impressive, so recently completed that leftover blocks of masonry were still piled around the base, and the dust from construction still filled the cracks of nearby paving stones. This is where the refugees seemed to be gathering, in a well-organised community of temporary huts made from timber, canvas sheets, and straw roofing. Men of the church were carrying buckets of water and distributing loaves.

Eparchius Avitus's town house was in a secluded corner of the city close to the north-west walls. Arvandus and Sidonius dismounted at the entrance, handing their mounts over to a stable boy, and were conducted through the front doors by the house steward. It was refreshingly cool inside the atrium. In front of the pool stood their hosts. The lady Severiana was just as Sidonius had described: regal, with a beauty that was dignified without seeming cold. Her girdled stola was of light linen, richly decorated with floral panels of green and red. Over her shoulders hung a wide necklace of emeralds and pearls linked by gold chain.

'Welcome, Sidonius,' she said, receiving her cousin with a kiss. 'I hope the journey hasn't been too difficult.'

'I think the army life is growing on me,' Sidonius laughed. 'This is my dear friend, Arvandus.'

Severiana smiled. 'Welcome. I believe you already know my daughter Attica, and this is my eldest daughter Papianilla.'

'I'm honoured to be a guest in your house, my lady,' Arvandus said, bowing. Sidonius had prepared him for the sight of the religious elder daughter, Papianilla, who was dressed in a plain, long-sleeved tunic, her hair concealed beneath a woollen shawl. He found it hard to believe that Attica was her sister. She was dressed no less elegantly than her mother, and had only grown in beauty in the two and a half years since Arvandus had seen her. She was taller and more graceful, having lost the awkwardness of adolescence. He felt sudden, unexpected guilt, recalling how he had tried to charm her in the forum of Arles, and again when she had caught him trying to sneak out of Lupiacum. That had been wrong of him. She had been a mere girl, and had not deserved to be used like that.

Finally, next to her, there was Felix. Arvandus had not missed his sallow face or those narrow, hunched shoulders. 'Welcome to Clermont,' Felix said with a smile. He extended his hand.

Arvandus took it in a brief, firm shake. It was only when they released hands that he noticed the ring on Felix's little finger: a garnet set in twisted gold. More than two years had passed, but there was no mistaking that ring. He had last seen it on the finger of the man who had mutilated him.

He felt a sudden chill. The memory of that night provoked a thumping in his chest, a tightness in his throat. He looked up at Felix.

The smile was still there, but it no longer seemed welcoming. It was cruel, triumphant.

XXVII

Ecdicius, leading a squadron of cavalry scouts, reached Bourges late on the fifth day before the ides of June. With his first clear view of the city he saw that both Aëtius and King Theoderic had arrived ahead of schedule and were already encamped along the main road. Not only that, but he saw squadrons of Alanic cavalry pitching camp in the neighbouring meadows. They could only be the soldiers of King Sangiban, who was meant to be defending Orléans. So he had not held the line after all.

Ecdicius rode into the Roman camp and found the commander's tent. His father was there along with Count Aëtius and some senior Roman tribunes. 'Protector Ecdicius of the First Gallic Horse reporting. Tribune Aegidius is about to arrive.'

'Good,' said Aëtius. He looked at Ecdicius's father. 'Avitus, you're dismissed. Go with your son. We'll have a war council in one hour.'

Ecdicius walked with his father from the tent into the bustle of the officers' encampment. 'Did you see the Alans by the road?' Avitus asked. 'Theoderic caught them heading south into Aquitaine. Sangiban left Orléans to the mercy of Attila and was trying to avoid fighting anyone, but rode right into the path of the Goths. "Turn around and fight," Theoderic said, "or we'll kill you ourselves." So he bent his knee to the Gothic king, and here we are, for all the good he'll do us.'

'Have the Huns taken Orléans, Father?'

'Not yet, as far as we know. But it won't be long now. I've sent Sidonius and Arvandus to Clermont for safety.'

They paused on a low bluff that presented a good view looking west over the camp. The army was now twice the size it had been at Lyons. There were countless tents, cooking fires, paddocks for cavalry mounts and pack animals, a teeming host thirty thousand strong stretching as far as the walls of Bourges, bathed in the shadowy glow of dusk. A trumpet blast sounded on the road below. Aegidius's column had arrived, bringing the last of the barbarian allies.

'Gaul has never seen the like of this,' said Avitus. There was deep pride in his aged voice. 'All these peoples brought together. Romans camped alongside Goths, Bretons, Burgundians, Suebes, Sarmatians, Franks . . . half of them have been at each other's throats for years.'

'We needed a miracle,' said Ecdicius, 'and we have it. Thanks to you.'

There was a dark cloud bank stretching across the southern horizon. From the distance, so faint it could scarcely be heard above the noise of the camp, came a long, slow rumble of thunder. The wind rose for a moment, lifting their cloaks and the cloth standards planted outside the commander's tent.

Avitus gave a sombre smile. 'If we're to defeat Attila, the greatest miracle is still to come.'

One hour later they returned to Aëtius. This time the tent was crowded with every commander: Aegidius, Marcus, Messianus and the rest of the Roman tribunes, as well as Theoderic of the Goths, Gundioc of the Burgundians and half a dozen other barbarian kings. Next to Aëtius stood a young cleric. He looked exhausted, his tunic and cloak covered in dusk and sweat. Satisfied that everyone necessary was present, Aëtius addressed the cleric. 'Go on. Tell them what you told me.'

The cleric swallowed. He cast his eyes around the room, taking in the daunting array of armour and weapons. 'I just came from Orléans,' he began. 'Attila has placed the city under siege. The bishop has organised the citizens into a defensive militia. We've bolted the gates and piled up earth ramparts in front of the walls.'

'How many Huns?' asked Avitus.

'We reckoned three thousand when I left, but that was two

days ago. Most of Attila's army is still raiding the country as far as Chartres.'

'And has he tried to negotiate?'

'Yes, my lord. He sent . . .' The cleric hesitated. 'He sent Bishop Lupus of Troyes. Attila has taken him prisoner. Through Lupus he demanded the surrender of the city. Our bishop refused. Then they attacked the north walls with battering rams and ladders, and flaming arrows. Bishop Anianus was up on the ramparts, urging the soldiers on, calling on God to protect them. They tried to shoot him down, but they couldn't. Not a single arrow hit him, praise be to Christ.'

'So the attack was repulsed?'

'Yes, my lord. They lost scores. But too many of ours fell, and part of the wall has been weakened. More of the enemy arrive every day. Our city cannot stand against another assault.'

King Gundioc, his enormous beard hanging low over his belly, spoke in a deep, grinding voice. 'Surely it's already fallen. We should hold back. We need more time to organise.'

King Theoderic laughed. He resembled his second son closely, with his prominent eyebrows and fierce stare. 'A Burgundian frightened of the Huns,' he sneered. 'Who would be surprised at that?'

'Frightened?' Gundioc straightened his back, swelled his chest, and met the Gothic king eye to eye. 'Yes, fifteen years ago the Huns butchered my people. But at least we stood and fought. *Your* ancestors didn't stand and fight in Scythia. When the Huns came for the Goths, they fled into the Roman empire with their tails between their legs.'

Theoderic grasped the hilt of his sword. 'Are you calling me a dog?'

'No,' said Gundioc. 'I'm calling you the descendant of dogs.'

'Enough,' snapped Aëtius, before Theoderic could unsheathe his sword. He glared at the two kings. There was history there, Ecdicius knew. The Burgundians had once had a kingdom on the Rhine, until Aëtius had destroyed it with the aid of Hunnic mercenaries. As a boy Gundioc had seen most of his family slaughtered in that war.

'The Goths will save Orléans,' declared Theoderic. 'I will take my cavalry north at first light.'

Aëtius nodded. 'Very well. I'll lead four mounted regiments with you. With luck we'll reach Orléans before Attila can muster the rest of his army there. The rest of our forces will follow as fast as they can. Everyone will receive marching orders once I've conferred with my staff.'

A tremendous storm rolled over the camp that night. By daybreak it had cleared, but the sky was still filled with heavy clouds and smears of rain to the north. Four thousand Roman and Gothic cavalry assembled, with Aëtius and King Theoderic in the van, and pressed hard up the north road.

It took them three days to reach Orléans, not knowing what they would find when they got there. More storms came from the south, the worst of them passing overhead and breaking beyond the hills. Ecdicius, riding with the First Gallic Horse at the head of the army, thought of what his father had said about a miracle. He wondered if this were it – God sending storms to hinder Attila, giving the Christian forces time to reach the city. Nothing slowed a siege like thunderstorms, which turned roads into rivers, fields into bogs, hillocks into islands. No assault would be possible in such conditions.

About noon on the third day Ecdicius saw the city, its battlements rising high on the north side of the Loire. The river was wide, at least three hundred yards across, with tussocky sandbanks stretching along the middle. When Aegidius called a halt on a rise overlooking the river, Ecdicius realised that both banks were teeming with many hundreds of men. His heart sank as he realised what was happening. They were Huns, with more pouring from the south gate.

'We're too late,' he said to Aegidius, who was riding beside him. 'They've taken the city.'

'Maybe, but they've not taken the river.' The tribune was grinning, viewing the scene with narrowed eyes. 'There's no bridge here. See, they're ferrying men across to build one from both banks at once.'

Ecdicius looked more closely. Aegidius was right. Attila must have realised that it would take days to ferry his entire host across the Loire, and so he had ordered the construction of a makeshift bridge, a causeway built from bundles of wood lashed together, pushed into the river and overlaid with a roadway of trunks and mud. But even from this distance Ecdicius could see that it was not going well. The current, bloated by the rains, was too strong, and was washing away the bundles of wood as soon as they reached a short distance from either bank. The Huns were disorganised, exhausted from felling trees and hauling timber into the treacherous mud of the Loire. Best of all, they were unmounted, their bows left unstrung. They were clearly not expecting the Romans so soon.

When some of the Huns did notice the Roman and Gothic cavalry drawing up along the crest above them, panic spread. Horns blew on both sides of the river. There was a confused scramble as hundreds on the south bank made for the ferry crossing. It was clear that the handful of barges would never get them across in time.

'Look at 'em!' Aegidius laughed gleefully. 'Boys – what do we call a Hun without a horse?'

This was a favourite joke of their tribune. Ecdicius and the men around him cried in unison: 'Dead meat!'

Down the line came horn blasts, the signal to move into charge positions. The four hundred troopers of the First Gallic Horse cantered to the far right flank. Ecdicius drew his horse into line, clearing his mind of distractions, of all thoughts of his father and mother, his sisters and brother. It would not be his first taste of combat in the last two years, but these were not the mere raiders and bandits he was used to. He made a brief, silent prayer. *Christ, let me do my duty.*

Tribune Aegidius drew his longsword and held it high over his head. At once four hundred more swords were drawn from their scabbards. Today there would be no javelin attack to soften up the enemy. It would be straight to the butchery.

Ecdicius felt the exhilaration rush through his body as the

horns sounded and four thousand Romans and Goths thundered towards to the river. Those Huns with strung bows were shooting arrows into the attackers with deadly accuracy, but they could not stop the avalanche. Aegidius, leading his regiment, peeled off to chase down a crowd of half-naked barbarians who were trying to flee along the riverbank. The battle line fragmented as it piled through the enemy. Again and again Ecdicius flashed his sword, riding down the fleeing Huns, cutting red streaks in mud-caked flesh. He saw a group seeking refuge on their incomplete causeway, and galloped towards them.

As soon as he charged onto the wooden planks he knew he had made a mistake. The bridge was unsteady, slippery with mud, its foundations incomplete. The fascines below tilted under the weight of his horse, and Ecdicius fell head-first from his saddle into the reedy brown water.

He forced his head back above the surface, coughing, thrashing, streams of water running down his face from beneath his helmet. Zephyros was still on the bridge, trying to get to his knees, whinnying in terror. A Hun had taken hold of his reins. Ecdicius found purchase in the river bed, only to find that he could not move a step. The mud had taken hold of his boots. He tried, but he could not loosen one foot without sinking the other deeper. He reached for the bridge, hoping to get purchase on the bound wooden bundles that underlay the planks, but his feet were too firmly held. He was buffeted by waves, weighed down by his armour. Panic rose in his gut. He was drowning.

Dark things flashed overhead, flying from the riverbank: javelins, he glimpsed, hurled by his comrades at the Huns, who had jumped from the bridge and were trying to swim across the river. A heavy object splashed in front of him, and he saw it was a looped rope. He grabbed it, pulled the loop over his head and under his arms. Within moments a terrific force was pulling on him – his feet shot free of his boots, and he flew from the water up the bank, sliding through mud and reeds, and came to rest on something warm and soft.

He turned over and coughed the remaining water from his

lungs and nose. He grappled with the chinstrap of his helmet, fumbling with the knot, and let the helmet fall away as he turned panting onto his back. His lungs were on fire. Gradually he tilted his head and became aware of others around him – elbows, hair, crooked legs. A pair of narrow, bloodshot eyes stared through him. He was lying on a pile of dead Huns.

With effort he climbed to his bare feet. Water ran down him in streams. The rope was still looped around his torso. It ran across twenty feet of hoof-mangled corpses up to the horns of a saddle, upon which sat Flaccus.

He stared down at Ecdicius, a sneer twisting his mouth. 'Looks like you'll need a new pair of boots, my lord.'

Ecdicius tried to speak, but his words became a coughing fit. He steadied his chest, breathing deeply. When he looked up, Flaccus had already moved on. He was relieved to see another trooper leading Zephyros by the nose back to dry land. Not a single Hun seemed to be left alive at the bridgehead. Ecdicius looked downriver to see that the slaughter at the ferry port had been even greater. No prisoners had been taken. Bodies lay in thick heaps all along the riverbank and bobbed face-down in the water. On the opposite bank there was a flow of barbarians back into the city, with boatloads of dismounted Romans and Goths already rowing and punting across the river after them.

As the breeze shifted, a great chorus rolled across the water. At first Ecdicius feared that the Huns in the city were slaughtering their prisoners; but then he realised that the voices were joyful, giving thanks to God. It could only mean that Attila was abandoning the city.

He fell to his knees, suddenly exhausted. After all those months of uncertainty, of anxious waiting, they had stopped the Huns crossing the Loire with only hours to spare. He began to cry. God had sent them their miracle. Orléans was secure, and the lands to the south, for now at least, were safe.

XXVIII

The loss of a few hundred was not crippling for an army of thirty thousand, but the appearance of the Roman and Gothic relief force had been enough for Attila to abandon his plan of crossing the Loire. Needing space and time to formulate a new strategy, he returned along his route of march towards the east. Count Aëtius now faced the same problem as had Attila, namely that it would take time to ferry an army of tens of thousands with all their pack animals and wagons across a river. While he remained at Orléans to supervise the crossing, he commanded Aegidius to take the First Gallic Horse ahead to snap at the heels of the Huns.

Ecdicius, now in the boots of a dead enemy, rode alongside his tribune. The road from Orléans was littered with scatterings of heavy treasure, reluctantly thrown aside by barbarians desperate to lighten their load. For the rest of that day the regiment followed the road through a stretch of thick forest, encountering a few abandoned carts whose owners had fled into the trees. On the second day, upon reaching more open countryside, Aegidius ordered Ecdicius to take a squadron of thirty troopers south of the road and screen the Hunnic rearguard, harrying stragglers and foragers and observing from a distance the disposition of the enemy.

There followed several days of steady progress, keeping pace with the Huns, avoiding any close contact. At the end of the fourth day Ecdicius returned to the main Roman column. He reported to Aëtius and Aegidius that the Hunnic force was still enormous and coherent, and had retreated in good order to Sens, where it had stopped for the night in a strong position overlooking the river Yonne.

Aëtius, mounted on his horse by the side of the road, listened to Ecdicius's report as he watched the last of his rearguard traipse into the Roman camp. The Goths and the other confederates had made their own camps nearby. A mere ten miles lay between them and the Huns.

'We should force him to battle,' Aegidius said.

Aëtius shook his head. 'He won't fight us here.' He was staring east, into the star-speckled shroud of evening that now cloaked Attila's army. 'He's making for the country past Troyes, the Catalaunian Plains. It's open grassland, perfect for horse archers. That's where he'll make his stand. Aegidius, I want you to ford the Yonne to the south at first light, and screen Attila as he continues east. Send me regular reports.'

Thus it was that the confederate force drew ever closer to the Huns over the next two days. Ecdicius heard of a few loose skirmishes taking place west of Troyes, and the first major clash between a regiment of Roman heavy cavalry and a contingent of Gepids who had broken away from the main Hunnic line of march. It was a total Roman victory that left a thousand Gepid dead on the field, and the Romans even thirstier for blood. The Huns continued their retreat.

The First Gallic Horse were the first to reach Troyes. They found the city deserted, its ramparts unmanned, its buildings ransacked. All the way along the central street were piles of horse dung, evidence of the passing Huns. As he rode through the city, Ecdicius noticed that the dung was still steaming. Attila was closer than ever.

They continued their advance past Troyes and up onto the grassy plains until, five days after the battle of Orléans, they spotted the enemy camp. As Aëtius had predicted, Attila had stopped on a well-watered plateau a few miles north of Troyes. The camp was in the form of a vast wagon circle, with Attila's palatial tent at the centre.

That night Ecdicius sat with half a dozen veteran troopers around a campfire until long after sunset. At first he left the talking to them. Since his near-drowning at Orléans he had kept his head down and fulfilled his duties with tireless determination, listening to everything, speaking only when necessary. Amongst his comrades there was little agreement about what Aëtius had in mind. Flaccus grumbled that the general had no intention of bringing Attila to battle, and merely wanted to nudge him back across the Rhine. The regimental chief of staff, a grizzled old soldier called Basilius, countered that Aëtius was merely being cautious, as usual.

Ecdicius ventured to express his own opinion. 'There'll be a battle tomorrow,' he said.

The other men stared at him. 'What makes you so sure?' demanded Flaccus.

'It's not just about Aëtius and Attila. I saw Prince Theoderic in Arles – he's desperate for a fight, so are the rest of the Goths.'

Flaccus scoffed. 'Who cares what some prince said in Arles? We're in the field now. The Goths always *say* they want a battle, then half the time they clear off the night before. I'll wager we wake up in the morning and find their camp empty and the whole lot of 'em halfway back to Toulouse.' The other troopers laughed.

'Then what about the booty?' Ecdicius asked. 'The Huns are carrying half the treasure of Gaul. Do you think the Goths will let all that gold just disappear across the Rhine? Would you?'

Basilius said, 'The lad's got a point. If Aëtius refuses battle now, he'll face a mutiny, sure enough.'

The officers murmured their agreement. Ecdicius caught Basilius's eye. The old soldier gave him an approving nod.

The next day was balmy and overcast. There was no morning call to battle assembly or to break camp. The Huns showed no sign of leaving, either. Ecdicius spent the day with the other officers, passing the time with dice and talk. Wrestling matches and races had been forbidden by Aëtius, who did not want any of his men to be tired or injured, and he had ordered them to be armoured and ready for battle at a moment's notice. Even so, the rank and file muttered that he was still hoping to avoid fighting Attila. Rumours of Hunnic flanking manoeuvres trickled through the camp. Some said that the Huns were slowly encircling the Romans and would storm them in their beds that night.

It was a day of tedium and false alarms. When the call to assembly finally came late in the afternoon, an enormous cheer went up from the entire army. Ecdicius sprang to his feet, mounted Zephyros, and cantered into position.

Slowly the two hosts assembled on the plateau. Ecdicius was with the First Gallic Horse on left flank, immediately beside a road that headed north over the chalk hills towards Châlon. Ahead was a long ridge of high ground that stretched the width of the battlefield. This would have to be the strategic objective for both armies. Aëtius was deploying the bulk of the Roman forces on his left flank, with King Theoderic and the Goths on the right, and the Alans and other federate peoples between them. Meanwhile it seemed that Attila had taken the centre of his own line, surrounded by his fearsome steppe warriors, and placed his subject tribes on the flanks. The First Gallic Horse were looking directly across at several hundred Franks, who were supported by the remaining Gepids.

'Seems we'll be dancing with the Franks tonight,' Aegidius said to Ecdicius. 'Just like old times.' He pointed to the far end of the enemy line. 'Do you see there? Those are the Pannonian Goths, under King Valamir.'

'Pannonian Goths? They're facing King Theoderic. Will they fight their own kind?'

Aegidius chuckled. 'Oh, yes. Goths hate other Goths even more than they hate the Huns. They'll fight, all right.'

Not all of the Goths were at the far end of the battlefield. Nearby Ecdicius saw Prince Thorismund, the eldest son of King Theoderic. He had agreed to fight with his personal warband alongside the Romans, at the opposite end of the line from his father. This heir to the Gothic kingdom was no less impressive to look at than his younger brother. His dark hair flowed and billowed like a cloak from under his gilded helmet as he trotted back and forth in front of the cavalry line, waiting impatiently for a signal from Aëtius to lead the advance to the high ground.

Ecdicius sympathised with the prince's impatience. With the muted sun already rolling down to the west, he was feeling the weight of his mail armour, the stifling press of his cheek pieces, and the strange fatigue that came from a day spent doing nothing. All was silent except for the odd cough from a cavalryman, or a snort from his mount. Ecdicius felt the need to commit some sudden, explosive action. He looked to the right, his eye following the bristling ranks of Romans, Sarmatians, Alans, Goths and all the rest of them, the muddled confederacy of nations that his father had helped create. They had come together to face the terror of the Huns. But would the alliance hold when battle was joined and the blood began to flow?

At last Aëtius, mounted with his personal guard ahead of the front ranks, gave the signal for the advance. A chorus of horns broke the still air. Slowly the cavalry on the flanks began to advance towards the ridge, building up to a trot and peeling in wedges away from the infantry in the centre. On the left Aëtius was leading the advance in person, with Prince Thorismund's heavy shock troops at his side; supporting them were the Roman light and heavy cavalry, along with horse archers, who screened the far left flank on their swift, nimble mounts.

The ridge ran at an oblique angle across the battlefield, and the First Gallic Horse reached its summit while the centre and right of the army were still climbing its lower slopes. From the crest of the ridge Ecdicius could now see Attila's entire army spread out on the plain, with the wagon circle in the hazy distance. The Huns were concentrated in the centre. The enemy right flank was coming up the slope directly ahead, a host of Frankish infantry supported by mounted Gepid skirmishers.

A shout ran down the line. 'Hold position!' Aegidius raised his hand to signal a stop.

From the right came a low rumble as the Hunnic centre advanced. A dozen dark streams, each containing a thousand riders, headed up and over the ridge towards the Burgundian, Saxon and Breton infantry in the allied centre. Ecdicius was unable to look away. The Hunnic mounts were kicking up white flurries of chalk dust that rose thickly and settled in drifting clouds overhead. A hundred yards from contact, each stream of Hunnic cavalry wheeled to the right, galloping parallel to the allied ranks and loosing thousands upon thousands of arrows into the massed infantry, before turning away and coming around to form a vast unbroken loop. Faced with these whirlwinds spitting ceaseless showers of barbed iron, the advance faltered; the rear ranks pushed into the front, who refused to advance, and as the dead piled up and men tripped over the bodies of their comrades, the arrows fell ever more thickly.

But General Aëtius, whether or not he had been reluctant to join battle, understood Hunnic warfare better than any other Roman. He knew that the Huns depended on space and mobility. Deprived of this, brought into close quarters, their small horses and lack of armour would be liabilities. Ecdicius now realised why he had placed Sangiban and the Alanic cavalry in the centre, behind the front infantry line. The Alans emerged from between the infantry regiments, riding hard for the Huns, who saw them coming too late. The Alans punched into the right-hand flanks of the Hunnic circles with lances and javelins, striking down the newly discharged archers before they had a chance to reload their bows. The whirlwinds collapsed into a chaos of tumbling horses and white dust. The allied infantry, lifting their heads to see that the deadly rain had paused, summoned their fury and charged headlong into the disarrayed Huns.

'Make ready!' The call from Aegidius brought Ecdicius back to himself. The Franks were nearing the top of the ridge, barely a hundred yards away. Franks were indomitable foot soldiers so long as they kept their shield wall intact; but these troops were pushing forwards too hard in their eagerness to capture the high ground, and chinks were already beginning to appear in their line.

The attack signal blasted overhead. Aegidius raised the javelin in his hand, and his regiment began to advance down the slope, one squadron after another in wedge formation. Ecdicius was near the front of the first squadron. As they neared the Frankish line, his wedge lengthened and wheeled to the right; and with shield held towards the enemy, Ecdicius flung his javelin down onto their heads. A throwing-axe spun past his face in a blur, missing him by inches. Through the juddering sound of hooves he sensed the mingled screams of horse and man behind him. He followed the man in front of him in a gallop back up the slope, reaching around for his second javelin. He saw the other squadrons pestering the Frankish troops, and the Roman horse archers engaging with the enemy cavalry on the far flank. His squadron made two more passes at the Franks, a frenzy of colour and noise during which he thought only of keeping behind the man in front, hardly even sparing a moment to aim his throw. Whether or not his javelins struck home, he could not say.

Only after the third pass, when his squadron withdrew and regrouped with the rest of the regiment at the crest of the ridge, did he look down and see that they had stopped the Frankish advance. The Gepid cavalry had also been dispersed, and the Roman horse archers were now peppering the Frankish infantry from the flank. The Franks were broken up into bunches, some already starting to flee. At this moment Aëtius and Prince Thorismund launched their charge. The horns sounded their long, ominous boom. Hundreds of armoured horsemen headed down the slope and tore through the Frankish line. Ecdicius and the rest of the light cavalry drew longswords and followed in their wake.

As he fell into the thick of battle, Ecdicius lost all sense of what was happening elsewhere. It seemed like the whole world had been filled with cries and slaughter. He rode after any Frank he could see, and did not stop until he had struck him down. Soon he lost count of how many had fallen to his sword.

The fighting continued until the sun was setting and the plains were sinking into darkness. Ecdicius looked around himself, and found that he and Flaccus had lost the rest of their squadron. During the pursuit of the broken Franks they had ceased to keep track of time and distance. Gloom lay all around, a shadowy, red-tinged veil that masked a distant hum of cries and clashes. The evening breeze picked up and troubled the tall grass of the plain, making the air suddenly cold.

'Come on,' said Flaccus. 'We must be a mile or two west of the road.' He turned his chestnut courser and began to ride slowly in a rough easterly direction, towards the darkest corner of the sky.

'We should head more to the north,' Ecdicius said.

Flaccus ignored him. Ecdicius buried his anger at his subordinate's disobedience and followed. There was no glow to be seen on any part of the horizon. The heavily clouded sky concealed all stars.

They had been riding a short time when an arrow came without warning from the blackness to their left, whipping sharply overhead. They both cursed, dug in their heels, and the two of them bolted forwards. This gallop brought them into the depths of the battlefield. Heaps of dead animals and men emerged before them, some piles lying so thick that they could not be jumped or ridden over. The ground was soft, sodden with blood. When his horse's hooves began snapping against wood, Ecdicius was confused, thinking that they had somehow entered a dried-out reed bed. He glanced down and saw that the ground was thick with arrow shafts, rising from the earth in place of the trampled grass.

Flaccus came to a halt. On the wind came the sound of distant shouting, the light clash of metal on metal, but it seemed to be everywhere at once, equally distant.

'The camp is this way,' said Flaccus.

Though Ecdicius could not say how far they had come, he was sure that his sense of direction had held true, and that Flaccus was wrong. 'We need to head south,' he said.

Flaccus did not stop, but called over his shoulder, 'This *is* south. Follow me, or I'll leave you to the Huns.'

'I'll leave *you* to the Huns,' Ecdicius shouted. Let the idiot get lost in the blackness, he thought. When Flaccus got back to camp and found Ecdicius already waiting there, he'd know his mistake.

Ecdicius struck in the direction he judged to be south, listening carefully. The noises of fighting seemed to grow louder, but were still incoherent. After a while he saw no more bodies. The ground began to rise gently. At the top of the slope loomed a great dark shape, and behind it a faint light. It was the Roman camp, he realised with relief. As he came closer, the dark bulk took the form of a covered wagon. It was deserted. Nearby was another, and then more, arranged end to end with small gaps between them. There were no men or beasts in sight. He rode to the nearest gap, and looked through to see the main camp a mere hundred yards ahead. It was a large crowd of fires and tents and more wagons stretching off to either side and far across the plain.

'You found the Hunnic camp,' came a voice. Ecdicius turned, hand on the hilt of his sword, and saw Flaccus coming up behind him. 'Do you believe me now?'

'I don't understand. I could have sworn this was south.'

'Look.' Flaccus was holding an arrow in his right hand. He held it out to Ecdicius, fletchings first. 'Hunnic, or Roman?'

Ecdicius looked at it. 'I don't know.'

'Roman. We paint our nocks, Huns don't. That's how you tell. Watch how the arrows stand in the ground. These were shot from the Roman lines, so most of them lean south. That's how you know which way to go.'

The sound of fresh fighting arose. It was nearby, distinct, coming from inside the Hunnic camp. At the very edge of the firelight, between the tents and the outer ring of wagons, Ecdicius saw a confused huddle of shadows, of men on foot and on horseback. He pulled on his reins, ready to start towards it.

'Where are you going?' said Flaccus.

'Where there's fighting, there must be some of our side. They might need our help.'

'Two of us won't be of much use. We should get back to our own lines.'

Ecdicius ignored him. He spurred his horse, urging it over the dark ground. He drew his sword. As he came closer he saw that the mounted figures, maybe two dozen of them, were wearing the tall helmets of Aquitanian Goths, and seemed to be pushing forwards into a larger crowd of Franks, thrusting with their oak lances and slashing with their swords. What were these Goths doing in the enemy camp? The way back was clear – why did they not retreat?

Ecdicius pulled slightly to the left and made for the nearest Franks, who were on foot and armed with spears, and were trying to form a coherent line to hold back the Goths. He spotted three Huns running towards the fray from the inner camp; they carried strung bows and clutched handfuls of arrows. In moments they would start shooting the Goths from their saddles. He changed course for the Huns, who failed to hear him approach in time; too late they turned to face Roman steel slicing out of the darkness. In moments the first Hun lay dead. The remaining two began to flee. Ecdicius went after the nearest. One perfectly timed slice, and the barbarian flopped to the ground, his neck half-severed. Before Ecdicius could change course, another rider sped past him in a blur and rode down the last Hun with a sharp downward cut. It was Flaccus.

Ecdicius looked back to the main fight just in time to see the Goths make a determined surge that broke through the Frankish shield wall. Only then did he see that the Goths had been trying to reach an unmounted figure whom the Franks had taken captive. The Franks now abandoned their prisoner, running for their lives as the Goths swarmed over them. Ecdicius and Flaccus galloped towards the fray, coming close to the Gothic cavalry. Flaccus hailed the nearest, a heavy cavalryman in a bronze helm and green cloak.

The Goth spotted him. 'With us, Romans!' he cried in Latin, wheeling his mount about. 'We have the prince! Ride, ride!'

Ecdicius and Flaccus followed the Goths as they galloped away from the Hunnic camp, back towards the ring of wagons and into the blackness beyond. Once past the wagons they slowed to a trot. The Goths began to laugh and sing, but Ecdicius did not understand their tongue.

'Seems that's Prince Thorismund we just helped save,' said Flaccus, alongside Ecdicius. He bowed his head, the closest thing to a salute he had ever given. 'Well done, my lord.'

XXIX

The safe return of Prince Thorismund to the Roman camp was the cause of much rejoicing. He was met by a crowd of dismounted Gothic warriors, who lifted him from his saddle and raised him on their shoulders. Cheering in triumph, they carried him through the glow of campfires towards their own encampment.

Ecdicius watched them go. Only now did he begin to feel the cost of so many hours of fighting: a torturous ache across his shoulders, the pain in his thighs, the hunger chewing inside his belly. He rode with Flaccus to the centre of the camp, searching for the command tent. All around were noisy groups of soldiers, most of them blind drunk. Some sat with women in their arms, others drank from jugs or ate from bowls of stew. Many had simply fallen asleep in the warmth of the fires. They were not celebrating a great victory, Ecdicius knew. They were just happy to be alive.

Outside the command tent Ecdicius saw the tall figure of his father. As soon as their eyes met, Avitus came hurrying towards him. Ecdicius jumped from his saddle and was immediately taken in his father's embrace.

'Thanks be to God,' Avitus said, weeping. 'Thanks be to God. When you didn't return with the others, I almost gave you up for dead. Are you injured? Let me see you.'

'I'm unharmed,' said Ecdicius, all of a sudden fighting down his own tears. His father had never before shown him such affection. 'I came in with Prince Thorismund.'

'Thorismund is alive? Thank God for that, too. The Goths have suffered enough today.'

'They had heavy losses?'

Avitus nodded. 'King Theoderic's been killed. Either fell from his horse and was trampled by his own men, or he was brought down by an enemy spear. No one seems to know. They haven't been able to find his body.'

'But did we take the field, Father? Did we win?'

'Oh, yes. We won.' There was little joy in his voice. 'Even after Theoderic fell, his Goths managed to take their end of the ridge. They routed the Pannonians, started to make for Attila in the centre. They almost got him, too, but he fled back into his camp. It was all over then. If it hadn't got so dark, we might've finished him off for good.'

Ecdicius was thinking of the Goths. The loss of their king would be a heavy blow. As for the rest of the army, the scale of the losses would not become clear until morning. For now there was nothing to do but sleep, or try to.

When the sun rose the next day, Ecdicius mounted Zephyros and rode him bareback to the top of the ridge. He was met by a ghastly sight. Across the entire ridge and plain, an area two or three miles broad, almost up to the wheels of the Hunnic wagons, countless dead were strewn amidst the shimmering dew. The heaps were thickest in the centre, where the Huns had first struck the allied lines, and on the far east flank, where the Aquitanian and Pannonian Goths had become bogged down in mutual slaughter. From the west flank lay streams of scattered corpses, tracing where Ecdicius and his comrades had chased down the fleeing Franks. Between the dead moved little specks: feral dogs and crows looking to fill their stomachs, and early-rising common soldiers looking to fill their purses.

As Ecdicius was watching, a series of horns sounded from the distant enemy camp. Soon afterwards hundreds of riders began to emerge from behind the screen of wagons. They rode forth into the battlefield, galloping over the detritus towards the looters, who hastily scurried back to the Roman lines. Most made it to safety, but some were ridden down or trapped, and either shot or lassoed by the Huns. When the field was clear, the

Huns gathered into regiments and started their swirling battle manoeuvres.

Ecdicius stared in disbelief. Despite having been routed the night before, the Huns had ventured from their camp to lay claim to the site of their defeat. It was an act of defiance, and it made Attila's intentions clear. He was not going to negotiate a surrender. If Aëtius wanted to take him, it would have to be by force.

Later that morning Ecdicius accompanied his father to the council in Aëtius's tent. As they entered, he saw that all of the Roman commanders seemed to have survived the battle, along with most of the barbarian leaders. The only king to have fallen was Theoderic. The younger Theoderic was present, but his brother Thorismund was nowhere to be seen.

Ecdicius followed his father as he moved close to Theoderic. 'Where's your brother?' Avitus asked him.

The prince's eyes were red, weary-looking. He had probably not slept the previous night. 'On the battlefield,' he said. 'Searching for our father's body.'

'Avitus,' said Aëtius, looking up and noticing that he had entered. 'Good. Let's begin.'

The men gathered around their general. He began by congratulating them on their loyalty and valour, of which poets would sing for a hundred years. He told them that Attila's invasion of Gaul was now conclusively finished, along with the legend of his invincibility. Yet he still lived, defiant in spirit, and his army was still formidable. There was little to be gained from another bloody engagement. The Huns were trapped, and no doubt low on provisions. The wisest course of action was to besiege them in their camp.

This plan won general support. The only dissenter was Prince Thorismund, who arrived as the others were voicing their approval of Aëtius's strategy. He came into the tent still dressed in his armour, although instead of a helmet he wore a blood-encrusted bandage around his head, covering a wound he had received in the enemy camp the night before. He had been weeping.

'I say *no* to a siege,' he declared, looking around contemptuously at the others, his voice thick with anger. 'I'll see those wagons burned to ashes, and every Hun butchered and thrown to the dogs and ravens, as they did to my father.' He looked to his younger brother. 'Theoderic, we have found him. He awaits the honours of burial. And when we have placed him in the earth, I will lead our people and avenge his death. Come with me.'

Theoderic did not move. 'We shall have vengeance, Brother,' he said. 'But our father ruled with prudence as well as courage. He wouldn't let grief drive him to rashness.'

'Our father always fought to defend his honour. If you or I had fallen in his place, do you think he would pause one breath before avenging us?'

'Be calm, Brother.'

'Look, Theoderic, look!' Thorismund held out his hands for all to see. They were stained with blood. 'This morning I have dug out our father's body from a mountain of dead. I have laid him on a bier, ready to give him to God. I can hear his spirit in my ears, demanding vengeance. Can you not hear his voice?'

Theoderic approached him. He took hold of his brother's bloody hands. 'I hear only the madness of grief. We shall have vengeance. But not now. Let's bury our father with dignity, mourn him, and then decide what to do.'

'You talk like a Roman,' said Thorismund, pulling his hands free. 'You always have. Small wonder you're here with them. *You* should have been fighting with the Romans yesterday, *I* should have stayed with Father. I swear by Christ, if I'd been with him, he would never have fallen.'

No matter how much Roman education he had received, nothing spurred a barbarian to violence like a slight on his honour. In the blink of an eye Theoderic had his hands around his brother's throat, and the two began to grapple and fling each other around the tent. They tumbled messily onto a couch, biting and spitting, sending an unlit brazier clattering.

The guards outside the tent rushed in and struggled to pull the cursing brothers apart.

'Stop this!' yelled Aëtius.

His fury, burning in his voice, stilled the Gothic princes. They let go of one another and stood like chastened schoolboys. Thorismund spat on the ground and wiped his mouth.

'Your father would be ashamed to see such barbarous behaviour,' Aëtius said.

'I'm now rightful king of the Goths,' growled Thorismund.

Aëtius waved his hand. 'Everyone but Thorismund, get out. I wish to speak alone with the heir of King Theoderic.'

The younger prince walked out. Ecdicius and the rest followed him. They stood outside the tent, talking in small groups. Only Theoderic kept himself apart. He was looking north, across the ridge to Attila's camp.

Aëtius and Thorismund were in private conversation for some time. When Thorismund emerged, he seemed subdued but resolute. He spotted his brother and called over to him. 'Theoderic, we must bury our father. Tomorrow we ride home.'

'Tomorrow?' Theoderic said, walking towards him. 'What of the siege?'

'There will be no siege. We ride home. That is my wish, as king.'

Theoderic, a puzzled look on his face, dipped his head. 'Very well.'

As the two brothers returned together to the Gothic camp, Ecdicius turned to his father. 'What do you think Aëtius said to him?'

Before his father could reply, Aëtius appeared at the entrance to the tent. 'Avitus!' he called, beckoning to him. 'Bring your son, too.'

'I know how Thorismund thinks,' Aëtius said as they entered, a satisfied smile on his face. He sat behind his desk, taking a mug of wine in his hand. A servant handed cups to Avitus and Ecdicius. 'It wasn't about his father's honour. He just wanted to show everyone he was the new king, not his brother. That's all he cares about. So I've convinced him that Theoderic is plotting against him. I said it was imperative that he return to Toulouse to seize the royal treasury before Theoderic does, and not risk his life or waste soldiers in a useless attack.'

'And is it true?' Avitus asked.

'Is what true?'

'Is Theoderic plotting to take the throne?'

Aëtius laughed. 'I certainly hope so. The more disunity among the Goths, the better for us.'

'And what about the Huns? Without Gothic help we won't have enough men to besiege their camp.'

'I have no intention of besieging it. I mean to let Attila go.'

Ecdicius coughed in surprise, almost choking on his wine. After everything that they had been through, after the weeks of negotiations and marching, the battles, and now having the most feared barbarian king in the world penned up at their mercy, just to let him ride away . . .

The count leaned forwards. 'Avitus, it seems that your son doesn't approve of my strategy.'

'Forgive me, my lord,' said Ecdicius. 'I was merely surprised.'

'Really? Ask yourself what we would gain from destroying the Huns.'

The answer to that seemed obvious. 'Security for Gaul, my lord.'

'And what kind of security can Gaul have while the Goths rule most of Aquitaine, and dream of ruling Provence? For thirty years only fear of our Hunnic allies – *my* Hunnic allies – has kept them at bay. If it weren't for the Huns, you'd already be kneeling to a Gothic king.'

Avitus spoke up. 'Do you mean those Huns of yours who fourteen years ago plundered the Auvergne, pillaged my lands, and murdered my secretary?'

It was an imprudent thing to say to the most powerful man in the western empire. Aëtius asked sharply, 'Do you also disapprove of my strategy, Avitus?'

'Consul, Gaul can never repay you for all you've done. I know that the Huns have served you well in the past. But King Theoderic is dead; Attila has been broken. Perhaps now is the time to find a new path, one of peace. Our alliance with the Goths—'

'With the Goths! The sons of Theoderic can serve us best by killing each other. And with their kingdom in confusion, I can use the Huns to finish them once and for all.'

'But Attila himself dreams of ruling the empire.'

Aëtius laughed. 'A dream from which he's been rudely awoken. He's no god as he claims, but nor is he a fool. He just needed reminding that all ambitions, even his own, have their limits. You'd do well to remember that, Avitus, next time you dream of living in peace with these Gothic animals. Go, now, both of you. I have an army to see to.'

As they left the tent Ecdicius could feel the restrained anger of his father. He had always said that the future of the empire depended on friendship with the Goths. He believed that they might be made civilised in a way that the Huns, savages who spent their whole lives on horseback, could never be. 'There would be peace,' he muttered, 'if only Prince Theoderic and I were the ones deciding the fate of the west.'

'But it's Aëtius and Thorismund,' Ecdicius said.

'I know. And neither of them has peace in mind.' The old general looked out over the camp. Ecdicius wondered how many times his father had seen a sight like this, how many times he had felt this hollowness that came the day after battle. 'Aëtius has spent his whole life fighting Goths and Franks and a dozen other races, even fellow Romans, always with the Huns at his side. He can't let go even now. He wants a Gothic civil war.'

'Will it happen?'

'I don't know. There might be a civil war, or Thorismund will attack the empire. Either way, everything I've tried to build will fall apart.' He shook his head sadly. 'We'll lose the best chance we've had for lasting peace in fifty years.'

At noon the Roman camp was haunted by the wailing and lamentations of the Goths as they buried their king. The Gothic army then marched in force back onto the battlefield, and spent the afternoon burying the rest of their dead and looting the corpses of their slain enemies. The Huns watched on horseback from a distance. That very evening, without holding the customary funeral feast, King Thorismund started the Goths on their long journey back to Aquitaine.

Sounds of celebration may have filled the Roman camp that night, but they were not the reason Ecdicius found so little sleep.

XXX

Clermont

Arvandus stood alone in the town-house garden, looking up towards the east. It was still there, just above the roofline: a comet, its tail stretching like a silver ribbon up into a darkening sky of cobalt blue. He had never seen anything like it. The portent had first appeared two evenings before, hours after news had arrived of the victory near Châlons. The meaning was clear to the whole city. Attila, terror of the east, had been defeated. His star had fallen.

It chilled Arvandus to see it. He was not inclined to religion; he only ever attended church on the saints' feast days, and that was so he could talk to girls in the breaks between services. A sight like this reminded him that one day he would have to start taking God more seriously. For now, though, he was glad that heavenly vengeance was directed elsewhere.

He became aware of movement in the shadows at the edge of the garden, and a form approaching down the path. It was Attica. She appeared not to have noticed him in the gloom. 'Good evening,' he said.

She stopped suddenly, bringing a hand to her throat in surprise. She relaxed when she saw who it was. 'Arvandus.'

'Yes, my lady. I'm sorry if I startled you.'

'That's all right. I just wanted to see it one more time before bed.' She came a few steps closer, stopping several yards away from him, and gazed up at the star.

Her handmaiden, Arvandus noticed, was waiting at the edge of the garden. Cyra, she was called; a pretty girl, though rather sombre-faced. Under different circumstances he might have tried his chances with her. For the last two weeks, though, he had been restraining those urges, and had not even visited any brothels. It was important to make a good impression, and so he had made sure to be the very image of the dutiful client, obeying Severiana's every command and helping Sidonius manage the accounts of the provisions brought for the refugees. It had felt good to have a sense of common purpose, to be working alongside the family of Eparchius Avitus. He knew he was still an outsider, unlike Sidonius; his low birth could not be ignored. But they treated him with respect.

He looked up at the comet. He was almost sorry that the war appeared to be over. Soon he would be returning to Arles, back to complete his final year of education. His carefree days would be done with, and the serious business of his career would begin. He might not see Attica again. Certainly not before her marriage.

He cleared his throat. 'You must be very glad that your father and brother will be coming home,' he said.

'Yes,' she replied, her eyes still on the star. She sighed. 'Of course, now I probably won't be carried away by a gang of rampaging Huns.'

'You sound disappointed.'

'Well, it was Felix's fear more than mine. But it would have been exciting.'

'Do you not want to get married?'

'Not every soldier wants to march into battle,' she said. 'But he must.'

He studied her features sidelong. Was she joking? He could not tell. 'Marriage needn't be a battle,' he said. 'Just look at your parents.'

Felix's voice called from the house. 'Attica. Where are you? Are you outside?'

Without saying another word, she turned and walked back along the path with hurried steps. She disappeared into the house with Cyra. Arvandus sadly watched her go. They had spoken little over the last two weeks; because of her engagement to Felix she had been treating him with polite reserve since his arrival, but he had come to admire her resilience and dry humour during the time of crisis. She had shown the same strength as her mother. The men of the family might have girded themselves with sword-belts and marched off to war, but it was the women who had preserved the spirit of home. It pained Arvandus to see Attica betrothed to Felix, who had refused to help with the refugees, instead spending his time with the gaggle of sycophantic friends he had accumulated among the local nobility. Arvandus had tried to stay away from him, not rising to his taunts, though he wanted nothing more than to put out the bastard's eyes.

He focused on the heavenly omen, clearing thoughts of Felix from his mind. That reckoning would come in time. For now, he would enjoy the peace they had won. Attila had been defeated, and the empire was safe.

The real victory celebrations happened two weeks later, with the return of Eparchius Avitus. He was received at the city gates like a triumphant emperor, escorted through the streets to the cathedral by cheering citizens who pressed close against his horse, surrounded by music and singing and the tears of the thankful. Arvandus waited outside the cathedral, standing close to Sidonius and the general's family. He saw Ecdicius riding behind his father, and was relieved to see that his friend was unharmed. There was a stab of envy, too, at how fine he looked, how heroic: the battle-hardened warrior, the worthy son of a worthy father, smiling as he rode through an ocean of adoring faces.

Bishop Namatius led prayers of thanksgiving at the cathedral altar, the crowd so thick that it spilled out of the doors into the streets. The noble households organised a public banquet that same evening. The forum was lined with tables that groaned beneath mountains of bread, meat, cheese, fruit, wine and beer, as the people feasted giddily on the stockpiled food that would no longer be needed.

Late in the evening Arvandus was sitting on the steps beneath the forum colonnade with Sidonius and Ecdicius, who had momentarily managed to escape the clutches of his admirers. It was long past sunset, but the banquet showed no sign of ending. Slaves had fixed blazing torches in sconces on the pillars of the colonnade. Nobles and commoners were drinking like Goths, as the saying went, and laughing as they were entertained by musicians and acrobats. Not far away Avitus was with his two daughters, talking to the bishop and other potentates of Clermont.

Ecdicius, watching them, seemed oddly subdued. Suddenly he said, 'My father thinks there'll be war with the Goths.'

'That's rubbish,' said Sidonius, slouched against a pillar. His words were slurred. He had never been able to hold his drink. 'The Goths love us. They love your father. We all love each other. And we all hate the Huns.'

'Aëtius doesn't hate the Huns,' Ecdicius said. 'He let Attila go after the battle. He wants to turn Thorismund and Theoderic against each other.'

'Well, that's good, isn't it?' said Arvandus. 'I mean, if Theoderic kills Thorismund and becomes king, that'd be good. He's friendly to Rome. Wasn't your father his tutor for a while?'

'Yes. But what if my father isn't around much longer? What if . . .' He hesitated, trying to find the words. 'I don't know. I think of what happened to my aunt and uncle, that's all.'

Sidonius sat up straight and put an arm around his cousin. 'Don't worry about that, comrade. Your father is too popular. Just look around. Look at all these people. Imagine what would happen if Aëtius tried to hurt him. Then there *would* be a war.'

Ecdicius did not reply. His worried stare was still on Avitus.

A shadow fell across them. 'Congratulations on your victory, Ecdicius,' said Felix. He was accompanied by two of his recently acquired friends, a pair of younger men from prominent local families. Arvandus did not know them, and did not wish to. Judging from their unsteady postures the three of them were drunk.

'Thank you,' said Ecdicius flatly. 'I should congratulate you, too, Felix. I'm sure your prayers helped us win the day.'

Felix studied Ecdicius carefully, as though trying to work out whether or not he was being mocked. Seeming unsure, he looked to Arvandus. 'Shame *you* couldn't stay with the army all the way north,' he said. 'Otherwise you'd be the one getting the parade.

Still, I'm sure you did a fine job helping the women with the refugees.'

The two friends standing behind Felix sniggered. Arvandus stared down into his half-empty cup. It took all his willpower to contain his anger. *Not now*, he told himself. There would come a time when he would make Felix suffer. He had to be patient.

Ecdicius stood up and faced Felix. 'My father sent Arvandus back here,' he said. 'He sent Sollius, too. So if you're mocking Arvandus, you must be mocking my cousin as well, and saying my father was wrong to do it. Are you?'

Felix tightened his lips, staring Ecdicius in the eye. 'I wasn't talking to you,' he said.

'You insult one of my friends, you insult me.'

'Let your friend speak for himself.'

'That's what you want, isn't it? There's nothing better than beating someone who can't fight back. Isn't that right, Felix?'

The two of them stood for a moment in silence, their stares locked as the revelry around them continued. Arvandus noticed that Ecdicius had his fists clenched.

Eventually Felix laughed. 'You're drunk,' he said in disgust. 'A typical soldier, always looking for any reason to start a brawl.'

Ecdicius smiled. He began to turn, seeming about to sit down, but the next instant his fist was flying towards Felix, who saw it coming too late. He tried to duck, and the blow struck him on the temple. At once he was on his back, his cloak splayed across the flagstones. His friends jumped in surprise, backing away. Nearby conversations stopped as people noticed the commotion. Arvandus and Sidonius scrambled to their feet.

Ecdicius loomed over Felix. 'You're a damned coward. You should have run off back to Arles like you wanted to.'

'I'll have you brought to court for this,' squealed Felix, pressing a hand to his temple. He rose clumsily, his friends now helping him. 'My father will hire the best lawyer. This will cost you a fortune.'

'No it won't,' said Attica, appearing between them. 'And if you even mention court again, you'll never have me as your wife.'

She put her arm through her brother's. 'Ecdicius, come with me. Father wants to talk to you.'

Felix watched them go. He spat on the ground where Ecdicius had stood. With a final contemptuous glance at Arvandus, he spun about and walked away, his friends following.

Sidonius was staring after him in confusion. 'What on earth happened there?' he said.

Arvandus said nothing. Ecdicius was now with his father, who at once began addressing him with some stern words. The bishop looked shocked, Papianilla and the other nobles embarrassed.

But it was Attica who had Arvandus's attention. She had been in his dreams again last night. In the dream they had not been speaking, or even close. He had simply been watching her, as now, from a distance. Ever since their brief conversation in the garden he had found himself studying her with what he knew was becoming a dangerous fascination. It was not even her beauty that captivated him. It was the animating spirit within, something that Felix did not deserve. With her every smile Arvandus seemed to catch a glimpse of spring: fresh, innocent, kind. When she laughed, as she had done even during the depths of crisis, all the bounteous warmth of summer sprang forth, and her eyes sparkled like the sun. Then were a shadow to fall across her face in a moment of distraction, he felt the soft, aching melancholy of autumn.

And when she was angry, as now, her features hardened into a wintry stare of terrifying beauty: for even in the most beautiful things, Arvandus knew, there could be depths of coldness.

XXXI

'I thought you'd decided to go,' said Attica.

'I've decided *not* to go.' Felix did not look up from the document he had spread on the desk before him. 'You know I don't enjoy theatre. Although I don't know if this performance should even be dignified with the term.'

'They've come all the way from Arles.'

'And they're being asked to perform on a ramshackle stage in the forum. I have work to do.' He cleared his throat and leaned closer to read a line of text.

'You know Cyra is sick,' she said. 'My mother and sister are in Lyons with Sidonius. Will you have me go without any escort at all?'

He made no response. Attica stood in the doorway watching him. She was wearing her long-sleeved tunic with gold-threaded bands around the wrists, a new linen shawl, her finest pearl necklace and earrings, and had spent the last hour having her hair set. The others were already in the entrance hall, waiting to take the litters to see the first public show in Clermont for years. The troupe of actors had been paid for and sent by special benefaction of her uncle the prefect, as a reward to the citizens of the Auvergne for their resilience during the invasion. It was true that the show would not be taking place in a grand setting. The actors had planned to use the old theatre outside the city, until during rehearsals a rotten trapdoor had given way and a dancer had fallen through it, breaking his leg. Not wanting to risk their lives for the sake of art, they decided to build a temporary stage in the city forum and hold the production there, with wooden benches for the audience.

Regardless, the people of Clermont were excited, and not just for the show itself. Count Aëtius would also be in attendance, having spent the last month trailing Attila back to the Rhine and securing the military situation in the north. Now on his way back south, he had arrived in Clermont earlier that day to a welcome even grander than the one her father had received. She had stood close to the count at the official reception, though she had not spoken to him. He had been smaller than she had expected, far less impressive to look at than his reputation suggested. Her brother had told her that the best cavalrymen were of medium stature. Even so, she could not see why everyone found him so frightening.

Including Felix. She suspected that Count Aëtius was the real reason he was refusing to attend the show. For all his pompous confidence over everybody else, Felix was intimidated by those few people who outranked him.

She was not in the mood to argue, and left him at his desk. 'He isn't coming,' she said as she came into the entrance hall. Three litters were arranged, each with four slaves ready to carry them. Her father and Ecdicius were supposed to take one, she and Felix another, and Arvandus was to take the third by himself.

'Well, we can't wait any longer,' said Avitus. He was irritated, already put in a dark mood by the presence of Aëtius in the city and the absence of his own wife. 'We only need the two litters, then. Arvandus, ride with my daughter.'

'Yes, my lord.'

Avitus and Ecdicius climbed into the first litter. Attica entered the next, settling herself on the cushioned seat as Arvandus sat opposite her. The slaves hoisted the litter and carried it out into the warm evening air. Attica opened the curtains on each side, partly for the sake of propriety, partly so that she might have something to look at besides Arvandus. She did not want a conversation. This was his last day in Clermont; tomorrow he would leave for Arles, and she would likely never see him again. With her marriage imminent it would do no good to indulge that old infatuation.

Nor was there any point in being frustrated by Felix, she knew, but it was hard not to be. He had come to Clermont so that he and Attica could get used to one another before their marriage in September. For her part, she had tried to get him accustomed to disagreement and disobedience, and herself accustomed to the idea of his physical attentions, unwelcome as they were. She wanted to marry him for his ambition, nothing more. That quality would be worthless if she could not benefit from it, and so she had taken pains to behave as his equal, and not to bow to his whims like so many did. More than once he had grown angry over some trivial disagreement and called her wilful. Lately, though, he had taken to withdrawing into a sullen indifference, and this irritated her. She preferred him to be angry, which at least showed strength of spirit.

It was not long before the litter was deposited amidst the noise of the forum. Ushers led the four of them to their seats on the front row, where cushions had been placed on the wooden benches. The stage was a wooden platform raised a couple of feet from the ground, with a makeshift façade rising behind it. Bundles of summer flowers and garlands were draped over the entire structure.

Arvandus bent his head towards her and spoke. 'Look to your right, at the far end of the bench. There's Aëtius and his wife Pelagia. Do you see? She's meant to be a princess of some sort.'

She glanced to where the count and the supposed princess were sitting. 'His wife is fat,' she muttered. When Arvandus laughed she flashed him an irritated look. She had not meant it as a joke.

The show was opened by acrobats, after which came a panto-mime performance that had the forum filled with laughter. Attica was determined not to find any of it amusing. The only sensible part of the show was a performance of the play *Phaedra*, which drew her in despite herself. By this time it was dusk, and the stage was illuminated by burning torches. She watched as Queen Phaedra, wife of King Theseus of Athens, fell in love with her stepson Hippolytus while Theseus was away in the Underworld. Phaedra knew that her love was forbidden, and yet she could not control it. She clutched both hands to her head and then flung them wide. 'What can reason do?' she exclaimed, her voice echoing around the torch-lit forum. 'Passion has conquered and now rules; it dominates my every thought like a god!' Eventually she confessed her passion to Hippolytus. He spitefully rejected her, along with all womankind, and stormed off. In her anger, Phaedra announced to everyone that Hippolytus had tried to seduce her. Then Theseus returned from the Underworld, just in time to hear the news that Hippolytus had been killed in a chariot accident. Phaedra dropped on her sword in grief. Theseus mourned his dead son, and cursed his dead wife. The audience applauded.

Attica was fond of Seneca's tragedies, especially *Phaedra*, and was sorry when it was over. As they got up to leave, Attica caught the gaze of Aëtius, who had also risen with his wife and companions. He looked at her quizzically for a moment, then beckoned her over with a finger. She walked to him and knelt at his feet. She greeted him with the usual formula. 'Illustrious Consul, I am unworthy of the honour.'

'On your feet,' he replied. 'Attica, isn't it? You're betrothed to Magnus's first-born. What's his name?'

'Felix, my lord.'

'Is this him?' He nodded in the direction of Arvandus, who was still standing at their seats. He beckoned him over too.

'This is Arvandus, my lord, a client of ex-prefect Alcimus.'

Arvandus came to them, and also knelt according to protocol. 'Illustrious Consul, I am unworthy of the honour.'

'Rise, boy.' He turned to Attica. 'Is your father not here tonight?'

She glanced over her shoulder to where her father had been. He was gone, but she spotted him a short distance away. 'He's over there, my lord, talking to some friends.'

'So I see,' he said. 'All right then, girl. Tell us what you learned tonight.'

'My lord?'

'What did you learn from the tale of Phaedra?'

Along with his wife, the count was accompanied by several

men from the military high command, all wearing their crisp tunics and flowing cloaks. From her brother's descriptions Attica recognised the red-bearded one as Aegidius, but the others she did not know. She would likely never see any of them again. Felix might hide at home in fear, but she would not cower before the man who had murdered her aunt and uncle. 'I learned that Phaedra was dealt with unfairly by just about everyone,' she said, looking him in the eye.

She could not tell whether Aëtius was surprised more by her words or by the tone in which she had delivered them. 'Sympathy for Phaedra?' he said. 'Well, I wouldn't call myself a professor of literature, but that is an odd view. I think you need to explain yourself, girl.' His companions chuckled. His wife looked on, unsmiling, her expression opaque.

'Gladly, my lord,' Attica said. 'I simply mean that Phaedra is condemned for a love she didn't choose. We shouldn't blame her for that. Right or wrong, it defeats her. So she confesses her love to Hippolytus – the poor woman, she grovels before him and professes herself his slave, she's overcome with a passion beyond reason, she declares that either her misery or her life must end that day. And what does Hippolytus do? He urges the gods to rend the heavens and strike him down with a thunderbolt, as though *he* were to blame, as though *anyone* were to blame. Then, which is even worse, he grabs her by the hair and wants to cut her throat in sacrifice to Diana.'

'But he doesn't do it,' said Aëtius.

'But *she* wants him to. Better to die than suffer rejection, that's what she's thinking. He doesn't stop himself because of compassion, but because he doesn't want to pollute his blade with her corrupted blood.'

'Does that justify accusing Hippolytus of incest? She casts her sin upon his shoulders.'

Every pair of eyes was glaring upon her like the torches of Phoebus. But she had begun to speak her mind, and she could hardly stop now. 'That was her nurse's idea. Anyway, at that point the whole affair becomes quite ridiculous. It seems to me that everyone in the play is mad except for her. Hippolytus behaves like a pompous idiot, full of hatred for womankind – odd coming from the son of an Amazon – and his father is even worse. You'd think Phaedra redeemed herself in the end by throwing herself on a sword, but Theseus curses her even in death! It's a sorry thing. Everyone gets what they deserve, except Phaedra.'

Aëtius chuckled indulgently. 'A spirited defence, girl, but the moral lesson is clear. Phaedra violated the bonds of matrimony, and paid the price. "May the soil lie heavy on her unholy head!"'

Attica frowned. 'My lord, I can only assume *you've* never been in love.'

There was a nervous pause as everyone waited for Aëtius to reply. So far the exchange had been good-humoured, but Attica knew that her comment, spoken without due thought, had been insolent. She found her breath trapped in her lungs. Aëtius was said to ruin reputations with a single word. In this case all he had to do was walk away. Word would quickly spread among the gossipers of Clermont, and Attica would become untouchable.

'I'm an old man,' he said at last. 'Luckily age and forgetfulness have hidden the follies of my youth.' His officers laughed politely. It was a joke. If Attica had offended him, she was forgiven.

Arvandus, standing beside her, let out a sudden gasp. He must have been holding his breath, too. Aëtius looked at him. 'Tell us, what do you think of Phaedra?'

Arvandus raised his eyes to meet the count's. 'I also believe she was unfortunate in her love,' he said. He spoke slowly, but with confidence. 'Her worst sin was to blame herself for it.'

'Well, you are indeed a confused generation,' said Aëtius, to the amusement of those around him. 'Give my greetings to your father, girl. Tell him I mean to call on him tomorrow. And my best wishes to you both for your matrimonials. Good luck to *you*, lad.'

Attica and Arvandus bowed and left the count's company, neither mentioning his mistake. They returned to her father and Ecdicius.

Arvandus did not speak again until they were in the litter on the way back home. 'I suppose we should let your parents know,' he said.

'Know what?'

'You heard Aëtius. The wedding arrangements have been changed by consular decree.'

She did not reply, although she wanted to be angry with him. It was not a joke. *He* was not the one due to marry Felix. He was lowly enough, and his parents were insignificant enough, that he would have freedom to choose his own spouse. With his rise in fortunes, and his charm, Arvandus would be able to choose his future bride from hundreds of girls, even senatorial ones. Attica would never have that freedom. She did not want to be betrothed to Felix, of all men. Why could he not be more charming, more courageous, kinder? Why could he not be more like Arvandus?

They dismounted the litter and walked behind Avitus and Ecdicius from the entrance hall into the atrium. Her father and brother kissed Attica goodnight, then headed together down the corridor that led to their sleeping quarters. Attica and Arvandus went down a different corridor. They came to Attica's room first. She placed her hand on the latch, and realised that Arvandus had stopped with her.

She turned to face him. They were close. He was looking at her in a way he had not since his arrival.

'I believe I can be worthy,' he whispered.

'Worthy of what?'

'Of you.' He reached out to touch her hand, which was still resting on the latch. She did not pull away.

It was unfair, she thought, that she was in this position; unfair that the course of her life had been determined by others in this way. It was unfair that such a thing as desire should exist, if it was all to be wasted, or would lead her only to ruin.

Cyra was not with her. There was no one who would know.

She lifted the latch. Slowly she pushed open the door. Taking Arvandus's hands in her own, she led him inside.

XXXII

Arles

That August was the hottest Arvandus had ever known. He sat in the stifling air of the basilica, sweat trickling down his brow and dripping onto the papyrus. He wished he did not have to wear his heavy, cumbersome toga, but such antiquated ceremony was expected at the Gallic Council, even for a mere clerk like him, sitting at a portable writing desk alongside other scribes as he made a record of proceedings for Alcimus, who was unable to be present. The councillors themselves were arranged on rows of wooden benches facing each other across the nave. Prefect Ferreolus sat on his throne in the apse, presiding over the discussions.

Every year this business of the Gallic Council consumed the city for a month, but it was the first time Arvandus had witnessed the sessions at first hand. Seven delegations of governors, city councillors, and the most powerful men of Gaul had assembled from the three provinces of Aquitaine, the two provinces of Narbonne, and the provinces of Vienne and the Maritime Alps, and were spending a full month debating and conferring and arguing. At the end of it all they would send a special envoy to the central government in Italy with their concerns and requests.

The members of the council wore the traditional garb of togas to make themselves feel important, but Arvandus doubted that the emperor paid much attention to them. He silently studied the faces and characters of the provincial governors and their staff as they bickered back and forth between their benches. Ferreolus kept a firm control of proceedings. One speaker he treated with special brusqueness: Paeonius, who had been appointed consul-governor of Vienne. It was the first time Arvandus had seen his former patron in open debate. He had so far proved himself to be irascible, tetchy and tactless.

Late in the morning Paeonius and Ferreolus became tied up in an argument over grain shipments to Rome. Paeonius was all sweat and shouting and folds of angry fat. He dabbed his round, flushed face with the hem of his toga. 'Perhaps the illustrious prefect could explain something to me,' he said, his voice edged with sarcasm. 'How are we supposed to send four hundred thousand measures of grain down the Rhône by the end of September, when we have only half the barges we need? Will the imperial court send us money to build more, or not?'

'Transportation is the responsibility of the provincial governor,' stated Ferreolus irritably, not for the first time. 'It is not for the count of sacred largesses to make good *your* financial misman-agement.' By now the rest of the assembly was weary and bored. Some had dozed off. Only a handful, the partisans of Ferreolus and Paeonius, were still paying attention.

'Oh, I see,' said Paeonius. 'I'm accused of corruption, am I?' His supporters expressed their outrage with jeers and boos.

'This is ridiculous,' said Ferreolus. 'I call this session to an end. We shall reconvene at the seventh hour.'

The usher jumped to his feet. 'The session is ended. Praise be to Emperor Valentinian!' The delegates echoed the acclamation half-heartedly, and slowly roused themselves from their benches, gathering into little muttering cliques. Arvandus followed Ferreolus and his attendants through a side door that led to a large barrel-vaulted antechamber. This room, part of the adjoining public baths, had been furnished with tables of food and drink for the refreshment of the delegates. It was where they mingled between and after sessions. Slaves stood in the corners and at the doorways, wafting the air with huge fans made from palm leaves.

Arvandus took a cup of watered wine and kept his eyes open for Sidonius, who had promised to join him during the interval. Nearby, mingling at the side of the room, was a group of a dozen other young notaries. They were all secretaries to the provincial delegations, excited to be in the famous imperial city, most of them for the first time. Over the past couple of weeks Arvandus had taken a few of them to his favourite taverns and brothels. It had proved to be a good way of gathering intelligence about the delegates. From Sextus, an excitable lad with a protruding lower lip, he had learned that the governor of the Maritime Alps was having an illicit affair with the son of the deputy procurator. Another had told him that the chief legal advisor to the governor of First Narbonensis had been pilfering from the provincial treasury – with the knowledge of the governor himself. The chief of staff of Second Aquitaine, meanwhile, was said to be two hundred and seventy pounds of gold in debt to a Gothic chieftain, and would likely end up in the Garonne with a dagger in his back before the year was out.

Alcimus would be much more interested in that sort of news than in the endless council debates. Arvandus did not look forward to the afternoon session, when he knew his head would be lolling and his eyelids as heavy as lead. He could not wait to get out of his damned toga and head for the cold pool in the public baths, maybe catch a pantomime show that evening.

Thinking of the theatre reminded Arvandus of the play at Clermont, and the night that had followed. The memory sent his pulse racing. For the last few weeks, ever since leaving Clermont, it had been a joy and a torture to think of Attica – of the sudden lust that had overcome them, had sent them stumbling to the bed with torn clothes, of the fumbled, muffled passion that had followed, every moment filled with the terror and excitement of imminent discovery . . .

He felt a red flush rise to his cheeks, and stifled those thoughts. It had been a mistake, a stupid, dangerous risk. He could only thank God that they had not been found out. Avitus, to protect the family honour, could have had him arrested and condemned to death for ravishing his daughter. The domestics, including Cyra, would have been tortured and questioned in order to discover how long the affair had been going on, and whether they had been complicit. Any found guilty would have been burned alive.

They had not been discovered. Instead, Arvandus had been able to retreat to his own room, stepping silently down the empty corridor. Neither Attica nor he had mentioned it again, and the following day they had reverted to their usual politeness. They both understood that it could not, must not happen ever again. It was bad enough that he had violated the trust of her father, a man he respected above all others, and he was deeply troubled by that guilt. But still it had pained him to leave her. She shared that pain, he had no doubt.

Arvandus tried to cheer himself up by thinking of how well everything else had gone. They had won the war, driving Attila out of Gaul. Arvandus had proved himself in public service to Eparchius Avitus. In a matter of weeks he would have completed his schooling, and would hopefully secure a junior post in the civil service. Then it would be a matter of getting an official post on the prefect's staff, going to Italy to hold some position at the imperial court, climbing the ladder one rung at a time until he reached high office – maybe even the prefectship of Gaul. Then he would finally put an end to the wasteful bickering of the Gallic Council, stamp out corruption, and restore justice to Gaul. It might take twenty or thirty years, but he would do it.

He sipped his wine and looked around at the councillors. Most of them were old, and would never live to see him achieve his dreams. He smiled. If only they knew what the innocuous young clerk standing at the side of the room would one day become.

Paeonius entered from the basilica, followed by his supporters, and went to a table loaded with cups of wine. His eyes passed over Arvandus, showing no recognition, of course. There had been no communication between them since Arvandus had gone over to Alcimus two years ago. It had not even been Paeonius who had sent those thugs to take his finger. Simeon's half-threats of 'consequences' had come to nothing.

As for Felix . . . Arvandus had waited this long to give him what he deserved; he could wait a few years more. It was pleasing to think that Attica had given him something that now Felix would never have, but he had not gone into her bed for that reason. He did not want rash, hot-headed revenge. One day he would make the bastard suffer, and then crush him to nothing.

'Arvandus, there you are!' It was Sidonius, approaching from the basilica door. 'Sorry I'm late, the city is heaving. How was the council session?'

'Hot.' He flapped a loose fold of his toga. 'This bloody frippery doesn't help, either.'

Sidonius laughed. 'I think it rather suits you. So, has Ferreolus strangled Paeonius yet?'

'Not yet. Give him a couple more days. Are you sure you don't want to take my place?'

'And rob my father of his most loyal client? You know I couldn't do that. Anyway, I have news for you. Two pieces of news, actually – one about you, one about me. Which would you like first?'

Indistinct shouts came from within the basilica. At first Arvandus assumed that some of the delegates were arguing. But there came the heavy tramp and clattering of soldiers, and an officer entered the antechamber, accompanied by two of his men. They were all fully armoured in helmets, mail shirts and cloaks, red-faced and breathing heavily. Every conversation in the antechamber stopped.

'Prefect,' the officer panted, his eyes darting around the room.

Ferreolus emerged from a group of toga-clad councillors. 'Here I am, tribune. Catch your breath. What is it?'

'The Goths, my lord. King Thorismund. His army is at the west gate. He's demanding the surrender of the city.'

The room was filled with panicked muttering. Ferreolus received the news in utter calm. 'I want every available soldier on the battlements,' he said. 'And you will now escort me to the west gate.'

'My lord, it may be dangerous.'

The prefect gave a good-natured smile. 'If I'm shot down, tribune, at least it will save me from another interminable council session. Lead the way.'

Marching behind the tribune and his soldiers, Ferreolus left the antechamber. His chief of staff followed, along with his chief deputy and two junior clerks, and another pair of soldiers from the prefect's personal bodyguard. Sidonius started after them, pulling on Arvandus's toga. 'Stick with me,' he said.

As they left the basilica the chief of staff, an ageing, stiff-backed bureaucrat called Sertorius, began to insist that Ferreolus summon his chariot, since it was unseemly for a praetorian prefect to be seen journeying through the city on foot. 'Damn the chariot,' Ferreolus snapped. 'We'll get there quicker if we walk. Tribune, lead the way.'

By the time they had crossed the bridge and reached the west gate, the midday sun beating down on their brows, each of them was panting and dripping with sweat. Arvandus unwrapped himself from his toga, unable to bear the heat for another moment, and bundled it under his arm. Sertorius and the chief deputy looked about to faint. Ferreolus, the tunic beneath his toga already soaked through and plastered to his skin, seemed not to notice the discomfort. He paused in the shadow of the gatehouse and wiped an arm across his brow. News of the Gothic army had spread throughout the city. Quite a crowd had flocked after them. Squads of soldiers hurried up the street, making their way to the western towers and battlements.

As soon as Ferreolus had caught his breath, he headed for a door in the gatehouse. Arvandus was the last to follow after him. They passed through a ground-floor chamber before entering a dark winding staircase. Inside it was refreshingly cool, filled with the noises of panting men and feet scuffing on stone. Eventually they emerged back into the light, the heat and brightness hitting Arvandus like a blow to the face. He raised his hand to shield his eyes. They were on the southern of the two protruding gatehouse towers. A handful of archers stood ready, and artillerymen were cranking a pair of scorpions, fearsome-looking bolt weapons of wood and brass that were now trained on the road leading towards the city. Ferreolus hastened to the edge of the tower, the rest of the group close behind.

Arvandus peered over the battlements. In the distance, spread across open fields in front of a forest perhaps a quarter of a mile away, stood a force of what looked like several thousand Gothic cavalry, shimmering in the summer haze. Sunlight flashed on the steel of their countless spears and helmets. Five riders were heading towards the city up the deserted road, the hooves of their mounts churning up a cloud of dust.

'Shall we shoot, my lord?' asked the tribune.

'Certainly not,' said Ferreolus. 'That's King Thorismund. Do you want to start a war? Command your men to hold fast.'

The tribune barked a command that was echoed by the troops on the northern tower, and then by the archers and spearmen down the length of the walls. The Gothic riders stopped thirty yards from the gate. Arvandus had never seen Thorismund, but he was easy to identify as the lead figure. His tall helmet was clad in sheets of silver gilt and studded with precious stones. A thick plume of green-dyed horsehair sprouted from the crest. He wore his own hair loose beneath the helmet, so that it fell onto his shoulders and over a cloak of rich red decorated with swirls of golden vine. Around his bronze scale shirt were wrapped a brass-studded belt and baldric, from which hung the bejewelled hilt and scabbard of his longsword.

Thorismund glared at the closed city gates. His eyes rose to the top of the south tower and fell on the group of toga-clad men observing him. He spotted Ferreolus. 'In the name of my departed father, King Theoderic,' he bellowed, 'I claim this city as my birthright.' His horse whinnied, rearing up and kicking the air with its front legs.

Arvandus felt a shudder of fear. Growing up in Bordeaux, he had heard tales of Thorismund. Of King Theoderic's six sons, he was said to be the fiercest, a masterful rider and dauntless warrior, commander of the royal guard, and the embodiment of Gothic strength. People were now saying that during the final battle against Attila he had pursued the broken enemy right into the heart of their camp. A man like that did not know the meaning of fear. And unlike his younger brother Theoderic, he was no friend of Rome.

'Great king,' Ferreolus replied, his voice carrying clearly over

the ramparts, 'we grieve for the loss of your noble father. We beg
you to show us mercy in your anger. Had we known of your
approach, we would have prepared a celebration, that you might
have entered the city amidst the joyful songs of its people. But
let me welcome you in peace, I pray, and invite you to my table,
where we might feast together as friends.'

Thorismund studied the prefect in silence for a long moment.
Finally he nodded.

'I will come down to welcome you in my own arms,' said
Ferreolus. He turned away from the battlements. 'Tribune, keep
the west walls fully manned for now. Let me know at once if the
Gothic army moves any closer.'

'Yes, my lord. Should we expect an attack?'

'Heavens, no. He may be an ass on the back of a stallion, but
not even Thorismund is that stupid. I was expecting him to do
something like this as soon as Aëtius was out of sight. He needs
to impress his army, and if that means parading up and down
in front of our city like Alexander the Great, we'll just have to
put up with it. I'll get him drunk and give him some trinkets,
and he'll be heading back home in a matter of days.' He pulled
a cloth from the folds of his tunic and dabbed his brow. 'I just
wish the fool hadn't waited until it was so damned *hot*.'

The rest of them watched from the battlements as Ferreolus
descended the tower, went through the gates as they were hauled
open, and greeted the Gothic king. Arvandus felt immense relief.
Now he understood why Ferreolus had seemed so unconcerned
by the appearance of an army on his doorstep. The Goths were
a pompous, prideful race.

'I can't see Prince Theoderic down there,' Sidonius said,
squinting at the other four riders.

'He must be holding court back in Toulouse,' said Arvandus.

'Maybe. Or there could be a rift between him and Thorismund.
That's what Ecdicius says, anyway.'

Having spoken a few words, Thorismund was now dismounting.
He walked to Ferreolus. The two of them joined in a loose embrace
and kissed one another on the cheek. The prince then climbed

back on his horse and Ferreolus led him through the gates. Three of the Gothic riders followed him, while the fourth headed back down the road towards the army.

'No war today, then,' said Sidonius.

Another cheering thought occurred to Arvandus. 'No more council sessions, either. They can't hold them without the prefect. Christ, that's a relief. What do you think, head to the baths?'

'Definitely. But I need to tell you my news. I'll tell you the bit about me first: I'm going to wed next month.'

'I don't believe it! Who's the unfortunate maiden?'

Sidonius gave a knowing smile. 'Papianilla.'

'Now I really don't believe it. I thought she was going to become a nun.'

'That was the plan. I persuaded her otherwise.'

Dumping his toga on the floor, Arvandus laughed and threw his arms around his friend. 'Congratulations, Sollius! This is suddenly turning out to be a much better day than I was expecting.'

'And it doesn't stop there.' From the pouch at his belt Sidonius withdrew a rolled sheet of papyrus and handed it to Arvandus.

He unrolled the sheet. It began by invoking Emperors Valentinian and Marcian, and went on to state that he, Arvandus, was to be appointed scribe on the staff of the Prefect Ferreolus. He read it through again, and then a third time. It felt unreal to see his name written in a document along with those of the emperors and prefect.

'Now it's my turn to congratulate you,' said Sidonius. 'I had it approved by the prefect's office this morning. You'll start as soon as Maximinus releases you from his class.'

Arvandus could find no words. He was sure that the grin stretched across his face made him look like an idiot, but he did not care. Even the heat no longer felt oppressive; it was radiant, glorious. The might of the Gothic army in the distance was a beautiful sight.

He laughed again, feeling as though he could jump twenty feet in the air. Life was good.

THREE YEARS LATER

Prologue

*O*nce he had been the most feared king in the world. Immediately after the battle of the Catalaunian plains, it is said that he commanded a pile of saddles and horse trappings to be built in the middle of his camp, and then set it alight. The plume of smoke rose to the heavens, and all who saw it understood. 'I shall flee no more,' Attila was saying. 'I will throw myself on this pyre sooner than be taken captive.'

But his old friend Aëtius let him go.

The king returned to his palace, and there he licked his wounds and he plotted. The men of Gaul had thwarted him. He had not expected them to stand united. And so he turned his eyes south, to Italy.

For one winter he waited, biding his time. Then, as soon as the snows had melted, he crossed the Alps and conquered Aquileia, and burned the cities north of the Po. Yet the Scythian gods had abandoned him, and suffered him to go no further; his men fell sick from the noxious air of that country, and died by the hundred, or became so weak they could not even mount their horses.

The Romans, fearing that the Huns might soon regain their

strength, sent an embassy. It was led by two of the noblest men from the Senate, Trygetius and Avienus, and by Bishop Leo of Rome. 'Leave our country,' they begged him, 'and we shall send you gifts of gold and silver.'

'By right half of the empire is mine,' grumbled Attila, but he knew now that he would never have Honoria as his bride, or the west as her dowry. He took his army from Italy and went home.

One more winter he waited in his home behind the Danube. It was time, he decided, to turn his attention back to the east, for the new Emperor Marcian had ceased paying the customary tribute, and Attila could not let this insult go unpunished. And so he told his Huns to rest well, to regather their strength, and to ready themselves to march once more on Constantinople.

In the meantime Attila became besotted with a slave girl called Ildico. Although he already had many wives, as is the custom among that barbaric people, she surpassed them all in beauty and charm, and so he determined to make her his bride. He ordered a great feast to be prepared for the wedding. Hundreds of his noblest warriors attended the celebration, drinking and singing with joy as their beloved king married the girl.

Late in the night Attila retired from the feast. His followers cheered as he took Ildico to his bedroom. As soon as he reached the bed, however, the countless cups of wine he had drunk finally went to his head; he fell on the mattress, rolled over onto his back, and fell asleep. Ildico climbed into the bed beside her husband and likewise fell asleep.

At dawn Ildico awoke to a terrible sight. Attila was lying beside her, precisely as he had lain all night. Dry blood was crusted around his mouth, down his scarred cheeks, and on the sheets. His eyes were open, but contained no life. He had choked to death on his own blood.

Terrified, too frightened even to raise the alarm, the girl did not move for many hours, but covered her head and wept. Eventually Attila's men began knocking on the door. Ildico was still too fearful to speak. Hearing no response, they knocked again. Then they started banging against the door. When there was still no response, they smashed through and came rushing into the bedroom.

They saw their king on the bed, saw the weeping girl, and realised what had happened. 'Oh, happy king,' they wailed. 'You who conquered half the world and struck terror into the empires of east and west – here you lie, at peace, having died in the midst of joy rather than at the hands of a vengeful foe!' Then, because to the Huns the only tears a man may fittingly weep are tears of blood, they took out their knives and began to cut their own faces, and tore lumps from their hair as they grieved the passing of their lord.

Emperors of east and west rejoiced when they heard the news. It is even said that Christ Himself had appeared to Emperor Marcian in a dream on the night of Attila's death. 'Behold,' He had uttered, showing Marcian a broken bow, 'see how the Lord has shattered His enemy.'

So died the terror of the world, and the judgement of God seemed complete. But those Romans who thought themselves spared were fools. For Attila was not the only man who would be judged. Soon there would be three more deaths; and these three deaths would shake the empire of the west to its very foundations.

XXXIII
Lupiacum, A.D. 454

'Am I holding her right?' Attica asked.

Papianilla smiled. 'Of course. You look very natural with her.'

Attica wished she felt natural. Perched on the couch with her back straight, her sleeping niece cradled in her arms, she feared that she would somehow slip and drop the quiet, loosely wrapped bundle on its head. She had forgotten that babies were so soft and fragile.

'I hoped this one would be easier than Alcima,' said Papianilla, on the couch beside her sister. 'She was worse, though. The poor girl didn't want to come out at all. I fainted twice. The midwife had to slap me to wake me up.'

'I bet she enjoyed that.'

'I'm sure she did. She was magnificent, though. You must ask me for her when your time comes.'

Attica studied little Severiana's features. She bore the name of their mother, and had some of her looks, too. Her big sister Alcima, named for Sidonius's father, was fourteen months old and sleeping quietly in the next room under the caring eye of her wet nurse.

A faint draught came through the open door that led out to the peristyle. Attica made sure that Severiana's arms were fully covered by the blanket. It was late September, three years since Attica and Papianilla had wedded their husbands. Papianilla had already given Sidonius two children. Attica had given Felix none.

'How often are you trying?' Papianilla asked, as though reading her sister's thoughts.

'It varies. Most of the time Felix is away in Narbonne or Arles. He prefers me to stay here in Lupiacum.' It was an evasive answer.

If Felix had not yet put a child inside her, it was not for want of trying. But Attica preferred not to think of those stiff, passionless nights when he pressed his weight onto her, his breath hot on her neck, and obliged her to receive his brief, awkward thrusts. She performed her wifely duties, he could not complain about that. By now she was so used to feeling revulsion at her husband's touch that she could not imagine marriage being any other way. It was only when she saw Papianilla with Sidonius, and saw the love they showed to one another and to their little daughters, that she was reminded of how different things could be.

Her mind drifted back to that night after the theatre three years ago. This was her only solace: a moment she had shared with no one but *him*; the two of them, lying together entangled in the sheets after their nervous, frantic explorations. A moment of peace and satisfaction, when even the fear of discovery had faded to nothing, as though they were the only two people alive. Even if she never saw him again, she would never regret what they had done.

It had been a different life then. Before marriage, before her life in Lupiacum, before she spent every day at the spinning wheel, suffering the paranoia of a jealous husband. She had dreamed of becoming great through him, but for three years he had scarcely let her breathe. When he took her to public events or dinners he never let her out of his sight. And yet he treated her with tenderness, after his fashion. He did not abuse her, and was never cruel to her. So far he had given her no grounds to annul their marriage. Only if Felix finally decided she was infertile would that happen.

She could not stop the tightening in her throat. She sniffed, using the baby's blanket to wipe the sudden moistness from her eyes.

Papianilla put an arm around her. 'It will happen,' she said. 'Sometimes it can take years.'

There were footsteps in the peristyle. Felix and Sidonius were returning. 'Here, you take her,' Attica said hurriedly. She did not want Felix to see her with the child.

Papianilla took her daughter in her arms. She looked at Attica with concern. 'If you want, I can pray for you and Felix,' she said.

'Please don't,' whispered Attica as her husband appeared in the open doorway. Sidonius was immediately behind him.

'There's my little treasure,' said Sidonius. He came to the bench and knelt before his wife. He brushed a finger down Severiana's nose.

Attica could sense Felix's envy as he watched the parents with their child. Suddenly he looked at her, and their eyes locked. She turned away, but she had seen the hunger in his stare. It was not hunger for her, but for what Sidonius had, and what she should have given him already after three years of marriage. She prepared herself for what was to come.

'It's almost sunset, my dear,' Felix said. 'We should let our guests retire.'

Attica smiled. 'Of course.' She had learned that there was no point delaying the inevitable. She rose from the couch, bending down to kiss her sister, her niece, and her brother-in-law in turn. Severiana chose that moment to stir from her sleep, squirm in discomfort, and open her eyes. She looked about vaguely for a moment. Then the crying began.

Papianilla hushed her, rocking her gently. 'She's hungry again,' she said. 'I'll take her back to the wet nurse. Goodnight, Sister.'

Attica walked with Felix to their bedroom. It was an uncomfortably large room, and dark. The windows were shuttered to keep in the warmth of the three braziers that burned in different corners of the room. A solitary lamp illuminated the table where Attica kept her personal possessions. Felix slipped his arm into hers and guided her to the foot of the bed. Once there he stood behind her and placed his hands on her hips, pressing himself close. She felt his stubble brush against the side of her neck, the wetness of his lips as he kissed her skin. She felt him slowly harden.

'Make yourself ready,' he muttered. 'First I need to see to Rebecca.'

'Why? What has she done?' Rebecca was one of the servant girls of the household. She was good-hearted, but simple. Attica had lost count of how many times Felix had whipped her for some careless mistake.

'She forgot to oil the legs on my grandmother's couch again,' he said. He left Attica and went to open a cupboard, reaching inside for his birch cane. 'She says she did, but they've cracked. I've told Servatus to keep her locked up for me. I won't be long.'

'Will another beating do any good? She's obviously a fool. You should just dismiss her instead.'

He pondered the idea. She could tell it appealed to him. 'You're right,' he said. 'She can leave tomorrow morning.' He swished the cane twice through the air. He scrutinised the shaft, a satisfied look in his eyes. 'After I've taught her a final lesson.'

As soon as he had left the room and his footsteps had receded down the peristyle, Attica went to the table. There would be just enough time to do what she needed to do. She opened the carved ivory box where she kept a few spare coins, and counted out ten silver pieces. Next she took a small sheet of papyrus and a pen, hurriedly dipped the pen in the ink pot, and scrawled a hasty letter in the steady light of the oil lamp. When she had finished she read it through.

To the lady Anastasia, Attica sends greetings in Christ.

Forgive the brevity of these words, my dear friend. I beg you to find the bearer of this letter, Rebecca, a place in your household, if at all possible. If not, I have given her ten silver pieces with which she can pay for her maintenance until you can find her such employment as you deem fitting. She is free-born but has no family, and is not kindly treated here. I beg you to help her.

Farewell.

She would have liked to write more, had there been time. Anastasia would understand, though. She knew what Felix was like.

Attica called for Cyra, and moments later the handmaiden glided into the room. 'Yes, my lady?'

'Take these,' she said, hurrying to Cyra and pressing the money and folded letter into her hand. 'Put them in a purse and make sure Rebecca gets it before she leaves tomorrow. Tell her to find the widow Anastasia in Narbonne. She lives in the south-west quarter of the city.'

Cyra nodded. 'I understand, my lady.'

'Good. Go, now. I'll undress myself tonight.'

Cyra bowed and left the room. Alone again, Attica removed her shawl, draping it over a couch, and began to untie the leather cord around her waist. She wished she could have done more for Rebecca, but she would be better away from this house. When Felix set his attentions on one of the servants, whether they were slaves or free-born like Rebecca, it did not matter what they did. He would find some fault, some excuse. Few things excited his blood like inflicting a whipping. He did not sleep with his girls like so many men did; Attica was sure of that, if only because she had never seen him do it, and he would not have taken the trouble to hide it from her. But she wished he did. At least then she might not have had to endure his attentions so often.

He would be back soon. She changed into a loose-fitting bed tunic and pulled the pins from her hair, letting it fall loose down her back. Then, after standing still for a moment to listen for any approaching footsteps, she hurried to the cabinet next to her desk. The jug was inside, hidden at the back behind bottles of cosmetics that she knew Felix would never trouble to inspect. She brought out the jug to see that it was almost empty. She would have to ask Cyra to refill it. Regardless, she brought the jug to her lips and drank the remaining wine.

It was undiluted, sharp. Strong. It helped.

Once she had replaced the jug she knelt beside the bed. She closed her eyes and held out her hands, palms upward, ready for prayer. 'Please, God,' she whispered, 'please, Christ and Holy Spirit, and blessed Mary, do not make me bear this man's child.' She repeated the prayer again and again, so many times that the words almost lost their meaning. She squeezed her eyes shut. Some women used potions, or enchantments, or amulets. This was the only way she knew. She was unworthy of God's mercy, but so far it had worked.

As soon as she heard Felix returning, she climbed onto the bed, slipping beneath the blankets and lying on her back. She stared at the painted bosses of the coffered ceiling, their bright colours subdued in the dull light of the braziers. *It will not last long*, she told herself. *And then I can sleep.*

He came into the room, closing the door heavily behind him. There was a clatter as he threw the cane on the floor.

She kept her eyes fixed on the ceiling. He was not in a good mood.

Something weighty landed on the blanket next to her feet. She looked down and saw that it was the small leather purse. One of her silver coins had spilled from the opening. He was glaring at her. 'Why would you insult me like this?'

'It's my money,' she said, grabbing the purse and the loose coin and clutching them to her breast. Her head was swimming; the wine taking effect. 'I can do with it what I like.'

'And you're my wife.' He took a step towards the bed, undoing his belt. He tossed it on the floor. 'I can do with you what I like.'

As he approached one side of the bed, she clambered out of the other. They stood facing each other across the sheets. 'Not tonight,' she said. 'Tonight you sleep elsewhere.'

'You are obliged to give me a child. I have my rights.'

'And I have my father. He will not be pleased when I tell him you forced yourself on me.'

He scoffed. 'Your father knows the law. It isn't possible for a man to rape his own wife.'

'Then you can explain the legal semantics to my brother,' she said, and noticed the flicker of fear in Felix's eyes. He had not forgotten the incident in the forum of Clermont three years earlier. Taking advantage of his hesitation, she pointed towards the door. 'Get out.'

At first he merely stared at her in bitter silence. Then, slowly, he said, 'As you wish.'

He left the room, closing the door quietly behind him. Attica went to the side table, extinguished the lamp with her fingers, and then returned to the bed. Pulling the blanket up to her chin, she closed her eyes and let out a long, slow breath. The calm with which Felix had left troubled her. She had been prepared for a rage, for shouting, even for violence. She had almost hoped for it. If he struck her, the marriage would soon be over; her parents would not stand to see their daughter abused even by the son of Magnus. But instead of raging, Felix had let her win. She could not understand it.

She had barely fallen asleep when she was awoken by a scream. She open her eyes, startled, unsure whether or not she had dreamed it. The next scream told her she had not. It had come from the dining suite next door.

In moments she had climbed out of the bed and was leaving the room. There was another scream as she came along the corridor, but this one was muffled, quieter. She found the entrance to the dining suite blocked by Ajax, the bald-headed, thick-necked ruffian who was captain of Felix's personal bodyguard. He stood there with his arms folded. When she tried to walk past, he stepped in her path and shook his head. She looked past him into the darkness of the room, which was illuminated only by the moonlight falling through the windows in the far wall. She could see Felix standing over the weeping, crumpled shape of Rebecca, whose tunic had been split open and torn down to her waist. The moonlight picked out the light ridges of old scars across her back, and gleamed on the wetness of fresh blood. A thick strip from the tunic had been stuffed in her mouth and tied around the back of her head as a gag. In his hand Felix clutched a leather thong.

'Leave her,' hissed Attica. 'In the name of Christ, will you beat her to death under our roof?'

'If I want to,' said Felix. 'She's the cause of all this.'

Attica's head was spinning. She had never liked her husband, but the shadowy form standing over Rebecca had become something inhuman. The cold of the marble floor was numbing her feet, and the chill of night was creeping beneath her nightdress. She shivered.

'You can have me,' she said. 'If you let her leave this house in peace with the money I gave her, you can have me.'

He turned towards her. His face was pure darkness, its expression lost in the gloom, but she heard the smile in his voice. 'I'm glad you are prepared to be reasonable,' he said.

XXXIV

Arles

It was the first time Arvandus had attended a gathering at the prefect's palace, and he had never been so nervous. He had bought a new tunic for the occasion, something elegant and well-made, but not too ostentatious; it was of light blue linen, with just a narrow ribbon of embroidered vines around the hem, and round shoulder patches of interlaced diamonds surrounded by leaf designs. His cloak was of undyed wool, fastened at the shoulder with the small bronze crossbow-shaped brooch that was his new badge of office.

He must have spent an hour polishing that brooch until it shone like gold. Perhaps he would be among the lowest ranking people there, but he must not disappoint his new superior, the curator of letters. Arvandus had worked hard as a lowly scribe for three years now, fulfilling his duties with speed and accuracy, slowly winning the approval of the senior civil servants, patiently waiting while high-born idiots were promoted ahead of him. But it had paid off at last. When the curator of letters had needed a new assistant, Arvandus had managed to get a strong recommendation from the registrar, and had been awarded the post. Silvius was a strict master, a traditional-minded bureaucrat with a dislike of novelty or innovation, but he was fair. Now Arvandus would accompany him to the prefect's palace, where the most noble people of Gaul were gathering.

Arvandus remembered the time he had been ejected from the consular ceremony. That had been five years ago. He smiled to think of his younger, foolish self. He had come so far since then. Today nobody would be able to throw him out. If he saw Felix, he would bow to him with every outward sign of respect. It would be worth it just to see the impotent look on his face.

It was past noon when he left his apartment and walked through the streets of Arles to Silvius's house, which lay in the respectable district to the south of the new cathedral. The curator of letters was not a senior member of the prefect's staff, but managing the official archive of correspondence was an important job, and well paid. Silvius also had some business interests, Arvandus knew, and over his long career these had allowed him to buy a comfortable house in the city, two storeys high with painted columns and pediment framing its double doors. Arvandus waited on the opposite side of the street until the doors were heaved open and Silvius and his wife emerged in a litter borne by four slaves. Silvius opened a curtain, gave him the briefest nod of acknowledgement, and Arvandus fell into step behind the litter.

The courtyard of the palace was bustling with horses, carriages and litters as the guests of the prefect disembarked and filed into the entrance hall. Spear-wielding soldiers stood on either side of the doors like statues, their helmets and mail armour gleaming in the sun. Arvandus followed Silvius and his wife through the entrance hall into the interior of the palace. Various guests were mingling in the atrium, with more beyond in a large dining hall. There was music of cymbals and cithara. House slaves carried platters of food and drink.

'Wait here,' Silvius said as they entered the dining room.

'Yes, master,' said Arvandus. Silvius and his wife left him standing by the door as they headed into the mass of guests.

Arvandus tried to ignore the familiar stab of frustration. He had hoped that Silvius was going to introduce him to people, but it seemed that he was here to act as a mere attendant. Well, he would put up with it. He had learned the virtue of patience. Given time, he would win the respect of his new master, and slowly the doors would begin to open.

To pass the time, he looked out for faces he recognised. Prefect Ferreolus was not far away. He had held the prefectship for almost four years now, managing Gaul with a diligence and honesty that had won him the devotion of the masses. When he had lowered taxes the people of Arles had been so delighted they had carried his chariot aloft through the city. He was about to retire, though, and his potential successors were crowding around him, all trying to win his favour. The most shameless of the sycophants was his long-serving chief of staff, Sertorius; but the post would most likely go to Priscus Valerianus, who was related by marriage to the Philagrii. Next to Priscus was his son-in-law Pragmatius, famed for his striking good looks and respected for his legal acumen. The military tribune Aegidius was also in the same group, standing out in his neatly trimmed red beard and heavy military cloak.

Looking across the room Arvandus noticed Paulus, a young man from a prominent family of Toulouse who had recently arrived in Arles as the Gothic ambassador. It was strange to see someone of senatorial rank serving the Goths. It used to be that only equestrians, those most hungry for advancement, would join the royal court. Most senators in the Gothic kingdom simply stayed in private life, keeping a respectable distance from the barbarians, or sought office in the empire. Paulus obviously did not care that most of his fellow nobles were trying to avoid his company, glancing at him in disdain.

The wind was changing, though. Arvandus could not deny that. Things had been different ever since the assassination of King Thorismund. Arvandus recalled that hot August afternoon on top of the western gatehouse three years ago, when he had seen Ferreolus welcome the king into the city. 'An ass on the back of a stallion,' the prefect had called him, and he had been right. A few gifts and a lot of flattery had been enough to turn Thorismund's head, and he had marched his army back to Toulouse. This had made his soldiers angry, because they had been given no chance to fight and had received no booty. Another campaign against the restive Alans of Orléans had been inconclusive. Some Goths had begun to grumble that Thorismund was becoming arrogant and complacent. He had tried to silence the grumblers by banishing them, which had made him even less popular. Eventually Theoderic and the next eldest brother, Frideric, had conspired with a faction of the nobility to murder Thorismund.

The plot had been successful, and the Goths had accepted Theoderic as their new king, with Frideric as vice-king. There were still three more brothers – Euric, Ricimer and Himnerith – but the eldest of these, Euric, was only fourteen, and so they had played no part in the coup. The news of Theoderic's rise had been greeted with relief in Arles. He was cultured and civilised, at least for a barbarian; he had not, like his brother, inaugurated his reign by marching on Arles and prancing about on a horse, but instead had sent generous gifts of gold and silver to the emperor and to the praetorian prefect. There had been no Gothic civil war, and no war with the empire. Theoderic was promising to uphold Roman law. He preferred to speak Latin over Gothic, and encouraged the Goths in his court to do the same.

He was also trying to fill his court with Roman advisors from the noblest families of Aquitaine. Many were still resistant, but some young men, like Paulus, had been seduced. He was ambling his way slowly through the crowd of civil servants, churchmen, officers, and noblemen and their wives, smiling at any who would meet his eye. Then he spotted Arvandus. It was too late to look away; at once Paulus was heading towards him.

'Arvandus, isn't it?' he said as he came near. His features were sharp, his eyebrows sloping down to a long, narrow nose. 'I understand you were recently promoted. Advisor to the curator of letters, if I heard correctly. Allow me to congratulate you.'

'Thank you,' said Arvandus, unsettled that Theoderic's ambassador should know so much about him. It suggested that he had been doing some investigating.

'And your patron is the former prefect Alcimus, am I right? A great man. A great Roman. You're lucky he found you. Not every patron would be so indulgent.' He smiled and glanced casually around the room, leaving the comment hanging between them.

Arvandus knew he was being baited, but could not resist. 'What do you mean by "indulgent"?'

'Why, nothing. It's not uncommon for young men like us to build up a few debts here and there. It must be difficult mixing in circles like these, without the means to make the best of it. Not on a junior clerk's salary, anyway. But you have a generous patron, which is as good as having a wealthy father.'

'Alcimus is a great Roman, as you said.' Arvandus kept his voice level, trying to conceal his annoyance. Who had told Paulus about his debts? He had suffered another run of sour luck at the races, that was all. Everyone went through bad patches.

'It's funny, though,' said Paulus. 'When I think of great Romans of our day, I think of Aëtius, of course, and Eparchius Avitus, Ferreolus, and so on. But then I can't help thinking of King Theoderic. Strange, isn't it? I know what you're thinking. How can a barbarian be a great Roman? But that's what he is. People forget that Aëtius himself has some Gothic blood in him. I think Romanness is a quality that lies in the soul.'

'I'm sure you're right.'

'The king is generous, too. He's started looking for poets and lawyers to bring to the royal court, and he wants to patronise the schools again. He's determined to make Bordeaux a greater centre of learning than Narbonne – "Let us lure Pallas Athena back to the Garonne," he says. Isn't that charming? Anyway, I thought that might interest you. King Theoderic is always looking for new advisors.'

'Thank you, but I serve the empire.'

'There's not much difference between serving the empire and serving King Theoderic. Think of him as another praetorian prefect.'

'I know what the difference is,' said Arvandus firmly. He left Paulus and pushed his way through the crowd, not heading in any particular direction. He had been in Arles long enough to know when someone was attempting to manipulate him, and Paulus had not tried to be subtle. It was better not to be seen talking to him. Even if everything else he had said was true, Theoderic was no Roman. The Goths had never built an empire. Rome's glory was not theirs to claim. They were parasites, nothing more.

'Arvandus,' came a voice that he had not heard for a long time.

As soon as he saw who had spoken, his heart began to thump as though gone mad. The strength drained from his legs. 'Attica,' he said. 'I mean, my lady.' He bowed.

'I wasn't expecting to see you here,' she said, the cheerfulness in her voice almost turning to laughter. Her eyes were wonderfully bright, shining with her pearl earrings and her necklace of gold and gemstones. She held a full glass of wine. Arvandus could tell that it was not her first.

'I'm advisor to the curator of letters now,' he said.

'That's wonderful! I always knew you'd achieve great things.'

Arvandus glanced over his shoulder, unable to shake the fear that they were being watched, but the guests around them seemed to be consumed in their own conversations. 'How is your husband?' he asked.

'Felix is as felicitous as always,' she said, laughing at her own joke. 'Sidonius has fathered a second daughter, did you know?'

'I didn't. That's wonderful news.'

'Isn't it? They're at Lupiacum now. If Sidonius had known you would be here, I'm sure he'd have come. I wish he had. I'd cut my arm off for someone interesting to talk to. But then, here you are!' She reached out and touched his arm. 'Tell me, whatever happened to those Frankish butcher friends of yours?'

He took a discreet step backwards. She was drunk. 'Thuringian. They're still in Arles, I believe. I haven't seen them in over a year.'

'You move in different circles now.' Again she touched his arm. He could not step back without colliding with another guest. She brushed her fingers up his sleeve, bringing them to rest on the bronze brooch at his shoulder. 'Personally,' she whispered, 'I think gold would look better on you.'

At that moment Arvandus noticed Felix on the other side of the room. He was looking about with his neck craned, clearly searching for Attica. He spotted her, saw her fingers were still resting on the brooch, and saw the owner of the brooch. He started through the crowd towards them, his nostrils flaring.

A loud voice suddenly interrupted every conversation in the room. 'I have an announcement.' It was Ferreolus. Everyone fell silent. Felix stopped where he was. Arvandus noticed a dispatch rider standing beside the prefect. 'News has arrived from Italy,' he continued, holding up a letter. 'Count Aëtius is dead. He has been slain by the emperor's own hand.'

There were gasps of horror and disbelief. At once the room filled with chatter. Arvandus saw someone take hold of Felix and start talking to him. Men flocked to Ferreolus and the dispatch rider, asking for more news.

Taking advantage of the distraction, Arvandus slipped away from Attica, ignoring her entreaties. He did not need the trouble of Felix chasing him down. He pushed through the pressing bodies to the atrium, and into the entrance hall. The doorman hauled open one of the doors to let him out into the courtyard.

The sky had become overcast. Soft autumn rain pattered on the flagstones. *Aëtius is dead*, he thought, the words echoing in his head. *Slain by the emperor's own hand.*

Was it even true? The letter had looked like an official report from Italy. It had to be true. He tried to calm his racing thoughts and work out what it meant for Gaul. Aëtius had always been a hero on this side of the Alps. He had spent thirty years defending Gaul's borders, protecting its cities, defeating its enemies, while Valentinian had sat in distant Ravenna and never once visited his Gallic subjects. No doubt the official story was that Aëtius had been plotting against the emperor. The people of Gaul would think it a pity he had not succeeded.

Figures began to emerge from the palace entrance, hurrying past him across the courtyard. The party was over. Within an hour the news would have spread to every house and tavern in Arles, within weeks it would have spread throughout Gaul, to the court of every last barbarian king. Everything Aëtius had fought for would soon be in the balance.

The only ones to celebrate his passing would be the Philagrii. Their oldest rival was gone at last.

XXXV

Attica had never seen her husband so happy. He entered their Arles town house with fast, energetic strides. He stopped in the atrium, pulled off his cloak, threw it into the arms of a house servant.

'A glass of water,' he commanded. He looked at Attica, grinning like a boy back from his first hunt. 'He's gone at last, the old bastard. I was starting to think that sorceress wife of his had given him a potion of eternal life.'

She thought of the wife, Pelagia, whom she had seen at the theatre show three years before. The official report, read out by Ferreolus to the party guests, had stated only that Aëtius and all of his co-conspirators and sympathisers had been justly punished. This, she suspected, meant that Pelagia and all of Aëtius's friends in Rome had been killed. She was not sorry to see the end of Aëtius, who had executed her aunt and uncle, but it seemed cruel to have slaughtered so many with him.

'This might be the one courageous thing our emperor has ever done,' Felix said. 'It'll be good for us, too. Did you see their faces at the party? I had to stand there and look distraught with the rest of them. After this, Valentinian will need to find friends in Gaul, and quickly. He's bound to approach our family, he knows what Aëtius did to us.' He came closer and placed a hand on her cheek. The coldness of his touch had an unpleasantly sobering effect on her. 'I told you once I'd make our family patrician again. This is the first step.'

A figure emerged from the door that led to the kitchen. It was Ajax. A long hooded cloak hung over his shoulders. 'What's he doing here?' she asked.

Felix ignored her. 'Did you find him?'

Ajax nodded. 'We caught him before he reached his apartment.'

'I don't need to know where you got him. Just bring him to us.'

'Yes, my lord.' Ajax headed back into the kitchen.

Attica was gripped by a nervous fear. 'Who is he bringing?'

'You want to be the wife of a patrician, don't you, my dear? Then you should know that with such status come certain expectations. The wife of a patrician behaves with dignity and decency. She obeys her husband. She does not prostitute herself to low-born scoundrels.'

There were sounds of scuffling from the kitchen. Ajax reappeared, pushing before him a struggling captive with bound wrists and a sack tied over his head. Ajax kicked him in the back of the knee, and he fell to the floor with a cry of pain. He raised himself onto his hands and knees, his heavy panting muffled by the fabric over his mouth.

'Take off the sack,' Felix said.

Ajax obeyed. Arvandus blinked in the daylight, gasping for air.

Attica looked at his face in horror. It was bloody, bruised, broken. *This is my fault,* she thought, her head swimming. *I have done this to him.*

Arvandus stared at her. One of his eyes was uninjured, but the other was swollen shut. A messy trail of blood ran from his nose to his chin. He reached out to her. 'Attica, please . . .'

Ajax kicked him in the stomach, making him roll over onto his back, clutching himself, his face screwed up in agony.

'Don't!' Attica screamed. 'Felix, what is this? Let him go!'

He laughed. 'Why should I? This rat tried to seduce my wife in public. I saw it with my own eyes. What do you expect me to do?'

'You know that's not true. It was me. I did it because I despise you.'

The humour faded from his lips, leaving only cruelty. He nodded to Ajax.

The bodyguard bent down, with his left hand he took a handful of Arvandus's tunic to lift his head from the floor, and then punched him.

'Stop,' Attica cried, her voice breaking in her throat. 'Leave him alone.' She reached out with both hands and gripped Felix by the shoulders. '*Leave him alone.*'

Felix nodded again to Ajax. Another punch. Arvandus made a grunt and a gargling noise. His head hung back limply, his good eye fluttering.

Mustering all her strength, Attica slapped Felix across his cheek. He stumbled, almost falling. At once Ajax dropped Arvandus and advanced to protect his master. 'Bitch,' spat Felix. He looked up at Ajax and gestured to Attica.

Ajax stepped towards her. He was enormous. For a moment he merely looked at her, like a wolf glowering over its prey. Then he drew his right hand back, and struck her.

There was a brief, black oblivion, and she found herself on the cold marble floor, her shawl tangled about her arms. She had been hit only once before, by Ecdicius, but not like this. She felt as though her cheekbone had been shattered. 'I'll tell my brother.'

'No you won't,' Felix said. 'If you do, I'll see to it that your sweetheart suffers a very slow and unpleasant death indeed.'

She struggled to her feet. At that moment Cyra entered the atrium, saw her, and cried out in shock. She came running to her mistress. Ajax grabbed her, lifting her from the ground as she struggled and screamed.

'Tell your girl to be quiet,' Felix said, 'or Ajax will silence her.'

Attica steadied herself on her feet. 'Do as he says, Cyra.' The handmaiden calmed, but Ajax did not let go of her. Attica rearranged her shawl. 'You'll let Arvandus go free?' she said to Felix.

'I will,' he said. He looked over at Arvandus, who was still on his back, groaning. 'But his career is over.' Felix went to Arvandus, and bent down to remove the bronze brooch from his shoulder. He studied it for a moment before tossing it into the atrium pool. 'Let the girl go,' he said to Ajax, then pointed at Arvandus. 'And get this creature out of my house.'

XXXVI
Orléans, A.D. 455

King Sangiban claimed that King Riothamus had started it. Riothamus claimed the opposite. Ecdicius did not care who was telling the truth. He cared only about the scores of towns and villages between Orléans and Rennes that had been raided, the hundreds of innocents who had been slaughtered or enslaved, the countless cattle that had been stolen. Within the last four months sporadic raids had grown into a full-scale war between the Alans and the Armoricans. It was an affront to Roman authority.

'It must stop,' Ecdicius said, looking at each king in turn. 'You are both sworn to preserve the peace.'

Sangiban slouched on his chair, legs spread apart. He had grown corpulent in the last couple of years, his age beginning to show in his sagging cheeks and white-streaked beard. 'I made a treaty with Rome,' he said. He gave a contemptuous nod in the direction of Riothamus. 'Not with *him*.'

The young king of Armorica, not yet twenty, sat straight-backed, his chest pushed out and his clean-shaven chin held high. He stared at Sangiban with fierce eyes. 'So you admit to starting it.'

'I admit to no such thing. *You* sent raids across the Mayenne. I merely defended my territory.'

Riothamus scoffed. 'You defended your territory by pillaging Nantes?'

'Enough,' said Ecdicius. A springtime breeze gusted through the open door of the tent, filling it with the sounds of the cavalry camp. The kings glared at one another in silence. In all likelihood neither of them had started the war. Probably some local chieftain, hungry for glory and plunder, had raided his neighbour. That had demanded retaliation, and so it had grown. But no king would admit to being unable to control his own vassals, and so there was nothing left for them to do but blame one another. 'Emperor Valentinian doesn't care how the war started. You've both lost too many men. Rome does not want her allies spilling each other's blood.'

'Rome doesn't care about our blood,' sneered Riothamus. 'Rome abandoned my homeland to the Saxon wolves. Rome watched as Britain burned from coast to coast, and my family were forced into exile. Ten thousand men, Aëtius promised us. Where are they?'

Ecdicius had no answer for that. He knew how Britain had fallen prey to the sea-roving tribes of Germany and Ireland, its citizens left to their fate. Those with the means had fled across the sea to Armorica, where they had roused the natives to open rebellion against the empire. Riothamus, the new king of the exiled Britons, spoke with all the bitterness of this legacy.

'Don't waste your time asking, lad,' said Sangiban. 'Rome doesn't have ten thousand men to spare for the likes of you. "Allies", he calls us. We're nothing but lambs to be slaughtered whenever it suits them.'

'As you like,' said Ecdicius, his patience wearing thin. 'Perhaps we don't have ten thousand men to spare. But King Theoderic does. He's as good as a brother to me. Do you want a Gothic army marching on your borders?'

'They'd never make it across the Loire,' Sangiban said.

The king's words were defiant, but Ecdicius could sense the fear behind them. Sangiban had wrestled with the Goths more than once in the past, and always come off the worse for it. 'And what about the Franks?' Ecdicius said. 'Count Aegidius need only say the word, and King Childeric will march on you from the north.'

Sangiban shifted in his seat. 'He wouldn't dare.'

Ecdicius was about to reply when a young staff officer entered the tent. 'Tribune,' he said, saluting. 'The count requests your presence.'

'Tell him I'll come shortly.'

'Apologies, tribune. He said you were to come immediately.'

Ecdicius nodded. It was frustrating, but Aegidius knew that he was talking with the kings. He would not disturb him if it were not important. He rose from his chair. 'Whatever your private disagreements,' he said, looking each king in the eye, 'Rome regards this violence as a breach of your treaties. It will come to an end, one way or another.'

He left the tent without giving them a chance to respond. There was little point continuing the discussion. Nothing short of such threats would keep them in line, but Ecdicius was not confident even of that. Sangiban was old and complacent, and Riothamus was young, with everything to prove and all the pride that came with youth. Neither of them feared Aegidius, who had been made count and appointed master of soldiers in Gaul only a year previously; Ecdicius had replaced him as tribune of the First Gallic Horse at the same time, and the kings feared him even less.

The personal guards of the two kings were lounging on the grass in separate groups, eyeing each other suspiciously. Ecdicius walked between them and continued the short distance to Aegidius's command tent. The walls of Orléans were fifty yards distant, still bearing some scars from the siege of Attila almost four years ago. Ecdicius could not believe that so much time had passed. His memory of the slaughter at the river was so vivid, as though it had happened yesterday.

The current unrest had followed the death of Aëtius. The petty war between the Alans of Orléans and the Armoricans had started as soon as news of his assassination had reached the north, just before winter. Spring had brought Saxon raids on the northern coast of Gaul, and there were reports of conflict on the Rhine. The barbarian tribes were like a pack of hunting dogs who had lost their master; without Aëtius to keep them in line, the snarling and snapping had already begun. Ecdicius could only pray that the empire would stand firm, and keep hold of what Aëtius had built. Otherwise it would not be long before the barbarians turned their greedy eyes towards Roman territory.

The staff officer waited outside the command tent while Ecdicius entered. He was about to salute when he froze in shock. It was a mess. The desk was lying upside-down, rolls of papyrus and wooden tablets scattered across the rug. A brazier had been knocked over. Platters and goblets were strewn in every corner. Aegidius was standing with his back to the entrance. In his hand he clutched a letter.

Ecdicius took a cautious step forwards. 'You summoned me, my lord?'

Aegidius turned. His eyes were blazing with fury. His mouth was tight, his nostrils flared. He was a man of strong passions, but Ecdicius had rarely seen him like this. When he spoke, his voice was strangely weak. 'The emperor is dead.'

Ecdicius opened his mouth, but no words came out.

'Assassinated on the Field of Mars,' Aegidius continued. He brandished the letter.

'Who?'

'Petronius Maximus, the senator. He's had himself proclaimed emperor.' He snorted in disgust. 'I can't say I'm surprised.'

Ecdicius glanced back through the entrance to make sure that no one but the staff officer was outside. He pulled the flaps shut and turned back to Aegidius. 'The kings must not hear about this.'

'They will, sooner or later.'

'They already think we're weak. If they hear that the emperor has been killed – losing Aëtius was bad enough, but this . . .'

'I know. They'll take advantage.' He shrugged. 'But if they do, at least it won't be my problem.'

'What do you mean?'

'I've been removed from my post,' Aegidius said. 'Your father is now master of soldiers in Gaul.'

'That can't be so. Why?'

'He's respected by everyone in Gaul, even the barbarians. He's safe. Petronius knows he can be relied on.'

'He won't accept the appointment. He's too old.'

'You know your father better than that. He won't refuse an imperial command, not even if it comes from Petronius

Maximus. I knew this would happen sooner or later. With Aëtius murdered, it was only a matter of time before I was removed. Majorian has already been called out of retirement and made count of the emperor's household guard. He's back in, and now I'm out. Aëtius trained both of us. We were like brothers. I never thought it would come to this.' He tossed the letter on the ground with the other detritus. 'Politics.'

Now Ecdicius understood Aegidius's anger. He was not sorry for the death of Valentinian, the slayer of Aëtius. He was angry because of his own dismissal. His purpose in life was being stolen from him. Ecdicius remembered how that felt.

But it didn't have to be that way. 'There's another option,' said Ecdicius. 'Take back command of the First Gallic Horse.'

'You're their tribune now.'

'My father will want me on his personal staff. I can recommend you to replace me. I know it would be a demotion, but surely it's better than retirement.'

'The emperor would never accept it.'

'He won't have a choice. Petronius has hardly any friends in Gaul, he'll need my father's support.'

Aegidius stroked his beard. 'Are you sure your father will agree to this? He knows I was one of Aëtius's men.'

'My father isn't a political man. He knows you're a good soldier, and loyal to Rome. That's all that matters to him. He'll accept you, if you accept him.'

Aegidius nodded. 'Very well, then. Tell your father I'm willing to serve him.' He picked up a small wooden tube from the ground and handed it to Ecdicius. 'This contains your father's letter of appointment. I suggest you bring it to him at once. Take my staff with you, and Messianus, too. He's an old friend of your family, and your father will want officers he can trust. I'll promote Secundus to replace him as tribune of the Senior Cornuti.'

It was difficult to leave his regiment so suddenly, but Ecdicius knew that time was short. With the situation in the north already so unstable, it was crucial that his father re-establish control as soon as possible. There would be difficult months ahead.

The journey to Clermont took a week. Tribune Messianus, a veteran of more than twenty years, proved to be a grim riding companion. He was balding, large-nosed, his weather-beaten face set in a permanent scowl that spoke of his long years of service. Ecdicius had never once seen him smile. It was rare for him to raise his voice, or to say one word more than was necessary. But he was tough and dependable, and that was what they needed.

Ecdicius did not find his father at Clermont. It was late April, and the weather was already warm enough that the family had withdrawn to their country estate at Avitacum, deep in the hills to the south of the city. The property had been part of Papianilla's dowry and so now belonged to Sidonius, but Avitus and Severiana still stayed there every summer. They had taken well to their roles as devoted grandparents.

As Ecdicius came within sight of Avitacum, Messianus and the dozen men of his father's new staff behind him, he felt the comfortable embrace of old memories. He had spent much of his childhood here, racing along the reedy shores of the lake, swimming in its cool waters, lounging on the portico of the villa and listening to the *ribbetting* of the frogs when the sun glowed heavy above the hills to the west. He knew every inch of the land, had climbed every tree, from the grey willows by the water-course, to the alders that loomed over sunken fields of bulrush, and the barren ash trees on the rocky heights above. Its meadows were where he had learned to ride, and where Zephyros was now enjoying a contented retirement. Even the sweet scent of manure in the fields stirred an old fondness.

This was what they stood to lose. If feuding barbarians dragged Gaul into war, there was no telling where it would end. This place might become another ruined shell, like so many he had seen in the north. That must not happen.

He spurred his horse down the track that led around the side of the lake to the villa. By the time he came to the courtyard, the sight of approaching soldiers had already drawn the house steward to the entrance. He bowed when he saw who it was. 'Master Ecdicius,' he said. 'This is a surprise – I regret that we had no news of your coming. We heard about the death of the emperor. When I saw soldiers approaching . . .'

'Don't worry, Vettius, it's all right. Where's my father?'

'Up on the high pasture, with the sheep. Lord Sidonius is there as well.'

At any other time Ecdicius would have laughed at the thought of Sidonius getting dirty in a sheepfold. 'Please take Messianus to my mother; he'll explain everything to her. We'll need stabling for our mounts, and food. Our men can bathe in the lake. I'm going to see my father.'

Vettius bowed, and with his customary efficiency clapped his hands to summon the stable boys, shouting out commands as the soldiers dismounted. Ecdicius set off up the track that led to the high pasture. As soon as he glimpsed the wooden sheepfold near the crest of the slope, he left the track and galloped across the open grass towards it. His father was standing outside the enclosure, leaning on the wooden fence with a handful of farm workers. Sidonius was inside, wearing the rough clothes of a commoner. The sleeves and skirt of his tunic were short, revealing his delicately white forearms and legs. He appeared to be attempting to catch a sheep while his father-in-law gave instructions, neither enjoying much success.

They noticed Ecdicius as he approached. He brought his mount to a stop before them and leaped smoothly from the saddle. He walked to his father.

'We weren't expecting you,' said Avitus, embracing him. 'Are you well?'

'Well, Father, very well. Sollius – you're learning the noble art of husbandry?'

'Slowly,' he said.

Ecdicius smiled. He reached for the satchel hanging around his neck, and pulled out the wooden tube containing the letter of appointment. He knelt before his father and presented it to him.

Avitus took the tube, opened it, and withdrew the rolled document within. He read the message in silence. When he was finished, he said: 'So much for retirement. Emperor Petronius has appointed me master of soldiers.' He stood there in his mud-smeared tunic and sandals, clutching the piece of papyrus that had made him the most powerful man outside Italy. Something in his demeanour changed: his chest tightened, his eyes narrowed, as though he saw the whole of Gaul suddenly laid out before him. Aegidius had been right; whatever he thought of Petronius, Avitus was a soldier. He did not have it in him to resist an imperial command.

'Messianus awaits you at the villa,' said Ecdicius, rising. 'The Alans and Armoricans are still at war. We've reports of Saxons raiding the north coast, Franks in Second Belgium and Alemanni west of the Rhine.'

Avitus nodded. 'Then we'll need to assemble a mobile force and march north as soon as possible. We have to show them the empire is still strong, establish new treaties.'

'What about the Goths?'

'Theoderic's treaty was with Valentinian. He's dead, so the treaty is void. Until Theoderic swears to a new treaty, our borders aren't safe.' He pointed the document at Sidonius. 'It seems I'm pressing you back into service as my secretary, this time officially. If you think sheep are tricky, wait till you try handling a barbarian.'

The three of them rode together back to the villa, Ecdicius telling them as much as he knew about the military situation. He then asked his father if he had more news about events in Italy.

'We heard that Petronius has already married the emperor's widow,' Avitus said. 'He's also made Princess Eudocia marry his son.'

'Do you know Petronius well, Father?'

'I've never met the man, but I've seen him speak in the Senate. He's very wealthy, very influential, a two-time consul, four-time prefect, and patrician. Ambitious. The unofficial rumour is that he wanted to be master of soldiers. Valentinian refused, so Petronius had him assassinated. The army in Italy supports him, and the Senate of course, but Count Marcellinus in Dalmatia has revolted. He was another old comrade of Aëtius

– a good man, loyal to his friends. As for the east, I'd be surprised if Emperor Marcian will accept Valentinian's killer as co-emperor.'

Ecdicius still found it hard to believe. 'Will there be civil war?'

Avitus gave a grim nod. 'Very likely. But for now our task is to keep Gaul secure. That's all that matters.'

XXXVII

May and June became one long military parade. Ecdicius, on the staff of his father, helped marshal the army at Lyons, and they marched north immediately. It was only a modest force of three thousand Roman cavalry and infantry, but the presence of Avitus was enough to subdue Sangiban and Riothamus without need of violence. By the time they reached Paris the Saxon raids on the north coast had abated, and so Avitus merely sent scouting detachments to assess the damage and see what could be done to repair it. Next the army headed north-east through the old province of Second Belgium, passing through Amiens and coming to Tournai, the capital of King Childeric of the Salian Franks.

Childeric had taken sorely the death of his foster-father, Aëtius, who had installed him as king after the defeat of Attila. When they went to him in the basilica that passed for his royal hall, Ecdicius found the long-haired king, who was no older than Riothamus, to be prickly and unpleasant. He was draped over a richly cushioned throne, a pair of beautiful slave girls at his feet, his vassal lords arranged behind him. Ecdicius would not have taken him seriously, had he not already proven himself to be a ruthless warrior. Only two months earlier he had captured a boatload of Saxons at Boulogne. He had ordered their hair shaved, their eyes put out, and their noses and ears cut off, and had put them back out to sea in their boat, stripped naked and bound, with neither oars nor rudder. The Saxon raids had stopped soon after that.

Ecdicius paid careful attention to his father as he talked with the king. Childeric was claiming a blood-feud against Petronius for conspiring in the murder of his foster-father, and spat with anger as he cursed the new emperor. It soon became apparent that his outrage was feigned, a mere negotiating tactic. Showing even temper and respect, Avitus promised Childeric dominion over several more towns to the south, and eventually persuaded him to renew his pledge to the empire. Then he ordered a barrel of Italian wine to be rolled into the hall, and they swore friendship with filled cups. Now Ecdicius saw why his father had ordered a wagon full of wine barrels to be brought with the army. The northern kings loved wine almost as much as they loved gold.

From Tournai they took the road south to Reims, and then east, through a country of thick forests and deep river valleys, to Trier. As they neared the Rhine they began to see evidence of the Alemannic raiding: a few burned-out farmsteads along the Moselle, acres of neglected crop fields whose owners had not yet returned, if they ever would. At Strasbourg, Avitus met with Prince Gebavult, the audacious young man who had launched the invasion. He feared the Franks, however, and soon agreed to a new treaty when he heard that Childeric had already done so.

It had taken many weeks of constant marching, traipsing thirty miles a day over roads that had not been repaired for years, or were drowned by springtime floods and barred by fallen trees, but at last the north was secure. They followed the road south along the Rhine, skirting the edge of the Burgundian kingdom – King Gundioc, at least, had remained loyal to Rome – and came west to the Saône. After a few days of rest at Lyons, they climbed back into the saddle and headed south-west for Aquitaine and the kingdom of the Goths.

On the twenty-first day of June they finally reached Toulouse, royal seat of King Theoderic. Ecdicius was about ready to fall from his horse with weariness. The city's encircling walls of brick lay beside the broad expanse of the Garonne; the river looked sluggish and dark in the evening light, the city itself half-asleep as dusk drew a shadowy veil over the east. They had covered a thousand miles in the last two months, a sweeping circle around

Gaul. Through all this his father had been tireless. Ecdicius had never once seen him give any hint of fatigue, even though he was over sixty years old.

'This will be the greatest test,' Avitus said to his son as they neared the city. Ahead of them Aegidius was leading a detachment from the First Gallic Horse as the vanguard. A Gothic host was assembling outside the gates of Toulouse, ready to receive them. 'The northern kings are troublesome, but they care more for raiding than conquest. The Goths are more like us – too much like us. Don't be fooled by the years of peace. They're the wolf in our midst, always have been.'

Ecdicius was surprised to hear his father describe them in such a way. 'I thought you believed in friendship with the Goths.'

'I do, after a fashion. Aëtius tried to chain the wolf and beat it with rods. I intend to tame it with kindness and make it our guard dog.'

Ecdicius prayed that his father would succeed. Not even he seemed to know which way the young Theoderic would turn. He might renounce all friendship with Rome. He might denounce Petronius as a usurper and claim all of Gaul in the name of the eastern emperor.

Ecdicius straightened his back, pushed his chest forwards, and tried to imitate his father's noble demeanour. It was important to show their strength, for awaiting them at the gates of Toulouse, mounted on a proud white stallion, a golden crown on his head, was King Theoderic himself. Ecdicius had not seen him in four years, when he had been a mere prince. Much had changed since then, but he had the same intelligent stare beneath heavy eyebrows, the same firm-set mouth, the same bear pelt around his shoulders. By his side, also mounted and crowned, was his brother, Vice-king Frideric, and behind them were the three younger brothers, Euric, Ricimer and Himnerith, all still youths. The royal Gothic horse guard were arranged on either side, a spectacle of gleaming mail, long cloaks and tall helmets, bronze horse trappings; their lances were topped with green pennants that fluttered in the breeze. The road beyond was lined first with the fur-clad Gothic elders, and then with churchmen and the leading Roman citizens of Toulouse, some of the older men wearing their traditional togas. The common citizens were packed along the rest of the road as far as the city gates, held back by Gothic foot soldiers.

Aegidius halted the vanguard in front of the Goths, and moved aside to allow Avitus to approach the king. Ecdicius watched as they saluted one another from horseback. Avitus was the first to speak. 'Most noble King Theoderic: I, Eparchius Avitus, master of soldiers, address you in the name of his excellency, Emperor Petronius Maximus. His excellency desires that the old friendship between Romans and Goths is renewed – and not merely renewed, but strengthened, so that our peoples, cousins by descent from Mars, will be joined for ever in alliance.'

It was a fine speech, composed to flatter. The mention of Mars had been Sidonius's idea. The Goths liked to think of themselves as descended from that old god, the traditional father of the Roman people.

Theoderic's reply was short. 'I accept the friendship of your emperor. Let there be for ever peace between our peoples.'

The royal guard cheered, thrusting their lances high; the foot soldiers clashed spears on shields; the people of Toulouse erupted with applause that filled the air and rebounded from the city walls. Ecdicius joined the Roman column in their own cheers. Avitus and Theoderic both dismounted, walked to one another, clasped shoulders, and kissed. They exchanged a few words Ecdicius could not hear. His father's face was hidden from him, but Theoderic was giving one of his restrained smiles.

The next morning Ecdicius was sitting bleary-eyed at a desk in his sleeping chamber. He had been able to grab a few short hours of sleep after the previous night's feast. It was not yet dawn, but there was work to be done. After sunrise he was to meet with his father and give him a complete summary of the rest of their forces, as far as he could understand it from the reports. Three burning lamps cast their warm light over the stacks of papyrus and wooden tablets on his desk. They were the latest reports from regular military units in Gaul, brought to the marching column by couriers

over the last few days. Camping outside the walls of Toulouse were
only one cavalry regiment and three infantry regiments: the First
Gallic Horse, the Lions, the Nervian Gallic Archers, and the
Brachians. They, at least, were up to strength.

As he sorted through the documents, Ecdicius realised for
the first time how dependent they were on their barbarian allies
for security. Between Lyons and the upper Rhine were the
Burgundians. The Loire was still guarded by King Sangiban
and his Alans. The cities north of the Loire had their own
militias, locally raised and funded, or relied upon contingents
of settled barbarians. None of those forces was represented on
his desk; they existed outside the command of the master of
soldiers. The reports were from field army regiments dispersed
through various southern cities, from Clermont to Arles.
Ecdicius knew that certain commanders inflated the numbers
under their command in order to receive more rations, but
even so, most units were severely under strength. Almost a
quarter of the regiments on the official list of the Gallic field
army appeared to be in Italy. Still others appeared to be nowhere
at all; either the couriers had not yet arrived, or the regiments
no longer existed and the official lists were out of date. Those
reports he had were inconsistent, with some listing sick and
injured men separately from able-bodied, while others making
no distinction.

This was not the kind of service he was suited for. He yawned,
leaning his elbows on the desk, and closed his eyes. They had
been given guest quarters in a wing of the palace that was near
the kitchens, and through the small window of his room Ecdicius
heard the sounds of the building waking up. A cockerel split the
still morning air. From the chapel came faint singing, as the king
attended his customary pre-dawn religious service with his Arian
bishop. In the courtyard outside, a surly steward was giving orders
for the bath house furnaces to be lit, and for the stables to be
prepared for the royal hunt.

It was discomforting to hear Romans, even mere servants,
rushing to fulfil the desires of a barbarian lord. Ecdicius found

it all too easy to imagine himself in Lyons, Clermont, even Arles. He thanked God that the new treaty was to be formally sworn today. The old friendship between his father and Theoderic would ensure peace. Gaul and Italy had accepted Petronius Maximus as emperor, and the barbarians had also recognised him. Count Marcellinus in Dalmatia was still the only rebel, and he had so far made no claim on the throne himself. Once the Gothic treaty had been sworn, Avitus would return to Arles and make a complete survey of his forces.

Ecdicius allowed himself an optimistic daydream. Perhaps things were not as bad as he had feared. There was now no major barbarian threat against Gaul. The Hunnic empire had collapsed upon Attila's death two years ago; reports from beyond the Danube were sporadic, but it seemed that the barbarian tribes he had pulled together were now tearing each other apart, too busy to cause Rome any trouble. With Goths and Burgundians by his side, perhaps his father could muster the forces he needed to bring the north back under Roman control once and for all. If anyone could tame King Riothamus and the fierce Armorican rebels, it was he. Roman forces might reoccupy the old forts of the Belgian and German provinces, and push the Franks back into their homeland. The Rhine frontier could be garrisoned again by regular troops. And maybe – this is where his daydream became fantasy – maybe Avitus could even cross to Britain like a new Claudius, crushing the Saxon invaders and bringing that distant island, so long fallen into darkness, back into the light of civilisation . . .

His thoughts were interrupted by a commotion somewhere deep in the palace. He heard shouting in Latin and Gothic, and footsteps echoing down corridors. Such disturbance was surely not normal even for a barbarian palace. He rose from the desk, about to investigate the cause.

Before he reached the door, it burst open to reveal Sidonius. He was freshly risen, wearing an unbelted light tunic, his dark hair a tousled mess on his head. The first dawn light was falling through the window, and Ecdicius thought he saw the glint of tears in his eyes. He spoke quickly, straining to catch his breath. 'Ecdicius – Rome – it's been taken. The Vandals. They've taken Rome.'

From a dream Ecdicius plunged into a nightmare. He ran with Sidonius to his father's quarters. Avitus was already awake. When Ecdicius told him the news, he asked at once, 'What about Petronius?'

'Dead,' Sidonius said. Ecdicius had never heard such fear in his cousin's voice. 'Killed by a mob as he tried to escape. The Senate has fled into the countryside. The city was undefended, King Geiseric sailed up the Tiber and landed at the docks.'

Avitus's body servant, a youth, came rushing into the room with his master's clothes. Avitus pulled the tunic over his head without removing his night shirt. The servant knelt to fasten the broad leather belt, his fingers fumbling. 'Calm yourself, boy,' Avitus said, resting a hand on his shoulder. He looked at Sidonius. 'How old is this news?'

'The Vandals attacked three weeks ago. They've been stopping any ships coming along the coast. The messenger had to come all the way by road.'

'So we don't know if Geiseric still holds the city. But is it certain that Petronius is dead?'

'It seems so. And Geiseric has captured Valentinian's widow and daughter.'

Avitus nodded. His expression was grave. 'So we have no emperor. The stupid fool. Petronius angered King Geiseric and then left the city open to attack by sea. I thank God that we're here in Toulouse. First Aëtius, then Valentinian, now this. It's more important than ever to keep peace with the Goths.'

'Will Theoderic still swear to the new treaty?' Ecdicius asked.

'With Petronius dead, there *is* no treaty. The best I can do is ask him for a personal oath to keep the peace until a new emperor is proclaimed. We need to get back to Arles, find out what's happening in Italy. By Christ, it's like the whole world is falling apart.'

A palace servant appeared at the door. Two armoured Gothic soldiers, members of the royal guard, stood behind him. 'Noble count,' the servant said, bowing. 'His Majesty King Theoderic requests your presence at his council.'

The soldiers escorted them to the palace basilica. They entered the great gloomy hall to the sound of vociferous Gothic debate. The voices were coming from the far end of the basilica, which was screened off by heavy green curtains. The soldiers drew the curtains apart to let them enter.

Theoderic was sitting on his throne in the apse of the basilica. Vice-king Frideric was on a smaller throne beside him. On the marble flagstones in front of them stood a crowd of twenty or so Gothic elders. As Ecdicius, Avitus and Sidonius entered, their voices faded and they turned to stare at the newcomers. The Goths wore their traditional costume: linen tunics fastened at the waist with leather belts, bearskin cloaks that hung down to the knees, tall boots of woven horsehair. Each man was bearded, dignified. They nodded at Avitus with respect.

'Count Avitus,' said Theoderic, beckoning for him to come closer. The elders parted to let Avitus approach the thrones. Ecdicius and Sidonius remained standing just inside the curtains.

'Your Majesty,' said Avitus, and bowed.

'Count, you said yesterday that Goths and Romans are cousins by descent from Mars. The treacherous Geiseric has violated Mother Rome, and today we are brothers in grief.'

'Thank you, Majesty. I never dreamed that God would punish us with such a disaster as this. You know I'm a man of peace. I was reluctant to obey the summons of my emperor and leave retirement. I came to you as his ambassador, and now I find that I have no emperor.'

'Indeed. So what do you intend to do?'

'For now, we must wait – we must all wait. I beg you to keep the spirit of peace. Remember how often I advised your father in the past. I negotiated the peace at Narbonne, I negotiated our alliance against Attila. When you were a baby I used to hold you in my arms, and you'd scream if the nurse tried to take you away.' He scanned the elders for familiar faces. 'Amalec, Theowulf – you remember how he used to be?' The elders nodded, and smiled. Avitus turned back to the king. 'When there is a new emperor, I'll return in his name with another treaty. But for now, in memory of my friendship with your father, in honour of the old love between us, I ask only that you keep the peace.'

There was murmuring among the elders, but Ecdicius could not understand their Gothic speech. He hoped that their mutterings were sympathetic.

Theoderic raised his hand, and the council fell silent. 'But with no emperor,' he said, 'there can be no peace agreement.'

Avitus clasped his hands together. 'I beg you, in honour of your father—'

Theoderic cut him off. 'You needn't invoke my father. I remember what you always said: "Gothic arms and Roman law are destined to rule the world." I swear in the name of God, in the name of Rome herself, that I desire peace with the empire. But an empire needs an emperor.'

'Yes, Majesty. Soon we'll have word from Italy. We just need to wait.'

'Why all this talk about waiting?' Rising from the throne, he lifted a powerful arm and pointed at Avitus. 'Am I blind, or do I see an emperor standing here among us?'

This time there was no doubting the attitude of the Gothic elders, who began to voice their approval. Avitus looked as though he had taken a blow to the chin. He stepped backwards, turning to face the elders with an expression close to panic. 'No,' he said. 'This is treason.'

'Treason?' said Theoderic. 'How can it be treason, when there's no emperor, when the imperial family has been taken captive, when Rome herself has fallen? I know we can't make you emperor. We can only propose it to you. You must be made emperor by the people of Gaul – your own people, your own soldiers. But I swear, in the presence of my elders, that there's no other man I'll suffer to see seated on the Palatine Hill.'

His brother got to his feet and voiced his agreement, and the elders began cheering again. A chant emerged, simple and plain: *Avitus Augustus.*

Avitus raised his hands, and slowly the chanting stopped. 'I do not accept your acclamation,' he said, 'but nor do I reject it. First I must discuss the matter with my staff, and consider the desires of the people of Gaul.'

'Do so,' said Theoderic. 'But be swift. The empire is in peril, my friend.'

Avitus turned and pushed through the curtains into the body of the hall, Ecdicius and Sidonius immediately behind. They found Messianus, Aegidius and a number of junior staff officers waiting at the doors, all in battle dress. Messianus spoke. 'Your troops are ready to proclaim you, my lord.'

'No,' said Avitus. 'I forbid it. Not here in Toulouse. If it happens, it must be in Roman territory, and there must be civilians, not just the army.'

'My father's right,' said Ecdicius. 'If he's proclaimed here, people will call him a Gothic puppet.'

'I agree,' said Aegidius. 'We'll need donatives for the troops, too. Five solidi and a pound of silver per head. It'll take time to gather it.'

Avitus nodded. 'We'll march east at once. I want messengers sent in every direction. Any who support us will be generously rewarded. Have them say that we'll assemble in Beaucaire. If the people of Gaul desire it, I'll accept their acclamation.'

'Done,' said Messianus. 'And after that?'

Avitus clenched his jaw and set off through the doors. 'Then we liberate Rome,' he said, his heavy footsteps echoing in the arched roof of the corridor.

XXXVIII

The imperial mills north of Arles

The noise of the mill was deafening: the angry grinding of the granite millstone, the squealing of the oiled wooden shafts, and the monotonous clunking of the spokes from the floor below, the rushing and sloshing of the water in the waterwheel outside, all of it colliding in a cacophony that choked the air along with the clouds of flour dust.

'You're three measures short,' Arvandus shouted again. The slave boy stared at him blankly, either stupid or feigning stupidity. Perhaps working in the mill for so long had made him deaf. Arvandus gave up, closed his wax tablet, and headed for the door, stepping aside to let another slave enter with a sack of grain on his shoulders.

The heat outside was searing. Arvandus removed his straw hat and wiped the sweat from his brow, blinking in the sun. He was standing at the bottom of a monumental staircase that had been built into the side of a rocky slope. The steep flight of steps rose fifty feet above his head, flanked on both sides by a cascade of two-storey millhouses – sixteen in total, each with its own waterwheel and millstone, its own slave crew, its own sacks of grain waiting to be ground, and flour waiting to be carried down to the barges. Slaves toiled up and down the stairs like ants, bent beneath their loads. These mills produced almost three hundred sacks of flour every day. Three full sacks from each mill every hour, every one of which needed to be checked and accounted for by Arvandus before it was loaded onto the barges below. It was all he could do to keep track of them. Every day spent running up and down those steps left him physically exhausted. It was a job for a slave, especially on a hot July day like this.

Four months he had been here now, having been promised that the job would last for just two weeks before he was transferred to the manager's staff in the city. That had not happened. He stayed here, taking his measly salary at this miserable flour factory in the hills five miles from Arles, only because he had no choice. After the curator of letters had dismissed him, the best post he could find had been this junior clerkship under the manager of the public mills, but it was a dead-end job. He had been unable to find another position on the prefect's staff. Felix had seen to that. No one was willing to cross the Philagrii, especially not in these uncertain times. Aëtius was dead, Valentinian was dead, and now the usurper Petronius Maximus was dead after just seventy-eight days on the throne – stoned to death and thrown in the Tiber, people said. Nobody knew who the new emperor was, or even if there was one. Rome itself had been captured by the Vandals. With the world on a precipice, it was not a good time to be upsetting the most powerful family in Gaul.

The worst part was being removed from everything that was happening in the city. He had to make do with whatever news filtered up on the grain barges. The frustration was tearing him apart. He needed to be back at the centre of things. Even a humble post in the manager's office would be better than this. Here in the hills, surrounded by slaves and sweat and dust, he was nothing. Felix would laugh to see him now.

He decided to talk to the mill overseer again, though he despised the man more every time they spoke. It was not just Bricianus's waddling gait or his drooping lip that offended Arvandus, nor even the casual cruelty with which he ruled his little kingdom. It was his predilection for the slave boys he employed to sweep the mill floors and clean the machinery of the waterwheels. Several times a day Bricianus would disappear with one of the boys into the lower storey of a mill, imagining that the noise was enough to conceal what he did down there.

Arvandus spotted the overseer on the concrete platform next to the canal, where a team of bargemen was unloading yet more sacks of grain to be carried up the steps. He was talking to a church deacon whom Arvandus recognised as the Bishop of Arles' estate manager. He began to head towards them. Their conversation did not seem to be a friendly one.

'This is unacceptable,' the deacon was saying. 'His grace will be sending five hundred measures of grain next week, as agreed. He expects it to be milled before the ides of the month.'

Bricianus replied in the whining, obsequious tone he always used when talking to churchmen. 'I can only beg the bishop's forgiveness, but there's nothing I can do. The imperial command came this morning: the army needs the mill. If I say no, they'll have me flogged.'

'Who sent the order?'

'It came directly from the office of Emperor Avitus.'

Arvandus froze. He could not believe what he had just heard. 'Did you say Emperor Avitus? Eparchius Avitus?'

The overseer scowled at him. 'Yes, there's a new emperor,' he snapped, 'or there will be as soon as he's proclaimed. I've received personal instructions from him. Get back to work.'

'Avitus will arrive in Beaucaire tomorrow,' the deacon said. 'His son-in-law is receiving all petitions. I'll meet with him, and make sure that this is sorted out.'

'Forgive the interruption,' Arvandus said, addressing the deacon. 'Do you know which son-in-law?'

'The one married to the elder daughter. Sidonius Apollinaris.'

'I told you to go back to work,' said Bricianus, raising a threatening hand.

Arvandus did not think through his next actions. Sheer instinct made him reach out and grab two handfuls of the overseer's tunic. 'And you go back to fucking your boys,' he snarled, and with all his strength pushed the big man over the edge of the concrete pier. Bricianus fell into the canal with an almighty splash.

The deacon stood in shocked silence. The bargemen laughed. The canal was only two or three feet deep, and Bricianus, after some flailing and spluttering, stood up straight. He was drenched.

'I'll have you convicted for this, you worm!' he screamed, splashing his arms in the water. 'I'll have you sent to the mines!'

Arvandus was already walking away, oblivious to the overseer's ranting. He went to his quarters in the small villa compound nearby, grabbed his clothes and money, and immediately set out for Beaucaire, a small town north of Arles. He would be there by evening, could visit the public baths to wash out the dust from the road, maybe find some lodgings for the night, maybe not; sleeping in the open would actually be pleasant at this time of year. And tomorrow he would go to see Sidonius.

Fresh energy filled his weary legs as he headed down the path that led to the main road. He felt as though he could run the whole ten miles. After months of frustration his luck had turned. Eparchius Avitus knew him personally, and knew his worth. Not even Felix could defy an emperor.

XXXIX

Beaucaire

The public assembly was to take place the following day in the basilica of Beaucaire. Avitus had pitched camp with his army outside the west walls of the town, waiting there until he was invited to enter by the representatives of the Gallic nobility.

Arvandus pushed his way through the crowd that lined the main street. The town was bustling with nobles, commoners, and slaves, thousands of whom had flocked here from Arles and the surrounding country. A little way along the street he spotted a derelict pagan temple whose front steps were quickly filling up with onlookers; slipping through the people, he climbed to the top step, finding a comfortable perch leaning on the base of a column. He had a good view of the street, from the west gate all the way to the basilica.

He had not been waiting long when trumpets blasted outside the town, and the gates were heaved open. At once the street erupted. There were cheers, chants, waving palm branches, wreathes and garlands flung from upper-storey windows. First came a contingent of Roman cavalry, their mounts walking in majestic order, their armour glittering in the sunlight. At their head rode Ecdicius, Arvandus saw with excitement; he yelled out to his friend, but of course went unheard. Eparchius Avitus himself came after the cavalry. He was clad in his military uniform, the heavy cloak hanging from his shoulders, but, to the surprise of the crowd, he was on foot and bare-headed. The confusion only lasted for a brief lull, before the people recognised it for what it was: a gesture of humility. It worked. They roared their appreciation. Avitus kept his eyes fixed ahead, his expression stern.

Next came ranks of infantry marching four abreast, followed

by his civilian staff officers, some mounted, some on foot. Arvandus was looking out for Sidonius when a boy next to him shook his arm and pointed in excitement to the town gate. 'Goths – look, Goths!'

Arvandus turned. The boy was right. A squadron of Gothic lancers was approaching, led by none other than King Theoderic. He had not expected this. It had to be a good sign, though, if Avitus already had the backing of the Gothic king.

The front of the procession had reached the basilica. Arvandus hurried down the temple steps, weaving through the crowd, most of whom were still staring at the Goths in astonishment and delight, and worked his way to the basilica doors. It was smaller than the basilica in Arles, and already packed with the nobility, but he was able to position himself close to the entrance, where he could peer inside and listen to what was said.

On the raised dais at the far end of the hall he glimpsed the praetorian prefect, Priscus Valerianus, take the floor. He had evidently been chosen as spokesman for the nobility of Gaul. As soon as Avitus reached the dais and the rest of the procession had come to a halt on the street outside, Priscus began his address. The crowd quietened as his strong voice carried out through the open doors, every man, woman and child listening to his words. He declared that Gaul was unanimous in its support of Eparchius Avitus. The long reign of the incompetent boy-emperor Valentinian was over, and the usurper Petronius Maximus had likewise fallen; a golden ray of opportunity was shining upon Gaul from Heaven. He used a pretty turn of phrase that pleased the crowd: 'The world lies captive in the city of Rome,' he pronounced. 'The emperor has perished, and now the whole empire has its head here.'

It was a short but powerful speech. When he finished, the pillars of the hall trembled with the applause of the nobles. A heartbeat later they were drowned out by the cheers of the people outside, so loud that Arvandus feared the roof of the basilica might collapse upon them. He shouted and applauded until his throat was hoarse and his hands were burning.

As soon as the applause died down Arvandus wasted no time heading for the military camp outside the city, where he had heard the imperial staff were to remain until they moved to Arles. He joined a crowd of dozens that had already gathered and was being contained by soldiers at the edge of the camp. Commoners, equestrians, and senators alike, they were all there to present their petitions and to beg favours, eager to take advantage of the first emperor to be seen in Gaul for more than forty years. The highest ranking petitioners, some of whom had come in litters or sedan chairs and were attended by slaves, naturally bullied their way to the front of the crowd. Arvandus kept himself near the back, close to the road. He wanted to catch Sidonius's eye as soon as possible.

It was at least three hours before the column of infantry and staff officers was seen returning from the city. The crowd had grown to over a hundred, and after sitting in the hot sun for so long its mood was impatient. Arvandus rose and stood on the edge of the road. Sidonius was near the front, riding a bay horse. Arvandus waved to him, calling out his name. Soldiers came to push him back.

Sidonius spotted him just before he rode by. 'Arvandus?' he said in surprise. 'By God, it's you! Let that man through,' he commanded the soldiers, and jumped from his horse. He took Arvandus in an embrace, and kissed him on both cheeks. 'A strange thing, to meet again like this! Come, let's talk in my tent.' Sidonius handed the reins of his horse to a junior staff officer, wrapped his arm around Arvandus, and led him into the camp.

His tent was close to Avitus's, sparsely furnished with a bed, travel chest, table, and two chairs. 'This is where I receive the lucky few,' he said, inviting Arvandus to take a chair. 'I interview them first, and then Avitus chooses whom he wants to see. Some were already here yesterday evening. Each one starts by uttering his undying loyalty to Avitus, then usually he mentions the time he won his patronage twenty years earlier. Then he might start crying. I had one old matron who fell on her knees and tried to kiss my feet.'

'Have any tried to bribe you?'

'A couple. Their names went to the bottom of the list. I promise you, comrade, I'm not looking forward to the rest of today.'

Arvandus laughed. It felt good to see his friend again, good to be away from the cursed mills. 'It feels like the war again,' he said. 'Don't you think? The military camp, the soldiers every-where, the tent. Except this time your father-in-law is the emperor.'

'Almost emperor,' Sidonius said. 'The army wanted to proclaim him in Toulouse, but he refused. He wanted the assembly to happen here, and the official acclamation in Arles two days from now. And then we'll be heading straight for Rome.'

From the tent entrance came a new voice. 'By God, it's true – here he is!'

Arvandus turned to see Ecdicius behind him, clad in immacu-late mail shirt and red cloak. Arvandus rose, and was about to reach out for an embrace when he hesitated.

Ecdicius looked concerned. 'What's wrong, comrade?'

'You're the son of an emperor now,' said Arvandus. 'Surely there's some protocol . . .'

'No, no. Not between us. I forbid it.' With that he stepped forward and took Arvandus in a hug that almost lifted him off his feet. 'In Christ's name, here we are again. Always in times of crisis, eh?'

'Sollius was just telling me about the plan. Straight to Rome, then?'

Ecdicius nodded. 'As soon as we can. We need to take hold of the city before anyone else does.'

'What about the Vandals?'

'They've already left,' Sidonius said. 'According to the latest report, Geiseric only stayed there for two weeks. He wanted plunder, not the empire. So he's taken whatever he could lay his hands on. Public buildings, private houses, the imperial palace, anything that the senators didn't take when they ran for the hills. It's been loaded on ships and taken back to Africa. People, too – thousands of them. Hostages from noble families, including Valentinian's widow and his daughter Eudocia.'

Arvandus could only shake his head. 'I can't believe it. How did this happen?'

'Weakness and pride,' said Ecdicius.

'And stupidity,' said Sidonius. 'Petronius cancelled Eudocia's betrothal to Geiseric's son. Of course Geiseric wasn't going to stand for that. True, I doubt anyone expected him to sack Rome itself, but Petronius should at least have made the city secure and guarded the mouth of the Tiber. If he had, pieces of him wouldn't be floating in it now.'

'So who's in charge of the city?'

'The Senate, at least those who aren't hiding in their country villas.'

'But there's no emperor in Italy?'

'Not yet,' Sidonius said. 'Nobody in the Senate seems willing to step forward.'

'Hardly surprising, that,' said Ecdicius. 'But there's a rumour that Majorian wants the throne and is trying to build up support through Italy. This is why we need to get to Rome. Petronius's mistake was not having enough military support. By killing Aëtius he alienated half of the army. But thanks to my father, we've got the Goths on our side.' There was excitement in his eyes. 'This is our chance, comrades. It isn't even just about Gaul. As soon as Italy is secure, we'll organise a fleet to invade North Africa. It's the richest province in the west. If we take it back from the Vandals, we'll have the strength to rebuild our armies. We can put right all the mistakes of the past fifty years.'

'I want to help,' said Arvandus. 'But Felix . . . he's trying to ruin me. He had me dismissed from the prefect's staff.'

His friends looked taken aback. 'Why?' asked Sidonius.

Arvandus hesitated. How much to reveal to them? He knew he must not bring Attica into it; for her sake, but also for his own. No one knew about that night in Clermont. Ecdicius must never find out. Nor did Arvandus want to mention the beating he had received at the hands of Ajax. One day he would get his revenge for that, but it would be his own work. 'Felix has always hated me,' he said at last. 'I don't have a great family name. I can't recite a list of my consular ancestors. I was born under a Gothic king. How many reasons does he need?'

'He is old-fashioned sometimes,' Sidonius said, giving a weak, apologetic smile. 'I know he's not an easy person to deal with. But it was unjust of him to have you dismissed. You deserved that post.'

'All I want to do is serve the empire. You both know that.'

'Then you will,' Ecdicius said. 'Sollius, you're the reviewer of petitions, aren't you? Recommend Arvandus to my father, make sure you get him a good post on his staff.' He placed his hand on Arvandus's shoulder. 'Leave it to us, old friend.'

Arvandus beamed his brightest smile. 'I can never repay you for this.'

Sidonius laughed, waving his hand. Ecdicius picked up a jug on his desk and poured out three glasses of wine, handing one to each friend.

They raised their glasses together. 'To the emperor,' Arvandus said.

XL

Arles

In the quietness of her weaving room, Attica felt as though her ears were still ringing from the acclamation. The memory was vivid. The day after the ceremony in Beaucaire they had made the long-awaited procession downriver to Arles. It had been a gloriously hot afternoon, and the whole ten-mile route had been thronged. The following morning the army and the people had assembled at sunrise in the upper forum. Her father had been led by Ecdicius and a troop of soldiers to a newly built wooden tribunal. Once he had climbed the steps and was looking out over the crowd, Ecdicius had gone up and placed the golden torc around his neck. Then Messianus had brought the purple cloak, draping it over his shoulders. Aegidius had handed him an ivory sceptre. Finally Remistus, the Goth who was now master of soldiers, had placed the golden diadem on his head.

Fully adorned in the imperial regalia, her father had seemed more than human. His eyes had been unblinking, staring into Heaven. He did not even flinch when the soldiers readied their spears and shields and showed the civilians how it was done. Attica was sure that there could be no other sound on earth like the din of an army proclaiming its new emperor.

Several days of games and chariot races had followed since then, to the delight of the populace, who had never seen a celebration like it. Attica sensed an air of delirious triumph about the city, as though the whole empire had already been won.

The last races of the evening were taking place at the hippodrome less than half a mile away, and the roars of the jubilant crowd seeped through the windows. Attica did not share the mood, with so many serious things happening around her. Amidst the frenzy of celebration and chariots there was the hectic preparation of the march for Italy. In order to travel more quickly and to avoid giving the impression of an invading usurper, her father had decided to take only a token force of about fifteen hundred troops, with more to follow if necessary. Then there was the recruitment of a new imperial court. It sounded like every man in Gaul was scrambling to get some post or other. Felix's father Magnus had been named master of offices, which made him the chief executive officer of the court. Felix himself was now first notary, head of the secretarial college. He bore his new golden brooch with excessive pride, wearing it even in their Arles town house, where there was no one but family and slaves to see it.

He could strut about all he liked, Attica thought, so long as it kept him satisfied with himself and uninterested in her. She continued to work her loom like the dutiful wife she was. She had hoped that the monotony of the task would help calm her frustration at being kept away from events, but it was not working. She had hardly seen her father since they had arrived in Arles. Felix had kept her confined to the house for months, and not even becoming the daughter of an emperor had changed that. Once she had dreamed of controlling her husband. How naïve that now seemed.

She just needed to be patient. Soon Felix would be going to Rome with her father, as would Sidonius, Ecdicius and the rest of the new court. Papianilla would be staying at Lupiacum with her daughters, who were too young for such a long and hazardous journey. Agricola was still only fourteen, and so would also stay behind. Attica would be joining them. She was anxious, of course, about everything that was happening. Her father had not accepted that diadem lightly, and part of her longed to go with him to Rome. She would have done so, had it not meant also going with Felix and leaving her sister behind. She could not bear the thought of Papianilla and the children being left at Lupiacum while most of the family headed across the Alps, still uncertain of what awaited them there.

She heard the front doors open, and voices in the atrium. It was Felix and Sidonius. Felix sounded angry, but that was nothing unusual. She got up from the loom and left the room. This would be her first chance to talk to Sidonius properly, and she was desperate for news of her sister and nieces.

'I forbid it,' her husband was saying. 'No, a thousand times no.'

'He's my friend,' replied Sidonius. 'You have no right to do this.'

Attica was surprised to hear Sidonius with his voice raised in such a way. He and her brother fell silent as she entered the atrium. 'I apologise for interrupting,' she said.

'No,' Felix said, pointing at her. 'No, you should hear this.' He turned to Sidonius. 'I have every right to forbid it. I'm first notary. I'm your superior. I won't have him on the imperial staff.'

'Arvandus is loyal to the emperor. He's our friend.'

'He's a grasping, devious little peasant. I'll have my father block the appointment if necessary.'

'Then I'll have the emperor approve it himself.'

'No you won't,' laughed Felix. 'Do you know why not? Because Avitus needs my father's money. Who paid for these celebrations? Who gave him those two hundred pounds of gold for the donative? I'd like to see how long the troops adore him when they stop getting paid.'

There was a pause before Sidonius spoke. 'That sounds like a threat.'

'It's a political fact, Sidonius, don't be such a pompous fool. You've let this weasel hang on to your cloak for years, and now you want to drag him all the way to Rome? Well, I say *no*. That's my last word.'

There was another silence. Attica waited. This was Felix's way of torturing her. She thought with pain of Arvandus, of what she had done to him. She wished she had some way to help him. Months ago she had thought of secretly sending him money, but had not done it, knowing that he would have taken it as an insult.

'Our new emperor has a talent for not making enemies,' Felix said to Sidonius. 'You could learn something from him.'

Sidonius did not reply, but stared at the floor for a moment before he turned and walked away. Attica called after him, but it was no good. He left the house.

'I wanted to talk to him,' Attica said. 'I was going to ask if Papianilla needed me to bring anything to Lupiacum.'

'He has more important things to worry about,' he said. 'And you won't be going to Lupiacum.'

'What do you mean?'

'I mean you're coming to Rome with me.'

'I'm not,' she said. 'I want to be with my sister. She needs me.'

'Do you honestly think I'm going to leave you in Gaul, after you proved yourself unfaithful? Do you think me a fool? I'd come back a year from now and find your belly swollen like a sow's.'

Her right hand jerked, driven by sudden impulse; she could almost feel the satisfying violence of it striking his face; but she held it back. She knew what would happen. She would hit him. He would be shocked for a moment. Then he would fix her with those cold eyes, and shout for Ajax.

'You're learning,' he said, a spiteful smile twisting his lips. 'Go back to your loom.'

She hated herself for doing it, but she began to weep as she walked back to the weaving room. She slammed the door shut behind her and raised a sleeve to stifle her sobs. The chariot races had now ended. It was growing dark outside. The loom awaited her in the shadows, the cursed machine that had become as hateful to her as a torturer's rack. She wanted to tear it apart, but what would that achieve? It would do her no more good than hitting Felix.

Slowly she waited for calm to descend. *Rule your hatred,* she told herself. *Do not let it rule you.* She grasped that hatred, holding it close, embracing it. It was what kept her strong.

That night Attica lay awake beside her sleeping husband. A pale glow of moonlight fell through the window above the bed, illuminating the ivory cosmetic box on her side table. It seemed to glow with unreal brightness. She remembered the time Felix had admired the carving of Queen Dido climbing onto her own funeral pyre, driven to suicide after Aeneas had abandoned her.

Of course that was the kind of woman he admired: one who offered mindless devotion, who had no purpose without her Roman hero, who would rather die than lose him.

Slowly, taking care not to disturb Felix, she slipped out from under the linen blanket. She stepped across the cold mosaic floor to the side table, carefully released the latch of the ivory box, and opened the lid. She peered inside, feeling for something cold and hard.

She found it. She took it out and held it in the moonlight. It was the small bronze knife Cyra sometimes used to open bags of cosmetics or cut loose threads from her tunic. The blade was no longer than a finger, but it was sharp.

Attica went to the side of the bed. She looked down at her husband, the knife clutched in her right hand. He was on his back, his mouth wide open, his throat exposed. It would be the work of a moment. This time he would have no chance to call Ajax.

She stood there for a long time.

It would be the work of a moment, true, but the consequences would last a lifetime. She would suffer exile. There would be scandal and outrage. She would bring disgrace down on the head of her family, on her sister, on her brothers. She would destroy everything that her father was fighting to achieve.

It was not the time.

Quietly she went back to the side table. She replaced the knife and closed the lid of the box. She returned to the bed, climbing beneath the blanket to find that a trace of her warmth still lingered.

XLI

A rvandus could remember the first time he had come to Arles. He remembered walking through the city, over the bridge, Lampridius introducing him to the exhilaration of the forum; he remembered craning his neck to see the soaring heights of the amphitheatre and aqueducts; he remembered his first games and his first chariot race, the first time he had gone to a brothel, the first time he was drunk. It had all been new and exciting. Now, six years later, the city felt like an old friend. He knew every corner of it, had drunk in most of its bars, thrown up in a fair number of its gutters. He would be sorry to leave. But he was going to a place that had hitherto only existed in his daydreams: Rome, the mistress of the world. Arles was said to be but a pale reflection of its wonders.

The day of the emperor's departure was close. Arvandus headed through the streets from his apartment to the house where he would meet Sidonius and Lampridius for dinner. Lampridius had returned home to Bordeaux after their schooling had ended, intent on living a life of ease and poetry. Arvandus had not seen him since then, although they had exchanged occasional letters. Now he was back in Arles and eager to meet his old friends. Every inn in the city was full and even private house owners had started to rent out spare rooms at exorbitant prices, so Lampridius was lucky that he had been able to stay with one of his distant cousins. Arvandus was excited to see him again, and looking forward to reliving the spirit of their student days. Most of all, though, he was anxious to learn what post on the imperial staff Sidonius had managed to secure for him.

His route took him past the taverns and market stalls clustered around the southern piers of the amphitheatre, which were even more crowded and raucous than usual. Through the celebrating crowd he glimpsed a group of three dark-clad, staff-wielding men, who looked around at the drunkenness and depravity with direful eyes. They were monks of Marseilles, another familiar sight. Normally they did not draw attention to themselves, quietly going about the city taking alms to the poor and caring for the sick; even the more fervent ones who occasionally harangued the people in the forum were regarded almost with fondness by most of the local people. Arvandus had heard enough of their doom-laden sermons that he no longer found them alarming. After all, the monk Salvian had forecast the destruction of Gaul during Attila's invasion, and that had not come to pass.

But today the monks were mingling through the crowd with purpose. Arvandus saw that they were handing out rolls of papyrus to any who would take them. He approached the nearest monk. 'What is it?' he said, taking the offered roll.

'The words of Brother Salvian,' the monk said. 'It concerns the present judgement of God. Read it, friend, and understand. May God go with you.'

Arvandus walked away, unrolling the papyrus. It was a single foot-long sheet filled with lines of small, tidy writing. He had heard of this polemic, which Salvian had written some years earlier. It had caused quite a stir in the city with its frank condemnation of the wealthy. This looked like an abbreviated version, intended to be mass-copied and distributed throughout the population. Arvandus smiled to think of Salvian's audacity. No doubt the monk had judged the Vandal sack of Rome to be an opportune moment to regurgitate his old argument that God was steering the empire towards its final destruction. Senatorial hotheads like Felix would not be pleased to see these rolls circulating in the city, that much was certain. Arvandus rolled it up and slipped it down the front of his tunic. It would make for amusing reading at dinner.

Following the directions on the note Lampridius had sent him, Arvandus found the house beyond the new cathedral. He knocked on the brass-studded door. It was opened, and a crooked old house steward invited him into the entrance hall. It did not look like an especially opulent residence, but it was clean and comfortably furnished, and Arvandus glimpsed some fine silverware displayed on the sideboard in the atrium.

Lampridius appeared through a doorway next to the sideboard. He came into the entrance hall. He had put on weight, and his beard was now a truly impressive hedge covering his lower face. He held out his arms in greeting. 'Three years, you dog, and still you haven't come home to Bordeaux to see me!'

'But Bordeaux is wet and cold, and so far away,' Arvandus said.

'Rubbish. Living in the south has made you soft. Ah, but you've been busy with your dreams of restoring the empire, I know. Come here!' He took Arvandus in one of his great hugs, almost crushing the papyrus roll.

Arvandus had freed himself from his friend's embrace when there was a hammering at the front door. The porter opened it, and in stepped Sidonius. 'There you are, Sollius,' cried Lampridius, grabbing him for another hug.

A friendly-faced, middle-aged couple came through the atrium. Lampridius introduced them as Teridius, his cousin, and Fabiola. They received their guests with almost embarrassing warmth, especially Sidonius, who had apparently blessed their abode merely by entering it. 'The emperor's son-in-law in our home,' the husband gasped, in between planting kisses on Sidonius's hand.

'Just like old times, eh?' laughed Lampridius. 'Splendid. Now, let's make ourselves fat and drunk.'

He had arranged a pleasant, private little dinner. Three separate couches had been set up around the low dining table. Sidonius was given the place of honour, having the left couch to himself, while their hosts took the right couch, and Arvandus and Lampridius reclined in the centre. Each couch was draped in a blanket that reached to the floor, concealing wooden legs that Arvandus suspected were a bit worse for wear. Across the table lay a fine linen cloth, rather too small to cover its chipped edges. When the dishes were brought out, he noticed that those placed nearest to Sidonius were silver, while the others were pewter.

There was a faint smell of paint in the air. But if their hosts were anxious about impressing their guests, they need not have worried. They were simply happy to be reunited with one another. Arvandus found the hapless attempts at sophistication rather endearing.

Once they had finished the meal, Teridius and Fabiola tactfully excused themselves so that the three friends could talk together. Lampridius called for more wine, and told the servant to keep their glasses full and undiluted. 'For we have many trivial matters to discuss,' he declared.

It was near to sunset when Arvandus, his head clouded with alcohol, remembered the papyrus roll that was still under his tunic. He dug it out excitedly. 'Listen, comrades, listen.' He scrambled from the couch and stood in front of the dining table. It was hard to declaim properly while holding a crumpled sheet in one hand, but he tried his best. 'Now hear the words of the holy man Salvian,' he said, speaking with ponderous authority as though about to recite a famous work of Cicero. He squinted to read the small writing. '"Certain people say that God is uninterested in human affairs, and virtually unconcerned with them, to the extent that he neither looks after the good, nor punishes the wicked."' Sidonius and Lampridius were already trying to contain their amusement. 'Pay attention there!' he snapped. 'I won't have giggling before the judgement of God. Where was I? Ah, yes. "And thus in this world many good are miserable, and the wicked are blessed. Now, since I am addressing Christians—"'

'Oh, most certainly you're addressing Christians,' said Lampridius.

'Quiet, I say! "Since I am addressing Christians, holy scripture should be enough to refute this idea. But since many still have some pagan disbelief in them, perhaps they will care to hear the testimonies of chosen and wise pagans . . ."'

Lampridius laughed, reached across the table to snatch the scroll from him, and continued the reading. Arvandus returned to the spare couch, taking a swig of wine. They took turns reading through the rest of it, their increasingly drunken recital broken by melodramatic pleas for mercy from Heaven.

'Oh, preserve us,' Lampridius said once they had reached the end. He tossed the sheet on the floor. 'We're all damned, my friends, we're all damned. Especially Sollius here. Look at him, son-in-law of the emperor. Look at the lust for worldly glory in his eyes. The wheel of fortune turns, my friend, the wheel turns. Beware.'

'Fortune,' scoffed Arvandus. 'Fortune is what we make for ourselves.'

'Oh no, no,' said Lampridius. He leaned back and spread his hands above his head. 'Our future is mapped in the stars above, not in the rantings of some monk.'

'Really?' Sidonius said. 'Then what's your destiny, Lampridius?'

'Soon I'll be able to tell you. There's a bunch of African magicians just arrived down at the east docks, refugees from Rome. I'm going to visit them tomorrow.'

Arvandus had also heard of those magicians. They had already attracted a good number of customers, much to the annoyance of the bishop. 'And ask them what?'

'Everything,' said Lampridius. 'I'm going to ask them if the girl I marry will have a big dowry and an even bigger pair of tits. I'll ask how many screaming babies she'll give me. I might even ask them when I'll die.'

'I don't think that's a good idea,' Sidonius said.

Arvandus understood his wariness. As students they had all studied the principles of astrology, but only out of scientific and philosophical interest. Any respectable professor would shun its practice, which was bound up with all sorts of arcane arts. Asking an astrologer about the death of a reigning emperor was a capital crime. Enquiring about one's own death was legal, but foolish.

'Why shouldn't I ask about my death?' Lampridius said. 'Sollius, your wife's father is emperor. There may be dark times ahead. Wouldn't you like to know your fate?'

'Not from those clowns down at the docks. They're charlatans, you'll be wasting your money.'

He jabbed his finger at Sidonius. 'My money is mine to waste as I like.'

When drunk, Lampridius could quickly become bellicose like this. Over the years his friends had learned how to handle him through distraction. 'Well, I can reveal Arvandus's future right now,' Sidonius said, 'and it won't cost him a penny.' He reached into his belt pouch and brought out a rolled and sealed letter. He leaned over the table to pass it to Arvandus.

He took the letter, giving a delighted grin. 'Sollius, I'll never be able to thank you for this.'

'Congratulations, you rascal,' said Lampridius. 'Well, read it, tell me what it says.'

Arvandus began to read aloud. '"Eparchius Avitus Augustus, father of the fatherland, grants to his servant Arvandus the post of exceptor in the bureau of petitions, under the authority of Alethius Renatus, most esteemed governor of First Aquitaine, given on this day . . ."' he stopped. He was no longer smiling. This was not what he had been expecting. 'Exceptor?' he said, looking across at Sidonius. 'A short-hand scribe? Sollius, I can't even write short-hand.'

'They'll teach you,' Sidonius said.

'Where, at the bureau of petitions up in Bourges? So I can spend the rest of my life in some backwater, with barbarians breathing down my neck?'

'Steady there,' said Lampridius. 'Sollius here is doing you a favour.'

Arvandus brandished the letter. 'You're tribune and notary to the emperor himself, and this is all you can give me? Nothing in the imperial offices? You'd rather pack me off to the provinces?'

'It's a start,' Sidonius said. 'From there you can work your way up to the prefect's offices . . .'

'That's where I was a year ago,' snapped Arvandus, more loudly than he intended. The disappointment coursed through him, a bitterness that was making his head pound. 'While you're tribune and notary from the very start, and go with the emperor to Rome. What have you done to earn that? I've been slaving away for years, while you've been sitting at home making babies and spinning wool.'

Sidonius got to his feet. 'You think I haven't earned it? The last months I've been all over Gaul, riding in the cold and wet, sleeping half-starved in a tent, barbarians in the hills around me. I was taken away from my wife and children. I didn't see them for months, and now I won't see them again for God knows how long – spinning wool! You have no idea what imperial service means, what people like me have to sacrifice.'

'People like *you*,' Arvandus said in disgust. 'People like you have tried to hold me down all my life. I'm there for when you have a use for me. As soon as I'm inconvenient, I'm shut out, ignored, spat on. Why get me a post on the imperial staff, when you must have a dozen cousins queuing up, and a hundred boys with rich fathers waiting to fill your pockets? I should never have saved you in that tavern. I should have let you be murdered. You don't think I know how to sacrifice anything?' He staggered to his feet, swaying as he held out the letter in both hands. '*Here's* something I'll sacrifice.' He tore the letter in two and tossed the pieces on the table.

Sidonius and Lampridius stared at him as though he had pissed on their ancestors' graves. He did not care. The fog of wine was around him; he had started angry, and ended angrier. There was nothing else to say. He made to leave, but as he turned he knocked his knee on the corner of the couch. Swearing at the sudden pain, he kicked the furniture and limped out of the dining room towards the front door.

Sidonius called after him, but he paid no attention. *Fuck them*, he thought. He waved the house steward aside, unbolting the door himself and staggering out into the street.

Fuck all of them.

Felix had mutilated him, beaten him, forced him out of the prefect's staff. Now his own friend – *the son-in-law of the emperor* – had tried to exile him to a shithole of a city at the far end of Roman Gaul.

So be it. If they did not want him, he would find someone who did.

XLII

Rome

It was said that a man never forgot his first sight of Rome. Ecdicius saw it in September of that year, the twelve hundred and eighth since the foundation of the city. After weeks of travel across mountains and plains, the column crested the road that led down to the Milvian Bridge. There was the Tiber, and beyond it, lying serene beneath a fuggy haze, were the walls and towers and marble gleam of the Eternal City, its fourteen districts spread over the rolling hills. Ecdicius had never seen such a place. It could have swallowed Arles twenty times over.

He rode at the head of the column, beside his father. With them were Sidonius, Felix, Magnus and the other officers of the court. Next were five hundred mounted Gothic warriors, the First Gallic Horse, and the infantry regiment of the Senior Lions. Finally came the wagon train, a rumbling city on wheels that stretched a quarter of a mile back along the road. Attica was part of it, accompanied by her household staff.

Few of the courtiers and staff officers had brought their wives with them, and Ecdicius would have preferred his sister to be back in Gaul. But Felix was her husband, and the decision was his to make. The presence of the Goths so close to his father was also unsettling. It could not be avoided, though. Back in Toulouse King Theoderic had established three conditions for his support. The first was that Avitus appoint the Gothic noble called Remistus as his master of soldiers. The second was that he accept a personal bodyguard of five hundred hand-picked Gothic warriors. The third was that this bodyguard be led by the fifteen-year-old Prince Euric.

Even after three months of travelling across the Alps and

down the length of Italy, Ecdicius had not yet got the full measure of the prince. He was a dark, handsome youth, well-built, who bore himself with uncommon gravitas for someone so young. He kept himself close to his Goths, who seemed to respect him. He rarely spoke to any Roman except the emperor or Magnus. Ecdicius could not decide whether Euric's reticence came from shyness or disdain. He would have preferred him to be more like his departed brother Thorismund: loud, boastful, and easy to read.

The column reached the city at the Flaminian Gate, where Bishop Leo and some members of the Senate were waiting to receive them. Crowds of commoners had also gathered along the processional route. They cheered, but their expressions were reserved, wary. There was none of the delirium Ecdicius had seen in Arles.

As they rode into the heart of the city Ecdicius turned his head this way and that, enraptured by the monuments and seemingly endless porticoes that stretched before them. It hardly mattered to him that Rome was clearly not what she had once been. It was now four months after the Vandal sack, and he could see evidence of the trauma all around. When they passed through the cattle forum he noticed the burned-out docks along the banks of the Tiber, and children and dogs playing in the ash. The towering colonnades of the septizodium stood empty and neglected, smeared with moss. But the imperial palace still rose on its rocky cliffs, a man-made mountain of marble and brick. The aqueducts that strode in majesty across the city, the Arch of Constantine, the monstrous heights of the Flavian amphitheatre and the temple of Venus and Rome that faced it – in comparison, Ecdicius realised, the monuments of Arles were mere playthings. This truly was the centre of the world.

Finally they came to the old Roman forum, where crowds stood on pavements that were unswept and overgrown with weeds. Columns and plinths stood in naked rows, robbed of their statues; the Vandals had left nothing behind but inscriptions and broken iron clamps. At the far end of the forum, standing outside the Senate House with a triumphal arch towering behind them, was a crowd of about fifty toga-clad senators. Many others who had fled in the face of the Vandals had evidently still not returned, preferring to wait out the political uncertainty in the countryside.

As Avitus brought his horse to a stop, one of the senators stepped forth to receive him. Ecdicius presumed that this was Flavius Rufius Opilio, who had already sent a messenger to Avitus on the road stating that the Senate was prepared to receive him as their new master. Opilio was swarthy-skinned and grossly overweight, a former master of offices and consul under Valentinian. He would be a useful ally as they secured their hold over the city, assuming he could be trusted.

Opilio gave a florid, predictable speech about how Rome, left destitute and violated by the Vandals on the bank of the Tiber, had raised her sorrowful brow to the north, where she had seen a new star of salvation rising above the Alps. Such tortured poetics had never moved Ecdicius. He was glad when it ended and Opilio offered to take the emperor and his court officers on a tour of the forum. They walked from the Senate House to the temple of Antoninus Pius and Faustina, entering through a fence of iron bars and climbing the front steps. Opilio lamented the loss of the bronze statues that had once graced the steps and the portico roof. The marble statues of Antoninus and his wife, seated on enormous carved thrones inside the temple, were still intact. Next Opilio led them to an enormous basilica, the grandest in Rome, its vaulted ceilings alive with colour and light. At the far end was an enthroned colossus, draped in a bronze pallium and holding a gilded orb in his left hand, a sceptre in his right. A pair of doves nestled in his lap. He stared down the cavernous hall with calm, otherworldly eyes, indifferent to the birds that cooed in the windows above, and to the new emperor and his entourage who chattered below. There was a strange and peaceful dignity about him, Ecdicius thought.

Prince Euric had so far been keeping himself at the edge of the imperial group, apart from the others. Ecdicius had noticed him yawning several times. Now, however, he was staring up at the colossal statue with something like admiration. 'The body is made of gold,' he said. His Latin was thickly accented; he had never been trained in the classics like his brother Theoderic, nor had he sought to cultivate a Roman demeanour.

'The torso is gilded bronze, yes,' said Opilio. Addressing the Goth, his voice was noticeably colder.

'Why didn't the Vandals take it?'

Opilio gave a patronising laugh. 'Why, this is the most holy Emperor Constantine. At Bishop Leo's entreaty, Geiseric ordered it not to be harmed. Even the Vandals have some respect for the man who made the world Christian.'

Euric grunted, his eyes still on the colossus. He was looking at it not in admiration, Ecdicius then realised, but with greed.

Once the tour of the forum was over, they took the road that led from the Arch of Titus up the Palatine Hill to the imperial palace. The route had been tidied up for them, but they entered the palace to find it stripped bare. As Opilio led them through the broad corridors, Ecdicius realised that every plinth was empty, with not a bronze statue or precious vase to be seen. None but the oldest and most cumbersome pieces of furniture remained. 'Before he left,' Opilio said, 'Geiseric even ordered the gilded bosses in the ceiling of the imperial bedroom to be removed, and the curtains to be torn from their railings. They had gold thread in them, you see. And what the Vandals did not take, I'm sorry to say, the palace servants did.' The state treasury, contained behind an iron-barred door deep in the palace, turned out to hold only dust. Opilio claimed that Geiseric had stolen its contents. He was equally apologetic that the Vandals had abducted the imperial concubines, and promised Avitus that he would supply more if required. 'That won't be necessary,' the emperor said.

Later that afternoon, as soon as Opilio had left, Avitus summoned his Gallic courtiers to an assembly in the palace throne room. He sat on the marble throne in the apse while Ecdicius and the rest of the court gathered before him. At the front were the three members of the consistory, the emperor's privy councillors. Felix's father Magnus, as master of offices, was the senior councillor; the post of quaestor, head of the judiciary, he had granted to his old friend Egnatius, while his nephew Camillus was now count of the sacred largesses, responsible for imperial finances. Ecdicius stood next to them. Consentius, who had spent the last few years serving on the staff of the prefect of Gaul, was now steward of the imperial palace; this had raised him to the second senatorial rank and entitled him to a prominent position. The lesser court officers, including Sidonius and Felix, stood further removed from the imperial presence. All in all, they numbered fewer than forty. In an audience hall built to hold a thousand, flanked by giant statues of shimmering green stone and by columns of Phrygian purple that thrust upwards to the ceiling a hundred feet above their heads, they seemed to Ecdicius a pathetically small huddle. *We must all be mad*, he thought.

His father thanked them for their loyalty, and ordered the distribution of largesse. As he had become emperor through their counsel, he said, so he hoped to reign justly through their counsel. They followed Magnus in heartfelt acclamations of the emperor's majesty and munificence, their voices echoing in the shadowy heights of the ceiling. Avitus endured their praise with sombre detachment, giving no hint of the discomfort that Ecdicius knew he was feeling.

After the acclamations Avitus dismissed the court, except for Ecdicius and the three members of the consistory. 'Majesty,' Magnus began at once. 'We need to discuss money. Without it we can do nothing. The treasury is empty. Opilio claims the Vandals stole it, but I've already heard a rumour from the palace staff that Majorian was seen taking it away before he abandoned the city.'

'If that's true,' the emperor said, 'we must ensure his loyalty.'

'He was count of the household guard,' said Magnus, a note of disgust in his voice. 'By leaving the emperor to die, he all but committed treason.'

Avitus waved his hand. 'That's a matter for another time. Majorian has soldiers and money, and we are short on both. We must make him our servant.'

'There is also the matter of the remaining appointments,' said the quaestor, Egnatius, who had been one of the most respected lawyers in Arles. Ecdicius found the man bookish and pedantic even by the standards of that profession, and had already begun to suspect that his opinions were for the most part directed by Magnus. 'Foremost, the city prefect. The last one fled, and hasn't been seen for months. Without a prefect, Rome will fall apart.'

'And he must be a Roman senator,' Magnus added. 'Winning the support of the Senate is crucial. I'd recommend Opilio. He seems to carry most weight among the conscript fathers.'

'Literally and figuratively,' said Egnatius, although the others seemed not to be in the mood for humour.

'Agreed,' said Avitus. 'Have him brought to a private audience tomorrow.'

'Yes, Majesty,' Magnus said, bowing. He glanced at his fellow councillors. 'But if I may return to the matter of Majorian . . . he is said to be still camped in the south. We understand that he's an old comrade of yours, but he could become a threat, and at the moment he is vulnerable. If we can lure him into a private meeting . . .'

'No,' said Avitus. 'Our reign will not begin with bloodshed. There will be no proscriptions, no assassinations. Is that clear?'

Magnus bowed in obedience, the reluctance clear in his eyes. He would need to be kept in line, Ecdicius knew. His financial support had been critical so far, but he seemed reluctant to accept that the master of offices answered to the emperor, not the other way around.

Once the rest of the priorities had been decided, Avitus dismissed the courtiers. Ecdicius left the audience hall by the north doors, wanting to see the view of the city offered by the balcony over-looking the palace forecourt. He spotted Sidonius standing a little way along the balcony, and went to join him. They nodded to one another, and looked over the deserted forecourt. Tomorrow morning the nobility of Rome would gather here to offer the first of their daily salutations to the new emperor. Very soon, no doubt, they would be buzzing around the palace like bees around a honey pot, hoping to snatch up any remaining posts in the judiciary, treasury, and palatine administration.

Neither Ecdicius nor Sidonius spoke as they stood there on the balcony, as though words could not express their thoughts. Ecdicius was sure that their feelings were the same. It was a pity that Arvandus was not with them, but there was nothing they could have done about Felix blocking his appointment; Ecdicius had pleaded with his father to allow it, but the emperor had been unwilling to anger Magnus over something so trivial. Sidonius had tried to get Arvandus the best position available at short notice. It was not their fault that he had overreacted. He had always been sensitive about such things.

So without their friend, Ecdicius and Sidonius had crossed mountains and rivers, and now, finally, they were here, in the imperial palace itself, scarcely able to believe that all Rome lay spread before them. Gables of basilicas and old temples glowed in the soft hue of the late afternoon sun. To their left was the Capitoline Hill, its great cliffs surmounted by the temple of Jupiter Best and Greatest, one of the wonders of the world. Geiseric had stolen half of its gilded roof tiles, but enough remained that it shone with ancient brilliance, a beacon above the shadowy depths of the Roman forum.

The senators down in that valley had seemed to Ecdicius a thin-blooded gaggle of timorous old men; this was not the age of Cicero, and the Senate of Rome wielded little power outside its own city. Least of all had he been impressed by Opilio, who struck him as an opportunist. The self-styled 'conscript fathers' deserved pity for what they had become. While they had sunk into frightened luxury, Gaul had become the crucible for true old-fashioned Roman virtues.

There was no doubt in his mind that the Fates were spinning his father's future in golden thread. Already they had achieved more than he had ever dared dream. They would soon put the empire back on its feet.

XLIII

It was late, almost dusk. Ecdicius looked at his bed. He wanted nothing more than to collapse into it. Another day with Aegidius sorting through the military paperwork of Aëtius, trying to reckon the latest disposition of troops throughout Italy, had left him exhausted. His eyes ached from reading sheet after sheet of strength reports and supply requests, most of them out of date. There was no telling where the loyalty of most Italian regiments now lay. Avitus had sent the Goth Remistus with a small guard to Ravenna in order to establish control over the remnants of the imperial court there. Majorian and his thousand-strong household guard were still somewhere in the south with Ricimer, another commander who had also served under Aëtius, but their intentions were unknown.

Since arriving two weeks ago Ecdicius had rarely left the imperial palace. Everything seemed to have been left a shambles: the imperial court, the military, the palace itself. He knew that Consentius was working hard to take control of the immense complex that sprawled across the top of the Palatine Hill, with its vast open courtyards, its audience halls and grand dining rooms connected by a maze of corridors and rooms, its enormous baths and enclosed gardens. He was leaving much of it to gather dust. Most of the palace staff had fled when the Vandals came, but the chief steward – or a man who claimed to be chief steward – had turned up, and over the last two weeks a trickle of servants had re-emerged from wherever they had been hiding. They were likely the ones who had failed to fill their pockets on the way out.

Ecdicius went to the basin and splashed water on his face. The bed was inviting, but he could not sleep yet, despite the late hour.

Senator Opilio, newly appointed prefect of the city, was coming
to dine, and the emperor's son was expected to attend.

They ate, as usual, in the small dining room adjacent to the
emperor's private quarters. Magnus also joined them, along with
Felix, Attica, and Sidonius. Opilio had brought his wife Salviana.
As the first dishes were brought in, Avitus thanked him for
accepting the post of city prefect. Opilio claimed that a sense of
civic duty had compelled him. 'I was more or less retired from
politics,' he said, fiddling through a plate of oysters with slippery
fingers. 'But in such times as these, I fear there's no such thing
as a private citizen.'

'Very true,' said Avitus.

'Majesty,' said Salviana, 'I hear that your wife will soon be
resident in the palace?'

'That's true. My wife Severiana. We expect her to arrive in the
spring. My younger children Papianilla and Agricola will remain
in Gaul for the time being.'

The frosty-faced Salviana gave an unconvincing smile. 'And
Felix, you must be overjoyed that you already enjoy the company
of your wife.'

'A woman belongs at her husband's side,' Felix said.

Ecdicius looked at his sister. She was staring at the piece of
bread in her hand, saying nothing.

'Oh, indeed,' said Salviana, glancing dutifully towards her own
husband. 'It's so reassuring that you feel Rome is safe for her. As
well you should. I hope you will all soon be joined by your families. You should all feel as safe here as though in your own city.'

Magnus cleared his throat. 'Naturally we do, my lady. Gauls
or not, we are all equally citizens of Rome.'

Salviana did not miss the indignation in his voice. 'Naturally,'
she said.

There was an awkward silence. It was broken by Opilio. 'Well,
the prefecture of Rome is a joyless post, let me tell you. Fourteen
urban districts to control, and fifteen bureaux to administer, not
to mention Portus and every other town within a hundred miles.
Oh, and the plebian guilds I have to deal with – the dockers and

the measurers, the bargemen, the bakers, the butchers, the builders and stone-cutters – it never ends, Majesty. Three months from now the grain will start arriving in Portus, and the warehouses below the Aventine are still a shambles. You'll forgive me, I know, for being so vulgar, but we simply need more *coin*.'

It occurred to Ecdicius that in such a time of emergency true patriots would be lining up outside the palace to donate their own savings to the imperial coffers; but it seemed that the Senate did not breed such men. He lay there on the dining couch, watching Opilio and thinking less of him with every oyster he popped into his mouth. He was wearing an old tunic, and his wife's only jewellery was a simple necklace. They certainly looked as though on the brink of poverty. Yet Ecdicius had heard that their city mansion, which lay near the Salarian Gate in the far north-east of the city, had not even been touched by the Vandals, and they had properties scattered the length of Italy. They were not short of money, however they chose to present themselves.

'Excuse me, Majesty,' came a voice from the door. It was Aegidius. He saluted the emperor, strode over to him, and bent to whisper something in his ear.

Avitus wiped his fingers and tossed his napkin on the table. 'I'm sorry to interrupt our dinner,' he said, his voice calm. 'It seems that Majorian and Ricimer are at the gates of the city with an army of six thousand men.'

The other diners sat in stunned silence. Ecdicius was the first to leap to his feet.

His father also rose. 'I want them summoned to our presence immediately.'

'It's late, Majesty,' said Aegidius. 'They'll be busy pitching camp.'

'Then they should have arrived earlier. Bring them to the council chamber. Ecdicius, go with him.'

Aegidius bowed and hurried out, followed by Ecdicius. As soon as they left the dining room, Aegidius gripped Ecdicius by the arm. 'Best if you let me go alone.'

'But my father—'

'I know, I know. But this is even more delicate than the emperor realises. Trust me, I know Majorian and Ricimer. If I turn up in their camp with you at my side, they might be inclined to keep you as a hostage. That's the last thing we want.'

There was some sense in that. Ecdicius knew that Aegidius, Majorian and Ricimer had all started their careers together as staff officers under Aëtius. There would be a bond between them that he could not fully understand. 'Very well,' he said. 'But be careful. I'll organise things here.'

Leaving Aegidius to his mission, Ecdicius found the master of admissions and commanded him to make the council chamber ready for an imperial audience, ignoring the man's protestation that it went against court protocol to have an audience so late in the evening. The biggest problem was simply lighting the chamber, which adjoined the throne room and was almost as capacious; servants scurried about the palace from top to bottom until they found as many ornamental braziers and hanging lamps as could be spared. Even so, when the court had finally been assembled an hour later, every man in his formal uniform, the ceiling above was hung with heavy shadows that fell and filled the corners of the room. There was light around the doors and the dais, but Ecdicius and the rest of them were standing in near darkness.

He was still not used to the sight of his father sitting on the raised throne, clad in the imperial raiment of diadem and purple cloak. To the left of the throne stood two members of his consistory, the quaestor and the count of the sacred largesses; Magnus was waiting outside the north doors to conduct Majorian and Ricimer into the imperial presence. Ecdicius and Felix stood against one side of the room with Sidonius and some other minor court officers. They would have been hidden behind curtains, had the Vandals not stolen them. Against the opposite wall stood Prince Euric, flanked by two of his Gothic soldiers.

The double doors opened. Another pair of Gothic soldiers entered, followed by the master of admissions. He approached the emperor and prostrated himself with ostentatious ceremony. After rising, he made some elegant swivelling backsteps that took him to the side of the dais. He swept his arm towards the doors and announced: 'Majorian, illustrious count of the household guard; and Ricimer, illustrious count.'

The two generals were conducted into the room by Aegidius and Magnus, who bore himself with his usual solemnity. But Ricimer and Majorian were in no mood for ceremony. They strode forward to the imperial presence, their hobnail boots clattering loudly on the marble floor. They were fresh from camp: unshaven, unwashed, still in bronze scale armour and red cloaks.

Of the two, Ricimer was the larger by far. He was descended from Gothic and Suevic royalty, and Ecdicius saw how those barbarian strains had reached their culmination in the thick bulk of his shoulders, the silvery hair that he wore brushed back over his ears, the savage blue eyes that he kept fixed on the emperor. True, he had been born in Spain and had spent his life in Roman service, but there was a fierceness in those eyes, a barbarous simplicity, that spoke to Ecdicius of chilly northern fens and barren shores bitten by frost. Wearing his uniform, standing in that court, he seemed a misplaced creature. Ecdicius thought of the aurochs he had once seen in the amphitheatre of Arles.

Majorian was in his late thirties, unimpressive in his looks, straightforward in his speech. 'So the Senate has accepted you,' he said.

Ecdicius bristled with annoyance. His father deserved respect. The generals had not prostrated themselves. Majorian had not even used proper address. 'This is your emperor,' he said, stepping forward. 'You should lie down before him.'

Majorian did not even look over. 'And you should keep silent until you're told to speak.'

Avitus gestured for his son to step back. Ecdicius obeyed, his anger undiminished.

'Count Majorian,' the emperor said, 'if you pledge yourself to us, we are prepared to confirm your post as count of the household guard. You will retain all honours bestowed on you by our predecessor.'

'And will my command include these Goths I now see running the palace?'

'Those are my personal guard. They will remain under the command of Prince Euric.'

Majorian laughed. 'A Roman emperor with his life in the hands of Goths. May I ask when this became tradition?'

'When you and your household guard abandoned the last emperor to die at the hands of a mob.'

'Petronius brought that on himself. If he hadn't bribed his way onto the throne . . .'

Ecdicius rarely heard his father raise his voice. Now he did, and the effect silenced Majorian at once. 'Be careful, Count. If Petronius had not bribed his way onto the throne – what? You would be sitting here now? You, who failed in your oath to protect the emperor? You, who fled Rome at the first sight of the Vandal fleet, and now come crawling back like a petulant child?'

Majorian seemed to shrink before the chastening. Ecdicius could tell that the surrender of Rome weighed heavily on his shoulders. So he had some honour as a soldier, at least. 'We've been fighting Vandal raids in the south,' he said.

'After leaving Rome at their mercy for two weeks.'

'It took time to gather our forces—'

'And you,' said Avitus, looking at Ricimer. 'We could lay the same charge at your feet. You two proud generals, protectors of Rome, who abandoned her to the ravages of a foreign foe. Who let her emperor be torn limb from limb and thrown into the Tiber. Why should we not strip you of all honours, and give you the punishment you deserve?'

Ricimer spoke for the first time. 'Because we have six thousand troops camped outside the city.' The threat was implicit in his words, and clear in his eyes. He was not going to be intimidated.

Now Euric burst forth from the shadows. 'And the emperor has the might of the Gothic army behind him.'

'Where are these Goths?' scoffed Ricimer. 'I see only you and a few palace guards. Where is your brother Theoderic? Where is his mighty army?'

'Our ally is defending our territory in the west,' said Avitus.

'We came to Rome as her emperor, not her conqueror. Now, you will pledge yourselves to us, or you will leave this room in chains.'

At this, Ricimer laughed, flinging his arms wide. His eyes sparkled like ice in the firelight. 'Do you hear him, Majorian? Do you hear him threaten us, with our men camped outside the city?'

'Calm, Brother,' urged Majorian, putting a hand on Ricimer's shoulder. He said to Avitus, 'We've been fighting and marching for weeks. Perhaps we should rest, and return tomorrow.'

'We agree,' said Avitus. 'But before you leave this room you will pledge allegiance.'

'Pledge allegiance to a Gothic puppet?' said Ricimer.

'My father is no Gothic puppet,' snapped Ecdicius. He was fast losing patience with the barbarian general.

'We will pledge allegiance,' said Majorian. He gave Ricimer a firm look. 'Both of us. Rome is weak, and we must be united. Majesty – we are yours to command.'

Majorian approached the throne, knelt, and then laid on his front, arms outstretched, forehead resting on the floor.

At first Ricimer did not move. He looked with scorn at Ecdicius and at Euric, who was staring back with triumph in his eyes. But then he, too, stepped closer to the throne, uttered the single word, 'Majesty,' and prostrated himself.

Once Avitus was satisfied, he commanded the pair to rise. 'Rome has need of your talents,' he said. 'Majorian, you are to continue as count of the household troops. Count Ricimer, you are to command the fleet and secure the grain shipments against Vandal piracy. If you both serve us well, you will be rewarded. Now go. We'll talk further tomorrow.'

The chief of admissions ushered the generals from the room. As soon as they were gone, the consistory came to Avitus and surrounded him with urgent whisperings. From what Ecdicius could overhear, Magnus seemed insistent on one point in particular: the Gallic field army was to be summoned to Italy at once, with as many barbarian allies as possible.

XLIV

A forest outside Toulouse, A.D. 456

Arvandus had always hated hunting. Sidonius had taken him several times to hunt marsh birds in the Camargue south of Arles, and he had never enjoyed it. The sport seemed to combine three of the things he most disliked: horsemanship, physical strength, and long stretches of tedium. It hardly helped that this time he was merely a spectator, here to admire King Theoderic's prowess along with two dozen others. They had set out from the royal palace an hour ago, as soon as the king had grown bored of his morning audiences. Most of the party was on horseback, with a few servants walking alongside carrying refreshments or hunting nets, bows and spears, or trailing leashed hunting dogs. Theoderic was at the front with several Gothic and Roman nobles. The rest of the riders were petitioners who had been granted the honour of accompanying the royal hunt. Each one of them was hoping for a moment with the king himself, but that was not guaranteed. It depended on Theoderic's mood. Paulus, who was riding behind the king, had already warned Arvandus that they might all return to Toulouse disappointed.

They followed a track into the depths of the forest that was a favourite hunting preserve of the Gothic king. It was a fresh, clear morning in early April. The trees were alive with birdsong, the branches were thick with fresh foliage, and every clearing was a colourful carpet of springtime flowers.

It felt good to be surrounded by the feeling of rebirth, Arvandus had to admit. The winter had been hard. More than once he had regretted not taking Sidonius's offer of the post at Bourges, which would at least have given him something to live on. During those cold, hungry weeks he had asked himself whether he had grown too proud, whether his expectations had grown too high. But even now he recoiled at the thought of accepting that humble post in the provinces while his friends were enjoying the luxuries of the imperial palace in Rome. If he regretted anything, it was not seeing Sidonius again before he had left Arles. That *had* been pride. There was nothing he could do about that now, though.

So he had turned his ambitions elsewhere. There was no future for him serving in the imperial administration. God knew he had tried. Felix had thwarted him once, and now Sidonius had insulted him. No matter what friends he made, he would always be the upstart peasant from the docks of Bordeaux, and someone would always stamp him down. Then he had remembered what the Gothic ambassador, Paulus, had told him at the prefect's party: King Theoderic was a great Roman of their day. Maybe that was true, maybe not; but he was a strong ruler, loyal to the emperor, and seemed enthusiastic to restore the schools and culture of Aquitaine. That was something.

Paulus had made it difficult for Arvandus, ignoring his first messages, then rebuffing his direct approach one day in the forum of Arles. But Arvandus had persevered. He went back to the forum every day and asked Paulus again and again to get him an audience with Theoderic. Eventually Paulus had given in. 'I'm returning to Toulouse in the spring,' he had said. 'Come with me. The king can make up his own mind about you.'

The hunting column stopped. All conversations were hushed. Arvandus, near the back, peered ahead to see that Theoderic had dismounted and was following a huntsman with a leashed hound off the path into the undergrowth.

Paulus came riding slowly down the column, his reins in one hand, an unstrung bow and four arrows in the other. When he came to Arvandus he held out the bow and arrows. 'Dismount and take these to the king,' he said.

Arvandus stared at the weaponry. 'I don't know how to string a bow.'

'Good, the king prefers to string it himself. Just take it to him – quickly, but quietly.'

Arvandus jumped from his pony, grabbed the bow and arrows, and hurried up the length of the column, feeling the envious eyes of the other petitioners on him. There was no sign of the king or the huntsman, but he crept into the undergrowth after them, avoiding twigs, treading as gently as he could.

He had gone about fifty yards and was beginning to fear that he was lost when he saw the king's dark cloak ahead. He was standing with the huntsman at the edge of a broad, marshy river bed. The huntsman was pointing at something in the reeds.

The leashed hound growled softly as it saw Arvandus approaching. The king turned and held out his hand. 'Give it to me,' he whispered.

Arvandus handed him the bow. Was he supposed to kneel in respect? He had no idea. The best thing to do seemed to be nothing, but to stay as still and quiet as possible.

The king's eyes were fixed on the distant reeds. Arvandus squinted and eventually saw them: two brown and white bitterns, well camouflaged in the reeds. The one on the left was about forty yards away. It was motionless, holding up its long beak almost vertically, its feathery fat throat jutting out. The other bittern was picking its way slowly through a reed bed a little further out.

Theoderic placed the strung end of the bow on his left foot. With a grunt he bent the bow, sliding the noose of the string up its length and fitting it over the nock at the top end. He did not take his eyes off the birds. He reached backwards to Arvandus, who placed an arrow in his hand. The king took the arrow, nocked it on the string, and said, 'Choose.'

Arvandus was not sure if he was being addressed. The huntsman caught his eye and nodded towards the birds. So he was to choose the target. He studied them again. The motionless bird on the left was closer, and the larger of the two. The other would be more of a challenge. 'The one on the right,' he said.

Theoderic raised the bow in his left arm, drawing back the arrow in a smooth motion. He exhaled slowly through his nose. For a space of several heartbeats he stood like that, with not a twitch or tremor.

He loosed the arrow. Arvandus followed its swift course across the reeds and into the belly of the furthest bittern. Its companion launched into the air with a sudden panicked flapping. The huntsman released the hound, which at once leaped into the marsh and began fighting its way through the reeds to the fallen bird.

'Well chosen,' said Theoderic, looking at Arvandus for the first time. His smile was restrained, his eyes giving little away. 'Paulus has told me that you want to serve in my court,' he said in crisp and precise Latin.

'Yes, Majesty,' said Arvandus, still unsure whether or not he should kneel. He felt like the moment for it had passed, but he did not want to cause offence. He was used to the strict rituals of Roman courts. Talking to a barbarian king on the edge of a marsh was a new experience.

Theoderic did not seem to care. He bent the bow to unstring it. 'Tell me why I should accept you.'

'Because I know Emperor Avitus well, Majesty. I served on his staff in the war against Attila. I know his family. I also served for two years under Tonantius Ferreolus when he was prefect.'

'And you're from Bordeaux?'

'Yes, Majesty.'

'I thought I could tell the accent, though you try hard to conceal it, I think. Very well. Now tell me why *you* should want to serve *me*.'

Arvandus had prepared words for such a question. He had not imagined delivering them in a setting like this, but he would make do. 'Majesty, your fame reaches from the shores of the outer ocean to the snowy peaks of the Alps. People sing of your victories in battle, and I've now seen with my own eyes your skill at the hunt. The glorious blood of the Gothic royal line has reached perfection in you. The nations tremble at the mention of your name . . .'

As Arvandus continued, Theoderic knelt down to receive the returning hound. It sprang from the marsh, dumped the bird eagerly at his feet, and shook itself dry. Theoderic laughed as he was soaked in the spray. Turning to Arvandus, he said, 'I think you meant to talk to my brother.'

Arvandus stopped speaking. He did not understand. Vice-king Frideric was in Toulouse, and the next eldest brother, Euric, was in Rome. Princes Ricimer and Himnerith were mere boys.

Theoderic spared him his confusion. 'Thorismund,' he said. He ruffled the neck of the panting hound. 'He always loved that kind of talk. A man of great passions and dreams. A good warrior. Not a good king.' He stood, handing the bow back to Arvandus and cradling the bird under his arm. 'Tell me again why you want to serve me. And know that in my ministers I value honesty far above flattery.'

Arvandus swallowed. He had indeed composed his speech as though for Thorismund, remembering his behaviour outside the gate of Arles. Clearly this king was different: cautious, cunning, not to be won over by pretty words. 'I was born under your father's rule,' he said. 'My family were poor and of no name. All I've ever wanted to do was restore the empire to what it used to be. It's said that your Majesty is the great Roman of our time.'

Theoderic smiled. 'But you just said Avitus was your old master. Why come to me? Why not serve him?'

Arvandus hesitated. He might have lied, but something told him that the king would be able to tell. He would risk the truth. 'I have an enemy close to the emperor.'

'I see. And if I take you into my service, your enemy will become my enemy. I may lose friends in the imperial court. Isn't that so?'

Arvandus could find no answer to that. The honesty had made him blunder. Even if he said more, if he admitted to the hatred between himself and Felix, it would not help. Theoderic could not afford to make enemies of the Philagrii.

The king did not say another word. He ducked into the undergrowth, heading back to the hunting party. The huntsman followed with the hound.

Arvandus went after them. He was dejected. With a few short words he had ruined his chances. If not even the Gothic king would take him, where else could he go?

Back at the column, he avoided Paulus's curious stare and

walked towards his pony. He would have to wait until they got back to Toulouse, and then decide what to do. There was little point returning to Arles, and he could not bear the thought of going home to Bordeaux. There was always the Burgundian kingdom. Nobody knew him there; he could make new friends and allies . . .

There was a hooded servant standing a short distance away, next to a horse belonging to a Gothic lord who had dismounted to speak to the king. Even though his face was hidden there was something familiar about him, enough to make Arvandus pause. He watched as the servant took a strung bow and a single arrow from a satchel behind the horse's saddle. Then the man lowered his hood and looked straight at the king, who was about twenty yards away.

Arvandus knew him. He recognised those thick shoulders, that bald, angular head, the protruding upper lip that almost touched the tip of the nose. Felix had called him Ajax.

And he was raising his bow.

Arvandus screamed: '*No!*' He charged across the space between them, pushing one of the other petitioners to the ground, almost stumbling himself, but somehow keeping his footing on the dirt and broken branches of the path; Ajax was distracted for an instant, long enough for the king and his nobles to look around and see the danger.

Ajax loosed the arrow at the moment Arvandus dived into him, wrapping himself around the big man's legs. They both tumbled into the undergrowth. Arvandus heard shouts of horror, the high-pitched whinny of a horse; Ajax cursed, fixed both hands on him, hurled him aside as though he were a rag doll. Arvandus's head collided with a tree trunk.

Everything became muffled, dark. There was shouting and movement all around him, Latin and Gothic jumbled together, barking and snarling hounds, the neighing of distressed horses.

Slowly his vision cleared. His head was throbbing. A servant was kneeling at his side, lifting a gourd of water to his lips. Arvandus drank and wiped his mouth. Ajax was on the ground nearby, face-down, writhing and cursing as two Gothic lords held him fast and a servant hurried over with a bundle of rope. Looking to the front of the column, Arvandus saw that the king's stallion was lying on its side, snorting in distress, an arrow protruding from its neck. The missile must have missed the king by inches. Theoderic knelt beside the beast, trying to calm it as the huntsman prepared to extract the arrow.

The king rose and walked over to Arvandus. There was shock in his eyes, even a trace of fear. 'I owe you my life,' he said.

'He's called Ajax,' Arvandus uttered, his voice shaking. 'He's one of Felix's men. Felix of the Philagrii.'

Theoderic turned to face Ajax as the Goths lifted him to his feet. 'You were sent to kill me?' he asked.

Ajax did not reply.

'Felix sent you?'

Still no reply. Ajax merely stared at the king, his thick lips clamped shut.

'You'll talk, I promise,' said Theoderic. He waved his hand, and the Goths dragged away the failed assassin. Turning back to Arvandus, he said, 'On your feet, Roman. It seems I may have need of your services after all.'

XLV

Rome

'It's a true temple of Pallas,' Sidonius said. 'The Ulpian library is the greatest in the west, without doubt. Ten thousand scrolls in the Latin hall, and just as many in the Greek hall. Just wait till you see it!'

'It sounds impressive,' Ecdicius said, trying to appreciate his cousin's enthusiasm for the famous library. They walked together through the forum of Trajan, the vast plaza stretching away on either side to monumental porticoes. They marched ahead and climbed the marble steps that led into the Ulpian basilica. Sidonius made sure that Ecdicius paused to admire its multi-coloured marble floor, and its double level of columns: polished granite below, Carystian green marble standing majestically in the upper arcade.

It was impressive. Rome was filled with such wonders. But Ecdicius found it impossible to forget the pile of paperwork waiting for him back at the palace. After making it through the winter, it was time to plan for the rest of the year. The granaries of Rome were running low, and the plebs would riot if they were not filled by autumn. Traditionally the grain had come from Africa, but for seventeen years now the king of the Vandals had been in control of the supply, cutting it off whenever he saw a political advantage in doing so. It was as though he had his foot on the throat of the city; he could starve it at will. This year the only ships he would send across the sea were likely to be war vessels.

So the grain would have to come from elsewhere, and that meant Sicily and Gaul; perhaps Spain too, if Theoderic managed to beat back the Suevic raiders who had attacked Tarraconensis.

All of this required coordination with Priscus Valerianus back in Arles. As prefect he would have to acquire the grain through extraordinary taxes that were sure to prove unpopular. Meanwhile the army also had to be fed. And when Theoderic finally sent reinforcements as promised, there would be even more mouths to worry about.

Ecdicius had seen the burden of all these uncertainties building up on his father's shoulders. Over the winter months they may have settled down into their daily routines, but there was a deep tension in the royal palace that was there at every dinner, every morning audience, and every meeting. Not even the arrival of his mother had helped. Avitus seemed to have aged five years since the autumn. It was not that Ecdicius ever heard him express doubt, even when they were talking alone in some private palace room; but there was a new seriousness in his demeanour that he seemed to have assumed along with the sceptre and crown of imperial authority.

Ecdicius tried to clear his thoughts. Problems were not solved by worrying. He forced himself to pay attention as Sidonius led him through the opposite door of the basilica into the library courtyard. The two separate halls of the library were to the left and right, their entrances closed off by screens of latticed bronze, while straight ahead was the temple of Trajan. In the centre of the courtyard was the enormous marble tomb of Trajan himself, surmounted by a soaring column that had been carved and painted with scenes from the famous emperor's Dacian conquest.

'Here I am,' said Sidonius, pointing towards a freshly installed statue that stood in the courtyard's colonnade. He stood gazing at it dreamily. 'With the poet Quintianus on one side of me and Merobaudes on the other, as though I deserve to be in their company.'

'Of course you do.' Ecdicius smiled to see his cousin's happiness. His father had commissioned the statue to reward Sidonius for the panegyric he had written for his consular inauguration on the first day of January. The ceremony had taken place in the forum of Trajan. It had been a cold, sluggish dawn, but there must have been ten thousand people in attendance, all cheering Avitus as he had donned the consular robe. They had filled the space between the porticoes, crowded the steps of the imperial podium, had been perched on the colossal equestrian statue that stood in the centre of the forum.

Even this happy memory, though, caused Ecdicius a stab of worry. His father had assumed the year's consulship, as was customary for a new emperor, but the east had still not recognised him as either emperor or consul. So long as Marcian withheld his approval, his father could be legitimately treated as a usurper by any who resented the rule of a Gallic emperor.

'Let me show you the Latin library,' Sidonius said. He led Ecdicius across the courtyard to the hall on the right. They passed through a gate in the bronze screen and entered a vast room beneath a light-filled vaulted ceiling. In the centre, on a gleaming floor of gold and granite, were rows of reading tables. Around the walls were columns of purple-veined marble, each fronted by a bronze bust, and between each pair of columns a set of steps led up to a tall wooden cupboard. Ecdicius saw an upper level of cupboards running around a balcony. There were four men at the tables, old professors or impoverished senators by the look of them. Their faces were bent low as they muttered through their texts.

'Forget the gold and statues and marble,' Sidonius whispered. 'This is the real treasure of Rome.'

Ecdicius gazed around the hall. He had never seen a library a tenth of this size. 'And the Vandals left it all?'

'They didn't touch it. Barbarians only care for things that glitter, Ecdicius. Just think of the generations of wisdom held in these cupboards. The other day I came across a complete set of Varro's *Antiquities of Human and Divine Affairs*. Even Eusebius has never seen a copy of that. Imagine if the Vandals had looted this place – or even worse, burned it. Just imagine what we would have lost.'

A gruff voice from behind them. 'Prince Ecdicius.'

He turned to see a soldier standing at the bronze screen, fully armed and armoured. 'Count Ricimer wishes to speak to you in private,' he said. 'Please follow me.' He went immediately to the Trajan's tomb in the centre of the courtyard, and entered through a door at its base.

'What does Ricimer want with you?' asked Sidonius.

'I don't know,' said Ecdicius. He had had very little to do with the count, who had remained in Rome while the fleet was readied at Portus for the spring campaign; apart from attending occasional military councils together, they rarely crossed paths. Ecdicius would have been happy to keep it that way. Ever since that first audience he had not trusted the man. His first impulse was to refuse the soldier's disrespectful command, but he did not want to seem like a coward. There were plenty of witnesses, at least. If Ricimer wanted to get rid of him for some reason, this was not the place to do it. 'I'll be back soon,' Ecdicius said.

He left the library, crossed the courtyard, and entered the tomb. Inside it was dark and cramped. The soldier was waiting for him in a small antechamber, at the foot of a narrow spiral staircase that led to the top of the column. He indicated for Ecdicius to ascend.

The soldier remained at the bottom while Ecdicius began to climb, carefully feeling his way up the stifling, winding space. He was quickly enveloped in darkness, the only light coming from tiny slits in the outer wall. For most of the climb he was blind, accompanied by the sound of his own breathing and the scraping of his boots on the marble steps. He could not shake the instinct to go back down, but the soldier would have stopped him – and anyway, he thought, why should he be afraid of a barbarian like Ricimer? He was the son of the emperor, and heir to the imperial throne.

At last he saw daylight above. The months of being confined in the palace had left him unfit, and he was panting from the exertion as he passed through a door into the open air. A narrow platform encircled the top of the column. He felt a strong gust of wind, and immediately clasped both hands on the waist-high iron fence that ran around the platform, the only thing protecting him from falling one hundred feet to his death. He tried not to look down. Straight ahead, over the roof of the Latin library, a busy clutter of buildings climbed the slope of the Quirinal Hill. Above them rose the mighty porticoes of the temple of Serapis, long abandoned but still a sight to behold; and beside it were the baths of Constantine, from which clouds of steam drifted up into the crisp April sky.

He could not see Ricimer, however. Gathering his nerves, he let go of the railing and followed the platform to the right. He found the general on the south side. He was standing close to the edge of the platform, muscular arms folded, his pale eyes looking over the bronze-plated roof of the Ulpian basilica and the imperial forums to the distant Palatine Hill.

Ecdicius spoke. 'You asked to see me, Count Ricimer?'

The count turned his head. There was something in those eyes – or an absence of something – that chilled Ecdicius; he stared at him as though he were not really there. He returned his gaze to the city. 'Did you ever see such a sight?'

Ecdicius stepped closer. 'She is the jewel of cities.'

'I remember when I first came to Rome,' Ricimer said. 'I was just a boy, five years old. My mother brought me here. My father was dead. The two of us were exiles, driven from Aquitaine by old Theoderic. This city became my new home. I must have been fifteen when Count Aëtius brought me to the top of this column, and we stood together, just like this. He showed me the city and said: "Ricimer, this is why we fight." I think of him every time I go into battle. He should not have died as he did, butchered by cowards. Rome does not need emperors like Valentinian and Petronius. She needs an emperor like Trajan – an emperor who can fight.'

'My father can fight. He served under Aëtius, too.'

'Yes. But he is not a young man.'

Unlike Majorian, Ecdicius thought. *Unlike you.* 'Count, may I asked why you summoned me?'

'Aegidius speaks very highly of you. Your reputation has spread through Rome, and many people are taking an interest in you.

"Who is this son of the emperor?" they ask. "What does he want?"'

'I want to serve Rome.'

'As do we all. Your father has proved himself to be a generous master – at least, so far as his means allow. How much more generous can he be, I wonder? The treasury is still empty. An emperor without coin cannot stay emperor for long.'

Ecdicius was becoming uncomfortable with the direction of the conversation. 'Imperial finances are a matter for the count of sacred largesses.'

'Even he cannot conjure gold out of thin air. There is still wealth in Rome, Ecdicius. The Vandals did not take everything. But the men who control this wealth will not simply give it up. They'll sit in the Senate dressed in rags and moan about the hardships of poverty, and curse the barbarians for ruining them, and all the while they have their treasures hidden away where nobody else can get at them.'

'Nobody except you?'

'Majorian and I have friends in the Senate. More friends than your father. They listen to what we say. But these senators would sooner lose their heads than lose their gold. They won't hand it over to the emperor, at least not to an emperor who is not one of their own. Now, were I to recommend such an emperor to them – that would be different.'

His talk was dangerously close to treason. Ecdicius felt his indignation rise. 'The Senate has pledged allegiance to my father, as have you.'

Ricimer looked at him sharply. Ecdicius was seized by a sudden visceral fear that the general was about to grab hold of him and hurl him over the railing; an irrational fear, but it was all he could do not to retreat. 'Do not doubt my loyalty,' Ricimer said. 'A soldier's oath is sacred. Your father has brought calm to the city; that is good. But he has no money. The Senate is unhappy to see the imperial palace filled with foreigners. Emperor Marcian in the east has not recognised him. Most of all, he is old. Can you deny any of this?'

'I don't care. He has honour and courage. He'll give up everything he has for the sake of the empire.'

'Then he should give up the throne. He should resign, and
retire to Gaul. I've sworn to serve him loyally, but I fear for his
safety.'

'He's well protected.'

'By Goths. Mercenaries. What will he do when he can no
longer pay them? You are his son, and I know he trusts you. All
I ask is that you talk to him, encourage him to act in the interests
of Rome. She needs an emperor who is young and strong.'

'You mean Majorian?'

'That's for the Senate and people of Rome to decide. I'm
simply a soldier. I can see a great future for you, Ecdicius. One
day you will succeed your father. I only ask, why wait?'

Ecdicius felt a stiff shudder down the back of his neck. So he
was being asked to depose his own father. The idea filled him
with revulsion. Were he even to do such a thing, he knew that
he would have no real power. Ricimer surely intended to make
him a puppet – and then a barbarian general would be dictating
the fate of the western empire.

Fighting down his outrage, Ecdicius smiled. It was better to
let Ricimer think he shared his lust for power. 'I've asked myself
that same question,' he said. 'Very well, I'll talk to the emperor.'

'Good. I hope this was the first meeting of many. Good health
to you, Prince Ecdicius, and to your father.'

Ecdicius went to the door and hurried back down the staircase,
his heart racing. It seemed that the whole world was against his
father: the eastern emperor called him a tyrant; the Senate did
not want him; the people of Rome would rise up the moment
their bellies were empty. And now, worst of all, his own sworn
generals could not be trusted. Ecdicius only prayed that Ricimer
had believed his lie. He needed time to tell his father that the
barbarian was plotting against him.

XLVI

Not until the following morning was Ecdicius able to speak privately with the emperor. Whether he happened to be in the country, city, or army camp, it had always been his father's custom to take a solitary walk at dawn, and since arriving in Rome he had adopted the palace gardens for this habit. Like everything in the imperial palace, the gardens were monstrous in their opulence. They had been built in the style of a race track five hundred feet long. Around the entire garden ran a covered arcade on two levels, brick arches below and marble columns above, and the enclosed space was so large that a timber amphitheatre had been built in the southern half. Prince Euric had taken over this structure as an exercise yard for his Gothic troops. The rest of the space was filled with rows of flowerbeds, paths, and tall hedges, a dense orchard of fruit trees in the centre, and an ornamental fountain where the northern turning post would have been.

Ecdicius walked with hurried steps along the lower arcade. Euric and his Goths had already begun their day, and barbaric grunts and the clashing of weapons echoed from the amphitheatre down the length of the formal gardens. Ecdicius soon spotted the tall form of his father on a gravel path near the northern end, wrapped in a fur coat against the morning chill, framed by the branches of apple trees. He was looking up into the heavens, at the last of the fading western stars.

Avitus heard his son approach on the sandy path. Seeing his urgency, he frowned. 'Ecdicius,' he said. 'Is something wrong?'

'I'm sorry to disturb you, Majesty.'

'Please, Ecdicius. Let's walk together.' As they began a slow stroll around the orchard, Avitus said, 'The German tribes believe that each new day starts not when the sun rises, but when it sets. Did you know that?'

'No, Father.'

'They believe night comes before day. The world is born in darkness, they say, and must struggle through the night before it ever sees the sun.' He looked again into the sky. Apart from a few fleeting clouds, it promised a clear day. 'The Germans are a grim people.'

Ecdicius glanced down the length of the gardens. Some Goths, their exercises over, were emerging from the amphitheatre gates. Their naked torsos shone with sweat as they laughed and flexed their arms. They were a grim people, true, until they picked up weapons. 'Father, I spoke with Ricimer yesterday. At his insistence.'

Avitus grunted. 'That is his custom. What did he have to say?'

Ecdicius had planned his words carefully. 'He's aware of our financial difficulties. He said that the senators are hiding their wealth and don't trust you. He also wants me to depose you.'

His father's eyes narrowed. 'He said that?'

'Not directly. But he wants you to resign, and he wants me to take your place.'

The emperor was quiet for a long moment as they continued their walk. Ecdicius knew that they would not be able to talk for long. The adoring people of Rome would already be assembling in the palace forecourt. Soon his father would have to receive their morning salutations from the balcony of the throne room.

Avitus reached out a gloved hand to touch the spindly twigs. 'I knew Majorian and Ricimer when they were junior officers under Aëtius. Aegidius, too. The three of them were like brothers. They certainly quarreled like brothers. Aëtius used to say that each of them was one third of a great general. Majorian was clever, Aegidius was bold, and Ricimer was ruthless.'

'I've let Ricimer believe I'm sympathetic to him. As soon as he realises I'm not, he'll try to replace you by force. I'm sure of it.'

'Nonsense,' said Avitus, as though shocked at the very thought.

'Ricimer may by ruthless, but he's a soldier to the bone. He understands that an oath is sacred.'

'Even so . . .'

'I've no doubt he'd prefer to see Majorian on the throne, with some justification.'

'Justification? Father, you're the inaugurated emperor. They owe you fealty.'

'Let me tell you about Majorian, son,' Avitus said patiently. 'A few years ago Emperor Valentinian wanted Majorian to marry his daughter Placidia, and thus become heir to the empire. But Aëtius wanted his own son to wed Placidia, so out of jealousy he forced Majorian to resign. Now, when Aëtius was murdered, Valentinian summoned Majorian back into service. And when Valentinian was murdered in turn, many people thought Majorian would become emperor after all – except Petronius took the palace first. And then Petronius was killed, and I became emperor. So now Majorian has been denied the throne a third time. Wouldn't you expect him to be a little disgruntled?'

'He had months to declare himself emperor before we arrived in Rome. If he wanted the throne, he should have taken it when he had the chance.'

'Indeed, so why didn't he? Either he doesn't want it, or he doesn't have the resources. All these rumours that he stole the treasury – it's all nonsense. If he had, he'd have raised another army with it by now. No, the treasury is in Africa, along with the rest of Rome's gold.'

'Except for the gold hidden away by the senators,' Ecdicius said.

'Which is why we must make the Senate our friend. Don't worry about Ricimer. He's about to set sail with the fleet for Sicily. Magnus is convinced that a victory over the Vandals there will persuade the Senate to give me a loan.'

'But what if Ricimer takes the credit for himself and Majorian?'

'They can take as much credit as they like. They're still bound by oath to serve me. Aegidius has vouched for them, and he's one of us. Those three are blood brothers. They'd never turn against each other.'

A palace servant awaited them on the path ahead. 'Majesty,' he said, bowing deeply. 'The Senate and the people of Rome await your pleasure.'

'Very well,' said Avitus. He turned to Ecdicius, placing both hands on his shoulders. 'Don't worry, son. Majorian and Ricimer will be kept busy fighting Vandals for the next few months. In the meantime, as soon as Theoderic has beaten the Sueves in Spain he'll send us another army across the Alps. These are delicate times. I'm relying on you to keep a calm head. Can you do that?'

Ecdicius nodded. 'Yes, Father.'

'Good,' he said. 'Now hurry and make yourself ready for the audience.'

Ecdicius watched his father walk up the path, the servant scurrying after him, and vanish into the shadows of the arcade. Perhaps his father was right about Ricimer and the others; perhaps the endless confinement in the palace and the anxieties of the previous months had made Ecdicius go mad with suspicion.

Yet it was so clear in his mind that Ricimer could not be trusted, he hardly knew how to express it. The memory of the conversation above Trajan's tomb, that look of emptiness in the general's eyes, haunted him still. The previous night he had dreamed that he was falling, and all around him was blackness; yet blind though he was, he had known that it was Ricimer who had thrown him, and that nothing was below but death. He had awoken breathless and close to panic, his sheets soaked in cold sweat.

Had this been a premonition, or simply a distemper of the mind? Ecdicius did not know. Certainly he could not present a dream as proof of treachery. Ricimer wanted his father off the throne. He had been frank about that. But he had also seemed determined to honour his oath. Ecdicius did not know what to think.

XLVII

Tarragona, Spain

A rvandus looked out over the calm waters to the city. Two piers stretched out into the sea towards him like a pair of welcoming arms, the lighthouse at the end of each guiding ships into the sheltered harbour of Tarragona. Above the wharves rose sheer cliff faces, and on top of those the city itself: towering walls, columns and pediments that shone bone-white in the sun, the curved roofs of the baths and the blazing red tiles of town houses and apartments, all climbing up to the citadel where King Theoderic had established his temporary court. Not even Arles could compete with the grandeur of this city, which stood like a mountain of marble over the blue waters of the Mediterranean.

He breathed in the salty air, relishing the breeze as it buffeted his cloak and billowed in the sails of the merchant ship. For three days they had hugged the coast south from Narbonne. Arvandus had enjoyed his own private cabin at the stern of the ship, furnished with a comfortable bed and as much wine as he could drink. At the start of the voyage the captain had actually apologised for the small size of the cabin; he had a larger ship, he said, unfortunately in dock for repairs, that would have made a more fitting vessel for a minister of King Theoderic. Arvandus had accepted the cabin graciously, not mentioning the fact that it was larger and more comfortable than most rooms he had rented on dry land.

Two months had passed since he had foiled the attempt on Theoderic's life. The king had rewarded him with four pounds of gold – almost three hundred solidi, a fortune beyond the dreams of most. The first thing Arvandus had done was buy a new wardrobe of tunics and cloaks from the finest merchants in

Toulouse, along with a heavy golden brooch to wear at his shoulder, a badge of his office as minister of the royal court. Next, with Paulus acting as intermediary, he had purchased a modest villa and vineyard outside the city. By now his parents would have received the money he had sent them. He smiled to imagine their reaction upon being presented with twenty solidi and instructions to move themselves to Toulouse at their earliest convenience. He had not yet rebuilt the family fortune, but he had overnight become a propertied man with seven servants. He was also still of equestrian rank, since senatorial status could only be granted by imperial authority, not by a barbarian king. In the Gothic realm, though, Paulus told him that such things mattered less with every passing year. The senatorial families clung on to their inherited titles, but what really mattered was how many acres a man had under his plough, and how much gold he had in his strongbox. By that reckoning, the family's future looked bright. Soon he might even start looking for a wife.

A deep voice came from behind him. 'Big city.'

Arvandus smiled. 'Yes indeed. King Theoderic is in the governor's palace at the top. We'll be heading there as soon as we dock. You should bring out the chest.'

The big German nodded and went back to the cabin, which Arvandus had been sharing with him and his brother Guntram. They had been the third thing Arvandus had bought with his newfound wealth. He had sent a messenger to Arles to find the two Thuringian brothers and invite them to enter his service as bodyguards. He had been pleased to learn that they were still in the city and willing to join him. At court he wanted two personal guards he knew he could trust. They had improved their Latin since he had last seen them. Better yet, their mother tongue was close enough to Gothic that they could act as translators when necessary.

Paulus was waiting on the wharves with his own two Gothic bodyguards when the ship came into dock. His eyes widened when he saw Arvandus walk down the gangplank followed by two enormous bearded Thuringians clad in short-sleeved tunics, breeches, and cloaks. Gunther came first, with a dagger and one-handed axe hanging from his broad leather belt. Guntram's weapon of choice was a *scramasax*, a one-edged short sword that hung in its scabbard horizontally across his front.

'I see you were able to find your friends,' Paulus said as Arvandus stepped onto the dockside.

'They were worth waiting for, as you can see.' They embraced and kissed each other on the cheeks. 'How was the march across the mountains?'

'Hard,' Paulus said. 'Come, we can talk on the way to the palace. The king's holding his morning audience.'

They set off along the docks, Arvandus and Paulus walking ahead, their bodyguards following, and a pair of sailors from the ship carrying Arvandus's chest at the rear. Dozens of ships packed the quayside, most of them traders from Gaul, the islands of the western Mediterranean, or elsewhere in Spain. Slaves laboured in their hundreds, bearing sacks and amphorae down gangplanks and across to the warehouses. The sky was filled with gulls, swirling and squawking in the salty air. Even so, long stretches of the wharves were empty, the warehouses seemingly abandoned. Tarragona had clearly seen better days.

Paulus explained how Theoderic had led his army on a long and difficult march across the Pyrenees during the weeks of May. This campaign was in retaliation against King Rechiar of the Sueves, who had taken advantage of the chaos in Rome and had left his own territory in the mountainous west in order to raid the Roman province of Tarraconensis. Theoderic had sent an envoy to the Suevic king commanding him to withdraw in the name of Emperor Avitus. Rechiar had responded by threatening to march on Toulouse itself. Thus war had become inevitable. To preserve the honour of Avitus, and to preserve his own, Theoderic had sworn to crush his rebellious brother-in-law. He had even made an alliance with King Gundioc of the Burgundians, who had marched from Geneva to Spain with his brother and two thousand troops.

'Where are the Sueves now?' Arvandus asked.

'King Rechiar still holds Saragossa, nine days inland. Theoderic will be heading for the city as soon as the army and supplies are ready.'

Arvandus remembered the war against Attila – the anxiety, the discomfort, his aversion to all aspects of military life. Strangely, he was not dreading this new war. He felt excited, almost ready to don a helmet and charge into battle himself. He had no doubt that Theoderic would destroy Rechiar if they met in open battle. With that victory would come plunder, slaves, and glory – and all of those who stayed true to the king would share in it.

It was a long, steep climb to the palace. From the boat the city had looked like a bustling metropolis, but that impression did not last long. Life seemed to be clinging to the docks and to the main streets that led up to the citadel. Overlooking the harbour was the back of an old theatre, now a broken ruin choked by trees and climbing plants. A little further on Arvandus glimpsed the roofless shell of what had once been a basilica, and entire side streets that seemed to have been abandoned to birds and dogs.

It became busier as they neared the citadel. Their path ended at a wide boulevard that cut across the width of the city. Along the opposite side of the street ran a single vast arcade, stretching as far as Arvandus could see in either direction, that Paulus explained was the south side of the circus. Between the arches of the arcade and all along the street, merchants shouted and sold their wares, children played, lounging men drank and debated chariots. There were quite a few soldiers, too, both Romans and Goths. Paulus led Arvandus to the east end of the arcade, through an entrance and up flights of stairs that eventually brought them past the circus to the largest forum Arvandus had ever seen. It was bustling with horses and Gothic troops. 'King Theoderic's army,' Paulus said, steering a path through the throng. 'Some of it, at least. On the far side are the Burgundians.'

At the top of the citadel was another plaza, surrounded by a grand portico. This area seemed to have been taken over by the heavy Gothic cavalry, the king's own warband of the highest noblemen and their retinues. In the centre was an old pagan temple, now evidently serving as a military headquarters. They went past it to the far end of the plaza, up a flight of stairs and through a row of enormous marble columns into a great hall.

This was where King Theoderic was holding court. He was seated on his throne in front of a curtain of deep vermilion, in discussion with a few of his elders. A pair of spear-wielding Gothic soldiers stood on either side of the throne. Around the hall were assembled groups of courtiers and petitioners, Romans and barbarians alike, all talking amongst themselves and hoping for a moment with the king.

As soon as Theoderic saw Arvandus and Paulus enter the hall he clapped his hands and gestured for them to approach. 'Arvandus,' he called. 'I'm glad you arrived safely. I have a surprise for you. A gift for your loyal service.' He turned to one of his guards and spoke a few words in Gothic. Then to Arvandus he said, 'He will take you to it.'

'Thank you, my king.'

Theoderic smiled and immediately renewed his conversation with the elders. Arvandus followed the soldier, glancing to the hall entrance and gesturing for Gunther and Guntram to remain there with the chest. The Goth led him through a different door at the back of the hall, along a corridor and down a narrow, torchlit staircase to the basement level. Here he lifted a torch from a wall sconce and set off down another corridor that had no light. The walls were unplastered, hewn from the rock upon which the citadel had been built. The air was cold and damp. It seemed an unlikely place for a gift. Arvandus felt the sickly grip of panic. *Don't be a fool*, he thought. *King Theoderic has no reason to harm you.*

They continued down the corridor. Heavy reinforced doors emerged from the darkness on either side. The Goth stopped at one of the doors and drew back the three iron bolts. He pushed open the door and entered the room, his blazing torch held high. Arvandus stepped in after him.

It was a small room, little more than a cave, windowless and filled with the choking stench of human waste. A shadowy huddle was slumped against the opposite wall. Arvandus heard the clinking of chains, and a face raised itself to the glow of the torchlight.

At first Arvandus did not recognise the prisoner. He had two months' growth of beard, and was screwing his eyes up against the light, his hands being too tightly manacled to reach his face. The angular, bald head, though, could belong only to Ajax. He was dressed in rags that hardly passed for clothing. Every inch of exposed flesh bore fresh bruises and scars. This was the fate of a failed assassin. Theoderic was surely keeping him alive as an example to others.

Arvandus crouched in front of him. 'Do you know who I am?'

Ajax squinted at him, studying him for a moment. He nodded.

'Has he taken your tongue?' Arvandus asked.

Ajax gave a hoarse cough. A whispery voice emerged from between his cracked lips and broken teeth. 'I can talk.'

'Tell me why Felix sent you to kill the king.'

Slowly he shook his head. 'Nobody sent me. I don't know any Felix.'

His words were flat, toneless, obviously well-rehearsed. Arvandus wondered how many times he had spoken them by now. Judging from his scars, a lot. Such resilience under torture was almost admirable. There was no point in Arvandus trying to interrogate him now. Sooner or later Theoderic would make him talk.

Arvandus got to his feet and spoke to the Goth. 'Give me your knife,' he said, pointing to the weapon in his belt. The Goth understood enough Latin to obey. Arvandus took the knife and knelt beside Ajax, grabbing hold of his right hand. Ajax struggled, but was too weak to resist.

It was harder to remove the little finger than Arvandus had expected. The knife was sharp, but he misjudged the angle and struck bone rather than slicing cleanly through the first joint. Ajax did not scream, but dropped his head back and let out an open-mouthed, rasping sound that was the closest thing he could manage.

It took quite a bit of twisting and sawing before the finger came free, by which time Arvandus's own hands were covered with blood. He stood, holding the knife in one hand, the finger in the other. Ajax writhed and slipped to the base of the wall until he was lying almost flat. The near-scream had not stopped. His eyes were now open.

Arvandus had expected to feel some kind of satisfaction. His first impulse had been to stuff Ajax's finger into his mouth, as Ajax had done to him, but that desire had evaporated. He felt no hatred towards this pitiable wreck of a man, whose suffering had only just begun. Harming him was like kicking a piece of furniture.

He tossed the finger on the floor, and handed the knife back to the Goth. 'Get some bandages for his hand,' he said.

Ajax may have done the deeds, but the crime was Felix's. He was the one who needed to suffer as Arvandus had suffered.

XLVIII

Rome

In the early days Attica had enjoyed the pomp of the morning audiences, the sight of her father on the throne in his glorious raiment, the stream of nobles and well-to-do commoners who came to offer obeisance at his feet. But now almost a year had passed and the novelty had worn thin. She was tired of seeing the same sycophantic faces each day, tired of being surrounded by the same muttering courtiers. It seemed to her that nothing of importance happened at the salutation. She had to attend every morning, though. Felix demanded it. 'The imperial family must be seen to be complete and harmonious,' he had told her. 'If you're not there, people will gossip.'

So long as they looked harmonious, Felix was happy. He did not care about the misery of his wife. The only times he allowed her to leave the palace were on religious feasts, when he would escort her to a church and stay beside her at every moment. By now she was used to standing through those long ceremonies like a statue, presenting an impassive face to the world. Sometimes she felt her insides turn to stone as well. It was for the best. If she allowed herself to dwell on things she would be driven mad. Her parents had troubles of their own, as did her brother. It would be unjust to burden them with her own unhappiness.

Her sole source of pleasure was the project she had been cultivating for months: she was paying for the refurbishment of the old basilica of Saint Lawrence. She had promised Bishop Leo, and so Felix had been unable to object. Every penny for the works had come from her own purse, in an act of public piety that she hoped would impress the nobility of Rome. She had had the basilica's roof replaced, the floors repaired, a new inscription placed on the façade. Most impressive, though, were the new ceiling mosaics in the apse that were almost complete. She had asked Sidonius to compose a short verse on the theme of Saint Lawrence, to be displayed in golden letters below the scene of his martyrdom. It would be her legacy to the city for generations to come. It was also the one thing she had managed to do without her husband's interference, although he still refused to let her visit the building works without him. After the audiences today she and Felix were to take their cousin to show him the setting for his poem. The thought of the excursion would help sustain her through the morning.

It was almost the end of the first hour. The public would be gathered by now in the palace forecourt. The imperial family was assembled as usual in the peristyle behind the throne room, the master of admissions casting his eye over them to make sure that all was in order. At the front stood her parents: her father in a diadem and gold-threaded cloak of Tyrian purple, and her mother, the empress, looking no less resplendent in her necklace of pearls and gemstones. Attica stood behind them, Ecdicius on her left and Felix on her right. In the third row were Sidonius and Magnus. At the rear came the train of personal servants and handmaidens, Cyra among them.

The master of admissions nodded to the attendants standing at the entrance to the throne room. They opened the great wooden doors. Inside horns blared. The imperial party processed along the peristyle and into the throne room, which filled instantly with the acclamations of the court, and continued down its length, emerging through the great doors onto the balcony to face the morning sun. More horns sounded, quickly drowned out by the cries of the people outside the palace. Lining the porch on either side of the balcony were Gothic soldiers. At the front of the crowd were a number of senators in their togas, the commoners filling the rest of the precinct.

The master of admissions stepped out onto the balcony and raised his staff. The crowd quietened. He gave the ritual acclamation: 'Hail Eparchius Avitus, pious and happy augustus!'

The people repeated his words again and again, the number of repetitions being a good measure of the emperor's popularity. Attica stared over their heads into the golden sky, wishing for it to end. It was early, but the late August sun was already hot, and she was beginning to cook beneath her under-tunic, ankle-length linen dress, and woollen mantle. The weight of her earrings and jewel-laden headdress were making her neck ache.

After the morning salutation came the imperial audiences, when a few lucky petitioners were allowed a moment in front of the emperor inside the throne room, while the court and the imperial family looked on. Italians struck Attica as an emotional and obsequious people, and today they brought the usual mix of legal cases, personal entreaties, and insipid flattery. Magnus stood beside the throne, whispering particulars of each supplicant into the emperor's ear. She knew her father hated it, but it was a necessary duty. It lasted for an hour before the master of admissions declared the audiences over. Again the trumpets blasted.

As she followed her parents out of the throne room back into the peristyle, Attica noticed that her husband was not with them. She had not seen him leave her side. 'Where's Felix?' she asked Sidonius.

'He disappeared during the audiences,' Sidonius replied. 'I think I saw him leave with someone.'

'He knows we're meant to be going to the church,' she said. 'We need to return in time for the midday meal.' It was a typically spiteful gesture, she thought. Felix hated the idea of her doing something independently of him, and this was his petty way of trying to control it.

'I suppose we'll have to wait for him,' Sidonius said.

'No,' she replied. 'Not this time. I'm paying for the building works. I say we go now, as planned.'

Sidonius was reluctant, but he could not match Attica's determination. She felt a small swell of triumph as she and her cousin climbed into the litter in the palace entrance hall.

The church was in the ninth district, to the north-west of the palace. They kept the curtains of the litter closed as they were carried down the slope of the Palatine Hill and through the Roman forum, accompanied by four Gothic guards on foot. Behind them was a second litter occupied by Cyra and Attica's new handmaiden, Honorata, a pleasant enough girl from an influential family of Rome. For most of the half-hour journey Sidonius excitedly recited the various drafts of his verses on Saint Lawrence, to which Attica listened with polite interest. She tried to suppress her habitual worry about how Felix would react when he realised that he had been left behind. *Let him react however he likes*, she thought. He had not brought that brute Ajax with him to Rome. He was too much of a coward to strike her with his own hand, and his words could no longer hurt her. This would be a useful lesson to him.

They dismounted at the steps of the church, which stood on a busy street of shops and apartments. Passers-by and traders watched as the emperor's daughter and son-in-law climbed the steps to the building, followed by the handmaidens and flanked by their bodyguards. The new façade had been completed, Attica was pleased to see, together with the inscription: *Attica, most esteemed wife of Magnus Felix, had this work built at her own expense.* It was a matter of convention to name her husband, but she had made sure that the credit for the rebuilding belonged to her alone. She ordered two of the Goths to stay outside with the litter-bearers while the rest of them entered.

Attica lifted her mantle over her head, Cyra and Honorata doing likewise. The church had been cleared of workers in antici-pation of their arrival, and they found themselves in a cool, tranquil space. The nave was empty except for some piles of wood and canvas sheeting that had not yet been cleared away. Attica led Sidonius to the apse at the far end, the guards and handmaidens waiting by the closed doors.

'It will be magnificent, don't you think?' Attica said. She gazed upwards into the half-dome ceiling, where the summer light gleamed brilliantly on the newly installed mosaic. Christ sat on a bejewelled throne in his imperial garments of gold and purple, the twelve toga-clad Apostles at his feet. Above them a cross rose into the heavens to join the four winged symbols of the Evangelists: lion and man, eagle and ox. An inscription ran around the top of the mosaic: *Holy, holy, holy is the Lord God Almighty, who was, and is, and will be.* Below the Apostles was a lower register that was still unfinished. In the centre was Saint Lawrence, striding determinedly towards a large grid-iron, its bars licked by yellow tongues from the fire beneath it. The mosaics to either side were yet to be installed, the scaffolding still standing in place.

'This is where I want your verse,' Attica said, with her hands indicating a line beneath the unfinished mosaics. 'What do you think?'

'I only hope my words do justice to the images,' Sidonius said.

She smiled, staring up at the mosaics in satisfaction. They were even more marvellous than she had been expecting. One hundred years from now, when she was long dead, all her worries and pains forgotten by the world as though they had never been, this piece of perfection would still be here. It was something Felix could never take from her.

Attica was distracted from her thoughts by shouts from the street outside. It sounded like a mob not far from the church. Chariot factions, she assumed, recalling that the stadium of Domitian was nearby. Then she remembered that no races were scheduled for that day.

She walked with rapid steps down the nave towards the doors, Sidonius close behind. She pointed to one of the Goths. 'You. Go and see what's happening. Bring the others inside.' As he hurried to obey, she addressed the other bodyguard. 'Take my handmaidens to the apse and guard them.'

The Goth was escorting the white-faced Cyra and Honorata to the apse when the first guard re-entered, bringing with him the other two Goths and the litter-bearers. 'There's rioting down the street, my lady,' he said.

'Don't close the door yet,' she said.

Sidonius, seeing her intentions, tried to obstruct her. 'Attica, don't go outside.'

She ignored him, pushing past and emerging out onto the top of the steps. A large woman hurried by with an infant clutched under one arm and a basket under the other. Other commoners, men, women and children, were running in the same direction, away from the odeon. As she looked down the street to the market stalls outside the grand arches of the theatre, some four hundred feet away, the mob came into sight.

It was not the first riot Rome had seen since their arrival, but it was the first time she had witnessed one. First of all appeared the dogs, running and barking like crazed heralds, their tails wagging in excitement. Then came the men in broken groups, chanting and swearing, the foremost waving clubs. She heard cruel-edged laughter as a market trader, too slow to flee, was stuck down in front of his stall. Missiles flew through the air: tiles and cobblestones, broken pieces of wood. The rioters hammered on doors and smashed the shuttered windows of buildings as they made their way up the street towards her.

'My lady!'

She heard the Goth's voice, but did not move. It was strange seeing such gleeful savagery with her own eyes; strange and terrifying, and between the two she was rooted to the spot. Only when a tile crashed into the façade above her head was she shocked into awareness. Her guard grabbed her by the arm and pulled her inside the building with such force that she almost stumbled on the hard floor.

As she steadied herself, she heard the doors being slammed and bolted shut behind her. The three Goths at the doors drew their swords, a flurry of sharp sounds in the quiet air of the basilica. None of them moved, listening to the chaos slowly come closer. Soon it was right outside.

The doors shuddered with a sudden impact. Attica's heart lurched into her throat. The mob was trying to break into the church. They might have been after the precious candlesticks and hangings, and whatever gold they could knock out of the mosaics. More likely they had seen the litters in the street and were after her and Sidonius. 'Is there another way out?' she asked.

'There's a door in the south aisle,' said one of the guards. 'But it's locked. We couldn't open it.'

'Give me a dagger,' Attica said. The nearest guard retrieved one from his belt and handed it to her. She raised the dagger and held the point against her throat. She felt no fear. She would not suffer the shame of rape.

'Attica,' Sidonius said, trying hard to keep his voice calm. 'Lower the blade.'

'I'll only use it if they break in.'

'They won't harm us. They wouldn't dare.' He spoke the words, but the fear was clearer in his voice than in hers.

'I won't take that risk.'

The door shuddered again.

'Please, Attica. Suicide is a crime against God.'

That was true. God was said to look on suicide as a kind of murder, which made it a mortal sin. She lowered the dagger. 'If they break in, you must kill me,' she said.

At once he broke into tears. 'I can't do that.'

'You must. Don't let the animals touch me. Promise me, Sollius.'

There was a third collision at the door, followed by shouts and muffled mayhem. It sounded like a battle was being fought outside. The guards tensed, weapons at the ready. Cyra and Honorata were holding on to one another, bearing themselves, Attica thought, with remarkable courage.

'I promise,' Sidonius said. 'Give me the blade.'

XLIX

Ecdicius, buckling his sword-belt as he ran through the throne room, feared that the palace itself was about to come under siege. He came through the great northern doors onto the balcony overlooking the forecourt, where Prince Euric was marshalling three hundred of his Gothic troops, both mounted and on foot. The riots had now spread from the ninth to the eleventh and eighth districts, and were slowly encircling the Palatine. Euric had sent the rest of his men to block the other approaches to the palace, meaning that the mob would be kept at a safe distance; but even so, Ecdicius could hear the tumult in the streets below, and from the balcony he could see columns of smoke rising from bonfires, settling in a pall that shone like gold in the summer sun.

He scanned the forecourt, but saw no sign of Attica. She must not yet have returned, which meant she was either still in the church of Saint Lawrence, or somewhere on the streets between there and the palace. 'Euric!' he shouted.

The prince ordered one of his officers to take over, and approached the balcony with too little haste for Ecdicius's liking. He was clad in scale armour, with immaculate cloak and helm.

'The princess hasn't returned,' Ecdicius said. 'Send some riders to the church of Saint Lawrence at once.'

Euric shrugged. 'Our task is to defend the palace.'

'Your task is to serve the emperor,' said Ecdicius, leaning over the balcony. Had Euric been within reach, Ecdicius would have grabbed hold of the arrogant little shit.

'My men don't know where that church is.'

'Then I'll lead them. Get me a horse.'

'I don't take commands from you.'

Ecdicius did not have time for this. He had not even bothered to don his helmet or mail armour before running from his quarters. He grabbed hold of the railings and launched himself over the balcony, landing on solid feet before the prince. Euric stepped back, taken by surprise, but Ecdicius resisted the urge to lay hands on him in front of his men. Goths were prickly even for barbarians, and the prince would take it as an attack on his honour. 'The emperor will reward you for this,' Ecdicius said. 'Give me a horse and twelve riders. That's all I need.'

It worked. Within moments Ecdicius was jumping onto the back of a Gothic mount, and a dozen cavalrymen were assembled. Ecdicius led them at a gallop down the street towards the forum. The rioting had not yet reached this side of the Palatine, and they had an unobstructed ride around the north side of the Capitoline Hill. They passed the first detritus of the riot outside the theatre of Pompey, and quickly saw the rioters themselves on the street ahead – a couple of hundred at least, Ecdicius judged, and they seemed to be gathered right outside the church.

He brought his squadron of Goths to a halt. 'Use the flats of your blades,' he commanded. 'Do not kill them. Ready, now – stay close!' He drew his sword, kicked his heels into his horse's flanks and charged down the street, a storm of hooves immediately behind him. Seeing the approaching cavalry, a few peasants on the nearest side of the crowd threw rocks and tiles, more threw curses, but most tried to flee. The furthest part of the crowd, however, had not noticed the horsemen, and refused to move. The stampede began just as Ecdicius reached them. Men stumbled or were trampled by their neighbours. Ecdicius kicked a youth in the side of the head, sending him falling to the cobbles where a moment later he was mangled by the hooves of a Gothic steed. Other Goths were spearing or slashing at the rioters, ignoring Ecdicius's command.

It was too late to do anything about that. The crowd was broken, fleeing away in both directions with Goths in pursuit. They had left behind a scene of carnage. Shattered wood was strewn on the church steps, along with strips of torn fabric: the remains of Attica's litters. On the street itself now lay several bodies, all blood-soaked. The nearest was on his back, an arm stretched across his face. A deep cut had almost severed his hand at the wrist. A deeper gash on his chest looked like the killing blow. An older man lay on his front, the back of his head caved in, his brains sprinkled on the cobblestones around him. But there were no women among the dead.

'Hold this position,' Ecdicius said, dismounting. 'They may return.' He ran up the steps to the church and hammered on the door. 'Attica! Sollius! It's Ecdicius, open up!'

Through the wood he heard the voice of his sister commanding her guards to unbolt the doors. He could have cried with relief. As soon as the doors swung open, Ecdicius pushed through. He saw his sister and went straight to her, taking her in his arms.

'You're hurt,' Attica said. She touched the side of his head, and he felt a sudden sharp pain. Her fingers came away bloody. One of those missiles must have glanced him.

'It's nothing,' he said.

'What about the rioters?' she asked.

'We've driven them off. I came from the palace as soon as we heard about the riot. Thank Christ we got here in time.'

'We must get you some water,' said Attica. She removed her head veil and used it to dab the blood from his temple.

'There's not time. We need to get all of you back to the palace. Come on.'

Both Attica and Sidonius gasped in horror as they came out of the church and saw the destruction. One of the Goths spoke to Ecdicius. 'They flee to river,' he said. 'We chase?'

'No.' Ecdicius jumped onto his horse. He reached out to his sister, and with one arm lifted her to sit in front of his saddle. Sidonius climbed up behind another Goth, as did the two hand-maidens. The four bodyguards and the litter-bearers would have to run and keep up as best they could. 'Back to the palace!' Ecdicius shouted.

They returned by the same route, finding the streets clear, and did not slow until they reached the Palatine Hill. The Gothic shield wall at the top of the street broke apart to allow them through to the forecourt. Ecdicius climbed from his horse at the foot of the palace entrance, and helped Attica dismount.

'Ecdicius,' Attica said, 'what's happening?'

'I don't know, there are riots in every direction. Go straight to the private wing, you'll be safe there. I need to speak with Euric.'

Attica took the hands of Cyra and Honorata and led them into the palace, Sidonius in pursuit. Ecdicius looked around the forecourt until he spotted Euric near the reassembling Gothic shield wall.

He went over to the prince, his face burning with anger. 'Your men slaughtered Roman citizens down there,' he snarled.

'They are warriors. What did you expect?'

'I expected them to follow my commands. I ordered them to shed no blood.'

Euric laughed. 'Few of them even speak your tongue, Roman. They saved your sister's life. You should be thanking them with gold. They will expect the reward you promised.'

Ecdicius turned and left him, knowing that if he stayed they would quickly come to blows. The very idea that Goths would demand gold for shedding the blood of Roman citizens made him sick. When news of the massacre spread, the city would be even more outraged. Few things could unite Rome's people, senators and plebs alike, better than a common hatred of barbarians; and that hatred would now be directed at the emperor's own bodyguard.

He was passing through the palace entrance hall when he encountered his father coming in the opposite direction, accompanied by Magnus, Aegidius, Consentius, and a cluster of other courtiers.

'Son,' Avitus said, his voice heavy with relief. 'I was told you'd gone down into the city. What were you thinking?'

'Attica was out there, Father. Sollius, too.'

'You brought them back?'

'I did.'

The emperor shut his eyes and sighed deeply. 'God be thanked,' he said. He opened his eyes. 'I'm told these are bread riots. A rumour has spread that the city granaries are empty.'

'Are they?'

'If they are, this is the first I've heard of it.' Avitus noticed the wound on Ecdicius's head. 'You've been injured. Go and have it seen to.'

'Father—'

'I command you. The palace is secure. There's nothing to do now but wait. Come back to me when you've rested.'

Ecdicius headed across the palace to his own quarters. He felt suddenly light-headed and weak. His father was right; he had to make sure that the bleeding stopped. He needed to think clearly. If the city had indeed run out of bread, then these would not be the last riots they saw.

He descended the steps to the courtyard of the private wing. He was walking along the peristyle to his own room when he heard a woman cry out and the clatter of furniture. The noises had come from Attica's suite, which neighboured his own. At once he went to investigate.

He found Attica in the bedroom. She was on the floor next to a chair that had been knocked over. Her two handmaidens were kneeling next to her, protecting her from Felix, who stood over her, his face bright red. He had taken off his belt, and was wielding it in his right hand like a whip.

As soon as Felix saw Ecdicius enter, he took a step back from Attica. He wiped his nose with his sleeve. 'My wife has disgraced herself,' he said, pointing the belt at her.

Ecdicius approached him. 'Did you hit my sister?'

'I told her not to go to the church without me,' he said. 'This is what happens when she disobeys me. She could have been killed, the stupid bitch.'

'Did you hit my sister?' Ecdicius asked again, stepping closer.

Felix did not answer. Ecdicius could see the panic in his eyes. It was the mindless terror of a trapped animal that was ready to lash out at anything.

'Leave him,' Attica said. Her handmaidens helped her to her feet. 'Ecdicius, don't. Please.'

'I just want an answer. Felix, did you hit my sister?'

Felix looked at Attica, then at Ecdicius. 'No,' he said. 'I hit my wife.'

The first punch caught Felix on his jaw and sent him staggering backwards against a cupboard. The next landed in his stomach. He fell to his knees and rolled onto his side, gasping, opening and closing his mouth like a fish. Ecdicius bent down to pick up the belt that Felix had dropped. He folded it in two, wielding it firmly in his hand. Then he began the whipping.

Even as he landed blow after blow on the screeching, squirming form of his brother-in-law, Ecdicius knew that his anger was not just because of Felix. It was Euric, and Ricimer, and Opilio, and the months of anxiety and dread; it was the lies that he sensed under the surface of everything but could not quite touch; it was the senseless waste of the Romans who now lay dead on the street outside the church of Saint Lawrence. All of it came rising together from deep within his gut and found life and force in his arm, and all of it was aimed at Felix.

He stopped only when Attica seized his arm and he found himself too tired to resist. He threw the belt down and let her pull him away. Felix remained on the floor, curled up in a shuddering ball, whimpering.

'That's enough,' Attica whispered, guiding Ecdicius to the door. 'God help us, that's enough.'

L

'**R**iots are simply the voice of the people, Majesty,' Prefect Opilio said, standing before the emperor in the council chamber. 'Often they are barely distinguishable from festivals. I understand that the experience must have been alarming to one unaccustomed to the ways of Rome, but I can assure you that the plebs never intended to attack the palace, let alone burn the city.'

Ecdicius, standing to the side of the apse, watched the city prefect with distaste. Sidonius was seated at a notary's desk keeping a record of proceedings. Magnus and Aegidius were also present, but Felix was still shut up in his quarters, nursing his bruises; for now, at least, he was pretending to be ill. With luck the beating had frightened him into silence. Ecdicius was not about to apologise to anyone for what he had done.

It was late, about the tenth hour. The riots had ended before dusk, the rioters drifting home after having turned several of the markets and public squares into wastelands of charred wood and broken pottery. Thankfully none of the bonfires had spread to the surrounding buildings. As soon as the streets had seemed safe enough, the emperor had summoned Opilio to the palace, having Aegidius and a detachment from the First Gallic Horse escort him from his mansion on the Esquiline. This time, presumably because he had been given no time to change into anything more humble, he was dressed in a very fine tunic. Griffins and serpents of silver and gold thread swirled along its hem.

'And the damage caused today was minimal,' he continued. 'A few cabbage stalls tipped over, some gangs taking the opportunity to settle old scores. As far as I'm aware, nobody of note came to any harm.'

Avitus glanced over at his son, knowing how close his own daughter had come to destruction at the hands of the mob. The anger was plain in his face, but he restrained it. 'We are told that a bread shortage provoked the riots,' he said to Opilio. 'Why is this? Why are the granaries empty?'

'It seems, Majesty, that while Ricimer was mopping up the Vandal fleet off Corsica, the latest grain shipments from Sicily were captured by a new group of Vandal pirates. It will be some weeks before the loss can be repaired.'

'What of the shipments from Gaul? We're expecting five hundred boatloads this month, are we not?'

Opilio gave a pained expression. 'I regret to inform Your Majesty that when the first grain from Marseilles was unloaded in Portus last week, it transpired that much of it was rotten. It is lamentable. It appears that many sacks had been deliberately half-filled with bad grain, and topped up with good to fool the customs officers. The deceit was only revealed when the guild of dockers was moving the grain into the warehouse. The clerks notified the prefect of provisions, and he notified me.'

'You did not think to report this fraud further?'

Opilio spread his hands. 'The mob did not think to warn me in advance of their rioting. I would not presume to trouble Your Majesty with every detail of grain shipments. The grain is spoiled. Nothing can change that.'

'And without bread, how are the people of Rome to eat?'

'If there are too many mouths to feed, perhaps that is because of the most recent arrivals.'

'My army, you mean?'

Opilio stiffened, pushing out his chest. 'Majesty, I must speak plainly. You now have five thousand troops in Rome by common report. Perhaps if they were Romans it would not matter so much; but these are Franks, Burgundians, Alans, all manner of nations, not forgetting the Goths.' He glanced at the guards standing by the doors. 'Of course, if Your Majesty is reluctant to dismiss the barbarians, perhaps the citizens themselves could be encouraged to leave the city. I have no doubt that your Gothic friends would relish the task.'

Eparchius Avitus, unable to contain himself any longer, got to his feet so quickly that Opilio flinched. The emperor glared at him. 'You – the prefect of Rome – would have the people driven from their own city by barbarian troops?'

'Forgive my flippant remark, Majesty,' said Opilio. 'I did not mean—'

'They are starving in the streets!'

The senator's mouth clamped shut. He looked at the floor as though studying the patterns in the marble flagstones. An awful silence filled the council chamber.

Avitus returned to his seat. 'The citizens must be fed. As prefect of Rome, it is your responsibility.'

'But Majesty,' Opilio said, his voice a pathetic whine, 'surely I cannot be blamed for Vandal pirates, or for corruption in Gaul.'

'Nor can the people of Rome be allowed to suffer for it. You have authority for one hundred miles in every direction. The harvests have been brought in, the granaries are full. It's your task to bring that grain here.'

'There are a hundred thousand plebs on the bread dole, Majesty. To find such amounts would require extraordinary taxes, by your decree.'

'You'll get whatever decree you need. Go now. Return to us tomorrow morning with a plan to feed our city. If you are not equal to the duties of prefect, we shall find someone who is.'

Opilio bowed, swinging his arms in ostentatious humility, and scampered out of the council chamber.

As soon as he had gone, Magnus spoke. 'He's lying. I can smell it on him like shit. That spoiled grain is safe and sound in Portus, I'd swear on it.'

'He's a worm, true,' said the emperor, still scowling at the door through which Opilio had left. 'But why would he want to starve Rome? The people will blame him as prefect.'

'The people will blame *you*, Majesty,' said Magnus. 'You're from Gaul. This supposedly rotten grain is from Gaul. You brought barbarians from Gaul who today shed Roman blood in the streets. Right or wrong, they will blame you.'

'The blame is neither here nor there. The important thing is to feed the people. We must make sure Opilio brings food to the city.'

'And in doing so, he'll pillage the countryside in your name, and so turn not just Rome against you, but half of Italy. Majesty, please – hiding bad grain beneath good! Priscus Valerianus is prefect of Gaul; he personally supervised the shipments from Marseilles. Would he fall for such an old trick as that?'

'Why would Opilio lie? Tell me, Magnus. Does he want to see the city ransacked by a starving mob?'

'He seeks wealth, Majesty. I know his type. No doubt he's hoping to hoard the grain for a few weeks, and then sell it at a profit. He might even be plotting to have you overthrown. It gives me no pleasure to say it, Majesty, but you can no longer treat him as a friend.'

Avitus leaned forward and shut his eyes, pinching the bridge of his nose. He muttered, 'God above, will you end this hammering in my head?'

'Majesty,' said Magnus softly, 'let me send an agent to Portus, I beg you. Such a quantity of grain cannot be easily hidden. A few discreet enquiries may reveal the truth of the matter. If Opilio is shown to be corrupt, by law you can replace him. I could recommend several men in the Senate who are not aligned with Majorian or Ricimer.'

The emperor stayed silent, with his eyes closed. He did not move. Magnus glanced at his colleagues in the privy council, a rare worried look in his eyes.

'Very well,' said Avitus finally. 'Very well. Send an agent to Portus. But be discreet. I don't want to cause a scandal if Opilio turns out to be innocent.'

It pained Ecdicius to see his father in such a state, sitting dejected on his throne, so unlike his natural self. All of a sudden it became clear how heavily the affairs of state had begun to oppress him. What Ecdicius had taken for the sombre seclusion of his office had started to resemble the miserable loneliness of a good man who cared too much about honour, and who longed to trust others, even knowing that his trust would be abused.

That night Ecdicius found little sleep. He lay on the bed in his small, plain room, watching through a solitary window at the turning stars. He saw the sea-beast slip by, followed by the long, winding Po, and then mighty Orion, frozen with his hounds in their eternal chase. He thought anxiously of what awaited them tomorrow, unable to forget the sight of those broken bodies lying outside the church, the Gothic hooves clattering around them. Not since the slaughter at Vicus Helena eight years ago had he felt like this. Suspicion of Opilio only deepened his worry. What if the prefect was manipulating the grain to turn the plebs against the emperor? It would be a clever scheme. It would at once get rid of the man whom many in the Senate still regarded as a Gallic usurper, and make Opilio a hero when the hidden grain suddenly reappeared. But who would be the new emperor? Opilio himself? That seemed unlikely; he was too clever to take such a risk. Nor would Ricimer be a candidate, for the people would never accept an emperor of barbarian descent. Besides, after his defeat of the Vandal fleet, Avitus had appointed him master of soldiers in a gesture of confidence and trust. That left Majorian, who was still busy in the south fighting the Vandals. But Aegidius swore that his old friend and comrade had no designs on the throne.

Ecdicius turned over onto his side, closing his eyes. It would do no good to dwell on such things. With luck Magnus's agents would discover the truth about the grain in Portus, and reveal whether or not Opilio could be trusted, at least.

The next day he rose later than usual, hurriedly dressed himself in the ceremonial garb of tunic and decorated cloak that his servant had laid out for him, and went to the peristyle behind the throne room for the morning audience. His parents and Attica were already present, along with Sidonius and the attendants. There was still no sign of Felix.

'Good prince,' said the master of admissions, bowing deeply. He turned to the emperor. 'We are ready, Majesty, at your leisure.'

Avitus nodded. The horns sounded, the doors opened, and they began the procession into the throne room.

Ecdicius leaned close to his sister. 'How is your husband?'

'As you left him,' she hissed.

She was angry with him, he realised. He said nothing more, containing his irritation. Now was not the time to discuss it.

They passed through the throne room and emerged onto the balcony for the public salutation. It was promising to be another warm day. The crowd was even larger than normal, Ecdicius noted, but this time there was no rapturous greeting. The hundreds of people looked up at the imperial family in eerie silence. Opilio, who normally stood at the very front of the crowd, was nowhere to be seen, and there were very few senators at all. Were Opilio and his allies refusing to attend in protest?

The master of admissions, looking unsettled by the quietness of the crowd, raised his hand. 'Hail Eparchius Avitus, pious and happy augustus!'

The mob began to echo his words. Today, though, something was not right. At first the crowd was repeating the right formula, but slowly the words changed.

Farewell Eparchius Avitus, they were crying. *Impious and unhappy augustus.*

Ecdicius exchanged a worried glance with Sidonius. Something flew through the air, clattering against the shield of a nearby soldier. A lump of brick bounced off the railing in front of them. Another hit a column to the side. Then suddenly the air seemed to fill with missiles.

Ecdicius yelled: 'Inside, get inside!' He pushed his parents back towards the doors, as the Goths scrambled to protect them beneath their shields, and he put his arm around the screaming Attica. Amidst the confusion Ecdicius heard someone shout that the emperor had been hit. Turning around, he saw his father on his hands and knees, blood streaming from his head. Ecdicius took one of his arms, Sidonius took the other, and together they carried him into the safety of the audience hall.

The doors thundered shut behind them. The shouts and screams of the panicking court resounded deafeningly all around.

'Euric!' Ecdicius cried, still holding his father, who seemed conscious but dazed. 'Euric!'

The young Gothic prince came running, pushing his way through the throng. 'The mob is storming the palace,' he said.

'Stop them,' said Ecdicius. 'I must take my father to safety. Bar the doors. Find Aegidius, and call out the whole guard.'

Euric nodded. Ecdicius thought he saw a grim smile on the prince's face as he turned about and yelled for his Goths to assemble.

Ecdicius and Sidonius carried the emperor the full length of the palace, leaving a trail of his blood from the audience hall through the two great courtyards and down a staircase into the private wing, where they laid him on the first couch they saw. Severiana knelt by his side, and commanded a shocked servant to fetch water, bandages, and the palace physician. Then she turned to the rest of them. 'Give us space. The wound is slight.'

Ecdicius was out of breath, his shoulder muscles on fire. His ears were ringing. The rest of the imperial family and a squad of palace guards had accompanied them from the audience hall. Nobody else appeared to be injured.

'Opilio,' gasped Ecdicius, wiping his sleeve across his brow. 'It has to be his doing. He wasn't in the crowd. He's turned the people against us.'

'Brother, is the palace safe?' asked Attica.

'I pray to God it is. The rest of you stay here, lock the doors.'

Ecdicius sprinted to his own quarters, where he grabbed a sheathed sword from a peg on the wall. He drew the sword and tossed scabbard and baldric aside, and ran back up into the main body of the palace. Courtiers and servants were racing along the peristyles in confusion, but Ecdicius could see no rampaging plebs. Back in the throne room, now deserted, the north doors were still bolted shut. So the mob had not broken in. It seemed weirdly quiet. There was still the sound of screaming, but it was faint, some distance away.

He went to the doors and heaved back the heavy iron bolts. Pulling one door open, he stepped out onto the balcony.

Detritus was strewn at his feet. He stepped over broken roof tiles, paving stones, bricks, lumps of wood. Nearby lay a motionless Goth with a wet hole in the centre of what had been his face.

The sight awaiting him below was far worse. Corpses were scattered across the blood-soaked flagstones of the palace forecourt. He saw no senators among them, but some of the dead were well-dressed, their linen cloaks and tunics torn by slashing swords. Most of the fallen, he could not count how many dozens, were commoners. Aside from the occasional dagger they seemed to have been armed only with makeshift clubs, if at all. His stomach turned as he listened to the screams still coming from the forum below, rising up through the morning mists: screams of Roman terror, and of unleashed Gothic fury.

LI

Near Tarazona, Spain

Arvandus had not been prepared for the heat. The late afternoon sun glared down on the scrubby grass and rocks as the Gothic baggage train of ox-carts and mules made its way up the valley. It was oppressive, like a great hand pressing down on the whole of this dry, dusty country. It sapped his strength and dried out his throat. The drivers and infantry escorts seemed too tired to speak; they stared at the ground in silence, only occasionally looking up through squinted eyes at the road ahead. The mules and oxen shuffled forwards with their heads sunk low between the bony ridges of their shoulders.

Arvandus was grateful to be mounted, at least, though he would have given a pound of gold to be inside a litter, shielded from the sun and the dust-filled air. But there were no such luxuries on campaign. It had taken them three hours to travel five miles from the mining town of Tarazona. The road was leading them into these sparsely populated hills and valleys, which seemed to become more barren and rocky with every turn of the path. It had been the route taken by King Rechiar's army only a day earlier as he fled the Gothic advance. Theoderic himself was in the vanguard some miles ahead, although Arvandus did not know how far. For the last three weeks the king had pursued the campaign against his Suevic brother-in-law with single-minded focus, leading the army of eight thousand Goths and Burgundians from the coast to Saragossa, from there to Tarazona, and then west into the hills, snapping at the heels of the Sueves at every opportunity.

Arvandus had spent most of his time with the baggage train at the rear, along with the rest of the king's civilian ministers and the camp followers. Paulus was alongside him, as he had been every day since leaving Tarragona. Arvandus glanced over at the young nobleman, whose face was almost hidden in the shadow of a wide-brimmed sun hat, his expression impossible to read. The longer Arvandus knew him, the less he liked him, without being sure why. So far Paulus had been friendly enough, and had helped Arvandus understand the workings of the royal court. He was an easy travelling partner, and seemed to be bearing the discomforts of the march with admirable stoicism. Perhaps that was the problem: nothing seemed to upset him. He was like a ship that sailed with unnatural calmness through the choppiest waters. Arvandus had never seen him drunk, and nor had he shown any interest in women – or men, for that matter. He rarely spoke unless it related to the king or to the politics of the court. He seemed to be devoted to Theoderic, but Arvandus wondered how deeply even that devotion ran. He could not sense what was happening behind those narrow eyes and delicate, pouting lips.

Paulus pointed at something ahead. 'Dead Sueve,' he said.

Arvandus looked to where he was pointing, and saw the twisted corpse lying in the scrub fifteen yards off the road. It wore a cheap tunic and pair of breeches, with no sandals, cloak or belt. The dead eyes seemed to fix on Arvandus as he rode past. 'How can you tell it's a Sueve?' he asked.

'There's been a battle. This one's been robbed and left for the birds, so he must be a Sueve.'

'I didn't hear about a battle.'

'Look at the sky ahead.'

Arvandus did so. Over the top of the next ridge, about a quarter of a mile further on, he saw clouds of heavy black birds circling in the air. Vultures. They would only gather in such numbers in expectation of a good-sized feast.

'Theoderic must have caught up with the Suevic rearguard,' Paulus said. 'The first blood of the war. And from the looks of it, we won.'

When they came to the ridge, the whole battlefield was laid out before them. It looked like it had been a skirmish; there were

no heaps of bodies where battle lines had been drawn, but individual bodies were scattered across the valley, from the high
slopes on the right down to the banks of the small river on the
left. They were infantry who had been surprised and chased
down, most likely stragglers of Rechiar's army. They had all been
stripped of their armour and left to lie in the sun. It would not
be long before they began to bloat and fester, if the carrion did
not finish them first. A few of the outlying corpses had already
attracted gangs of squabbling vultures.

It was the first time Arvandus had seen the aftermath of battle.
He had been secretly anxious about how he might react to the
grim reality of something he had only ever encountered in poetry,
but he felt nothing. These Sueves were dead. He did not know
who they had been as men, and did not care. He wanted only
to stop and rest, to put some food in his grumbling belly, to fall
asleep in the cooler air of the evening.

They continued for another four hours, climbing onto a high
plateau before following the winding road down the side of a
valley, where the army had halted at a ford. This would be the
camp for the night. Most of the soldiers were strung out along
the river in either direction, some enjoying its refreshing waters
while others lounged in the shady copses on its banks. Troops
of cavalry still patrolled the high ground all around. Arvandus
spotted the king and a group of his nobles gathered on a rocky
bluff beyond the river, and so this is where he and Paulus headed.

Theoderic had dismounted and was standing alone, looking
out over the country to the west. It was a land of isolated farmsteads set amidst undulating hills, with taller peaks rising in the
blue haze on the horizon. It looked to Arvandus like goat country,
but there were neither goats nor people to be seen; some of the
livestock would have been stolen by the passing Suevic army,
and the remainder spirited away by locals into more remote
valleys.

At the top of the bluff one of the mounted Gothic nobles, a
broad-chested and full-bearded man of about forty, raised his
hand to stop Arvandus and Paulus coming any closer. 'I have a

letter from the emperor to the king,' Arvandus said, holding out the document tube that had arrived in Tarazona that morning. 'Tell him that Hesychius brought it from Italy, along with a gift of two pounds of gold for His Majesty.'

The Goth took the tube. 'Wait here,' he said. He dismounted and walked over to Theoderic, handing him the message.

Arvandus and Paulus watched as the king opened the tube and read the letter. Arvandus had been wondering what it contained. The latest news from Rome had been encouraging; Ricimer had defeated the Vandals near Sicily, crushing the remnants of their fleet off the coast of Corsica. Majorian had beaten the last of Geiseric's raiders on the Italian mainland. Both generals seemed to be fighting willingly in the name of Emperor Avitus. He still lacked the recognition of the east, which was a cause for concern, but Emperor Marcian had not made any efforts to remove him. Arvandus could only pray that things were going as well as they seemed. His acquaintance with Avitus had been formal and slight, but enough to teach him respect for the redoubtable old Roman, who seemed as free from envy or guile as anyone Arvandus had ever met. It was a rare thing in so powerful a man. For the sake of Ecdicius and Attica, too, Arvandus could wish him well. He could not believe that Avitus had had anything to do with the assassination attempt. That reeked of Felix alone. Just what Felix had hoped to accomplish, however, was an utter mystery.

Theoderic, having finished the letter, waved for Arvandus and Paulus to join him. They both climbed from their saddles, leaving their mounts with their bodyguards, and walked over. They knelt together at the king's feet.

'Rise,' Theoderic said. He wielded the letter. 'News from Magnus, in the name of the emperor. He wants me to end the campaign and bring six thousand troops to Italy at once.'

Arvandus was stunned. 'Does he say why?'

'No, merely that the emperor requires it. It can only mean one of two things. Either Marcian has invaded Italy with an eastern army, or the Italian army itself has turned against Avitus.'

'But Majorian and Ricimer have been fighting for him against the Vandals,' Arvandus said.

'Of course they have. They wouldn't risk a civil war while Geiseric still controlled the sea. They've dealt with the Vandals, and now they're ready to turn on Avitus. I can't say I'm surprised.'

Arvandus was taken aback by the calmness with which Theoderic spoke. It was almost as though he had not himself placed Avitus on the throne. 'If you're right, Majesty,' Arvandus said, 'we must make for Italy at once. Rechiar has been driven out of Tarraconensis, hasn't he?'

'Driven out, yes,' said Theoderic. 'But not punished. I swore I'd crush him. I must keep that oath.'

'You swore an oath to the emperor first,' protested Arvandus.

'Majesty, if I may,' said Paulus. 'One might well ask whether that oath is still valid. We must not forget the attempt on your life so valiantly foiled by Arvandus here, who himself identified the assassin as a servant of Felix, son of Magnus – the very man who wrote the letter in your hand.'

'But Avitus had nothing to do with that,' Arvandus said. 'He would never have allowed it.'

'Are you so sure?' asked Paulus. 'Do not underestimate the influence of Magnus. It's well known that he has personally financed the emperor's reign so far.' He turned to Theoderic. 'Besides, Majesty, consider the feelings of your army. They will not be happy to leave Spain so soon after tasting blood.'

'An army should obey its king,' snapped Arvandus. He was losing patience with the obsequious courtier.

Theoderic silenced them both with a raised hand. 'The point is moot; it's too late in the year to leave for Italy now. We don't have enough ships to travel by sea, and the land route would take months. We'd get back to Gaul to find the Alps closed by snow, and we'd have to sit there through the whole winter, having achieved nothing in Spain. No, the campaign goes on. Rechiar must be punished, or else next spring he'll be raiding Aquitaine while half our army is in Italy. I will consider my reply to Magnus. Both of you find a place to camp down by the river.'

They left the royal presence and returned to their horses. As they began the ride back down the bluff to the river, where the carts and mules of the wagon train were being unloaded, Arvandus thought with frustration of how he might change the king's mind. It would not be an easy march to Italy, but it was possible. Surely the safety of the emperor was the priority. Rechiar was little more than a bandit king, capable of petty raiding and not much else.

Paulus spoke. 'Where do you think the Gothic kingdom is, Arvandus?'

Arvandus gave him a sidelong glance. He was not in the mood for patronising questions. 'In the provinces of Aquitaine.'

'No.' Paulus nodded towards the teeming mass of soldiers, horses, mules, wagons and servants along the river. Piles of supplies were being built up, tents and canopies erected. 'This is the Gothic kingdom. The *army* is the Gothic kingdom. Without his army, Theoderic is no king at all. He's brought them across mountains with the promise of glory and plunder. These are not Roman troops; they receive no salary. If tomorrow he were to tell them that the war against Rechiar was finished and he was taking them to Italy instead, what would happen?'

'I don't know.'

'Revolt. He would be dead in an instant, and probably the two of us with him. Frideric would be fetched from Toulouse and declared king in his place. The war against Rechiar would continue regardless. And as for the Burgundians – who knows what they would do? There's a simple lesson here, Arvandus: don't ever go against the interests of the army. If you do, it'll be the end of you.'

'So we leave Avitus to his fate.'

'To put it bluntly, yes. I know you admire the man, Arvandus. I do, too. But for now, we cannot help him.'

Paulus continued the ride down to the river, leaving Arvandus alone. Unpleasant as it was, he knew that Paulus had spoken sense. This had to be why Theoderic had pretended that there was simply no time to reach Italy before winter. A king could not seem to be intimidated by his own troops, but that was the truth of it.

Not that this made it any easier to accept. Were it not for Felix, Arvandus would be in Rome now, able to help the emperor any way he could. He would be with Sidonius and Ecdicius. With the three of them together, he felt that they might have overcome anything. And there was Attica, too. The thought of her being harmed was too awful to bear.

A deep, sick fear clutched his stomach. He feared what would happen to his friends if Avitus fell from power. Everyone knew that when usurpers fell, they rarely fell alone.

LII

Rome

'The barbarians must go.'
Subdued murmurs of assent ran around the floor of the Senate House. A few bold senators spoke out more clearly. It had been a shameful slaughter, one said. The Goths were savages and heretics to boot, declared another. But for the most part, although their anger was clear, they were still cowed by the six Gothic guards standing at the main entrance, and the two standing at each of the doors flanking the emperor's platform.

Ecdicius stood to one side of the platform, Magnus to the other. The low tiered seating that ran down either side of the hall was half empty, since many senators had chosen to absent themselves once again from the city following the massacre a week earlier. Opilio, who as urban prefect was also president of the Senate, had disappeared. Rumours placed him in every corner of Italy. In his place the senators had elected as their spokesman Gennadius Avienus, who had helped negotiate Attila's withdrawal from Italy four years earlier. He was a level-headed, softly-spoken diplomat and ex-consul, the sort whose voice commanded the respect of all.

'The barbarians,' Avienus repeated gently, looking at the emperor, 'must go.' There was a likeable earnestness in his eyes. His tone was firm but pleading. 'Rome is weeping, Majesty. The very saints are lamenting in their holy tombs. Hundreds are dead. Such inhuman violence – has the city not suffered enough at the hands of savages?'

The emperor hesitated, sitting on his throne as though frozen. Ecdicius could see that he was unsure how to respond to this appeal. He had convened the Senate at the suggestion of Magnus.

Yes, the Goths had committed a regrettable atrocity, and almost two hundred Roman citizens had died at the hands of Euric and his men; yet Magnus had insisted that now was the time not for hesitation, but to show strength and determination and the righteous anger of an emperor whose palace had been attacked. 'We must prevent further bloodshed,' Magnus had argued after the massacre. 'If Rome is afraid of the Goths, all the better. We can use that fear.'

They had been expecting a terrified Senate or a furious Senate, but Avienus was presenting something trickier: a sorrowful Senate. He was appealing to the emperor's humanity and reason. Avitus had both in abundance, and that was why Magnus was now watching him nervously.

'We saw few of you among the crowd that morning,' Avitus said. 'The mob came armed, intending to assault the imperial family. This was an open revolt planned by Opilio, and our guards behaved as imperial guards should.'

'The mob is an emotional beast,' said Avienus. 'Disrespect to the imperial family must of course be punished. But such indiscriminate slaughter, Majesty! The dead were heaped up in the streets of the forum, up to the very steps of this hallowed chamber. As to Opilio's guilt – the people say, Majesty, that barbarians came to seize him in the night. Is it any surprise that the city is alarmed, if none of us may sleep soundly in his bed?'

There was the kind of unjust accusation that could hurt an honest man. 'Those rumours are false,' Avitus said. 'Opilio has not been proscribed. I cannot explain why he has fled.'

Magnus spoke up. 'One might conclude, however, that only a man with something to hide would flee in such a manner.'

'With respect,' said Avienus, 'a senator cannot be called guilty until he has been tried and condemned by his peers. To do otherwise is libellous.'

'Do not lecture me on the law,' snapped Magnus. 'I know that to hoard grain intended for the people of Rome is embezzlement. I know that to steal from the imperial treasury is theft. And I know that to conspire against the reigning emperor is treason.'

There were some outraged shouts from the senators. Avienus raised his hand to calm them. 'Then let us have a trial, and examine the evidence. Where is the grain, and the treasure? Are there witnesses to this conspiracy?'

'My agents returned from Ostia this morning. They discovered the supposedly rotten grain from Gaul in Opilio's own warehouse. As for the treasury, I have no doubt that it was secreted away immediately before the Vandals took the palace. By fleeing, Opilio has now declared his guilt.'

'No.' Avienus was entirely calm. He spoke as though this were a hypothetical legal case. 'By fleeing, he has declared his *fear*, and with good reason if Goths are running wild through the streets. True, the grain may be evidence of embezzlement and corruption. But where is the treasure he supposedly stole? I have yet to see evidence of treason.'

'Spare us your legal technicalities,' said Magnus. 'You know as well as I, as well as everyone in this room, that Opilio is a traitor.'

'Traitor or not,' said Avienus, 'the law is the law.' He looked at the emperor. 'Does Your Majesty not stand for the law?'

The hall waited. Once again, Avitus did not speak. *Say something*, Ecdicius thought. *Anything. An emperor can be good or bad, vengeful or merciful, but he cannot be hesitant.*

Still his father said nothing. Eventually Avienus said, 'The Senate and people of Rome have pledged themselves to Your Majesty. By recovering the lost grain, you have eased the famine, and for that we thank you. If Opilio is found, tried and legally condemned, we shall rejoice that justice has been served.' He paused, and lowered himself slowly to his knees. He raised clasped hands to the throne. 'But Majesty – free us, we beg you, from the savagery of foreigners. Please send the barbarians home.'

The entire assembly watched the emperor. Ecdicius glanced across at Magnus. He had his jaw set in frustration, knowing that a response to this appeal had to come from the emperor himself. Anything the master of offices said would only make the emperor look weak. But there was no clear answer. If his father refused the request, he would look like a barbarian puppet. If he granted it, he would make enemies of the Goths.

Avitus cleared his throat. 'Your appeal has moved us,' he said. 'We will dismiss Euric from our service.'

The Senate erupted into chatter. Amidst the babble, someone began to chant the traditional formula: *May our emperors enjoy life for ever. May our emperors enjoy life for ever. May our emperors enjoy life for ever* . . .

The procession from the Senate House back to the imperial palace was orderly. The senators even followed the emperor with their continued cheers and acclamations. Ecdicius was not smiling, however. He did not know about the law, but he felt in his gut that Opilio was guilty to the bone. As soon as the senator had realised he was found out, he had surely fled to join Majorian or Ricimer. It was only a matter of time before they declared open revolt. The emperor needed the support of the Senate and the Goths, yet it seemed that he could not have both; and if he failed to retain either, his cause would be lost.

As soon as the palace doors were closed behind them, Magnus ordered an attendant to bring Prince Euric to the audience chamber. Then he leaned close to the emperor. 'Majesty,' Ecdicius overheard him say, 'I suggest you issue orders for the First Gallic Horse and the Lions to come to the palace in strength at once.'

Avitus nodded. He looked around at the surrounding courtiers and Gothic soldiers as though in confusion. Ecdicius caught his eye for a moment, but he passed over him without any look of recognition. He seemed almost in a daze. Having pledged to dismiss his Gothic bodyguard in front of the Senate, he could not go back on his word. But the consequences of this pledge were becoming clear to him only gradually. To Magnus, and to Ecdicius, the reality was all too clear. The Goths would not be so easily dismissed.

Yet when Prince Euric appeared before the emperor and the privy council and was told that his services were no longer required, he did not rage as Ecdicius had feared he might. He was sixteen years old now, a hard-faced young man with deep eyes and a quiet arrogance. 'It is a strange Roman custom,' he said, 'for a lord to dismiss a warrior who has fought so hard to defend him.'

'Noble Prince,' Avitus replied, 'this is no slight on your honour. You know the esteem in which I hold you and your people. It's merely a political concern. Your brother will understand, I'm sure.'

'Theoderic? He thinks like a Roman, of course he'll understand. But my men are warriors. They will take great offence if they are sent away without reward. It will be a badge of shame.'

'You and your men will be fully paid once we recover the imperial treasury.'

'My men and I will be paid *now*. Ten solidi per man.'

The members of the privy council gasped. 'Don't be absurd, boy,' said Magnus. 'No Roman soldier is paid so much. You commit murder on the streets of Rome, and expect to be rewarded with a fortune?'

'Be calm, Magnus,' said the emperor. 'Noble Prince, you must understand that such a sum is out of the question, but you have my pledge that the wage of four solidi per man will be paid in full within a year.'

'All right. But we require two solidi now. Otherwise I may not be able to control my men.' Even at so young an age, Euric evidently knew what it was to hold the balance of power. He had the same twisted smile that Ecdicius had seen on him a week earlier, just before the massacre in front of the palace. His blood was still hot from that butchery. What other sixteen-year-old would dare blackmail a Roman emperor in his own palace?

'Two solidi per man,' said Avitus. 'Then you will return peacefully to Gaul.'

Euric nodded and left the audience chamber. Watching him leave, Ecdicius felt like a fly trapped in a web, the size of which was beyond his comprehension. It did not seem possible for them to free one foot without trapping another. He knew as well as anyone that his father did not have even the thousand solidi required to pay Euric and his men.

Magnus was the first to give voice to this problem. 'Majesty, we cannot afford this.'

'I know,' said Avitus. 'We'll need to raise the funds quickly. There are still bronze statues we can take – from the temple of Rome and Venus, from the amphitheatre, the basilica of Maxentius. Have the Lions remove anything they can find and get it melted down, then sell it to metal merchants.'

'Those are public monuments, Majesty. When the Senate—'

'I am tired of the Senate!' shouted Avitus. 'I am tired of the Goths, and of this city, and of you questioning me at every turn. By God, Magnus, I gave you an order – carry it out.'

Magnus bowed. As he walked out of the chamber, Ecdicius saw that his hands were shaking.

It did not take long for the people of Rome to realise what was happening. The riots began later that afternoon when some citizens, outraged that their city was being stripped of its few remaining ornaments, pelted the soldiers trying to break the statues from their moorings on the temple of Rome and Venus. They continued as fresh soldiers came down from the palace to protect their comrades, and only worsened as the gangs arrived from the Aventine wielding hammers, clubs and hatchets. The people were hungry, full of hatred for the Goths, and all of the anger and fear of the last few days erupted onto the streets of Rome. The emperor's other barbarian troops, summoned from their quarters outside the city, arrived to crush the uprising.

It was the worst slaughter yet. Ecdicius remained in the private wing with his father and the rest of the family, his sword by his side in case the mob broke into the palace. His father sat on a couch, his aged head hung low, with Severiana beside him. Magnus was outside in the courtyard, where he spent the entire afternoon pacing back and forth. Sidonius was seated on a chair by the door, trying to read some codex, although it looked to Ecdicius as though his eyes were merely resting on the words, and he never seemed to turn the page. Attica and Felix were sitting on another couch, neither looking at the other, but the fear was plain in their faces as they listened to the rolling madness of the riot outside. None of them spoke. They could not bear to eat. They could do nothing but wait.

The mob did not enter the palace. It was all over by nightfall, by which time it was too dark to see anything from the windows. There was only the wailing of the bereaved, and the excited howls and yelps of the dogs as they fought over the fresh meat.

Eventually Ecdicius went to his own quarters to find whatever sleep he could. He kept his sheathed sword on the mattress next to him, right hand resting on the hilt, thinking of the news that had arrived just before the riots had broken out: Aegidius had refused to bring his regiment to the palace when ordered. Instead he had taken the First Gallic Horse and left Rome for the south. The only reason could be that he intended to join his old comrade Majorian in revolt. He had betrayed them. The news had left Ecdicius in dumb shock. He still could not comprehend it. He had ridden with Aegidius for years, served on his staff, fought by his side. It was impossible to imagine that he could have abandoned not only the emperor whom he had sworn to serve, but one of his most loyal comrades. And yet he had.

The following morning Ecdicius awoke with a sickly taste in his mouth and a nervous anxiety that reached into every part of his body. As he got to his feet he felt his head sway and his empty stomach turn over itself. The memory of yesterday's horrors flooded into his thoughts, joining the waking nightmare in which he had been living for weeks. All his dreams of Rome had crumbled, leaving only this tangled mess of intrigues, plots, greed, and death. Where amidst all this, he wondered, was something worth fighting for?

He needed to walk, to breathe in the open air.

It appeared that overnight the palace had become the quarters not only of the Goths, but of an entire army. As he walked along the upper colonnade of the imperial gardens he looked down to see that the Senior Cornuti had turned the lawns and orchards into a single giant stable. Passing deeper into the palace, he found that the western peristyle and banquet hall now served as barracks for the five hundred troops of the Lions. Eventually he reached the northern balcony to see the rest of their forces camped in the palace forecourt and the surrounding temples

– a couple more regiments from the Gallic field army, along with two thousand barbarians from various tribes. The Palatine was now a military camp. The halls and peristyles behind him rang with the clinking of weaponsmiths. German voices bellowed in the dawn light, echoing across the forecourt.

He heard footsteps approaching along the porch, and Sidonius appeared at his side. He rested his hands on the marble balustrade. Ecdicius could see the worry in his eyes. 'Good morning, Ecdicius,' he muttered.

Together they watched the milling army camp. Soldiers rose from their sleeping blankets and kicked apart the remains of the fires they had set up on the flagstones of the forecourt. Some emerged yawning from the old temple buildings, stretching as they stood on the marble steps.

Ecdicius thought of all the history he had learned through his life, and remembered how the fate of the world could turn on the events of a few hours. He had always thought that he understood this. Living through such events, though, was something else. Hearing stories had not prepared him for this awful uncertainty, for the simple, fearful ignorance of not knowing what was going to happen next. It occurred to him that he had not eaten properly for days. He had grown so used to the anxiety that he could hardly remember what it was like not to feel it.

Over the din of the camp came the sound of galloping hooves on stone. A solitary horseman was riding hard up from the forum, whipping his mount as it brought him between campfires and drowsy soldiers towards the palace entrance. He spotted Ecdicius on the balcony and rode over, coming to a stop below him. His hair and face were soaking with sweat. 'My prince, I bring news from the coast,' he announced, tugging hard on the reins to bring his mare under control.

'Have you come from Portus?'

'No, my prince.' The despatch rider reached into the satchel slung over his shoulder and brought out a sealed tablet, which he handed over. 'I set out from Cerveteri last night. This report arrived from Civitaveccia.'

Ecdicius broke the seal and read the message. 'Ricimer is heading for Portus,' he told Sidonius. 'His entire fleet is sailing down the coast. They'll be arriving today.' It took a moment for the meaning of his own words to become clear to him, as though the letter were a riddle. Ricimer was sailing to Portus. Had not Avitus ordered him to go to Sicily? He had disobeyed the emperor. *An emperor without coin cannot stay emperor for long.* That was what he had said to Ecdicius months ago. The missing treasury, the flight of Opilio, Aegidius heading to meet Majorian, the man who three times had failed to win the throne . . . they had run out of time.

'I need to take this news to my father,' Ecdicius said.

'He won't want to abandon Rome,' Sidonius said. 'But we must.'

Ecdicius nodded. 'We don't have nearly enough men to defend her. We don't have enough to meet Ricimer in the field, either. Even if we march to Portus now, Majorian might attack us from the rear. We need to head north immediately, meet with Remistus at Ravenna, get reinforcements from Gaul. We need King Theoderic to bring his army.'

'And if he doesn't?'

'We'll make a stand. My father is the rightful emperor. Do you think we're going to let them take all of it, and lose everything we've tried to accomplish? No. They must not be given the empire. My father will fight.'

He had forced determination into his voice, as though he were trying to convince himself as much as his cousin. But his father was no longer the man Ecdicius had known all his life. He had become hesitant, erratic, confused. Yesterday, as Rome had torn itself apart around them, Ecdicius had watched him sitting on the couch, cradled by his wife, a weary and lost old man.

Yet he was still the emperor. 'I must give him the news,' Ecdicius said. 'We don't have any time to waste.'

LIII

Four days later they were fifty miles north of Rome, on the tallest bridge in the world. From the stone balustrade Attica looked into the depths of the mist-laden valley, its forested slopes falling down to the tumbling Nera. Through the trees she glimpsed slaves at the riverbank filling buckets and leather bladders with water for the baggage train. To her right, at the south end of the bridge, the turrets and walls of Narni rose up to catch the golden morning light. It was early September, and the leaves were starting to turn.

She knew they could not afford to stop here long, but it was pleasant to leave the carriage and breathe the clean air. The Goths of the royal bodyguard waited patiently for the column to start moving. Wagon drivers chatted, courtiers strolled along the bridge. Attica remembered crossing this bridge a year ago, when she had looked down from its heights with tremulous excitement, thinking of the even greater wonders that awaited her in Rome. Now she trembled less from excitement than from fear of the perils that still lay ahead.

Their escape from Rome had been close. Ricimer had landed with his army at Portus and sent an embassy to demand her father's surrender, but by the time the embassy arrived they had already abandoned the palace and were heading north on the Flaminian Way. The plan was to head across the Alps to Gaul, where they would marshal the combined might of Romans and Goths, before returning to Italy and winning back Rome before the onset of winter. The master of soldiers Remistus, who was in Ravenna raising local Italian forces to her father's cause, was charged with holding the north until they returned. They could not allow the Senate time to install a new emperor. It was to be a hard march; taking the coastal road would have allowed Ricimer to intercept them by sea, and so they had to cross the Apennines and head up the east side of Italy.

Yet Attica's immediate concern was her father. She looked back at the large enclosed carriage that contained both of her parents. Despite its gilded wheel hubs, despite its rich decoration of purple and red and the bronze lions that reared proudly on either side of the driver's seat, she knew that the man inside was emperor in name only. He had hardly eaten or spoken since leaving Rome. Most of the time he had spent staring through the window with the look of a man in a trance. By day he stayed in the carriage, by night he went into his tent wherever they made camp. He refused to let his wife leave him. During the journey she had been holding his hand and whispering in his ear as though he were a child.

Her mother said he was heartbroken from having to leave Rome. Attica put it down to the betrayal of Aegidius. She remembered how he had staggered, his knees suddenly giving way, when he had been given the news that the tribune of the First Gallic Horse had gone over to the rebels. Ever since then he had been a shadow of the father she had known all her life.

She heard a horse approaching from the rear of the column, and turned to see Felix riding towards her. They had not spoken for the past few days; she had stayed in the company of her father, and he in the company of his, busying himself with the administration of supplies for the marching column. The flight from Rome seemed to have given him renewed purpose, at least. After a week of skulking in the private wing of the palace pretending to be ill and letting his beard grow as though in grief, he was now clean-shaven and clear-eyed.

He reined in his mount as he reached her. 'Wife,' he said, nodding by way of greeting. He looked down at her as though she were a stranger.

She was not surprised that he was forcing distance between them. She had not told anyone of the beating he had suffered at the hands of her brother, and she doubted that he had, either. It would have caused him too much shame to admit to it, especially to his father. But she had seen it; she had nursed his bruises and held him in her arms. She had been a witness to his shame, and that surely frustrated him. He was not the sort of man to search for faults within himself when he could invent them in others. 'Felix,' she said. 'I hope you are well?'

'Well enough.' Behind his accusatory tone there was still a trace of fragility. Despite everything, she felt tenderness towards him. It came from pity rather than affection, but it was there. His beating had taught her that she could never enjoy the sight of pain being inflicted on another, no matter how well deserved. 'My father has received news from our scouts,' he said. 'He wants to talk to the emperor.'

'The emperor is not well.'

'He hasn't been well for days, but he must still rule.'

More horses approached at a hurried canter. It was Magnus, together with a group of Gothic soldiers. Noticing his son talking to Attica, Magnus dismounted, walked over to her and bowed. 'Princess,' he said. 'I must speak with your father.'

'I'll take you to him,' she said. She led him to the carriage, climbing the steps between the wheels to enter the side door. Inside were two facing benches, her mother and father occupying the rear one. She sat on the empty bench, leaving room for Magnus to join her.

There was no room to kneel, but he dipped his head. 'Majesty,' he said. 'Our rearguard scouts have reported that Majorian's army has reached Capua. Aegidius must have joined him there by now.'

Avitus gave no response. He was staring through the open door of the carriage.

'We believe they intend to chase us north,' Magnus continued. 'We'll need to cover at least twenty miles a day to stay ahead. I suggest that you order our troops to forage whatever they can along our line of march, and to burn everything they can't. We must leave nothing for the rebels.'

Still the emperor was silent.

Severiana spoke in his place. 'By forage,' she said, 'you mean loot.'

'An army marches on its stomach, my lady,' replied Magnus. 'We had no time to build up provisions in Rome.'

'The Italian people already distrust us. If you burn their fields and granaries during the harvest, you'll turn that distrust into hatred.'

'This is war.' He produced a rolled document from the purse at his belt. 'I have the orders for the tribunes already drawn up. I have added a command that any soldier caught attempting to desert should be executed in front of his comrades. The document need only be sealed by the emperor.'

'He is in no state to consider these matters now,' said Severiana. 'Bring them to him tonight.'

'Empress, we do not have the luxury of time. It is imperative that we maintain discipline on the march and slow the enemy as far as possible. We cannot show weakness. Until the emperor is fit to rule, I respectfully suggest that I take on the authority of government.'

There it is, thought Attica. Magnus had orbited close to her father ever since the acclamation, so close that sometimes she could hardly tell which of them was truly at the centre. He had exercised control over all appointments, handling his colleagues in the privy council like puppets. Now his intentions were plain to see. He did not dare assume the imperial title, but he did desire its power.

Severiana looked tenderly at her husband, her lips firm. Then she reached down and gently slipped the seal ring from his finger. He did not resist. She gave it to Magnus. 'Only until he is well again,' she said. 'And I wish to read everything you seal with that ring.'

'Of course, Empress. I am the emperor's loyal servant, as always.'

Although it made Attica sick to watch Magnus climb out of the carriage with her father's ring clutched in his fist, she could not bring herself to object. She knew that Magnus was as grim, resolute and cruel as his son. But right now the army needed such a man to hold it together, or they would never reach Gaul alive. That goal was all that mattered – not just for herself, nor even for her mother and father. More than anything, it mattered for the child growing within her.

Her mother noticed the distress in her eyes. She reached across to take Attica's hands. 'All will be well,' she said. 'Once we're safe back in Gaul, all will be well.'

Attica could only smile. She wished that she could believe those words.

'Have you told him yet?' her mother asked.

'I'm waiting until we reach Arles,' Attica said. 'Things will be calmer then.' Her mother did not enquire further. Perhaps she understood the true reason Attica was waiting: soon she would not be able to keep her pregnancy hidden, and would have to tell Felix. But for these precious weeks, at least, even though she could not hold it in her arms, the child would be hers alone.

The march continued. For a few more days there seemed to be a desperate optimism among the troops. The soldiers sang their marching songs, and each night at camp she could hear them drinking to the health of her father. Such was his reputation in Gaul that Romans and barbarians alike were still ready to march wherever he led. They were not to know that Magnus, not the emperor, was now doing the leading.

Within a week the songs and nightly toasts had ended. North they went, leaving behind a trail of burning granaries and slaughtered livestock. Outside Foligno Attica saw Alanic horsemen swirling around a meadow, shooting goats as though for sport. Near Fano on the Adriatic coast Euric and his Goths, whose thirst for blood seemed never to be sated, committed a massacre of the local people after they put up a noble and useless resistance. The Goths were stripping and throwing the bodies in the river Metaurus as Attica's carriage trundled by. She looked away to hide her tears.

A week after that massacre, as they neared Piacenza, Magnus

brought more bad news to the carriage. Remistus, the master of soldiers in Ravenna, had been assassinated. There would be no north Italian troops to join their cause. Those he had raised had gone over to the rebels.

Dejected, they turned their weary faces west and moved on, unwilling to pause, knowing that their foe was snapping at their heels and waiting with slavering jaws for them to stumble or pause. The air of the Po valley was known for being noxious, and scores of men, especially Franks unused to the southern climate, began to suffer from fevers and vomiting sickness. Tortoni, Asti, Chieri, and other smaller towns whose names Attica never learned – they passed by each of them in turn, skirting their walls without stopping even to hammer at their gates. Word of the emperor's flight had by now travelled throughout Italy, and it seemed that the locals were only too happy to see the back of the Gallic pretender. At Turin, just before they entered the Cottian Alps, the people jeered from their ramparts. 'Go back to Gaul,' Attica heard them shout. 'Go back to your foggy wilderness.'

LIV

Arles

I t was strange to think that eight years ago he had approached
this city gate with worn-through shoes and clothes so ragged
that only the dirt held them together. He remembered how he
had stood in the line by the side of the road with the other
commoners, baking in the summer heat, and watched as rich
men had gone by on horseback or in their carriages and litters.

Now he was among those rich men. He twitched open the
curtain of the carriage window to see the dusty, sweaty faces of
the peasants. City guards patrolled up and down the line, keeping
their eyes open for pickpockets or troublemakers. They did not
concern themselves with Arvandus in his two-horse carriage, with
his pair of Thuringian bodyguards riding immediately behind.

He closed the curtain and relaxed on the cushioned seat. This
carriage had been another worthwhile investment, especially after
the king's recent generosity. The campaign in Spain was going
well; Rechiar was in full flight, and the Gothic army had pillaged
a wide swathe of Suevic territory in Galicia. Theoderic had made
sure that his ministers did not fail to share in the booty. Arvandus,
as a new member of the court, had received a modest gift of
twenty pounds of pepper and a decorated pepper-pot looted
from one of Rechiar's estates. He had soon sold the box of
pepper to a Goth for gold, but did not have the heart to sell the
pepper-pot, which was in the form of a rather graceful gilded
swan. It would make a pleasing centrepiece to his dining table
when he began entertaining guests. It had once been a favourite
ornament of King Rechiar, he would tell them, and would then
describe how he had received it from the hands of Theoderic
himself.

The carriage darkened briefly as it passed through the gate-house tunnel. Such pleasures of life as dinner parties would have to wait. He had come to Arles on the king's business, with a message for the prefect that the Gothic army would be staying in Spain until the war against Rechiar had been concluded, however long that took. Arvandus was not looking forward to delivering this news. He had been instructed to present it as a necessary and rational course of action, but all his powers of rhetoric would not be able to hide the truth: it was a denial of imperial authority. To make matters worse, only in Narbonne six days ago had he learned that Avitus had abandoned Rome in the face of rebellion and was retreating back to Gaul. He had not realised how desperate the situation had become. It gave him some pleasure to think of Felix running away from the city in terror, until he remembered that Ecdicius, Attica and Sidonius were also fleeing. If Eparchius Avitus were caught and executed as a usurper, his entire family would suffer with him.

Arvandus tried not to think of them. He would have followed Avitus to the ends of the earth, had Sidonius allowed him. But he had been rejected, and the Philagrii had gone to Italy without him. That had been their choice. What happened to them was not his concern. His master was now King Theoderic.

Needing distraction from these ugly thoughts, he opened the slot at the front of the carriage. 'Driver, take me to the forum.'

'Yes, my lord,' came the reply. 'We'll be there shortly.'

It was his first time back in Arles since entering the king's service, and so his first chance to promenade in the forum as a man of real importance. It amused him to think that he was now more of a foreigner in the city than ever, despite the years he had spent here. He descended from the carriage at the forum entrance opposite the prefect's palace, making sure that his golden brooch was clear for all to see and not hidden by the folds of his cloak. It was early October, that pleasant autumn time before the chill of winter set in, and the lower forum looked busy. Arvandus was not sure how many faces he would recognise, since most of his student friends had left Arles years ago. It would do

no harm to walk the market, though, and to recapture some old
memories.

He walked through the entrance hall into the forum. Little had
changed. The vegetable traders were on the left side, the fishmongers and butchers on the right. Boys walked about with trays
of shellfish or roasted chestnuts suspended from their necks,
calling out for customers. On the east side of the forum, past the
vegetable stalls, Arvandus spotted the statue where he and his
friends had idled away countless hours between lessons and baths.
It had been colonised by a new group of students who looked
like they were still to grow a whisker between them. In the far
left corner a large crowd had gathered, as always, to see the
slavers show off their wares. Arvandus remembered how he and
Lampridius would sit and ogle the pretty barbarian girls, dreaming
of the day when they would be able to buy one for themselves.
Many times back then he had pictured himself walking through
the forum clad in sweeping cloak and followed by bodyguards,
just as he was now. Yet he had never expected to be a minister
of the Gothic king.

He felt unexpected melancholy as he thought of his former
self sitting on the steps beneath that statue. How innocent he
had been. That was before the war against Attila, before the death
of Valentinian, before the Vandals had sacked Rome and turned
the world upside down. His head had been full of ambitions for
imperial service. Sidonius had been by his side, a true friend for
ever, or so he had thought.

One of the students on the podium steps, a pimple-faced
youth wearing a low-cut tunic to show off his necklace, met his
eyes. Arvandus realised he was staring, and looked away. Perhaps
it had not been a good idea to visit the forum, a place filled
with memories and dreams long dead. He should head for the
house that Theoderic kept here for his ambassadors, deliver his
message to the prefect tomorrow, and return to Toulouse as
soon as possible.

'I see Fortune has smiled on you, Arvandus.'

He knew the voice as soon as he heard it, though it was for

the first time in many years. 'Greetings, Simeon,' he said, turning to face him.

Simeon smiled. 'We haven't seen you for a long time. We thought you were finished with Arles.'

'I'm here on business.'

'Your own, or somebody else's? You've obviously done well for yourself. Trading, perhaps? I never had you down as the merchant type.'

Arvandus knew that this meeting was unlikely to be a coincidence. 'Let's assume you know why I'm here,' he said. 'What do you want – or more precisely, what does Paeonius want?'

Simeon feigned shock, placing a hand over his heart. 'What, I'm not allowed to greet an old friend in the forum?'

'Of course you are, except that we're not friends. Nor am I friendly with the Philagrii these days, so I'll be of no use to your master. I've found my own way in the world.' He began to walk back towards the forum entrance.

Simeon's voice came after him. 'So I see; your companions are most impressive. The company of barbarians suits you, Arvandus.'

He stopped. Turning to Simeon, he said, 'And what do you mean by that?'

'Exactly what I said. A man who hops from one lord to another like a frog, draping himself in whatever gold he can find – isn't that the behaviour of a barbarian? I'm surprised you haven't grown a beard yet. Perhaps you're not able to.'

Arvandus resisted his rising anger. Maybe once he would have lost control and struck out against such deliberate provocation, but he was no longer a boy. Keeping his voice calm, he said, 'I won't stand here and let a Jew accuse me of not being Roman.'

Simeon snorted. His sarcastic smile became a sneer. 'Jew as I am, I'm more Roman than you ever were. Why do you think the Philagrii rejected you? They could see it.' He stepped closer, glaring down at Arvandus. 'I'm only surprised it took you so long to scurry back to where you belong – sucking on the teat of a

Gothic bitch.' With those words he brushed a contemptuous hand against Arvandus's chest.

At once Gunther and Guntram surged forward and grabbed Simeon, one brother on each side, and forced him roughly onto his back, knocking the back of his head on the flagstones. The surrounding market-goers cried out in surprise, stepping back at the sudden commotion. Guntram had whipped out his *scramasax* and was bringing it up to Simeon's throat.

'Leave him,' Arvandus shouted. 'Let him go.'

Slowly the brothers released Simeon and got to their feet. Guntram sheathed his sword. Simeon winced, touching fingers to the back of his head.

Arvandus was relieved to see no blood. He held out a hand, offering to help Simeon to his feet. 'That was a mistake,' he said. 'My men—'

'Are savages,' spat Simeon, ignoring the hand. He clambered to his feet and cast his eyes around the onlookers. More had joined the crowd. Arvandus noticed that the boys had left the statue and were hurrying over to see what was happening. 'Do you see what kind of men serve the Gothic king?' Simeon said. 'My master Paeonius gave this scoundrel, Arvandus, everything he has. He lifted him out of the dirt like a loving father. See how his son repays him – by going over to the Goths, kneeling to the Gothic king, and now returning to Arles with these two barbarians in order to attack Roman citizens in broad daylight!'

Arvandus saw the hatred of the crowd building up. One man called him a whoreson. Another called him a traitor. The curses kept coming. 'It's not true,' he protested. 'King Theoderic is loyal to the emperor . . .'

An elderly woman carrying a child spat at his feet. 'Then where is Theoderic's army?' she demanded. 'My first-born son is with the emperor. The Goths have betrayed us.'

'Let me speak,' pleaded Arvandus. The crowd was closing in. His bodyguards stepped in front of him, drawing their weapons. A pair of soldiers at the entrance to the upper forum noticed what was happening, and began marching towards them.

There was a long, low blast from across the city, towards the east gate. It was a military horn. The crown quietened briefly. There was another blast, and then a third.

'The army,' one man said. 'The emperor has returned!'

The people surged towards the forum entrance, heading for the main street. They abandoned Arvandus as though he were invisible. Only Simeon remained. 'A lucky escape for you,' he said. His smile had returned. 'I told you once that Paeonius has a long memory. I hope this has reminded you of that.'

With a brief, polite bow Simeon left him, following the mass of people streaming from the forum. Arvandus could now hear cheering rising from the direction of the amphitheatre. So Avitus had returned. He swallowed, waiting for his heart to calm itself. Part of him wished that the crowd had finished him off. Now he would have to deliver Theoderic's message to the emperor himself.

LV

Ecdicius reached Arles with the vanguard on the second day of October. Desertions and sickness had taken their toll, but the army was still in one piece. He was pleased to see that reinforcements from the Gallic field army were already camped in the meadows outside the city walls. He recognised heavy cavalrymen from the Lancers, along with the banners of several infantry regiments: the bronze impaled head of the Valentinians, the silver laurel wreath of the Salians, the curling serpent heads of the Batavians. There were Nervian archers, along with sizeable Frankish, Alemannic and Burgundian warbands. Messianus, the master of soldiers in Gaul, had done well to assemble such a force.

The people of Arles, hearing the trumpets sound as the army approached the east gate, had filled the streets. They waved from every window; children were perched in every tree, on every roof, in the upper arches of the amphitheatre. It was as though the emperor had returned in triumph instead of undignified retreat.

Ecdicius was simply relieved to be back. Finally, after all these weeks, he could let go of the fear. He could forget about Majorian and Ricimer, whose cavalry scouts had followed them like spectres right up to the Cottian Alps. He could forget about the betrayal of Aegidius, and the worry he had seen every day in the faces of his parents and sister. They were back in their city, and now there would be time to rest.

As he rode into the palace courtyard with the vanguard, he saw the rest of the imperial family. His brother Agricola, fifteen years old now, was standing on the steps of the palace. Papianilla was next to him, holding her two daughters by the hand. Magnus's wife Egnatia was behind them.

Ecdicius jumped from his horse, handed the reins and his helmet to a groom, and went over to them. Agricola came running down the steps and took his brother in an embrace. 'Look at you,' said Ecdicius. He grabbed Agricola's chin, where the first wisps of a beard were sprouting through. 'You're becoming a man already!'

'I had my first shave,' said Agricola, evidently proud of his new, deeper voice. 'I'll be able to ride with you and Father when we take back Rome!'

Ecdicius laughed, pulling him close. He did not want to disillusion his brother. Whether or not they returned across the Alps depended on how many troops they could gather, and how soon. Even if they did, Agricola would be unlikely to join them. One prince was enough to risk in battle.

Sidonius had also arrived in the courtyard, and was rushing to embrace Papianilla. Ecdicius smiled to see his cousin pick up his two girls, one in the crook of each arm, and spin them around until they screamed with laughter and he almost fell from the dizziness. The emperor's carriage came rolling through the courtyard gates, together with the imperial guard. The sight of Prince Euric wiped the smile from Ecdicius's face. There had been no Goths camped outside the city, which suggested that Theoderic had so far ignored the request for reinforcements. If Gothic support was waning, Euric might also decide it was time to abandon the emperor. Ecdicius would not be sorry to see the back of him, but they could not afford to lose five hundred skilled warriors.

There was little time to enjoy the family reunion. Within the hour Ecdicius was summoned to a war council in the office of Prefect Priscus Valerianus. The dour-faced master of soldiers in Gaul, Messianus, was present, as were Magnus and Tribune Marcus of the Eighth Dalmatian cavalry. 'Where's my father?' Ecdicius asked.

'The emperor is resting,' said Magnus, seated at the head of the table. 'We're meeting to discuss the tactical situation.'

Ecdicius took a seat next to Messianus, who began the discussion. 'We now have seven thousand men assembled,' he said.

'Eight hundred cavalry and two thousand infantry from the field army, the rest barbarian auxiliaries. One thousand Franks, and smaller contingents of Bretons, Alemanni, Sarmatians, Taifali, and Alans.'

'And we have money in the treasury,' said Magnus. 'Prefect Priscus has been very efficient with taxes.'

Priscus nodded. 'As soon as I heard what was happening in Rome I stopped all further grain shipments, so the granaries at Marseilles are full of provisions for the army. For once feeding and paying the soldiers won't be the problem.'

Ecdicius sensed a note of irritation in his voice. 'Then what is the problem?'

'Finding enough soldiers to feed and pay,' said Magnus. 'It does not reflect on Messianus that our barbarian allies have been unwilling to send more men. At the moment they are concerned with defending their own lands from each other. We don't have time to raise conscripts for the field army, let alone train and equip them.'

'And what of the Goths?' asked Ecdicius.

There was a brief silence. Magnus stiffened, and drew himself up in his chair. 'Theoderic's ambassador is waiting for an audience. He says he bears a message from the king.'

'Then let us hear it,' came a new voice.

They all looked to the door. Ecdicius rose as soon as he saw his father, and the other men did likewise. He looked almost like his old self – tall, his chest firm and chin held high. It was as though a few breaths of the city's air had returned the strength to his limbs and the clarity to his eyes.

'Majesty,' said Magnus, bowing deeply. 'Forgive me, I believed that you were resting.'

'I was,' said Avitus, stepping into the room. 'I've rested enough. Gentlemen, I intend to win back Rome before the onset of winter. Any longer and Marcian will likely send an eastern army to steal the throne. We must crush the rebels before that happens. Now, let us meet with the ambassador. As soon as Theoderic's army arrives, we march.'

The audience chamber was hastily prepared. It was the very same room where Ecdicius had first seen Theoderic, at the start of the Hunnic war. Back then his father had sat on the throne as a mere citizen; now he was emperor, wearing the diadem and heavy purple cloak, with two Gothic soldiers in mail armour standing on either side. Sidonius had been summoned to keep a record as notary, and was sitting at a writing desk at the side of the chamber. Ecdicius went over to him. 'How are my nieces?' he asked.

'They're well,' Sidonius said. 'A pair of angels.'

'I'm very glad to hear it.'

At that moment Magnus, positioned at the entrance, declared that the imperial audience was in session. Ecdicius returned to stand next to Priscus and Messianus. When Magnus announced the name of the ambassador, Ecdicius almost gasped aloud. 'An audience is granted to Arvandus, minister of King Theoderic.'

Ecdicius watched his friend enter and kneel before the emperor. He was wearing a golden brooch in the style of an imperial official, though without any badges on his tunic to denote his office. When had he gone over to serve the barbarians?

Arvandus rose, his expression cold. 'I bring word from King Theoderic of the Goths,' he said.

The emperor raised his hand. 'Speak.'

'The king thanks you for the gifts you sent by Hesychius. He regrets that he cannot supply Your Majesty with any men. The situation in Spain is at a critical stage, and he must commit all his forces to protect your interests there.'

There was a nervous silence among the audience. Every pair of eyes watched Avitus.

'I see,' he said. 'My interests in Spain, you say?'

'King Rechiar of the Sueves is still at large in the west. King Theoderic is confident of victory within a month.'

'A month will be too late. We intend to return to Italy and defeat the rebels before winter.'

Arvandus bowed his head. 'I regret, Majesty, that for now the king cannot spare any men.'

'Then King Theoderic is an oath-breaker.'

Perhaps such an accusation would have touched the pride of
a Gothic envoy; but Arvandus was no Goth. He took the insult
in stony silence. 'The king will keep his promise. It is simply that
current circumstances prevent him from doing so.'

Magnus spoke up. 'Majesty, the only interests that King
Theoderic is defending in Spain are his own. If he'd dealt with
Rechiar months ago like he was supposed to, we would never
have had to leave Rome in the first place.'

'Forgive me,' said Arvandus, 'but were it not for King Theoderic,
Your Majesty would not be emperor at all.'

'That is outrageous,' snarled Magnus. 'The emperor was
acclaimed by the people of Gaul and by the Senate itself. And
you miserable worm, you stand here in the service of a barbarian
king and dare to insult His Majesty?'

'King Theoderic is a loyal friend of Rome,' said Arvandus.

Magnus stared at the young envoy with wide, unbelieving eyes.
His nostrils flared. 'You miserable, treacherous . . .'

The emperor thumped a heavy fist on his armrest. 'Quiet! By
God, I'll make Theoderic himself answer for this. I'm only
emperor because of him, he says? Who was it taught him to be
king when he was hardly out of swaddling? Well, here's a message
you can take back to your master, and tell him to remember it.
Tell him we'll march to Rome without him, and take back the
throne; and when we've finished with the rebels, we'll come back
to teach him the lessons he has forgotten. Tell him that we need
only stamp our foot upon the ground anywhere in this country,
and armies of infantry and cavalry will rise. Now go, Arvandus
– make sure you tell him that!'

Arvandus's face was grim as he bowed and left the imperial
presence. He was no doubt thinking the same thing as Ecdicius.
It had been an inauspicious choice of words by the emperor, for
they had first been spoken by Pompey at the start of his war
with Julius Caesar. Theoderic, of all barbarians, would know how
that particular war had ended.

As soon as Arvandus had gone, Magnus stepped forward. 'I
always knew that one was a traitor.'

'Arvandus is no traitor,' snapped Ecdicius. 'It was your son who drove him out of the imperial service. Nor is he responsible for the decisions of the Gothic king.'

'How do we know? He's clearly slithered his way into the royal court. Who knows what secrets he's betrayed?'

'Arvandus would never betray us. He served my father with honour.'

Avitus rose from the throne, sweeping his cloak over his shoulder. 'And now he serves my enemy.' He looked to the master of soldiers. 'Messianus, ready the army to march in five days.'

'Majesty, that gives us very little time to make preparations. The men need rest.'

'They will have five days of rest. We'll strike back before Majorian and Ricimer expect it. I want that traitor Aegidius's head on a pike before winter, along with the rest of them. Then we'll deal with Theoderic.'

Ecdicius watched his father stride from the room. Every step seemed fuelled by anger, as though he had woken from the weeks of stupor a different man. Yet Ecdicius knew that he was right – returning to Italy so quickly might catch the rebels unawares. Majorian had not yet been declared emperor, and it was imperative that they struck while there was no other claimant to the western throne. The enemy would also have to consolidate their hold in the south against a potential Vandal counterattack, which meant that the Alpine passes were now open, but within a month they would be blocked by snow, and after the snow melted they would be blocked by enemy troops.

Attacking now was their best chance for victory, slim though it was.

LVI

Piacenza, Italy

Two weeks later Ecdicius was in the command tent with his father, watching the two magistrates of Piacenza grovel in the dirt.

'May God and all the saints bless Your merciful Majesty,' the first said, his voice an irritating nasal whine.

'Our city will shower a thousand prayers upon Your Majesty's blessed countenance,' added the second.

'Very good,' said the emperor. 'Return to your citizens. Tell them that their faithfulness will not be forgotten.'

The magistrates struggled to their feet and were escorted out of the tent by two soldiers of the Lions, who were now acting as the imperial bodyguard. Ecdicius watched the civilians go, then glanced at Sidonius. His cousin looked up from his writing desk, met his eye, and pulled a face. Ecdicius smiled. So they both had the same opinion of the snivelling magistrates of Piacenza.

Count Messianus approached the throne and began a private conversation with the emperor. The other occupants of the tent started talking amongst themselves. For the most part they were the leaders of the various barbarian contingents, ambitious young lords and princelings who had been sent by their respective kings to win glory at the side of the Roman emperor. The large Frankish army was led by a minor prince called Chlodoric, a sinewy, sharp-eyed warrior whose hair had been braided into an elaborate carpet down his back. In charge of the Alanic cavalry was Prince Eocharic, nephew to the corpulent, cowardly Sangiban. Under his arm he clutched his gilded helm, from the top of which sprouted a horse-tail plume laced with silver bells. On the march so far the youth had proved himself as flamboyant and belligerent as his uncle; Ecdicius hoped that when it came to battle he would prove to be made of tougher stuff.

Sidonius left his desk and came over to his cousin. 'So, what did you think of the Piacentini?'

'Brazen sycophants,' said Ecdicius.

'I quite agree. One can hardly blame them, though. It's in their blood. Piacenza has been sacked and re-sacked so many times by Gauls, Ligurians, Romans and Carthaginians that they've become very pragmatic when it comes to loyalty.'

'"Pragmatic" is a good word for it.'

'Are you surprised? The Torinese were hardly any better.'

That was true. Turin had been the first city they had reached upon crossing the Cottian Alps. Ecdicius had not forgotten the insults the Torinese had hurled at them a few weeks earlier when they had been retreating west. This time, shocked at the sight of seven thousand unexpected troops descending from the mountains, the people of Turin had flung open their gates. Their councillors, at least those who had not fled in surprised terror, had been quick to prostrate themselves in the dirt. It had been a wise decision. Avitus had refused the advice of Messianus to sack Turin as punishment for their earlier treachery. At this early stage in the campaign, he had said, a wealthy and servile city was more useful to them than a destitute and angry one.

After Turin they had continued east at a good pace, covering the next hundred miles in five days. The air of the Po valley was less virulent than a month previously. Earlier that morning they had crossed the Trebbia and arrived here at the city of Piacenza, where the air was clear and dry, and the ground fresh with the scent of newly turned clods. They had pitched camp to the south of the city. Piacenza, Ecdicius knew, was to Italy what Orléans was to Gaul: the hinge between north and south, the city that any would-be conqueror had to control.

The army was already in triumphant mood, encouraged by

the easy capitulation of the north, and had almost forgotten about the absence of the Goths. Euric had abandoned them at Arles, ostensibly because of the emperor's insult to his brother, but Ecdicius suspected that the young prince's nose had simply been turned by the smell of plunder elsewhere. Why risk death fighting Ricimer and Majorian when there were easier spoils to be had in Spain? He had not been surprised when the Goth had deserted.

Still, Ecdicius had been disturbed by the sight of Arvandus riding back to Toulouse alongside Euric. He would have liked to speak to him first; not that he would have known what to say.

'You look distracted, cousin,' said Sidonius.

'Forgive me. I was thinking about Arvandus. We could have used him on this campaign.'

'Arvandus has made his own choices,' Sidonius said. 'His ambitions were never going to be constrained by anyone.'

There was frustration in his voice, but regret, too. Sidonius had been one of the few civilians to accompany the army, at his own insistence. Both Magnus and Felix had chosen to remain in Arles until the victory was assured. Unlike a year ago, this was no parade of pomp and magnificence, but an invasion. The army mustered under the command of Messianus represented every barbarian tribe in Gaul except the Goths. Ecdicius could not help but admire his cousin's quiet courage. He had certainly toughened up since their student days. They both had. This was not about glory for either of them, as it might have been once. It was about justice. The rightful emperor had been plotted against, betrayed, forced out of Rome. Opilio had let the people starve and provoked them to riot on the streets. Aegidius had broken his oath. All of these crimes would soon be punished.

A soldier stepped into the tent. 'Majesty, a scout from the Eighth Dalmatians has returned.'

'Show him in,' said Avitus.

All conversations stopped as the cavalryman entered. He pulled off his helmet and quickly fell to one knee, dipping his head almost to the ground. 'Majesty.'

'Rise, soldier.' Avitus snapped his fingers, and a servant offered the scout a ladle of water. 'What is your report?'

The scout swallowed the water too quickly, almost choking on it. He cleared his throat. 'We've skirmished with the enemy at the river Nure, Majesty. We took a prisoner, who claims that Ricimer's army is camped seven miles east of us.'

'And Majorian?'

'He is said to be still in Rome, Majesty.'

'Ricimer is by himself?' said Ecdicius. 'Father, we have to fight. Now's our chance to defeat him.'

Avitus looked to his master of soldiers. 'Messianus?'

'Your son is right, Majesty,' said Messianus. 'If Ricimer is here we must fight him, or else turn back. It seems that he was not expecting us to retake the north so soon.'

The emperor nodded. 'Tomorrow, then. Make sure the men are well fed and rested. And let them know that the man who brings me Ricimer's head will receive a pound of gold.'

That night Ecdicius was walking along the ramparts of Piacenza, looking over the moonlit gloom of the plains to the south. A calm, cool wind breathed out of the darkness. Down in the city his father was sleeping in the house that the magistrates had offered as his residence. The rest of the army was still camped outside the walls. Finding himself kept awake by the same old twisting nerves in his stomach, Ecdicius had ventured up to the walls with a gourd of wine, hoping that a little drink and light exercise would help him settle down. It was cheap wine, army issue, but it felt good to have the warmth inside him. He had passed a few sentries, when he spotted someone standing further along the ramparts. He seemed to be studying the constellations overhead. Although he was cloaked and hooded, Ecdicius could tell that it was his cousin.

'Sentry duty, Sollius?' he said as he approached.

Sidonius turned to him in surprise and grinned. 'Too excited to sleep.'

Ecdicius handed him the leather gourd. 'Have some wine. It'll soothe the stomach.'

Sidonius took the gourd and swigged a mouthful. He winced as he swallowed, and wiped his mouth. 'I can never sleep on nights like this,' he said.

'I don't think I slept at all on the Catalaunian Plains,' said Ecdicius. 'Not before the battle, hardly after it either. Then once Attila left I must have slept for three days straight.' He chuckled. 'By the time we got to Clermont I was sleeping on the back of my horse.'

'Are you afraid?'

'No,' Ecdicius said. 'I've been afraid before, but this isn't it. This is anticipation. Excitement. You've never ridden into battle, Sollius, but let me tell you, there's nothing else like it. You know how you can get your nose stuck inside a book for hours, and it becomes your whole world? That's what battle is to me.'

'With the added excitement of possible death.'

'When it starts, I don't think about anything else. Honestly. I don't have time to be scared.'

Sidonius took another swig of wine, and handed over the gourd. 'Speaking of books,' he said, 'we're standing in the shadow of history. This was the site of one of Hannibal's great victories.'

'Which victory was that?'

'Ecdicius, you should have paid more attention at school.'

'And you should have paid less attention.'

Sidonius laughed. 'It was the winter after he'd crossed the Alps. He had one consular army trapped in those hills to the south, when another came to see him off, led by Sempronius. Hannibal knew that Sempronius was a good general, but headstrong, so he taunted him into sending his legions across the Trebbia, somewhere to the west there. This was the depths of winter, remember. The Romans came out of the river shivering and numb, hardly able to hold their weapons, the warm, well-fed Carthaginians fell upon them, and that was that.'

Ecdicius nodded. 'Were there elephants?'

'I believe so, yes.'

'We could use some elephants.'

'Elephants aren't so good. You just shove a spear up the arse and they go crazy.'

'I'll remember that when we invade Africa.'

They both looked out over what would be the arena of battle. They could not see far into the darkness, but on the southern horizon, silhouetted against the stars, there was a black line of mountains that their scouts had reported lay some ten miles to the south. To the east lay the Nure, to the west the Trebbia. It was mostly pasture and newly ploughed fields, with only a few patches of light woodland: a flat, open battlefield that would favour cavalry above all. At the military council that evening Ecdicius had pointed out that cavalry was their weakness; without the First Gallic Horse or the Goths, all they had were three hundred heavy cavalry, five hundred light cavalry and one thousand Alans and Sarmatians. Both his father and Messianus had decided that they would have to engage with the enemy as soon as possible, taking the initiative and breaking Ricimer's centre.

'Do you think we'll win tomorrow?' Sidonius asked.

'Oh, yes,' Ecdicius said at once, smiling.

'How?'

'I have no idea. Nobody knows how a battle is won until it's been won, and even then sometimes you don't know. A thousand things might happen. Ricimer might slip and crack his head on a rock. Now, wouldn't that be a sign from God?'

'Let's hope that doesn't happen to our side.'

'It won't. My father will be staying here in the city, along with you. He's too important to risk. Should things start to go against us, we'll head west across the Trebbia, back to Gaul. Ricimer won't follow us so close to winter.'

'But that won't happen.'

Ecdicius yawned. The wine was beginning to take effect. 'Of course not. Well, I'm going to try to get some sleep after all.' Before he left, he reached out and placed a hand on his cousin's shoulder. 'Thank you, Sollius.'

'For what?'

'For sticking with us until the end. You might have stayed back in Arles with the others.'

'You know I'd never desert your father.'

'I know. But thank you all the same.'

Ecdicius walked back along the ramparts, looking out at the star-filled sky. It was the wine, perhaps, but tonight he felt as though the constellations were smiling down on them.

LVII

'Keep the line steady. Keep the line steady.'

The emperor was whispering to himself as he watched the battle line advance to the east, wading through the low morning mist. Trumpets and horns bellowed to one another like forlorn beasts, and the line came to a halt. From the city ramparts Ecdicius could make out the regimental standards of the Lions, the Valentinians, the Salians, and the Batavians. These regular units held the centre behind a skirmish line of Nervian archers, and were led by Count Messianus himself. On the right, their weakest flank, Messianus had placed the Bretons, Alemanni and mounted Sarmatians. On the left were the Franks, supported by the Burgundians, Taifali and mounted Alans. Their meagre heavy cavalry, the three hundred Lancers, had been divided between Messianus in the centre and Ecdicius, who was about to leave his father and ride out to the left flank.

For almost a mile across the plains stretched this force of glittering iron and steel. Even so, it seemed to Ecdicius painfully delicate; except in the centre where the Valentinians brought up the rear, the infantry line was only four ranks deep, almost ribbon-thin. Were it to break, there would be nothing between Ricimer and Avitus but the walls of Piacenza.

Beyond their lines was the approaching enemy, still too far away for Ecdicius to make out any details, but it was clear that they had considerable forces of cavalry on both flanks. This was what he had been afraid of. Even so, the rebel line did not seem any wider than theirs, and was perhaps even a little shorter. 'We might outnumber them,' he said.

His father was also studying the enemy. 'Something isn't right,' he said. 'Ricimer is too careful to risk this. If we outnumbered him, why isn't he retreating south?'

'Could it be an ambush? Perhaps Majorian is bringing his army from the north, to cross the Po behind us.'

'Our scouts haven't seen any trace of him in the north, or anywhere else.'

'Ricimer's being over-confident, then.'

Avitus said nothing, but continued staring at the enemy lines as though searching them for a secret message.

As a new chorus of horn blasts rolled across the plain, Ecdicius felt the fire surge through his limbs. 'Father, it's time,' he said. 'I need to join the men.'

Slowly, reluctantly, Avitus nodded. 'It's time.' He turned to his son, clasping him on both shoulders. He stared deep into his eyes for a moment, then pulled him into a powerful embrace. 'Fight bravely, son. And may God watch over you.'

Ecdicius donned his helmet and fastened the neck strap. 'I'll bring you victory, Father,' he said. Nodding farewell to Sidonius, he descended the rampart steps to where the groom waited with his horse and shield. He mounted, took the shield, and turned to face the one hundred and fifty Lancers who were to be his personal guard. 'With me,' he cried. 'For the emperor!'

The Lancers echoed his words, thrusting their thick spears into the air. Unlike Ecdicius they wore heavy mail and plate armour that covered them from head to toe. Ecdicius had kept to his usual light armour of short-sleeved mail shirt. In the depths of battle he would need to move quickly. He could not afford to be constrained or weighed down.

He led the Lancers at a bracing trot across the meadows to the left flank, where he would lead the Frankish, Burgundian and Taifali infantry, along with the Alanic light cavalry. They would be facing the enemy heavy cavalry, who would pose a deadly threat to the infantry if the line were broken. The shield walls had to hold.

Riding through the gap between the centre regiments and his own, he wheeled left and spurred his horse along the front rank, holding his sword high. The Franks cheered when they saw him. 'Keep your ranks closed,' he urged. 'Make your shield wall like iron, and the enemy will break on it like water! Stand your ground – stand your ground, and when victory is yours, go home with your hearts full of pride and your satchels full of gold!' That was what barbarians wanted to hear, and with swords and axes and spears clashing on shields they raised a deafening din. 'Stand firm,' Ecdicius cried, 'stand firm,' and he galloped past the Franks, past the cheering Burgundians and Taifali, with his guard of Lancers thundering close behind, until he came to the far left of the army. Then he stopped and looked back down the line to see that it was straight and strong, the infantry regiments formed up in close order with shields ready to take the enemy charge.

This was what he loved. The purpose, the resolve, the feel of hot blood coursing through him. There was no feeling like it in the world.

The enemy line was close now, two hundred yards away. Ecdicius watched as the skirmishers in the distant centre began to pepper one another with missiles. Ricimer seemed to have twice as many archers, and it did not take long for the tide to turn in the enemy's favour. At the sound of a horn from the centre, the Nervians sprinted back to friendly lines, filtering through the infantry ranks and reforming at the rear.

Ricimer's forces tramped on, their marching a low thunder on the earth. In the enemy centre Ecdicius saw the standards of the palatine sister legions, the Jovians and Herculians, the elite of the Italian field army. Two thousand legionaries against their two thousand battle-hardened Gallic regulars: these odds were not impossible. Directly ahead, facing his own troops, he could now make out one regiment of auxiliary infantry, one of heavy cavalry and another of light cavalry. Again, not bad; Ricimer had mounted superiority, but his infantry was weak on this flank. Ecdicius started to feel something more than excitement: elation. This was a fight he could win. If only the Franks held, he could win.

There was time for one more pass along the front. Always show the men that you are still with them, that was what his father had taught him; show them you are not afraid. He kicked his horse into a gallop, and once more a cheer rose from the barbarian ranks. 'Stand firm,' he screamed, over and over again until he could not hear his own voice above the roar of the men and the blood pounding in his ears. He reached the end of the Frankish line, and wheeled about to return. The Franks began their war-cry, the rumbling chant that started low and quiet and climbed into a fearsome roar, accompanied by the clattering of steel. Not to be outdone, the Burgundians and Taifali began their own chant before the Franks had finished, at which the Franks redoubled their efforts and the Alans behind them joined in, until two and a half thousand barbarian voices seemed about to break open heaven itself.

Ecdicius, riding with his guard to the rear of the Frankish line, laughed to hear them. If only shouting won battles, the German tribes would be masters of the world.

He turned to look for the commander of the Alans. With his plume of silver bells, Prince Eocharic was easy to spot at the head of the lightly-armoured skirmishers. Ecdicius raised his arm. Eocharic saw, saluted in return, and with a high-pitched yell spurred his horse towards the left flank. The earth trembled as his five hundred Alans followed, javelins at the ready. Their task was to harry Ricimer's cavalry, pester them with missiles, to break them up and draw them off with feigned retreats.

There was no pause in the enemy advance. The auxiliary regiment came on at a steady pace, now only a hundred yards ahead of the Franks. The enemy cavalry was forming up to charge the Burgundians and Taifali, as Ecdicius had expected. 'Win this day,' he cried, 'and all of Italy will be yours!'

Eocharic and his Alans, splitting into groups and spreading out to cover the enemy horsemen, began their swirling attacks that brought them hurtling toward the tips of the enemy spears before loosing their javelins and turning away. There was only so much they could do, five hundred against one thousand, but it would be enough to delay Ricimer's cavalry for a while.

That was when Ecdicius saw the yellow, blue and black cloth

streaming from the dragon-head standard of the enemy light cavalry unit, and spotted the shield design of the First Gallic Horse. He felt his nerves tighten. It meant that Aegidius himself was commanding the opposing flank. Flaccus, Basilius and the rest would be there with him. Ecdicius had hoped not to face his old comrades.

He cleared those memories from his mind. They were not his comrades now. They were the enemy, and they had to die along with their treacherous commander.

Fifty yards, and the auxiliary troops halted. Ecdicius barked a single word: '*Shields!*' With a fierce clatter a roof of linden-wood appeared above the Franks, and Ecdicius found himself surrounded by his guard, almost crushed as they packed around him and lifted their own shields as a shell, blocking his view; he hated to be closed up like this, even though he knew what was about to happen. The darts of Mars were about to fall.

First, from within his darkness, he heard a thick rush as the lead-weighted darts were hurled upwards from the enemy ranks.

Ecdicius froze. He waited. The breathing of his guard was thick and heavy beneath their shields. The mounts shifted restlessly.

Like a deadly hail, the darts hit them. He heard guttural Frankish cries as the lethal barbs punched through shields and helmets and mail coats, knocked men to the ground, shattered bones, plunged into soft flesh. Many thudded into the ground around them. None struck the shields above his head, but one horse next to him screamed in anguish and collapsed, sending its rider tumbling from his saddle. Ecdicius looked down to see the fat weight and brightly-coloured flights of a dart protruding from the beast's rump. It rolled onto its side, delirious with pain, but this served only to twist the barb within it, and as its muscles were ripped apart it tossed its head from side to side with frenzied, frothing squeals, kicking at the legs of the tightly-packed horses around it, which in turn began to panic; the dismounted rider, his heavy spear thrown aside, drew his longsword and stood over his tormented companion, and brought the blade down in a wide arc that bit deep into its neck, and finally the horse shuddered and lay still.

On one side, the side where the horse had died, Ecdicius was still exposed, and he saw the Franks lowering their shields to wrench darts from the wood or to help their injured companions. Others were hurling their throwing-axes towards the enemy line. There was no coordination to them, no discipline.

'Shields up!' cried Ecdicius. 'Shields up, shields up!' These Franks had clearly not fought Romans before; they did not know that each enemy soldier would have five darts behind his shield, and would pause between each throw so the enemy might let his guard down.

Ecdicius's guards, thinking themselves addressed, hurried to close the gap and tighten the shell around him, and he found himself in darkness once more, just as the next rain of darts fell. More screams, worse this time, as those Franks too slow to react were struck. '*Keep your shields up!*' Ecdicius roared, even though the Franks would not hear.

The darts ceased falling, and the cries of the injured continued. This time he heard the Franks themselves yelling at each other to keep their shields high. They had learned their lesson. A third rain fell. More screams, even more curses. The Franks believed that the only honourable missile was the axe: bows, slings and javelins were the weapons of cowards. But their curses did not prevent the fourth rain of darts. By now their shield arms would be tired, their fear mounting. The final flight of darts would come moments before the enemy charge struck home. Ecdicius pulled the nearest shield to one side, giving him a gap into fresh air. 'Keep your shields high,' he shouted. 'After the darts will come the charge!'

He let the gap close again. 'Keep steady,' he said to the men around him. 'As soon as the sky is empty, two-rank formation.' They echoed his command, passing it to the rest of the unit. He trusted the soldiers of this regiment, having ridden with them before, when he was in the First Gallic Horse. The barbarians, though – that was another matter. They followed him only because he had promised them loot.

For a fifth time iron and lead fell upon them, hammering, splintering, tearing. Before the last dart fell, the sound of the enemy charge rose up like a storm. This was it. 'Now, two ranks,' he said, and the shell flung apart and sunlight fell in, blinding him for a moment. He squinted, shielding his eyes, and saw the enemy infantry charging towards the Franks with their helms and blades flashing, and the Franks pulling themselves into order, bellowing hatred and flinging axes into the faces of the enemy, and then the two lines met with a sound almost like the surf sucking through a shingle beach, a drawn-out, tumbling collision. After this rose the noise of battle: of steel on wood, of shouts and cries, pushing and panting. The Franks were holding their ground, rooted to the spot by their battle-fury. There had been casualties from the darts, some corpses now trampled underfoot by their comrades, injured men dragging themselves from the fray, but they still outnumbered the attackers. The line would hold. Over to the left Eocharic and his Alans were harassing the enemy cavalry, and had successfully loosened up their formation and stalled their advance. The Burgundians and Taifali, seeing the milling cavalry within striking distance, seemed impatient to engage them. Ecdicius saw some of them urging the rest to hold position as they had been ordered, but the thirst for blood and glory was growing too great, with some waving their blades and edging forwards, and then all at once the formation broke, and the Burgundians, followed by the Taifali, started their roaring charge towards the enemy.

Ecdicius watched his left flank peel away and screamed uselessly at their ill-discipline. He almost started to ride in their direction, ready to drag each barbarian back into line in turn, but stopped himself. The enemy cavalry was disorganised and distracted, vulnerable to infantry attack. It was not good to break formation, but things were going in their favour, and unrestrained barbarian ferocity could work to their advantage. The enemy advance had been halted, and the Franks were now shield to shield with the auxiliaries, slowly shoving them back inch by bloody inch as men fell to spear thrusts from the second and third ranks, or to axes thrown from the rear.

Ecdicius allowed himself a glance to the centre: there battle had also been joined.

But something was not right. The Jovians and Herculians were in a melee with the Gallic troops, but behind them Ecdicius could now see more troops – many more, and standards rising that before had been lowered. He counted four new banners. Four legions behind the first two, hidden from view by the flatness of the plain, their banners kept down so they would not be seen until it was too late.

Four thousand more legionaries: Ricimer had six thousand men in the centre, a steel fist to punch a hole through their army. No wonder he had kept his flanks so weak.

Ecdicius stared in frozen horror. He spotted Messianus and his mounted guard at the rear. The general seemed to have spotted the new banners also, for he was craning up in his saddle, trying to get a clear view. But what could he do? His centre could not possibly stand its ground against so many.

There was only one thing to do, and it appeared to Ecdicius with sudden clarity.

'Wedge, on me!' he shouted, drawing his sword and holding it high. The Lancers repeated his cry, bustling themselves into formation even as he started off at a gallop towards the left, away from the centre. This was not a parade ground, and there was no time for finesse; his men would have to form themselves into a wedge behind him at speed, and as he sped past the Franks and across open ground to help the Burgundians and Taifali in their struggle, he was pleased that the Lancers had found their places before they struck like an arrow into the flank of the First Gallic Horse.

The force of their charge took them deep into the enemy cavalry, where faces Ecdicius knew turned first in surprise, then in horror. He swung his blade, catching one rider on the elbow and half-severing his arm with a violent spray of blood, and yanked on the reins to veer left, then with a back-handed swing struck the shield of another rider, whose own blade came rushing down and glanced his helmet, missing him only thanks to his mount, which gave a sudden jolt backwards, but Ecdicius kept his balance and saw an opening and thrust his blade point-first into the other man's armpit, pushing deep inside his chest. He pulled the blade out, the man tumbled dead from his horse, and Ecdicius looked around and found himself surrounded and hemmed in by friends and foes in a chaos of Roman cavalry and barbarian infantry and the hurtling javelins of the Alans. He knew that to be trapped in such a place would be to die; his horse reared, frantic amidst the smell of blood, and Ecdicius pointed his sword into the depths of the enemy, who he saw were starting to pull away from the fight to reform around a yellow-plumed rider that could only be Aegidius.

They must not be given the chance, he thought; they had to be driven from the field now, or all would be lost. 'On me – for Avitus!' Scores of voices, Roman, Burgundian, Taifalian and Alanic, cried his father's name and followed him in the headlong thrust deeper into the disordered enemy throng, where they wreaked havoc, for the First Gallic Horse were facing a combined onslaught of javelins, spears, axes and swords, and even with the screaming commands of Aegidius they could not form a united defence against so frenzied an attack. Ecdicius pushed on, guiding his horse around collapsed riders who were speared where they fell, taking a sword from the left on his shield, and then another, but not stopping until he found his path blocked by a foe who raised his sword ready to strike; the blade came down, and Ecdicius caught it on his own with a clash that made his arm shake in its socket, but before either could aim another blow a press of Burgundian spears appeared around them, and the enemy rider was pierced from three different directions and died in his saddle.

Not far away now, perhaps forty yards, Ecdicius saw Aegidius turn about, raise his hand and signal a retreat. They had done it. The remains of the enemy cavalry began to pull away, those still in the fight breaking off if they were quick enough, or falling to barbarian steel if they were not. The Alans were pursuing the fleeing cavalry in their flight to the east; the infantry were standing about to get their breath, roaring victory, laughing with one another, or already looting the dead and dying that lay strewn across the field of slaughter. And it had been a slaughter: the First Gallic Horse and the other enemy regiment had taken heavy casualties. The Lancers had survived largely unscathed, and the barbarians still looked strong. But the battle was far from won.

'I swear there will be time for plunder,' Ecdicius shouted. 'Gather yourselves, and follow me!'

By now he was exhausted, his thighs on fire with the fatigue of keeping himself in the saddle, his chest heaving to suck in air, but he ignored the pain and led the Lancers and the barbarian infantry at a steady pace back towards the Franks, who were still engaged with the Italian auxiliaries. They were winning the fight, but not quickly enough. He looked back to see the Burgundians and Taifali lagging behind, some having to stop and catch their breath. 'Move, move!' he screamed. 'Are you waiting for your mothers? Move!' The taunt worked, and the men hoisted their shields and spears and pressed on.

Plenty of strength, these barbarians, but not enough stamina; they were used to short, pitched fights, not great battles that could last half a day and range across a mile of ground. Yet one way or another, this battle would not last that long. Beyond the Franks and the auxiliaries, the enemy legions were grinding down and overwhelming the Gallic centre. Ecdicius knew that if he did not finish off this enemy flank and bring help to Messianus soon, it would all be over.

He led his force around to the rear of the enemy auxiliaries, who were fighting hard, but the superior Frankish numbers were forcing them back and soon they would break. As soon as he reached charging distance Ecdicius bellowed the name of his father, and his Lancers joined his charge. The auxiliaries heard them too late to run, soon enough to show some panic. Their line loosened, a few stepping back from the fray, not knowing what to do except hold their shields and raise spears in a desperate attempt to defend themselves. The cavalry tore into them, sending men falling to the ground, while others were impaled from behind by the thick oak lances that plunged through mail and leather. Ecdicius spotted the standard bearer, headed for him, swung his sword down on the man's head; the steel cut straight through his helmet, embedding itself in his skull, and he dropped the shaft and crumpled to his knees. The enemy banner fell to the ground and in moments was trampled into the bloody mud. A triumphant cry went up from the Franks. Like a single creature, with fresh strength they made one great spontaneous push that broke the resistance of the auxiliaries. This was the moment when shoving and cursing would give way to open slaughter.

Ecdicius broke away from the fight, not wanting his cavalry to obstruct the Franks as they stormed over the broken enemy, or to waste their remaining strength in pursuit when there was so much fighting still to be done. The Burgundians and Taifali had now caught up, but were themselves too weary to chase the fleeing auxiliaries. The Alans were nowhere to be seen; they must have been drawn away by Aegidius. Ecdicius raised his sword. 'Hold here,' he cried, trying to get the attention of the Franks. 'Hold here, form your lines!' The Frankish chiefs, those who commanded the separate warbands, heard him and started to kick and drag their men back into a new line facing the enemy centre. The Burgundians and Taifali were forming up to their left. Their numbers still looked strong, well over a thousand in total; but now they would have to face the palatine legions, and they were a different breed of soldier. Their only hope was to hit them on the flank with such force and savagery that they caused a panic.

Yet even as Ecdicius prepared to command the advance, he saw that the centre was lost. The legions were about to break the Gallic regulars, some of whom were already in shambolic retreat back to Piacenza. Ecdicius could not see Messianus or any of his mounted guard. Somewhere in that maelstrom the general must have fallen. It would not be long before Ricimer, wherever he was, saw that his own left flank had collapsed and redeployed his central regiments to encircle Ecdicius. That could not happen. They had to pull back and gather their remaining forces.

'Back to the city,' Ecdicius shouted, his throat hoarse. 'Keep together – back to the city!'

But there was no such thing as an ordered retreat in the heat of battle. When the foot soldiers realised what was happening, the ranks broke apart. Some barbarians stopped to seize weapons or rings from the dead; others of weaker nerves dumped their own heavy shields and helmets, even tugged off their mail shirts, and started to run across the plough-rutted fields towards the walls of Piacenza with all the speed they could muster. All of their bluster and confidence had evaporated in a moment.

Ecdicius did not waste his breath on them. He had to lead the Lancers back as quickly as possible. 'Head for the city,' he yelled, and dug his spurs deep into his horse's flanks. Looking over at what had been the centre of the battlefield, he saw that the enemy were being cautious, slow to press their advantage. The Italian legionaries were reforming into lines. That was good. It would give Ecdicius enough time to reach the city gates first.

But as he neared the city, he saw a solitary rider leaving the gates and heading straight towards the enemy centre, even as retreating infantry swarmed past him in the opposite direction.

It looked like his father. He must be mad to leave the city. Could he not see what was happening?

Ecdicius veered left, galloping to intercept the rider. He had left behind the slow, heavily-armoured Lancers, but that did not matter. He had to get the emperor back to safety before he came within range of the enemy archers. 'Father,' he yelled, waving his arm. 'Father!' The rider came to a stop. Ecdicius hurried the remaining fifty yards to join him.

Emperor Avitus was glaring at the retreating soldiers. They raced past him as though he were not there. He tugged off his helmet and flung it to the ground, his face alive with fury. 'Cowards!' he screamed. 'Damned cowards and traitors!'

'Father,' Ecdicius said, 'we must pull back. The battle is lost.' He reached out to take the reins of his father's horse.

Avitus slapped his hands away. 'No – no! Messianus will hold the ground. He's still out on the field. We'll find him.'

'Messianus is fallen.'

Avitus seemed not to hear him. He drew his sword. 'The bastard Ricimer – we'll drive him all the way back to Rome!'

'Father, please. We must return to Gaul. This battle is lost.'

Suddenly his father was no longer emperor, and hardly even a general. He was merely an old man on a horse, abandoned by all except those closest to him. Ecdicius thought he saw a moment of hesitation in his eyes, and hoped that his urging was at last having some effect. Avitus opened his mouth to speak, but before any words came out there was a series of sharp whizzes and thuds, and arrows sprouted from the earth around them. The enemy archers had their range. Any moment they might be hit. Ecdicius reached out again to grab his father's reins, to pull him in the direction of the city.

It happened in an instant, but every detail was as clear to Ecdicius as a fresh painting. He saw the whites of the horse's eyes, and the reins wrapped in his own fist. It was a bay gelding, sleek and well-muscled, unarmoured. The arrow struck it in the throat just below the jaw and pierced right through its neck. Sharp fountains of hot blood sprayed from each side. It tossed up its head in shock, almost pulling Ecdicius from his saddle before he released the reins as it fell back on its haunches with an awful gargling whinny, and began to topple over. There was no time for Avitus to dismount. As the beast rolled over, it trapped his leg beneath its crushing weight.

Even as Ecdicius leaped clumsily from his saddle and scrambled to help his father, more arrows thudded into the earth. The horse was dead, its inert body pinning Avitus to the blood-soaked ground. He gripped the saddle horns and tried to lift it even an inch or two, but it was no use. Rushing feet appeared around him; he looked up to see the last of their soldiers fleeing the battle. He yelled at them to help, but whether or not they realised that it was their emperor trapped beneath the horse, not one man stopped. Their sole thought was of escape.

After them came the enemy: the vanguard of the Herculean legion, bloody and fierce from the battle, advancing in a broken formation. They saw Ecdicius struggling with the horse.

Avitus gripped his son's sleeve. 'Leave me,' he snarled through gritted teeth.

Ecdicius pretended not to hear. He drew his longsword and faced the enemy. The oncoming legionaries, now less than thirty yards from him, merely laughed. Here is an easy kill, they were thinking.

They might have been right had the Lancers not charged into their flank. Legionaries fell to spear and sword, or were barged aside or crushed as the wedge pushed through them like a ship through water. Shocked at the suddenness of the unexpected attack, the enemy officers halted the advance and began barking orders to reform the ranks. As the enemy milled about in confusion, the Lancers formed a protective barrier around Ecdicius and his father.

He pointed at the two closest riders. 'You, you – help me!'

Together they were able to lift the dead horse enough for Ecdicius to pull his father from beneath it. Avitus cried in agony as his smashed leg was dragged free. Ecdicius climbed back into his own saddle and commanded the horsemen to lift the emperor up behind him. The horse snorted unhappily at the extra weight, but Avitus was still conscious enough to wrap his arms around his son and hold fast as he began the ride back to the city. The remaining Lancers followed, leaving behind the field of devastation and defeat.

Sidonius was mounted, waiting outside the city gates. 'Thank Christ,' he said when he saw Ecdicius, tears rolling down his cheeks. 'Your father took a horse and rode like a madman into the field. We couldn't stop him.'

'He's injured,' said Ecdicius. 'Where can we take him that's safe?'

'The cathedral. Follow me.'

Ecdicius and the Lancers rode after Sidonius as he led them through the gatehouse. Inside the city all was disorder. Some officers were trying to form their units and bring them up to the ramparts, but most of the soldiers had decided to pillage the shops and houses of the city. It was as though a curse of insanity had fallen on the army. Ecdicius saw two soldiers of the Lions barge through a locked door; from the shattered doorway came female screams, followed by one of the soldiers dragging a young woman by the hair. He did not look back to see what became of her. On the opposite side of the street a private house was being ransacked by a group of Valentinians. Already there were civilian bodies in the street, adults and children, male and female alike.

Ecdicius rode through the madness with his father. As soon as they reached the cathedral, Sidonius dismounted and went to hammer on the heavy oak doors, shouting that he had the wounded emperor and would smash his way in if they were not opened. Almost at once the bolts were drawn back and the doors swung open. Ecdicius ordered two Lancers to lift his father from the horse and carry him inside. He dismounted and followed through the doors after them.

'Towels and water, now,' he said to the nearest cleric, a young, petrified-looking deacon. They must have been a terrible sight: muddy, bloodied, panting with exhaustion. While the deacon ran off to fetch water and cloth, a priest and another deacon drew together two benches so that the emperor could be laid upon them.

Avitus grimaced as he was placed on his back and a priest began to inspect his leg. 'Leave me here,' he said. 'Leave the city. Go back to Gaul.' In his face Ecdicius could see the effort of speaking, the waves of pain he was fighting to subdue.

'Not without you,' said Ecdicius.

'I'm not going anywhere. I'll be safe here. I have sanctuary.'

'Ricimer won't care. He'll kill you.'

'No. Majorian won't let him. He'll want to show mercy. Listen to me, son.' He reached out and clasped Ecdicius's hand. 'Go home. Protect your mother, and your brother and sisters. Make peace with the Goths. Do you hear me?'

There was a strange peace in the cathedral. The sounds of chaos in the city seemed distant, unreal. Ecdicius felt a sudden surge of tears, and fought to keep them down. 'I hear you, Father.'

'There must be peace with the Goths. This was a mistake. It was all a mistake. If only I had waited . . .'

His voice was growing weaker, his eyelids fluttering. The deacon reappeared, hurrying over with a bowl of water and some towels draped over his arm. Ecdicius took one of the towels, dipped it in the water, and used it to cool his father's brow.

'Ecdicius,' Sidonius said, 'your father's right. We must return to protect the family.'

Ecdicius turned to him. 'We can take him with us,' he said. He could no longer hold back the tears. 'We'll find a wagon. There must be a wagon somewhere in this fucking city.'

The priest shook his head. 'His Majesty must not be moved.'

Sidonius knelt beside Ecdicius. 'His leg is shattered. He'd never survive the journey.'

'We can't leave our emperor.' He spluttered now and began to cry, an open, boyish wail that echoed around the rafters of the basilica. He buried his face in his father's tunic and sobbed. He did not believe any of it was happening. The stars had smiled on him . . .

He felt a hand rest on his shoulder. 'We must go now,' Sidonius whispered. 'We'll be back, I swear. Ricimer will pay. But we must return to Gaul to protect the others.'

Ecdicius knew his cousin was right. There was still his mother and his brother and sisters. They would need him. He raised his face and sniffed, and wiped a sleeve messily across his nose. He leaned forward to kiss his father. 'We will see you again, Father. We'll take you back to Rome in glory.'

He could not tell whether or not his father heard him. His eyes were closed, and though his lips were moving no words came out. When Ecdicius rose from his side, Sidonius also leaned over to kiss him, and said, 'No harm will come to your daughter or your grandchildren. I swear it.'

An officer from the Lancers appeared at the open doorway. 'My prince,' he said, 'the enemy is forming up outside the city to the east. The west gate is still clear.'

'Ready our horses outside,' said Ecdicius. To the priest he said, 'Heal my father's injury. Protect him. Do not trust Ricimer.'

The priest bowed. 'His Majesty has sanctuary; no harm will befall him here.'

Ecdicius kissed his father one more time, and then knelt on both knees. Sidonius knelt next to him, and the two soldiers with them followed suit. 'Hail the emperor,' Ecdicius said.

'Hail the emperor,' the others repeated.

LVIII

Toulouse, A.D. 457

Arvandus had witnessed grand public ceremonies before, but not anything quite like this. The pomp was nothing new, and neither was the enthusiasm of the citizens, who crowded the forum of Toulouse in their thousands. The triumphant arrival of the king was familiar, too, except that he rode a horse instead of the chariot normally used by Roman emperors and prefects, and was escorted by Gothic rather than Roman cavalry. They came riding towards the wooden platform where Arvandus stood with other ministers of the court, the clatter of hooves mingling with the cheers of the people. Theoderic dismounted, along with his brothers, Vice-king Frideric and Prince Euric, and together they climbed the steps to the top of the podium, where three thrones awaited them. Each of them was clad in full ceremonial dress of bronze scale armour, gilded helmet and flowing cloak, swords hanging in bejewelled scabbards at their hips. They sat on their thrones, Theoderic in the centre, as the cavalry escort split and formed up on either side of the podium.

Then came the unfamiliar part of the ceremony. The next figure to enter the forum was also a king, but he came on foot. He also had a military escort, but they were his captors. Instead of armour and cloak he wore rags and chains. Rechiar, King of the Sueves, came shuffling towards the podium, his hair unkempt and eyes downcast in the disgrace of defeat. The king who less than a year ago had threatened to march on Toulouse was now jeered at and spat upon by its people.

Arvandus watched in silence, simply glad that the Spanish war was finally over. After leaving Arles he had spent the autumn here in Toulouse, waiting through many anxious weeks for news

rom Italy and from Spain. News from the first had finally arrived
n the kalends of November: Emperor Avitus had been crushed
y Ricimer at Piacenza. The remnants of the Gallic field army
ad retreated in disarray back to Arles; many of the barbarian
llies had set off to pillage northern Italy, but had soon been
unted down and wiped out. The invasion had been a disaster.

Yet all hope was not lost. Ecdicius, Arvandus had been relieved
o hear, had survived the battle and was safe in Arles. Ricimer
ad captured Avitus in the cathedral of Piacenza, but the bishop
f Milan had interceded on his behalf, persuading Ricimer to
ppoint Avitus Bishop of Piacenza instead of executing him. This
vas a clever move, Arvandus knew; by sparing Avitus's life Ricimer
nade himself look merciful, but by forcing him into the church
e had politically neutralised a dangerous enemy. Once ordained,
 bishop was bishop for life, and no consecrated member of the
hurch could hold government office, let alone claim the throne.
Avitus's career was well and truly over, and he was unlikely ever
o leave Piacenza again. But he had his life, and his family might
et be spared.

Arvandus had still been recovering from this news when a
eport of victory had arrived from Spain. After weeks of pursuit,
Theoderic had finally brought Rechiar to battle near the city of
Astorga and had inflicted a conclusive defeat on the Suevic king.
Rechiar had escaped, but Theoderic had pressed on and sacked
is capital of Braga, and then captured Rechiar himself as he
ttempted to flee Spain by boat. Other Suevic prisoners had been
ut to the sword. Rechiar himself had been dragged across the
nountains back to Gaul, thrown in prison, tortured through the
ong winter months, and now, on the kalends of March, brought
ut for this final spectacle.

Arvandus watched the captive king being led by his guards to
he space in front of the podium. A pair of servants placed a
eavy wooden block on the flagstones. The executioner, a thick-
rmed Goth bearing an unsheathed longsword, waited as the king
vas pushed to his knees and forced to lay his chest on the block.

Paulus stepped forth from the crowd of Theoderic's ministers and raised his arms. 'Behold Rechiar,' he cried, 'enemy of King Theoderic.'

And of Rome, he should have added, but this time did not. Even though winter had passed, still no report of a new emperor had reached Toulouse. Majorian had not claimed the title for himself, as everyone had expected. Until some new claimant came forward, the Gothic king had resolved to act in his own name alone.

Theoderic now rose from his throne. An expectant hush fell over the forum. With a single nod he gave the order to the executioner, who positioned himself next to the block. He raised his sword, and held it there, hovering above the neck of Rechiar.

'Behold vengeance,' Paulus declared. 'Behold justice!'

The executioner brought the blade down in a swift, precise arc. There was no need for a second blow. The people roared. The soldiers clashed their shields and spears.

Arvandus cheered, too. However much he wished things had turned out differently, he was glad to be serving Theoderic. He knew that the king was angry about the fall of Avitus, and behind his proud exterior was perhaps even feeling guilty about his refusal to send reinforcements. But without Gothic support, they had all expected Avitus to wait out the winter in Gaul; it had been rash of him, foolish, to invade Italy alone. If only he had waited.

After the ceremony came the feast. This was one ritual where Theoderic had stayed true to Gothic custom. The diners did not recline, but sat at two rows of benches and tables arranged down the nave of the palace basilica, with the king and his brothers occupying a table set across the width at one end. The food was plain, but abundant: roasted pork, stew and bread, lentil soup, fish and oysters. Servants hurried to keep cups overflowing with the spiced wine captured from Rechiar's cellars.

Arvandus sat with Paulus and the handful of other Roman courtiers on the table furthest from the king, close to the doors. The other hundred or so guests were barbarians, and their guttural, drunken voices filled the hall, echoing between marble pillars and the fading frescos that had once shown the great deeds of Roman heroes. On the opposite side of the hall, above the heads of feasting warriors, Arvandus noticed a painting of a spear-wielding female. The colours were pale or blackened by soot, but he could make out the golden Greek helmet pushed back upon her head, the cuirass fringed with coiled snakes, and the towers of a city upon which she cast her benevolent gaze. It was Pallas Athena, goddess of arts and wisdom. Once, long ago, she had been worshipped as the divine protector of Toulouse. Now she was forgotten even by her own people, soon to be smothered by the cobwebs that were spreading down from the ceiling. The Goths who sang and laughed beneath her had likely never heard her name.

Arvandus felt a hand on his shoulder. 'You seem in poor spirits, friend,' Paulus said. He and Arvandus seemed to be the only two diners who were still sober.

'I was admiring the goddess.'

Paulus looked at the painting and gave a sad smile. He raised his cup of wine in a toast. 'Alas, Athena. For all your wisdom, Arachne will have her revenge.'

The attempt at humour only depressed Arvandus further. Theoderic claimed that he wanted to cultivate learning in his kingdom, but so far Arvandus had seen little evidence of it. The king's interest in poetry did not seem to go beyond sponsoring Latin panegyrics in praise of his own greatness. He certainly seemed most at home here, surrounded by his feasting lords and warriors. 'I just wonder,' Arvandus said, before hesitating. A new thought had occurred to him, and he needed to let it take shape in his mind.

Paulus looked at him with a quizzical frown. 'You wonder what?'

Arvandus waved his hand down the hall. 'I wonder if this is all they'll ever be. You said yourself, the king must please the army. This is what the army wants. Feasting, drinking, fighting. The Goths may be a people, but can you truly build a nation on this?'

Paulus shrugged. 'You've seen Roman soldiers. Are they really any different from the Goths? These are dark times, my friend, I know. But give Theoderic time. Rome itself had to be built on the bones of its enemies before it reached the ages of silver and gold. Dear old Athena isn't quite vanished yet, you'll see.'

Arvandus took little solace from Paulus, whom he had resolved not to trust more than he had to. It was the same with all of the Romans who had recently flocked to Theoderic's court. Each one was friendly and pleasant to the others, including Arvandus, but he understood the stratagems of charm too well to be fooled. For Paulus was wrong: these were not dark times, not for them. The king had returned from Spain laden with glory and gold, and they had all shared in it. They had wealth and respect. When the gold ran out, when Theoderic lost a war and his courtiers began to fear for themselves, Arvandus knew that the smiles would quickly fade.

He drained his cup of wine, gesturing to a jug-wielding servant for a refill. To survive he would have to learn the rules of the game better than the rest. He could not afford to rely on anyone. Sidonius had taught him that.

It was early in the following morning when Theoderic summoned Arvandus. The king had just attended the morning service with his bishop, and was in his private bedchamber, preparing for the morning audience. The guard brought Arvandus into his presence.

'You sent for me, Majesty,' Arvandus said, bowing.

Theoderic was standing with his arms outstretched as a boy buckled a thick leather belt around his tunic. In one of his hands he held a papyrus letter. 'Yes,' he said. 'I need you to take a message to Arles at once. News has arrived from Italy.'

'Majorian has been proclaimed emperor?'

Theoderic shook his head, his expression sombre. 'Eparchius Avitus is dead.'

Arvandus could only stare at the king, struck dumb. *Avitus, dead . . .*

The boy finished arranging the belt, and went to fetch the sheathed sword and baldric that were laid out on the bed alongside a green embroidered cloak and golden brooch. 'This letter is from Majorian,' Theoderic said, handing it to Arvandus. 'He says that Avitus was taken ill during winter, and died of a fever in Piacenza last month. Given the sensitivities involved, he has asked me to keep this a secret for now, and requests that I make an expression of personal loyalty. Needless to say, I mean to do neither. Avitus was like a father to me.'

Arvandus scanned the letter. It was just as the king said. 'I understand, Majesty.'

'I don't think you do. I've known Avitus my whole life. The man was built like an ox, and was never ill for a single day. His sudden demise strikes me as very convenient. Do you not agree?'

'Perhaps, Majesty. But if he was wounded, and the wounds festered . . .'

'It is still too convenient.' He took the weapon from the boy, lifting the baldric over his head. 'While Avitus lived, there was a chance for peace. Now he is murdered, my honour forbids me to ally with his killers. I want you to take this news to Arles. Tell Ecdicius that I will stand with him against Ricimer and Majorian.'

Arvandus bowed. 'I will, Majesty. I can leave within the hour.'

'I have only one condition,' Theoderic said. 'I require Arles.'

Arvandus was not sure if he had heard correctly. 'Majesty?'

'I require Arles,' the king repeated. 'If my kingdom is to be worthy of the name, strong enough to avenge Avitus, it must have defensible borders. I need the rest of Aquitaine as far as the Loire, and First Narbonensis as far as Narbonne and Arles.'

'Majesty, that is a considerable . . . I don't believe Ecdicius can possibly accept. The people of Arles will not tolerate a Gothic—'

'The people of Arles do not concern me,' said Theoderic. 'This choice is for Ecdicius to make. Remind him, if necessary, that his father's army has been destroyed. His father has been murdered. He should consider whether or not I will be a better friend to him than Majorian and Ricimer.'

Arvandus did not know what to say. This was a cold political act, with not a shred of honour in it. Theoderic was merely seeking

to expand his own territory. But Arvandus could see the realitie
of the situation well enough: Ecdicius would need the help of th
Goths. He was bold, proud, popular, and heir to his father. I
Majorian had murdered Avitus, he could not afford to let such a
son live.

Theoderic took the cloak from the boy and flung it around
his shoulders. He fastened the brooch on his right shoulder a
he spoke. 'Go now, take my message to Ecdicius. Tell him I griev
with him like a brother.'

LIX

Arles

It was remarkable, Ecdicius thought, how swiftly those nobles who had clamoured for his father's attention when he was emperor had scurried into hiding at his capture, as though he were already dead. After the defeat at Piacenza, Ecdicius had returned to Arles with the sixty remaining Lancers and other troops, fewer than two thousand all told, to find the city already half empty. No parade had greeted them as they trudged through the rain-drenched streets. Even during the cold winter months, when it was customary for the nobility to move to their town houses, his father's old supporters had remained skulking on their country estates. The quaestor Egnatius, the count of sacred largesses Camillus, Consentius, and almost every other member of the court were nowhere to be seen.

A deep grumble of thunder broke outside as Ecdicius walked through the entrance hall of the prefect's palace, escorted by one of the guards. *Let them hide,* he thought. He brushed a hand through his sodden fringe, wiping the water from his eyes. *When we rescue my father and return him to Rome, we won't forget who was faithful and who was not.*

He was here to meet with Magnus and Priscus Valerianus, who were among the handful still prepared to acknowledge him. Priscus's term as praetorian prefect had officially ended in December, but the lack of a western emperor meant that no new appointments had been made this year, and he had reluctantly agreed to remain in his post – for now, at least. Ecdicius knew that he was wavering. Magnus, meanwhile, was giving little away. So far he had merely insisted that they wait until winter had ended, and see what would happen.

Now it was spring, and Ecdicius was impatient for action. As far as he knew his father was still prisoner in Piacenza; its bishop, supposedly, but captive all the same. Yet he was alive, and no western emperor had been named. There was still time to fight back against Majorian and Ricimer, provided that Ecdicius could win enough support. He remembered how his father had built the coalition against Attila. Such things were possible, he knew. But they would have to move quickly.

The palace guard brought him to the private office of the prefect, where he saw that Priscus and Magnus were already waiting. Priscus was sitting behind a large, tidily ordered desk. Magnus stood at one side of the room, next to what Ecdicius recognised as the insignia of the prefect's office. Upon an ornate carved side table stood the codicil, the leather-bound book that contained the prefect's charter of appointment. On either side of the book were two burning candles. Next to the table was the *theca*, an ornamental, gold-plated inkwell that stood as tall as Magnus's chest.

'Greetings, Ecdicius,' said Priscus. He gestured to one of two chairs facing his desk. 'Please sit.'

Ecdicius removed his damp cloak, handing it to an attendant. He took one seat, nodding briefly to Magnus, who took the other.

Rain hammered on the tiles of the roof above their heads, oppressive and grim. The older men looked at him, waiting for him to speak. Something about their silence made Ecdicius uncomfortable. He had the sense that they had already predicted what he was about to say and had decided how to handle him.

Perhaps that was so, but it changed nothing. 'It's now March,' he began. 'The situation hasn't changed, but soon it will. We must rebuild the field army.'

Priscus gave a slow, sceptical nod. 'A defensive force, I presume?'

'That depends on Majorian and Ricimer. If they invade Gaul, we'll defend it. Otherwise we'll be the invaders.'

'Another invasion of Italy?' said Priscus. He looked at Magnus. 'Would that be prudent?'

'Most imprudent,' Magnus said. 'For one thing, Messianus is dead. Who would lead this army?'

Ecdicius was prepared for that question. 'Tribune Marcus of the Eighth Dalmatians. He's the most experienced commander left in Gaul.'

Magnus was unconvinced. 'A hothead and a martinet. A master of soldiers requires a more temperate character.'

'Marcus may be hot-headed, but he listens to good counsel when the time comes. As for discipline, it's better to have too much than too little. We'll need discipline to raise a good-sized force before the summer.'

'That is another matter,' said Priscus. 'Where will these new recruits come from? Instituting a draft will be the surest way to lose the support of the landowners. They won't stand to see their strongest young labourers taken away by the army. And how many will you need?'

Ecdicius noted with irritation that Priscus had said 'you', not 'we', but decided to make nothing of it. To win them over, he needed to maintain the presumption that they were united. 'Ricimer took heavy casualties at Piacenza, and Majorian must still be busy in the south, or he'd have taken the throne by now. There's still time. I believe the Burgundians will support us, maybe also the Alans.'

'And the Goths?' said Priscus.

'They betrayed us once already,' Ecdicius said, keeping his voice calm despite the anger he felt coiling inside him like a snake. His father had insisted on friendship with the Goths, but he could not do it. Theoderic had disobeyed an imperial command and cost them victory at Piacenza. He had abandoned the man who had treated him almost like a son. He had no honour. Like Aegidius, he would eventually pay for his treachery. 'Without the Goths,' Ecdicius continued, 'we'll need to raise five thousand troops for the field army.'

'Impossible!' exclaimed Priscus. 'As praetorian prefect, I can tell you that we have neither the coin nor the means to raise such a force in, what, three months? Four? This is hardly the time to start a new war.'

'It isn't a *new* war,' snapped Ecdicius, his patience wearing thin. 'So long as my father lives, the last war hasn't finished.'

'New or old,' Priscus said, 'wars are expensive. This would require the levying of heavy taxes across the provinces of Gaul.'

'Then levy them. The provinces of Gaul owe everything to my father. Who was it who saved them from Attila?'

'Attila is long dead,' said Magnus. Anger was edging into his voice, too. 'I've already spent a mountain of gold on this war, with nothing to show for it but defeat. Why should I risk even more?'

Ecdicius stared at him, scarcely able to believe his words. 'Because of *justice*,' he said. 'My father – *your emperor* – is held by the rebels. Does that mean nothing to you?' He looked to Priscus. 'Does that mean nothing to either of you?'

They had no response. Ecdicius then saw the truth: they were frightened for their lives. They were bureaucrats, not soldiers. Nothing was more precious to them than their own existence. More than ever he missed his father, who knew how to deal with such men.

A soldier's voice came from the doorway. 'My lords, an envoy from King Theoderic.'

They all turned. Standing beside the palace guard was a short figure in a dripping woollen cloak. A puddle was collecting at his feet. 'I'm here to see you, Ecdicius,' he said. 'I just arrived. I went to your house, and they sent me here.'

Ecdicius got to his feet. 'Arvandus.' He had not expected to see his old friend. 'You never told me you were coming.'

'There wasn't time; the king sent me with an urgent message.' He glanced warily at Magnus and Priscus. 'It concerns your father.'

Ecdicius felt a sudden lump rise in his throat. His heart began to pound, sending a shudder through his whole body. Somehow, before Arvandus even spoke the words, he knew.

'Your father fell sick with a fever,' Arvandus said. The pain was clear in his face. 'I'm sorry, Ecdicius. He died in Piacenza last month.'

The room swayed. The din of the rain grew deafening, a smothering pillow around his head. Ecdicius clutched the back of the chair and eased himself back into the seat. He closed his eyes. When the others spoke their voices were dim, distant, as though heard through a wall.

'There it is, then,' said Priscus with a sorrowful sigh. 'It's over.'

'May God rest his soul,' said Magnus. 'He was the noblest of men.'

You damned hypocrites, Ecdicius would have said, had he been able to speak. *A moment ago you were ready to leave him to this fate.*

Arvandus had more to say. 'The news came to Toulouse by secret courier, together with a demand that King Theoderic pledge himself to Majorian. Theoderic will refuse that demand. He suspects that the death was unnatural. He's offered to stand by you, Ecdicius, if you will accept his friendship.'

'It's too late in the day for Theoderic to talk of friendship,' scoffed Magnus. 'We all know what that means, coming from a Goth. What is his price?'

Arvandus hesitated. He swallowed slowly. Then he said, 'Land.'

'Land? How much land? I expect he wants Narbonne?'

'Narbonne. The rest of First Narbonensis, and the rest of Aquitaine, up to the Loire. And Arles.'

Magnus jumped from his seat. 'That is outrageous! Priscus, are we going mad?'

'Theoderic is mad, not us,' said Priscus. 'He might as well ask for Rome itself.'

'I believe the king will be amenable to negotiation,' Arvandus said, but his voice was weak. 'Ecdicius, he wants to avenge your father, I swear it. He says he grieves with you like a brother.'

The others waited for Ecdicius to respond. He was still in his chair, his eyes closed. An image had risen in his mind like a memory, as clear as if he had seen it for himself. It was his father lying on a bed, pale and brokenhearted, an old man exiled from his home and family. Over him loomed a barbarian with cold eyes and silver hair, who slowly reached down and gripped both hands around his throat.

Ecdicius opened his eyes. He saw the floor mosaic, with its calm geometry of black and white. The rain seemed to have softened, and was pattering now, a soothing hum above them.

There was still anger, but of a kind he had never before felt. It had sunk deep within him, into his bones, into his gut. His head was clear.

He looked up at Priscus, and then at Magnus. Their faces were hard with indignation, but it was self-righteous, nothing but a performance. Ecdicius saw at once where it would lead. They had half-forgotten his father when he was captured; now that he was dead, they could forget him entirely. This threat of Gothic annexation would give them the excuse they needed to treat with Majorian.

As for Arvandus . . . Sidonius had been right. He had made his choices.

Ecdicius rose. He straightened his tunic and faced Arvandus. 'Go back to your king,' he said. 'Tell him his friendship means nothing to me.'

'Ecdicius, please think about this. I can wait a few days. About your father, I—'

'Go back to your king,' Ecdicius said. 'That's all I have to say, to him or to you. Leave now, or I'll have you put in irons.'

Arvandus nodded. He turned, his lips tight, and left with the guard.

'The audacity of it,' grumbled Magnus as soon as he had gone. 'Every year more of his type go crawling to the Gothic king.'

'Disgraceful,' agreed Priscus. 'To bring such brazen demands before us.'

Magnus returned to his chair. 'True. But at least it makes our choice clear. With Theoderic threatening us, we now have no option but to open negotiations with Majorian. If we take the initiative, he'll more likely be inclined to mercy.'

Ecdicius remained standing. 'You talk of mercy? He's murdered my father.'

'Your father, may God grant him peace, died of a fever.'

'And if we treat with Majorian, will I also die of a *fever*? Will my mother, my brother and sisters?'

'Listen to reason,' Magnus said. 'You must surrender. I understand that you fear Majorian—'

'I don't fear Majorian, or Ricimer.'

'But you fear for your family. Let me negotiate on your behalf.'

'So you can betray me?'

Magnus stiffened. 'That sort of personal abuse is uncalled for, Ecdicius. To talk in such a way shames the memory of your father.'

'Do not dare speak of his memory,' said Ecdicius. 'You don't honestly think he died of a fever. Not even Theoderic is fool enough to believe that.'

'I don't know for sure, I admit. The wisest course of action will be to enquire into the matter when we have the chance. But to do that, we must make peace with Majorian.'

'You must also consider the alternative,' Priscus said. 'As we already discussed, it would be impossible, quite impossible, to rebuild the field army by the summer. Without troops, you have no hope of resisting Majorian and Ricimer. I completely agree with Magnus. Surrender is the only option.'

Their eagerness to capitulate disgusted Ecdicius. They were not even pretending to be reluctant. He had no use for such men. 'Surrender is never the only option,' he said.

LX

The winter in Gaul had been long that year. The waters of the Rhône shimmered silvery and cold in the light of dusk, and if the wind that whispered along the wharves of Arles carried a promise of spring, Attica did not hear it. To her it felt as though the seasons themselves had come to a stop. She was tired, worn out from the months of dread and by the weight of her swelling belly, by the aches, by the constant hunger and the sleepless nights. The news brought by Ecdicius a few hours earlier had almost been a relief, a longed-for breathing out. Amidst the shock of the household, her brother had provided a calm focus. She had wept, but the grief had quickly exhausted her; she had been half-asleep when Cyra had helped her change into the black mourning gown, and had dozed for most of the journey down to the docks.

There would be time for grieving. Soon they would be on the barge, and she could rest for the week's journey upriver to Lyons. Her child would arrive in a month or two. That was as far ahead as she could see. Ecdicius and her mother could take care of everything else. They had been doing as much for the past few weeks, since she had moved from Felix's town house to her own family's for the final stages of the pregnancy.

Cyra approached from across the wharf. 'The cabin is almost ready, mistress. Your mother has made sure it's clean.'

'Thank you,' said Attica. Sitting in the open-top sedan chair, she looked at the river barges, the pair tethered in a row. It would be crowded with all of them sleeping in two cramped cabins, but they had no choice. She saw her mother and sister talking on the nearest barge, both of them also clad in black.

Agricola was with them, holding his two nieces by the hand. The girls were too young to understand what was happening. At first Agricola had wept more bitterly than any of them, but his reddened eyes were now narrowed below a determined, manly frown, and his jaw was clenched. Ecdicius and Sidonius were still on the front barge, supervising the crewmen as they stacked the crates and chests and prepared to haul leather sheets over the heap. They had loaded clothing, food, tableware, smaller pieces of furniture and other portable valuables – whatever they had been able to collect from their family town house, not knowing if they would ever come back. Ecdicius had hired the barges and the crew, and paid them extra to help carry the cargo down to the docks. They had to leave Arles at once, he had said. They had no friends left in the city. Their best hope was to take the river north to Lyons and throw themselves on the mercy of the Burgundian king.

Ecdicius climbed out of the front barge and spoke a few words with the officer leading the half-dozen armoured cavalrymen who had escorted them to the docks. They were Lancers, part of a unit that Ecdicius had led at Piacenza. Since October Ecdicius had garrisoned them in an empty military warehouse across the river, with a few of them serving in the town house as private guards. Attica certainly felt safer for their presence. Thanks to them, the groups of curious commoners milling on the dockside had kept a respectful distance as the barges were loaded.

Ecdicius finished talking to the commander and came over to Attica and Cyra. 'We're almost ready,' he said, touching his sister's hand. 'How are you feeling?'

She had almost grown used to the way he now frowned and softened his voice whenever he spoke to her. Agricola was the same, and Sidonius. She doubted that they even realised they were doing it. Women understood what she was going through; men did not understand, but seemed driven by instinct to protect her. 'I can walk,' she said. 'I just need a moment.'

'Whenever you're ready. I've commanded the guards to wait here until we're past the bridge, and then they'll join the rest of the unit to follow us on the north road. They'll be able to keep pace up to Lyons, so if anyone tries to stop us, they'll have to deal with sixty heavy cavalry. I'd say we'll be safe.'

'Mistress,' said Cyra, sudden alarm in her voice. 'It's your husband.'

Cyra was right. Attica saw Felix emerging from a side street onto the wharves. He was mounted, and followed by three of his retainers on foot, who lately had taken to wielding blades instead of clubs. Felix dismounted, left his horse with the retainers, and came striding towards her.

'Do you want me to stay?' Ecdicius asked.

'No,' she said. 'I'll deal with him, go and wait by the barges. You too, Cyra.'

Attica had hoped that they might escape the city without Felix hearing about it, but obviously it had been impossible to keep secret the evacuation of an entire household. She straightened up in the chair, grunting briefly at the pain in her lower back. As she shifted, she felt the baby stir inside her.

'I forbid you from leaving with my child,' Felix said, pointing at her as he came to a stop. 'Have your things unloaded from the barge at once. You're coming back to stay with me.'

'I'm going with my family to Lyons,' she said.

'I forbid it.'

She sighed. 'And what will you do, Felix, if I refuse?'

'I can have you kept here by force. Legally the child is mine.'

'No it isn't. Until it is born, legally the child is part of me.'

'Then as my wife, you must obey me.'

'No,' she said. His assumption of her ignorance was becoming tedious, but she kept her tone reasonable. 'With my father's death I have become legally independent. I'm taking nothing with me that I do not own.' She watched him stand there in frustrated silence, his mouth clamped shut. 'I realise,' she said, 'that I have no grounds for a divorce, but nor do you have power over me. My father is dead. You can no longer threaten to hurt him.'

'I never threatened to hurt your father. How could you—'

'I'm tired, Felix. Please accept that you cannot make me stay. If you truly loved me or our child, you'd come with me.'

'You know I can't do that,' he said. 'Unless you renounce your father, you and the rest of your family will be condemned for treason. If you stay here, I can protect you. Attica, please, think of our child.'

Tired as she was, she laughed to hear him say that. 'Felix, I think of nothing else.'

He stared at her, frowning in consternation. His mouth twitched as though he were about to say something, but couldn't. He held out a hand, let it hover for a useless moment, then dropped his arm back to his side. 'Please stay,' he said at last, the words escaping as little more than a whisper. 'Please, Attica. I have not been a good husband. But I will be better.'

She shook her head. 'Neither of us believes that.'

Now he began to cry, his eyes narrowing as he attempted to fight the tears. She tried to feel compassion for him, but could not. Nor did she despise him as she once had, much less fear him. He was simply irrelevant, his worth measured only in respect to her unborn child. On that score, she would be content never to see him again.

'Here,' he said, sniffing as he reached into the purse on his belt. He took out a golden ring, and placed it in her hand. 'I want you to take this.'

'What is it?'

'It's a *chnoubis* charm. My mother wore it when she bore me. I should have given it to you months ago.'

She examined the ring. It was engraved with a crude face, from which stretched seven tentacle-like rays. *Chnoubis* was an ancient Egyptian god; this one had small Christian crosses etched above and below the face. An inscription around the band read: *Lord, help her who wears this.*

'It will protect you,' he said. 'And our child.'

She slipped the ring onto the middle finger of her right hand. 'Thank you, Felix.'

A gull screeched overhead. Attica looked over at the barges to see that the loading was complete, the bargemen ready to cast off and take to the oars. Ecdicius and Cyra stood together, waiting for her.

'This sedan chair belongs to you,' Attica said, lifting herself from the seat. 'You may take it back.' Ecdicius and Cyra came rushing over, one going to each side. They took hold of her elbows. 'Goodbye, Felix,' she said, not looking back. She let them guide her to the barge, where her mother and Papianilla helped her make the awkward step down from the dockside onto the deck.

'The cabin is ready for you, my dear,' her mother said.

'I'll stand for a while. I'd like to see the city one last time.'

Ecdicius helped Cyra step aboard, and then hurried to the front barge to join Agricola and Sidonius. He yelled for the barge captains to cast off.

Attica stayed on her feet, steadied by her sister and mother, as the barge was pushed away from the dockside. They drifted out into the flow of the river, the steersman keeping the bow straight ahead. She kept her eyes on the receding wharf, on the six cavalrymen and the crowd of onlookers who were now dispersing to go about their business; on the dockworkers and ships further down the jetty, and on the fishing boats bringing the day's catch from the sea; on the sloping roofs of the wharfside shops and taverns, beyond which rose the great marble edifice of the prefect's palace. Its portico, like the seabirds that circled overhead, shone like gold in the light of the setting sun. And in the midst of it all, next to an empty sedan chair, stood a solitary figure whom she acknowledged as the father of her child.

When there was enough distance from the wharf, the captain ordered the crew to lower the oars. With a few soft lurches the barge began to move upstream. Attica started towards the wooden cabin at the stern. It would be a slow, difficult journey, but in Lyons there was safety and hope.

Acknowledgements

Thanks are due first and foremost to Jim, Laura and Nick, for their faith and ever-helpful guidance, and to Charlotte for her careful eye. Thanks to Ant and Tiff for providing a writing refuge in Colorado, where the shadow of the Rockies provided unlikely inspiration for a novel about ancient Rome, and to David, Edward, and (of course) Duncan, for making me feel so welcome in Minneapolis that same summer. Nate deserves much gratitude for his willingness to read an early draft and for the welcome respite in the Lost Creek Wilderness, and with Vikki he shares my thanks for their wonderful hospitality. Thanks to Giles for reading a *very* early draft, and for his support in difficult times. To all family, friends, and students new and old, my thanks are too many to list; but in particular thanks to Noel for his abiding advice, to Ludmilla and Elizabeth for flying my flag better than I can fly it myself, to Teams Aëtius, Galla, Euric and Clovis for exploring fifth-century Gaul with me, and to Eleanor for the peacocks and more. Finally, there is much I would now say to my brother Edmund, if I only had the chance. Instead I dedicate this book to his memory.

Historical Note

My first novel, *The Lion and the Lamb*, was a simple beast. All of its characters and major events were pure fiction played out before only the loosest backdrop of historical fact. In this second novel, the lines are more blurred. Of the protagonists, Ecdicius and Arvandus are based on – or rather, inspired by – real historical figures. Various other characters are also inspired by real people, to a greater or lesser extent. Sometimes all they have left to posterity is a name and a list of accomplishments, sometimes a few biographical snippets, but never enough to rebuild a life. Take Ecdicius's uncle, Ferreolus. We know that he served as prefect of Gaul during Attila's invasion, and that he wined and dined the pompous King Thorismund when the Goth rattled his sabre before the walls of Arles. We know one or two other things from later in his life, but none of it adds up to a human being. There is plenty of room for the novelist's imagination to clad him in a peacock-bright cloak for his trips to the forum. On the other hand, we have a precious pen-portrait of King Theoderic which tells us, for instance, that he preferred to have his hunting bow handed to him unstrung because he thought it womanly not to string it himself. What historical novelist could resist picking up such a biographical gem?

It would be tedious to list every instance like this from the novel, but it is only fair that I own up to some important liberties. First of all, we know nothing about the part of Arvandus's life portrayed here – not even his place of origin or his social class. I doubt that the real Arvandus would thank me for dropping him in the dockside slums of Bordeaux. Only later in life does he appear on the pages of history, fully formed. His character in the novel can therefore be treated as entirely fictional, but heading on a trajectory to coincide with his historical counterpart. The same is true of Ecdicius, to a lesser extent; we do, at least, know something about his family background. But with Attica I must confess my guilt. There was a noblewoman called Attica who paid for the renovation of Saint Laurence in Damaso in Rome, as is recorded by an inscription. She was married to Felix of Narbonne and had children by him. These two sentences encompass her contribution to history. Everything else about her in this novel is fictional, including that she was sister to Ecdicius. The enclosed family tree of the Philagrii is at least half guesswork.

Still, where the novelist of the late Roman empire is forced to sketch out character portraits almost from scratch, he or she is somewhat better served when it comes to the landscape they inhabit. For this was the age of Attila the Hun, whose exploits fascinated writers of his own day and have done ever since. Thus the 'big picture' of emperors, battles, invasions and assassinations painted in this novel is (I hope) historically faithful, at least as far as the fragmentary sources allow. This is not to say that there is no room for invention; indeed, like a jigsaw puzzle missing most of the pieces, one must guess how to put the remaining few back together, and fill in the blanks as best one can.

So much for historical facts. These, for the novelist, are really only a colourful excuse to explore what was *really* going on in the improvised drama of human life. What was it like to wake up one day to the news that Attila and his Huns had crossed the Rhine? What was it like when people you knew were swept up by the whirlwind of history – and when you found yourself swept up, too? Or, as was surely just as often the case, when you longed to be swept up, but were left sitting frustrated in the dust? My protagonists are young because young people, those who stand on the threshold of adulthood, feel such excitement and disappointment most keenly. But this is only half of the story, for if the Huns were a passing whirlwind, there was also a deeper, more ominous rumbling within the foundations of fifth-century Europe.

In this novel Ecdicius, Arvandus and Attica are trained, even *bred*, to play some role or other – soldier, bureaucrat, matron – in a Roman world that has lasted for centuries and, for all anyone knows, might last for centuries more. When the ground beneath their feet, once so sturdy, shifts in ways that they can neither predict nor control, and the world around them starts to fall apart, they are forced to make painful decisions. This is where we find the human drama at the end of the western empire.

List of Characters

Status and position of characters are described as at their first appearance.

Philagrii

Eparchius Avitus, *vir illustris*, former praetorian prefect of Gaul
★ Severiana, *femina illustris*, his wife
Ecdicius, their eldest son
Papianilla, their eldest daughter
Attica, their second daughter
Agricola, their second son
Magnus, *vir spectabilis*, nephew of Eparchius Avitus
★ Egnatia, *femina clarissima*, Magnus's wife
Felix, son of Magnus and Egnatia
Probus, son of Magnus and Egnatia
Araneola, daughter of Magnus and Egnatia
Camillus, *vir illustris*, count of the sacred largesses, nephew of Magnus
Lupus, Bishop of Troyes, first cousin to Eparchius Avitus

Servants of the Philagrii

★ Cyra, handmaiden to Attica
★ Soranus, secretary to Eparchius Avitus
★ Vettius, steward in the household of Eparchius Avitus
★ Stephanus, groom in the household of Eparchius Avitus
★ Rebecca, servant in the household of Magnus
★ Ajax, bodyguard to Felix

Other Romans

★ Papianilla, *femina illustris*, sister to Severiana

Tonantius Ferreolus, *vir illustris*, her husband

Sidonius Apollinaris, first cousin once removed to Papianilla and Severiana

★ Roscia, *femina illustris*, his grandmother

★ Alcimus, *vir spectabilis*, his father

Paeonius, *vir clarissimus*, former consul-governor

★ Simeon, his secretary and agent

Consentius, *vir clarissimus*, tribune and notary at the imperial court

★ Frontius, a student in Arles

★ Marcus, a student in Arles

★ Maria, a landlady in Arles

Salvian, a monk of Marseilles

★ Maximinus, rhetor

Eusebius, rhetor

Astyrius, *vir illustris*, consul, former count and master of both services

Syagrius, *vir clarissimus*, cousin to Tonantius Ferreolus

Namatianus, Bishop of Clermont

Anianus, Bishop of Orléans

Patiens, Bishop of Lyons

★ Silvius, *vir perfectissimus*, curator of letters

Priscus Valerianus, *vir spectabilis*

Pragmatius, *vir clarissimus*, his son-in-law

★ Bricianus, manager of the imperial flour mills at Barbegal

★ Teridius, *vir perfectissimus*, cousin to Lampridius

★ Fabiola, *femina perfectissima*, his wife

Flavius Rufius Opilio, *vir illustris*, former consul and master of offices

★ Salviana, *femina illustris*, his wife

★ Egnatius, *vir illustris*, quaestor

Gennadius Avienus, *vir illustris*, former consul

Romans from the Gothic Kingdom

Arvandus, a common student
* Flacilla, his mother
* Patroclus, his father
Pontius Leontius, a noble student
Lampridius, a noble student
* Concordius, grammarian
* Sedatus, orator
* Lupus, a common merchant
* Galenos, physician
* Frontinus, Bishop of Bordeaux
* Paulus, *vir clarissimus*, a minister of the younger Theoderic

Members of the Roman military

Aëtius, *vir illustris*, patrician, former consul, count and master of soldiers
Majorian, *vir clarissimus*, tribune of the First Gallic Horse
Aegidius, *vir clarissimus*, tribune of the Senior Honorian Horse, nephew to Syagrius
Messianus, *vir clarissimus*, tribune of the Senior Cornuti
* Marcus, *vir clarissimus*, tribune of the Eighth Dalmatians
* Flaccus, primicerius of the First Gallic Horse
Ricimer, *vir illustris*, count of the household infantry
Remistus, a Goth, *vir illustris*, master of soldiers

Barbarians

Attila, King of the Huns
* Wulfilas, Count of Bordeaux
* Gunthar, a Thuringian butcher
* Guntram, his brother, a Thuringian butcher
Pelagia, a Gothic princess, wife to Aëtius
Theoderic, King of the Goths

Thorismund, his eldest son
Theoderic, his second son
Frideric, his third son
Euric, his fourth son
Sangiban, King of the Alans
Gundioc, King of the Burgundians
Riothamus, King of the Armoricans
Childeric, King of the Franks
Gebavult, an Alemannic prince
Rechiar, King of the Sueves
* Chlodoric, a Frankish prince
* Eocharic, an Alanic prince